MOCCASIN TRACE

A Novel by

HAWK MacKINNEY

MOCCASIN TRACE

A Novel by

HAWK MACKINNEY

Copyright 2006 by Hawk MacKinney

ISBN: 1-59507-148-2

ArcheBooks Publishing Incorporated
www.archebooks.com

9101 W. Sahara Ave.
Suite 105-112
Las Vegas, NV 89117

Hardcover First Edition: 2006

ArcheBooks Publishing

DEDICATION

to my blood-kin
who taught me the treasures
of growing up Southron

ACKNOWLEDGEMENT

Thank you, Lygia

OTHER BOOKS BY HAWK MACKINNEY

White Sodom

Poison at the Pinnacle

1865

1

Thinning white hair and slumped shoulders hung poorly on the tall, haggard frame of once dignified, stalwart Rundell deWorthe Ingram, IV. Like lots around and about, the past was a mingle of blurred fog-and-mist memories. Rain or shine, day after dreary day, before sunup, a wheezing Rundell labored out of bed. After an early breakfast, he shuffled along a porch that stretched across the front of the house that was Moccasin Hollows—home to him, his grandparents, parents and Hamilton, Rundell's lanky, broad-shouldered son born in this dogtrot, ancestral land of the Nordmadhr Norman-Scottes Ingrams.

Rundell slouched into his worn, cane-back rocker, staying there 'til late night, sometime all night except for a call of nature. Now and then, he'd slap at the pesky whine of a mosquito, most times paying them no mind. He no longer greeted the rare passerby, and made even fewer visits into town. Like Rundell, Queensborough Towne seemed to have pulled in on itself, as though chastened at having become unseemly to the point of being unneighborly.

Any time Hamilton tried to cajole his papa to go for a buggy ride into town, Rundell would shake his head and mutter, "Town's full of undone folks and beady-eyed outsiders in store-bought show-off clothes. Maybe tomorrow—the day after."

At spartan mealtimes, Rundell might nibble. He seldom bothered. His mind wandered desultory and aimless in a past more pleasant than this disquieted, downside-up world he could do nothing about.

On one particularly balmy afternoon, sandy-haired Hamilton and his young wife, Sarah, came out of a shabby-curtained parlor with its missing window panes, boarded with scorched roof shingles salvaged from the blackened skeletons of the outbuildings. Faint lines creased the young woman's once exuberant face, crinkling deeper at the corner of sky blue eyes. As they continued down the wide front steps, she tucked and pushed tawny gold braids up under one of her worn bonnets. Its frayed pink and blue ribbons were faded to a drab sameness, matching the lackluster color in her cheeks.

Seldom breaking his self-imposed solitude, puffy-faced Rundell's raspy voice boomed through the still afternoon, "Where you two off to?"

He sounded more crotchety than he was. The whole parish never doubted how he doted on his daughter-in-law.

"Sarah'n me thought we'd go for a walk." Hamilton's calloused hand gripped the cane pole with its frazzled line. "Mayhaps fish a bit. Anything you need?"

As though he hadn't heard, Rundell shook his head, continued slowly rocking.

"I patched most of the leaks in the kitchen roof," Hamilton said. "With the sawmill tore up I'll split new shingles for the smokehouse when we get back. Chicken house will have to wait."

"Chicken house don't need a roof. Don't need no chicken house. Got no chickens."

As they headed across the yard, Hamilton called back, "We'll be back in a while."

Short walks with Sarah, a little fishing, checking his rabbit snares, being any distance from the house left Hamilton uneasy. Hadn't been safe for some time. Doubly so if Mother Greer was away and Sarah and Papa were there alone. Not sure what he'd do if he came face to face with a pack of ghost-eyed raiders. As lawlessness and *incidents* increased, Hamilton knew if there was to be a fight, the farther it stayed from the house, the more warning those at the Hollows might have. By any measure it was a reedy-slim plan, but the only one he could muster. If he saw he was going down he'd take as many with him as he could. His greatest fear being something happening he might've prevented by being close by. But, for the time being, everything was as alright as he could make it.

"Fish not gonna bite," Rundell yelled. "Sun's too bright, too warm. There's blackberries. Berries and muskydines ought to be sweet for pickin'." Rocking steady, his fixed look off to nowhere. "Get 'em 'fore the deer strips 'em clean."

For as long as Hamilton could remember he and Papa had always liked the plump, sweet blackberries served with thick cow's cream. Hadn't told Papa most of the wild vines not trampled by Sherman's bummlers were long ago picked bare. The last time he and Papa had gone pickin' had been some of the last good days—for lots of folks.

"Me'n Sarah might sit a spell."

He took special care to have quiet times for Sarah, 'specially since night before last. He got real excited when she told him she might be with child again. She hadn't been sleeping well, often wanted him to rub her aching back. Now he knew why.

Threadbare clothes and unshorn hair gave Hamilton Bothington Graeme Ingram the look of a run-down, unkempt derelict instead of heir to one of the largest non-slave plantations in Saint George Parish. He ducked under what was left of the split-rail fence with its crooked corner post. Rails and most posts had long gone up in the smoke of hoards of campfires.

"Step wide." He reached back to help her through. "I don't want the mother of our children to step on a canebrake rattler catchin' sun on this fine day."

"Lord have mercy." Sarah clutched her bonnet in her hand so as not to get it snagged in the coiled tangle of wire. "I suppose it's up to me to get used to your hoverin' over me again."

"Yep," he grinned. "Reckon my favorite sweetheart will have to do just that."

"Your favorite sweetheart?" She giggled, wrinkled her nose at him. "Just listen to you and your Ingram fiddle-faddled talk."

He grinned as she brushed back strands of the golden hair Hamilton loved to run his fingers through. She gathered her mended skirt, slipped her hand into his, and quickly stepped wide over the fallen post.

"C'mon…" her voice lilted soft, and she squeezed her grip on his hand. "Let's hurry."

Her singular tenderness refused to let the devastation around them blight their few alone-times. In the spoliation around them, such times when they managed to make it just the two of them held a more-than-special meaning.

"Don't you get too tired now." He gave a chuckle low in his throat.

"Hamilton Ingram, I don't know why I bother, but why in the world must you treat me like I'm about to break?" She gave him her reassuring but exasperated look.

His hand tightened on hers, he pulled them to a stop, his hazel eyes looked dead into the pale blue of hers. "If anything happened to you…"

He let his words fade, remembering another sunshine mirage of a day that seemed to be only whispers of another life. Times he and his papa walked this same field, checking the stalks of corn in these sections to see if they were beginning to tassel-out. He'd peel off one young ear of sugar corn, its glossy smooth silks barely poking out from green husks.

"Looks to be the makin's of a good crop this year," Rundell had said as he shucked the ear, took a bite. "Ought to make enough to put up winter feed for that new team you were looking at the last week."

Those days now seemed unreal. Hamilton and Sarah continued across the unplowed furrows, his worn boots puffed up dusty little dirt devils between tufts of weeds. They skirted the flattened thickets, through fields of corn stubble, and angled around the stand of thick canebrake and scrub between Moccasin Trace and the river. The talk of blackberries made Hamilton think of once-upon-a-time bowls of chilled berries swimming in thick cream that had been skimmed from yesterday's milk, and his stomach growled loud enough for Sarah to hear.

Sarah giggled. "Me too."

He wasn't the only one hungry in these parts, not by a long shot. A whisper of a coquette smile shadowed across her face. To him she looked young again, out for an evening's walk with her beau—halcyon days become fond memories.

"Maybe we'll catch a big bluegill," she said.

"Not likely. Last week I walked two of the cut-acrosses. Water's still runnin' muddy and churned. Banks're tore up by the plank bridges they threw across for wagons and artillery caissons. Lots of suteler's junk in the water, odds and ends, old saddles, burnt, rusted pans, broken wagon wheels. Brim beds churned and trashed, even mud-lovin' catfish don't like water that messy. Bluegills and red-bellies might bed again late this fall. I doubt it, though. Most anything left has been pretty much fished out."

He thought of past Thanksgivings, him and Papa, Sarah's family, the Greers, and the best eatin' in the parish...bar none. Last week he'd killed their last Rhode Island Red hen. She'd quit laying the daily egg and lost most of her neck feathers. Bessie tried to help him with storing eggs in what little lime water they had. It worked 'til the salt ran out. It was either eat the eggs or let 'em spoil. Old bird was stringy and tough chewin', hardly filled the stew pot. Stew needed fatback, which they hadn't had since the hogs were taken. Their last cure of venison jerky tasted wild, like it'd turned bad. It needed salt, too. Besides salt costin' money they didn't have, it wasn't readily available. Just as well they didn't have hogs. No way to age or cure the hams without salt. Hamilton'd had a few middling-meat johnnycakes soaked with chicken broth. He left most for Sarah and Papa.

Rundell liked munching raw potatoes. He favored the smaller, fresh-dug ones he called *new potatoes*. He'd use the bent kitchen knife that'd lost its handle on the withered moldy ones that hadn't been taken by foragers. Sometimes he didn't peel them, just rubbed off the dirt and gnawed away.

The Hollows had been spared, but damn little else had.

Growing up a gangly towhead on the sprawling acres of Moccasin Hollows, Hamilton never gave much notice to outside goings-on. On his seventeenth birthday, near four years ago, he had gotten his first notion of the world beyond.

Rundell usually kept his feelings close to home, seldom using strong language, but that day his disgusted papa'd remarked, "Damn few prudent heads among the lot of them," as he flung down the Augusta newspaper. "*Constitutionalist* editors and those pigheaded politicians. They couldn't get off a water moccasin if it was chewin' on their big toe. Fools got no idea what they're stirrin'. Most likely don't care neither."

"What happened?" Hamilton had never seen a turmoil fret his papa so.

"I suppose it's gettin' to me more'n I thought. Benson Crouder stopped by, that's what. All gussied up in his top hat and new attire like some up-town Beau Brummell, that fancy rig of his hitched with his matched bays, their mane and tails all curried. Cain't figure some folks. Let them get money in their pockets, they act like their sweat don't stink. All fired up, heading into Queensborough for the big meet, asked if I was going. I told him I didn't see no point to another meetin'. Far as I could tell too many done decided they were finished with talk."

Not many days went by before Rundell swallowed his distaste for politics, and got knee-deep in the middle of the commotion at the capital in Milledgeville. Hamilton harnessed and hitched the buggy for his Papa.

Rundell climbed into the buggy, took the reins. "Don't see my bein' there'll make much difference in that brew of catfish stew." Looked at this strapping son, he added, "Suppose it cain't do no harm neither."

Hamilton remembered that day, watching Papa drive off, and how at the time the day hadn't seemed different. Now, when he thought back, he could think of no one thing which seemed to've change, except he recalled the yellowish-orange morning light seemed sharper with a change to the air.

Now, for way too many folks, stench and fear rode the breezes, carrying the smell of char and ashes. Each day had become a hunt for food and shelter. Tending the meager gardens at the Hollows barely managed enough food, but it was food. The lawless churning mayhem, moving far and near, sometimes too close to the Hollows for Hamilton's liking—his wife and their unborn son, Papa, Mother Greer and Sarah's brother, Benjamin. Gaunt chimneys haunted the ashes of Wisteria Bends, Hamilton's second home, the grand plantation manor where Sarah and Ben had grown up. Without money there was no point going into town. Except for land speculators, gold jingling in their pockets, there wadn't that much food to be had in Queensborough nohow.

A blizzard of thunder and hell-hot hate had smashed most homes in the countryside around Queensborough Towne. With Sherman and his army gone, worse than carpetbaggers and a lot more dangerous were the lawless bands of white trash infesting the countryside. No questions asked, easier to kill anyone that happened in their way, and get on with the stealin'. Human locust pillaging what they could get their hands on, torching homes, farms, what was left of the Queensborough courthouse. With parish land records in ashes a fair number of low-lifes claimed land which was never theirs.

Sarah broke Hamilton's quiet reverie. "A bungtown copper for your thoughts."

"Guess I'm not very good company." He slid his arm around her, hugged her. "Word from Milledgeville is bad. Seems no end to the ruin."

"I saw smoke off in the direction of the river this morning." She snuggled to him. "Seems that's all we smell now'days."

"I feel so helpless." His hand gentled across her belly where their new baby was. "...Afraid for you."

"Sometimes me, too, but," she laid her head on his shoulder, "there's no point frettin', working yourself up when you can't do nothing about it."

This woman was his whole being. Usually no matter the problem, her comfort was there for him. But lately nothing had been soothing.

With her usual impetuous excitement, Sarah sat up straight and burst out, "Let's go wadin'." She jumped up, kicked off her sandals, most of their soles worn-gone, gathered up her skirt, and splashed into the murky sandy waters that flowed between Ingram land, Brier Creek and the Ogeechee river. "Come on," she squealed, kicking her feet, wading out deeper. "*Oooo...it's* so cold! Feels so good." She wiggled her toes in the Georgia red clay sandy bottom. Then, pulling her skirt higher, she hopped up on a fallen log. "Water seems to've cleared a bit."

Hamilton knelt, fingered the mud and sand. "Silt seems to've settled some." Studying this enchanting wonder of a wife dangling her feet from the log, he let the sand dribble through his rough fingers.

"You are amazing."

Sarah caught his look and stopped kicking her feet, her hand resting across her belly. "What?"

"How lucky I am to have you."

"You sweet silly man...you'll always have me."

He pushed up his worn shirtsleeves and sighed, "Always is full of tomorrows where anything can happen."

With the hogs gone, they had no rendered hot fat for making lye soap, and scrubbings with the red clayish muddied water had stained his hands and arms.

Just the other day Sarah had said, "Your skin looks so coppery. That Cherokee blood of yours is showing through."

His skin was chafed by the coarse hoe handles, weeding their small garden patches or straightening used fence wire or nails he dug from the ashes. Just as well the mules were gone. Early rains had come up short. Meager corn hadn't tasseled good enough to feed them. Each day seemed to bring something else to do without.

Sarah slid off the log and sidled down next to him. He laid his hand on her belly. "You felt him move yet?" Ever since they'd lost that first baby, he'd enjoyed the thought of having children, of being a father.

Sarah beguiled with a coquette tease, pressed her hand atop his. "And tell me, Mister Know-it-all Daddy Ingram. Just what makes you think it's another boy?"

Hamilton turned quick mock-serious. "Have to be a boy to come into a world like this."

"Mmm—now you are being truly silly. You're always telling me how strong I am. Our daughters will be strong." She gave a toss of her tawny unbraided wave of hair and wrinkled her pert nose at him in a sassy smile. "Just like their father."

"And their mother." He kissed her cheek.

Sarah slumped back against him, closed her eyes, and murmured, "It's so peaceful here."

Hamilton laid is hand in her lap. He wanted to stay right here with her, here where a bit of serenity had managed to linger. He pined to laze away afternoons like this in the shade of the bayou beneath the leafy branches, and let the peace of this moment hang into forever.

"This is about the only place that's not changed."

"Our special place," she sighed, "that no one else knows about."

Half-listening, he went on, "Everything's topsy-turvy. They're makin' sure to keep it nice and legal while they steal an' grab all they can."

Sarah sat up. "You're not talking about the Hollows?"

"Don't matter whose land. Using their kind of bandit laws to make it legal. Gives me a whole understanding why Papa never liked politicians and lawyers. Taxes howling through the roof, and gold about the only payment they accept. Paper money won't do it. Like us, nobody has any gold. Typhoid and dysentery and gangrene, and having little to eat are a world difference from that Charlestown cotillion."

"Glistening sabers and beautiful gowns, all those uniforms with their gold braid..." Sarah's eyes grew misty. "When I think about those days, it somehow feels like it happened to someone else."

Hamilton dabbled the tip of his still-green cane pole in the water, its hook still stuck in the bobber. Hadn't dug any worms, didn't feel like fishin', just smackin' the water. He wondered who were the luckiest...the dead people or the ones struggling to stay alive. "Lots of things different, and would never be the same. Quicker folks get used to it, the better."

He slouched back against the trunk of the water oak. Its mossy rotting bark soaked a cool feeling against his back. His eyes drifted toward the purple wisteria twisted in the dogwoods and tulip poplars above them. Like idle ghosts braided among the limbs, lazy Spanish moss swayed in a green cathedral. In the serene stillness his eyelids grew heavy, the gurgle of water reminding him of Sarah's gay laughter that last time they went wading.

A soul-deep sorrow caught at him, for her, for their young son and yet-to-be children. The smell of her hair stung his nose, the yearning as strong, even stronger. Other good memories crowded in, the all-night hunting parties with friends from plantations around Queensborough Towne. Being a hometown boy, he was forgiven just about anything.

"Young bucks just feeling their oats," the sheriff once said after one wild drinking melee.

Lives sundered spirit from body. Such rememberings left him with an aching hankerin' for Bessie's strong corn whisky. Ingram men had a weakness for good whisky, some couldn't stop. It made for a seductive escape until he had to face another empty dawn. Hamilton fought the uncertainties in uncertain tomorrows. Others had run. Pulled up stakes, and *git*. He'd never run from nothing his whole life. Ingrams hadn't been run off their land by the British. He wadn't being run off now neither.

The reedy slim figure of Alexander Stephens had admonished, "Secesh means ruination." By the time the blind began to see his words, the choice was pitifully clear, "Either quit or keep fighting." Like most, Ingrams and Greers stuck with Georgia, keeping crops and livestock growin' to feed Johnny Rebs far and near.

Andrew Greer, Sarah's father, hoarded cotton. "Let Yankee merchants get hungry for Dixie's white. They'll back off, an' leave us be once England lets it be know she means to have the cotton."

Hadn't happened. Lots that was supposed to happen didn't. Lincoln's armies kept comin'. Blood flowed, casualties rose, a growing list of Hamilton's friends buried in unmarked graves if they'd been buried at all. Lamentable few came back in pine boxes. Lots of those that did make it back were broken husks of the starry-eyed happy-go-luckies gone off for glory and adventure. Hamilton sometimes felt guilty not totin' bayonet and rifle. No amount of sweat, hard work and sunburned shoulders took that from him.

Sarah unfolded her bundle, slipped into a pair of Ben's throw-off britches, breaking into his thoughts with her soft Georgia drawl. "You hungry?" she asked as she tightened up a makeshift belt.

"Why you change into those? You'll be all hot an' sweaty by the time we walk home."

"My dress was wet. I hate that feelin'."

Even her brother's rumpled riding pants hanging oversized and baggy on her didn't dim the wonders of this woman Hamilton loved with all his heart. Both enjoyed riding the vast acres, Hamilton about raised in the saddle. Roads being sparse, horseback was the only way to reach some of the backland gullies and sweet water springs of their family lands. Her hair flying free, Sarah scandalized the whole county riding like a man, not side-saddle like a proper lady should. Even worse she wore britches with her blouse stuffed inside. Riding prim and proper in a buggy with starched crinoline hooped over yards of linen did not fit to her liking of a saddle. She reveled in knowing Hamilton liked her willful behavior. It distressed Bessie, the house maid of Sarah's mother, Corinthia Gresham Greer. Like any daughter of opulent landed gentry, being one of the parish's own Sarah enjoyed position with status. Corinthia kept a watchful eye on her daughter's share of Greer contrariness. The young'uns, Ben, Sarah, Hamilton, and Samuel, Bessie's son, played together. Bessie had midwifed 'em all. Took off a whole day for her Samuel's birthin', then swaddled him and propped him beside her in the big kitchen back of the Bends.

Wisteria Bends, the Greer Plantation, thousands of acres of cake-icing cotton rolling over the gentle foothills of east Georgia that bordered the somewhat lesser acreage of Moccasin Hollows. The Hollows and its vested lands weren't extensive by cotton standards. Hard worked by Rundell and Hamilton, and jealously guarded with the usual Southroner passion for land. Ingrams and Greers were bred, borne and nurtured on old family crown grant lands. Money was vulgar. All that had mattered was the land.

On the walk back home they cut across the pasture. Hamilton's favorite sorrel chestnut stallion came trotting toward them with Sarah's bay gelding not far behind. The two horses were just about all they'd managed to hide and salvage.

Sarah said, "At least our picnic spot isn't torn up."

"It's about the only place left with any peace and quiet," Hamilton mumbled. "It tears at Papa all the time."

1860

2

A ndrew paused, Caribbean cigar in hand. "Rundell...if I didn't know you better, I'd think you was scared of that bunch of citified gasbag dandies the North has way too many of."

It was a heady, hot July, trigger-ripe with ready politics. At Wisteria Bends, salt-and-pepper haired Andrew Greer was hosting his lavish annual July 4th dinner on the ground for several landowners from East Georgia and parts of Alabama. Even the imported Seychelle *coco-de-mer* leaf porch fans along the shaded veranda didn't do much more than stir the sultry Deep South humidity.

"North don't have a corner on blowhards," Rundell chortled. "We got a fair crop of our own homegrown ones."

"You truly believe the odds be against us if we go for independence?"

Rundell was quiet for the longest, then softly said, "Favored way against us, but the main weight is economic." He swirled his glass of amber liquid, clinked the icehouse lumps of block ice against his drippy tumbler, and took a long swallow. "You know as well as I, that I'm not the only one thinkin' so. North and South both stirring the pot. No one's takin' a hard look at how things are. It's not just the South. Feelings are way harsh. Each camp makin' demands with no considerin' of consequences that cain't stand side by side." Another swirl, another guzzle.

"Rundell's put his finger right to the tender spots," Alex Stephens said. "Hotheads could cost us the very things we're trying to preserve." He'd buggied down from Crawfordville for the shindig, not only for the politics; he wadn't about to miss the renowned spread of food as well as the gracious and charming Corinthia Greer. "Slaves is only part of it and not a big part, but the chattel issue makes for an easy thorn. Jab us in front of the rest of the world. Not that I care what the rest of the world thinks, but Lincoln's election makes a good lightning rod for coddlin' up to the abolitionists. That Massachusetts bunch won't leave it be 'til the whole mess is a logjam with no guarantee those doing the jammin' will be around at the unjammin'. Crowin' fight is one thing, and startin' one is even easier, but keepin' that sort of scuffle to where you want it don't always shake out in the doing."

"That's the main reason we ought to get out now," Andrew contended. "Washington is a southern city squeezed between Virginia and Maryland. Northerners can leave." His words spit out like they were some kind of blasphemy. "Go their own way."

"Most of the talk is about the other fellah doin' the gittin'," Rundell said. "We don't take to being told what we're gonna do, and I avouch a goodly number of Northerners feel the same."

"Don't matter," Andrew snorted. "Federal capital cain't sit inside another country." He took a gulp of his drink and swallowed it down hard. "Virginia won't set still for Federals marching across her borders. Georgia neither."

"Andrew, if this separation is goin' to be so peaceable, where you coming up with this *marchin' across Virginia borders?*" Rundell contended.

"Might take a couple of weekend frays, but Maryland'll go along. Georgia won't stand alone. South has thoroughbred men and pure-blooded horses. North cain't match us."

"There's lots they got we can't match," Hamilton added.

"Let 'em yell," Andrew said. "There's not a damn thing they can do about it once we pull out."

"There's blockade talk out of some Ohio and New York conclaves about what they'll do if the South engages in what they're callin' renegade actions."

"That's poppycock scare talk," Andrew grunted. "Our coasts and shores are way too long with too many harbors. It'd take more ships than the whole United States Navy has just to plug up Charlestown or Savannah."

"They got shipyards," Hamilton said. "Big enough to build what they need."

"Then we build shipyards, build ships. Any ports or harbors they try to shut, we keep open," Andrew said. "No one can plug the whole damn Southern whisky jug."

"Funny thing about jugs..." Hamilton looked into his half-empty glass. "Ram the cork in tight enough, you bust the jug."

Alex Stephens said, "Could come to that."

Rundell said, "They won't turn loose just 'cause we tell 'em to let go."

"Georgia's militia can hold its own, hold open Savannah," Andrew glared at Stephens. "Docks, warehouses wharves at Augusta can hold the cotton 'til we're ready to ship. Same for Wilmington, New Orleans and Florida. Make the mills up north and in England hungry for it."

"Don't matter where a squabble starts," Rundell said. "Once it does it'll likely domino in lots of places. With trade as widespread as it is, it'll touch everyone."

"It's done started!" Andrew roared. "Look at Kansas. Union buttin' in where they got no right."

"Missouri's in it just as bad as Kansas," Rundell pointed out. "There's all manner of high soundin' words about what should or shouldn't be, or who ought to do the tellin'. Mark my word, livelihoods are bein' threatened, and that could take us where none of us have looked."

"The yards at Norfolk and Mobile and Pensacola are state properties," Andrew said firmly. "Central government has no right holding them if a state asks for 'em back."

"And if they don't give for the asking?" Hamilton threw in.

"Take 'em!" Andrew slapped his knee. "That's why states keep a militia. No cause for Washington City to say different." His neck pulsed blood-red.

"It's not only ships," Hamilton said. "Where's the..."

"All we want is for them to leave us be," Andrew interrupted. "The constitution leaves states with the final say-so. Powers not given to the federal government remain with the states. Too much control in the hands of the royal governors was the same problem."

"You sayin' words about leaving peacefully is just for show?" Hamilton asked. "We talk about poking guns in their face if they don't give. Where we gonna get the guns to take the forts they won't give up?"

Andrew was incensed. "I'm not eating crow 'cause of Yankee meddling! Georgia is *our* state, *our* land. Any man here will fight to defend ourselves."

"We're not ready, neither is the North." Hamilton had listened to other parleys with the same fever and disliked its drift. "Both sides're bent on arguing without looking where it's going."

"Andrew..." Rundell swirled his drink. "No one's trying to make the South eat crow. No one can force us to do what we don't want. South's too big. There's nothing to be lost by sittin' down an' trying to resolve it."

"Forcing it down our throats is exactly what those high and mighty falsifiers riding Lincoln's coattail are trying to do!" Andrew blustered. "Give 'em a couple of good set-to whuppings, they'll change their tune. We don't need riffraff factories and the likes messin' up what we got. Puttin' in a rail spur between here and Millen Junction is bad enough, ruinin' good farm land."

"North won't let go." Alex refilled his glass. "It's a little about jealousy and a lot about money. They want to enlarge the government, use the power to line their pockets."

"And pilfer a proper way of livin' they no longer got in their dirty cities," Andrew said. "If new territories come in as free states, we'll be outnumbered in congress. Once they got the majority it won't be long before they'll start passin' laws against us."

"We take ourselves out, we got to go peaceable," Stephens

maintained. "If it comes to a contest of arms, which is exactly where it looks to be headed, we best make double sure Federals do the startin'. Otherwise they'll make that we're the ones going against the flag."

"Damn Union's no longer like it was settled upon," Andrew muttered.

"True...sad, but true," Stephens nodded. "But that fact has little to do in the bluster and twist of words."

"Ever'day is more like King George squeezing the colonies," Andrew said. "Time we was rid of the whole lot."

Stephens gave Andrew a firm look. "Majority of people in the South, 'specially the upper South and border states, are against breaking up the Union. To lots of them the stars and stripes is a symbol."

"Stripes on that rag is gettin' to look more like prison bars. No longer something I'm proud to claim. Founding fathers wouldn't like it neither," Andrew said.

Stephens said, "Go against it for what appears to be no reason, it'll rile a good many who're straddlin' the fence, leave 'em little to no wiggle room."

"While they screw down tight," Andrew added.

"Don't fool yourself. Push come to shove, one battle won't settle it," Stephens said, "'specially if we win, and at first we likely will. In the long run it's up in the air. North thinks we're bluffing. That's a blinder both sides are wearin', a goodly bit of it our own doing. We snorted about seceding before, then never carried through. Another thing you best chew over. I'm not so certain leaving the union is a good pick, but whether it is or it ain't, it sure looks to be on its way. If so, there's a heap to be got ready. States cain't do it by themselves. If things were all nice and perfect, states could stand independent, but that's not the way it's shapin'. A southern government will be forced on us out of the need to have one. An' we better make up our minds from the start to have one that'll stand for what we want, or we'll face the same problem we got with Washington—states' rights. States got to have the last say, otherwise we end up headin' for unlimited executive power, same our forefathers had with royal governors. That's the barb bustin' the bubble. A state's first purpose is to guard its citizens against such a government." He gulped a full swallow of ice tea. "We don't handle this exceedin'ly judicious, Bob Toombs is of the mind it could draw out long an' nasty."

Hamilton drifted out onto the porch, away from the fried chicken and heated words. He gave out a slow sigh, ran fingers throw his windblown hair, crossed his arms, and leaned on the porch railing. His gaze roamed out over the surrounding roll of fields that made up the rural plantations and farms around Queensborough Towne. From beneath great, sprawled-limb live oaks, lush green fields spread far beyond the squabbles of committees and presidents and politics—or so it once seemed. He and Papa were busy with the running of the Hollows, he and Sarah and Ben no longer carefree kids playing kids' games. He'd never given politics much thought, but even his inexperience in the debating arenas could see conditions were crowding levelheaded thinking out the door.

His thoughts returned to a childhood playmate grown voluptuously enticing. A seductive tawny-haired lover who ate his nights and entangled his feelings. For Hamilton the Hollows, and Queensborough Towne, was his whole world. Yet, he couldn't shake Papa's fateful words of ugly clouds blowing around Georgia and the heart of Ingram and Greer hard-won land.

•

Warm weeks slipped into a stifling summer. One Sunday afternoon short, spry Bessie had a twosome picnic basket all wrapped and ready for Sarah and Hamilton.

"Missy Sarah, they be a stoppered bottle of lamp an' camphor oil against them redbug chiggers. Stirred fresh early this morn, wrapped it tight, stuck in the side corner of the basket." Bessie cautioned, "Ain't havin' you two come home, scratchin' in the night 'til you bleed."

"Thank you, Bessie," Hamilton said as he grabbed the basket.

She watched Hamilton help Sarah up, snug the basket under the seat, and climb up next to her. Bessie'd been around Hamilton almost as much as her Greer chirren. From the porch she continued watching Hamilton, his long, hurried strides toward the waiting carryall. "Somethin' sure be eatin' at you," she muttered to herself, and then waved as they drove off.

The buggy ride to their favorite shady spot on the creek bank took hardly no time. As Hamilton unloaded, Sarah pulled off her flared coal-scuttle cabriolet bonnet and shook loose her long, wavy hair. Humming a sprite ditty, she smoothed the picnic blankets, picked off stray pine needles, and laid out Bessie's fixin's. A spirited smile danced about the corners of her mouth, her sparkling, translucent blue eyes tinted with devilment a kelly green.

Hamilton slouched down on their pallet, nibbled a piece of Bessie's homemade cheese, and put it down. "Bessie packed us enough food for six people."

"Hamilton Ingram, if you don't beat all. Bessie fixes us this nice basket, and ever since you came over this morning you've had a case of mope-around. What's the matter?"

"Just me, I suppose." He nibbled the cheese again.

"If it's so unimportant why the sourpuss face?" She flounced as she put out the fresh baked bread. "I simply refuse to sit here and let your grumpiness ruin a perfectly glorious day. You just make your mind up right now to get over it. I won't hear of it, even if I have to tug you in the creek." She fixed her gaze on his lean body, liking the thought of skinny-dipping with him, seeing his body, touching him. "Every time you get around political talk you come away feeling truly awful. I believe you men like eggin' on all that talk, and I won't have it ruinin' our picnic. So stop it this very minute. You hear me?"

"I'm not very hungry." He rolled over and lazed on his back.

"You usually eat like a horse. You want some of Bessie's mince pie, or a sandwich?" she asked, slicing the homemade bread. "Bessie made your favorite." She set out a bottle of last year's wine.

Sarah then smeared camphor oil on her ankles, just in case there were any harvest-mites. She knew Bessie would put the picnic quilt through a boiling wash pot before it went back into the main house.

•

The year before, the Thanksgiving feast had been spread out on the broad grounds of Wisteria Bends with its majestic white columns and formal gardens. This year was the Hollows' turn to hold their annual sportive feed. The weather dipped just above a light frost the night before and left a refreshing coolness in the sunny air.

The Greers arrived with Ben driving his papa's pair of matched grays hitched to one of their shiny, black phaetons. Behind him in the second carriage, Sam was in the front driver's dickey seat of the double Brougham-Clarence.

After everyone was seated, at the head of the outdoor table Rundell Ingram finished the prayer with a solemn, "...And for what we are about to receive. Amen."

"I do hope there's enough," Corinthia murmured.

Bessie looked around at all the food, the decanters of homemade wines and corn squeezin's, and said, "Mistress Corinth'a, they be 'nough food here for us'uns an' ever hands at the Bends."

Hamilton's mother, Victoria Bothington Graeme Ingram, had died three days after Hamilton's birthing. Whether at the Hollows or Wisteria Bends, Corinthia was hostess for these family get-togethers. Weeks before each gathering, she always made sure they'd fatted up a nice, plump, roasting goose, maybe two. Have them ready and dressed out to stuff with sweets and relishes, and candied yams.

The cornucopia of eats never failed to assume sumptuous, unrestrained proportions. Food a rooted tradition, frugality a vice when it came to hearth and hospitality. Foodstuffs overflowed onto the great round table with its checkered cloth. More stacked inside on the parlor sideboards and in the dogtrot hallway—sweet meats, candied and baked sweet yams, spiced peaches with thick, sugary syrup, apple butter and fatback bannock cakes, beef dodger corncakes filled with minced beef, baked hams and roasted pork sides. If hunting was good, a fat turkey was shot just for the occasion. If not, then a big, roasting goose. This year their luck held. The turkey looked big enough to be more suckling pig than bird. Pickled cucumbers, baked pumpkins, muscadine jams, blackberry jellies, basted asparagus, and more desserts than any two congregations could eat.

With its gabled roof and three chimneys Moccasin Hollows had been built above a huge cellar of deep, wide divided bins, the dryness of the bins protecting Rundell's two favorite vegetables, stored potatoes and onions, against mildew and rot. Graceful steps led up to wrap-around, deep-shaded summer porches. It gave the impression of exactly what it was, a peaceful countryside home with more than enough room for widower Rundell and his only son.

With Hamilton's mother passed on, Bessie made certain to come over from the Bends with Corinthia's family. Sometimes come over by herse'f. Bessie was protective, pretty much had the say-so of both places. No one took care of her famblies 'cepting her, an' she saw to it they was took care of proper. Greers and Ingrams were as much blood to Bessie as the flesh of her own body. Anytime she dropped in on the Hollows, Bessie made sure her poultice satchel was in the buggy with her.

Bessie'd knowed for some time Mister Rundell had weak lungs, more'n once she'd stewed, "Mister Rundell, what I gonna do with you? You don't take care of yo'self one smidgen like you ought to. Cain't have you feelin' poorly." Checked the weather anytime she knowed he was gonna be outside for any length of time. "Knew when I spotted that shimmery circle 'round the moon last night it was gonna git muggier an' come up a thundery summer shower. No need a body riskin' a chill, come down with the achy banes an' lumbago ague. Hollows got no suitable house help, nothin' 'cept bargained hands for he'pin' with plantin'.''

Young Hamilton was as special to Bessie as eighteen-year-old sassy Sam, her blood son. Didn't take but a few butt-whallopin's from Rundell for youngster Hamilton to learn mouthy back—talk to any grownup, including Bessie brought swift retribution.

When Samuel come into the world, Corinthia gave Bessie a pledge Sam would never be sold away from her. Came down to as simple as Bessie and Sam were family. No fancy reasons or ugly mixed-blood skeletons. Corinthia loved Bessie, and it flowed both ways. Bessie would've gotten consider'bly riled if anyone say she was part of what needed changing. The Bends was her home, too.

Sarah passed Hamilton the silver-legged chafing dish. "Have

some more mincemeat shortbread stuffing. Bessie showed me how to roll the crust so it baked out light 'n flaky."

"I ate too much," Hamilton patted his stomach. "I'm stuffed."

"Wouldn't hurt to git some meat on your skinny bones," Bessie said. "Wouldn't hurt Mister Rundell, neither."

By late afternoon the cool of the evening was settin' in, the outdoor tables were cleared, and everyone retired to the roomy parlor, logs ablaze in the great fireplace. From now through the end of the season the fireplace would be kept stoked hot with Yule logs.

As Andrew and Rundell settled around the fire, Rundell handed Andrew several Virginia tobacc cigars. "Here, picked these up when I took my last cotton load to Augusta. Got to admit, they've a right good taste."

"You know those are one of my favorites."

"Yeh..." Rundell grinned. "Reckon I do."

Hamilton and Benjamin fired up stogies as well. Ben coughed and sputtered and his cigar went out. He took a swig of bourbon, re-lit and puffed away.

Rundell snipped off one end of his cigar. "Andrew, you putting in more tobacco next year?"

He reached to the fireside, took out a short piece of smoking lightwood. Blew on the end 'til it was red, and pressed it to his cigar. He drew several hard puffs, 'til his cigar glowed, then tossed the kindlin' back into the fire.

"Think I'll keep it about the same," Andrew said. "Maybe a few acres less. Prices come down some. I'm thinking it's too hot around these parts for tobacco. Besides, the last tobacc fields took the life out of the soil. Had to let them go fallow and pasture out for a couple of years, and they still weren't good for much but thistles and Egyptian millet."

"You might want to try some clover on those fields," Rundell said. "Bees have a real likin' for it, and it makes for tasty honey. Seems to pick up the soil right well. I'm thinkin' on increasing my sorghum acreage. Tried some last year. Made good forage and fodder."

"I don't know about grain." Andrew pulled a couple of puffs. "But you were right about it cuttin' down on feed I had to buy.

Still, the savings don't make up for the cotton yields I lost. I'm looking at buying those upper sections on the east side of the Bends."

"I heard they were up for sale."

"Got good water, good drainage."

"Land prices are high." Rundell blew smoke. "Too high for small farms. Several are selling out, moving to Texas. East Texas has prime land almost for the taking."

"Wish I had those fresh water springs you have."

"Hamilton an' me've been looking at puttin' in some dams, irrigate a good bit of our crops with the flow. Good drinking water, too. Doctors at that medical school in Augusta tested the water, said it was clean. Lots of iron—good for the blood. Comes out of the ground cold enough to raise goose flesh."

"Glad that squabble about Texas statehood is over."

"That fracas isn't over." Rundell spit into the fire. "Not by a long shot, not with the smell of Kansas in everyone's nose."

Andrew stabbed the air with his cigar. "I tell you, Rundell," his salt and pepper chin whiskers bobbed, "if that abolitionist, Lincoln, is elected, there's talk among several states about bein' shed of that bunch of instigators. South Carolina's hot. Governor Pickens already signed the call for a convention."

"I'm not so sure Lincoln's as bad as they say."

"Maybe not. But them cantankerous Republicans behind him sure enough are. They keep squeezin' and pushin', it leaves us little choice."

"There's always choices," Rundell reflected. "Spec'ly before things narrow down serious and get where they don't need to go. I tell you for a sure certainty." He sucked his cigar 'til it glowed. "North's got no corner on lamebrains lunatics like John Browns."

Andrew was adamant, "That rump session of democrats in Baltimore last April didn't do nothing except hand the republicans the election."

"We brought a lot of this on ourselves, things that are a bunch more important issues than slavery. Andrew, you're a good business man. You make every penny count, but you spend more money on keeping up slave hands than you do on buyin' land. With land prices climbin' higher ever year, investing in field hands idn't the best profit for your money. Cotton prices wiggle up and down. More farms are puttin' in more cotton, prices got nowhere to go but tumble. The money you pour into bond servants could be used for other things. I pinch corners myself. Cotton's like tobacc, it bleeds the land. We got to broaden our crops." He chewed off a butt and spit it out. "You an' me know lots of owners here 'bouts in debt up to their ears to northern banks. That's the worm stirrin' the pot. Agitators down here are doin' and saying things to stir trouble, but they don't say nothing about the real reasons. Politics follows the money. This secesh nonsense is as much about sidlin' out of debts owed as it is about slaves, and in the long haul it could end up eatin' more money than anyone's lookin' at."

Andrew squinched shut his eyes. "Secesh ain't nonsense." He stubbed out his butt, knocked it against the brass spittoon, reached for another stick, and fired up again.

Rundell said, "Lincoln admitted he's got no authority to touch slavery."

"Makes no difference," Andrew cut his eyes toward Rundell. "We take our leave, Lincoln can go to glory."

"It makes a whale of a difference," Rundell fired back. "Suppose a fight gets stirred, and we don't make it stick."

"Cain't trust politicians."

Hamilton and Benjamin quietly listened, with dark-haired Benjamin trying to master the strong cigar. Scarcely a year younger than Hamilton, more brother than brother-in-law to-be, Ben mirrored his father. Bluster-eager peppery to show Georgia boys could take care of themselves. Have done with it, get on with running things.

He looked at Hamilton. "What you think'll happen?"

Bluish smoke made slow corkscrews around Hamilton's head as he replied, "North won't leave us alone whether we secede or not." He blew another puff. "*Augusta Constitutionalist* said Virginia sent a delegation to meet with Lincoln, try to cool things off before the slide got too steep. An independent South has to have Virginia, Tennessee, Missouri, Maryland. Texas. For sure Georgia'll get plenty attention. Even then, it'll be an uphill struggle."

"Georgia can go it alone," Andrew butted in. "We got the

26

land, raise our own food."

"You're right farm-wise. But maybe we ought to look at history's lessons. In past contests between agricultural and industrial societies, the more developed side carried the bigger punch. What we got to stop them?"

"We fought George the Third and won," Andrew said. "British had industry. We had farmer soldiers, same as Georgia today."

"Colonies weren't all of the pieces. Without the French it might've turned out different."

"North try to stop us, we give 'em a good whup. That'll put an end to their buttin' in."

Ben took another long puff. "Y'all ready for the Christmas Cotillion in Charlestown?" asked Hamilton, weekend war talk put away. Hamilton stretched. "Your mama's been planning for Charlestown for the last six months." He rubbed his stomach. "Sarah mentioned it, too. Never know what your sister and Mama will cook up."

"That's for sure," Ben said grinning.

3

The last days of November lazed into December. Shorter Indian-summer warm days teemed with indolent blusters of multi-russet golden leaves. After a couple of hard frosts, chilly ev'nings became chillier. It made perfect weather for Rundell and Andrew's annual hog-killing week with plenty for the coming holidays—hams, rump roasts, middling meat, ribs and salted pork bellies.

After they'd finished up the last harvests Hamilton kept busy with things he'd put off, fences needing fixin', new tongues for the wagons and buggy, shingles for the barns and house. Sarah felt neglected. Pouty she was being taken for granted, she decided to remedy that, her snatches of being peevishly fractious failed to see exactly what her willful girlishness would do.

Never accustomed to being at anyone's beck and call, her petulance baffled Hamilton—and put him off. Which was exactly what spoiled Sarah wanted. The thought of getting his attention and being the center of his attention delighted her. Instead, in the weeks following Thanksgiving, she got a different taste of the Ingram's Welsh stubbornness as he kept more to himself, out in the fields, shodding and trimming the mules and horses, clearing new fields—wherever needed doin'.

At supper one evening at the Bends, Corinthia said, "Sarah, we haven't seen Hamilton lately."

Sarah gave her mother a silent I-don't-wish-to-talk-about-it look. Sarah felt if Hamilton truly was interested in her, he was staying way too busy.

Andrew reached for another thick slice of sugared ham. "Rundell and Hamilton been haying right heavy these weeks. Same as us. Wet season could set in any day." He dished another helping of mashed potatoes and cream sauce gravy onto his plate. "Dangerous putting too much wet hay in silage."

All during supper Sarah toyed more'n more with thoughts she'd been having. Of course she made sure Corinthia didn't catch her half-poutiness. Decided making Hamilton jealous was just exactly what she needed to do to bring him around. The next afternoon on their sashay stroll in Queensborough Towne, she made sure he caught her flirting with a casual familiarity. Unlike most of her other young acourting squires, his aloof stare at her was thunderingly silent. For the next few weeks Hamilton kept himself even busier around the Hollows. It wasn't at all what Sarah expected, and she never forgot her miscalculation. Some days later when she rode over to the Hollows, she received another eye-opener.

Rundell in the garden, saw Sarah riding up, leaned the rake on the fence rail, and greeted her with, "And how're you this fine mornin'?" He pushed up his hat and wiped his forehead. "Reckon you're looking for Hamilton?"

She slid out of the saddle and dropped the reins for the sorrel to graze. "I haven't seen him in weeks." Then with her sweetest face, added, "I positively hope he's not feeling poorly."

"I hope not either, since he's been off in Alabama for a month looking to buy some mules. How's your folks?"

Somewhat taken aback, she murmured, "They're fine."

"You like a glass of ice tea? Made fresh this mornin' with plenty sugar."

"That sounds perfectly wonderful, I'm terrible thirsty." She fanned herself nervously. "By the way, Mama reminded me to be sure and tell you that she asked about y'all," she smiled obligingly to hide her surprise. "Hamilton didn't mention he was going to Alabama."

They chatted a while, then gathering the reins, she said, "I must be getting back."

"Soon as Hamilton gets back, I'll tell him you paid a visit."

She nodded and spurred the horse into a canter. As she rode, Sarah wasn't sure which she felt, slighted or angry or a good bit of both.

The following afternoon as she sat with her mother in the sewing room, Sarah confided, "Hamilton ran off over to Alabama and didn't even bother tellin' me he was goin'."

"I'm sure there's a great many things Hamilton hasn't told you." Corinthia smiled and kept stitching the lace on the petticoat. "And being as intelligent as he is, he likely never will."

"Mother!" Sarah pretended to sulk. "If he loved me he'd've told me."

"My darling daughter, you just cut out actin' the little girl pouty act right the very minute. You're not foolin' anyone but yourself. You're not very good at it, except where your father's concerned, and he doesn't count. You're his sweet daughter. Which is a very good reason for Hamilton not telling you everything." Corinthia rested her sewing in her lap and looked at the eager-eyed daughter, who was so much like her father. "You have your heart set on Hamilton Ingram, and your father and I wholeheartedly approve. We couldn't be more proud. He's like another son to us, and most importantly, comes from a fine family. You couldn't find a better man, except perhaps your father." A knowing flash of fire swept Corinthia's eyes with her smile. "You know I love you, but you certainly have yet to understand a few things about men, 'specially one as complicated as Hamilton."

"Mama, whatever in the world do you mean?"

"You most certainly have seen that all those run-of-the-mill dandies who cluster about you at church socials are very unlike Hamilton. Of course you were drawn to him. Any woman in her right mind would be. When a man's upset he pulls inward. If he wishes to discuss it with anyone, he will, otherwise it's a closed matter. Such contemplation can last quite some time. Much longer than with a woman. If they're pushed, they can pull away entirely, and never reveal why. I find it quite charming. Your father's not at all like that, but Rundell most definitely is, and along those lines Hamilton takes after his father. Hamilton has a big heart, and takes things much more serious than he lets on. Men, and Ingrams in particular, keep their feelings to themselves. He gets that from Rundell and their French deWorthe blood. Ingram pride is monumentally infamous," she chuckled. "They can be relentlessly stubborn. Hamilton's mother, Victoria, knew it only too well. She loved Rundell, and made sure no one ever had to deal with that part of him. I've seen it in both Ingram men, Hamilton a bit more than Rundell. However, like you, Hamilton is young. It will come to no good for you to continue to play with him."

"I've never—"

"Sarah..." Corinthia's voice was sharp. "Just you stop it this very instant. My sweet, I've seen you enjoy the doin' of it. Which accounts for a great deal of the misunderstanding between you and Hamilton. He likely picked this time to go to Alabama because he didn't want to be around you. He's told you he loves you. For him it seems pointless in repeating it every day. That may not strike your fancy or your daydream idea of romance, but Hamilton and his father are truly one of the very few romantics. He respects you, and equally important, he respects your position. You'd best learn to appreciate what a true gentleman he is. Unlike a lot of lesser young men, he doesn't run around behind your back and has never been seen with those loose women in Queensborough."

Sarah was shocked her mother knew about those kind of men or the kinds of women she and Ben whispered and giggled about.

"And get that silly look off your face," Corinthia gave a nod. "You think your mother wouldn't know about such things? Any mother who cares about her family makes a point of knowing such things. You may tease other young parish rakes all you wish, but if you don't wish to drive Hamilton away, you will stop behaving as the spoiled daughter of Andrew Greer. And you are

31

spoiled—which I must take considerable responsibility for." Her face showed the slight warm genteel smile that was distinctively Corinthia Greer. "I love the endearing, willful child that is my daughter, but this very day, I wish you to put away this foolishness with Hamilton that I've seen when you flirt with other young gentlemen."

Sarah gaped. Her mother had never spoken to her like this, not ever.

Corinthia put down her crochet needle, leaned over, quickly kissed Sarah softly on the forehead, and picked up her hooked needles. "I trust we shan't have need to speak of this again."

•

As the day to pack and leave for Charlestown and the Christmas Cotillion drew nearer, the Bends was in a hustle-an'-bustle flurry to get ready. Corinthia was in an utter flutter, until the bolts of linen cloth she'd ordered from Savannah finally arrived. Bessie had all three bolts unfolded, sized in vinegar wine and hot water, bleached, soaked and rinsed twice, set overnight, stretched to fluff dry, readied to be cut to pattern, then sewn and stitched into frilled pantaloons and petticoats. Smaller bolts of gossamer satin were made ready to be encrusted with hand-sewn seed pearls for the dazzling fringes.

"Thank heavens the Balmoral shoes arrived. I'm so relieved they fit," Corinthia said. "But we've still to do the linings for the capot evening hoods, and we simply must do something about the lace for the gowns. It won't do, it doesn't match the bonnets. For the life of me I don't see how we can possibly have everything ready with all that's left to be done. These bonnets will simply have to be sent back." She held up the silver trimmed Trafalgar white satin evening gown.

Bessie said, "Mistress Corinth'a, that be the grandest gown I ever did see, an' they no need troublin' to send them off. Restitchin' that lace won't take half the time it'd take to traipse into Queensborough Towne and mess around with mailin' it. 'Sides, you might never see it agin. You know how the mails be."

"Mother, these bustles are so frumpy, they make me look

simply dreadful." Sarah tossed them back in the box. "And surely you don't expect me to wear one of those outlandish *Apollo knot* hair styles." Then she quickly asked, "We taking two carriages?"

"Three. Hamilton and Rundell will take theirs." Corinthia stretched another length of the material, while Bessie held it straight.

"Oh, goody!" Sarah exclaimed. "Hamilton and I can ride in one, Papa and Mister Rundell in one, and Ben can drive you."

"Sarah Greer..." Corinthia stopped smoothing the cloth. "There are times you behave like a brazen, citified hussy from Mobile."

"Mistress Corinth'a!" Bessie went goggle-eyed at the language.

Corinthia turned an austere eye to the unbending line between proper and unacceptable. "You'll ride with your father, like a proper young lady from one of the oldest families of Queensborough Towne should." Propriety simply was not to be infringed. "Young ladies have often amused themselves making eyes at young men. However, as your mother, it most definitely is my place to remind you of your obligations to your father and to this family. We may have been born to this position. Nevertheless, one has one's duty, and it behoves each of us to take care to see those duties are properly attended to."

Sarah rolled her eyes. "Being *proper* is what you always say when you can't find any other reason for me to do what you want."

"And I shall keep saying it until you behave accordingly." Corinthia looked at Bessie. "Bessie, what am I to do with this child? She has a mind like a piece of Georgia granite."

"Sam be the same. Headstrong as any Georgia mule that ever plowed. Here them silk hair nets you was lookin' for."

As she brushed her hair, Sarah asked, "How long we taking for the trip?" They'd be going through Augusta, and she'd make her own plans. What Mama didn't know wouldn't hurt nobody.

"Depends on the weather. Your Father is thinking six, perhaps seven days. Longer if we stay a spell with the MacLennans at their town home in Augusta."

"Weather won't matter," Sarah said excited, thinking, having all the time with Hamilton, he couldn't ignore her.

"Weather too so matter—git wet an' ketch a death," Bessie muttered. "Pray the good Lord see fit it don't rain, an' best makes sure my remedy bag be packed with 'nough poultices. Never know when a body need doctorin'."

"Bessie, by all means let's not forget that," Corinthia mumbled through her mouthful of pins. "Mercy me, I'm glad you remembered. However in the world would I get along without you?"

Bessie knotted the last stitch. Then smoothed the hand-starched, white collar of her new polka-dot dress she'd sewn from cloth Corinthia had seen her eyeing one day during a sojourn into Queensborough Towne. She snipped the short thread, and as she rethreaded her needle, Bessie said, "Sam be proud bein' head of the livery hands to South Carolina an' back."

"Sam's a good son." Corinthia checked her double-stitching along the seams. "Sarah, your father and I are considering stopping for a bit at the Clayborne place at Windsor Springs. I haven't seen Annie Clayborne in far too long."

Corinthia Greer was an exception to the social pretentiousness that plantation wives never worked. Red satin libertines of Savannah or Memphis bought ready-made, but Queensborough country folk made do. Buxom Corinthia used every trick of the latest fashions to keep her dumpy, hard-to-fit high-waisted figure from being too obvious. She religiously copied styles from pictures she'd seen from Paris and London or Richmond, always to compliment the curves of her ample bosom and hide what she most decidedly did not wish to draw attention to.

Corinthia hung the gown on its frame, taking extra care with the loose basted seams and ruffles pinned along the sleeve edges.

She stepped back. "Bessie, don't you think that ought to be enough gathering at the waist?" She fluffed the sides and the pointed bodice.

"Maybe a tad more tuck here," Bessie pulled a pin out of her mouth and added a pleat. "Not much though."

"Overnight in Augusta," Sarah murmured.

She laid her brush on the dressing table and walked out through the French doors of the sewing room onto the upper balcony. The thick, gnarled limbs of the huge trees speckled her with a breezy afternoon leafy shade. She thought of being with Hamilton the whole way to Charlestown, and thought of the time she'd spied on Ben skinny-dippin' in the creek. Her sassy thoughts replaced Ben with a shimmering vision of a wet Hamilton.

She turned back into the sewing room, and with a singsongy lilt to her words she said, "Charlestown will be such fun."

Bessie threw a glance at this rascal, tomboy daughter, which had become a fine-figured young woman. She brushed at the hairs straying from her pulled-back bun an' kept stitchin'. Missy wadn't foolin' her one dinky bit.

•

As soon as it arrived from Savannah, Hamilton tried on his new cotillion attire. Before his first fitting, he'd decided against wearing a hat. He liked the darker green velvet of the jacket with its satin lapels, pocket panels and stripe down the trousers, which matched the darker green of his pants. The maroon and matching green Welsh Gwyddelic designs in the brocade of the vest made it even sharper. He turned in front of the full length cheval mirror, the tailored cut of the britches, the dashing snug fit across his butt that showed off the muscled promise of his broad shoulders, fitting like a second skin. The smoothness of the velvet to his stout thighs interrupted by the swell across his belly was way more than some folk would call decent, leaving little imagining to the promise of this stalwart, robust scion of Clan Ingram.

His was a patrician, unbearded, rugged face, not necessarily handsome, but, like the rest of him, put together well. He liked the look. His pale hazel eyes, sandy bush of hair, even teeth, arched brows and the Ingram square jaw—the total package dressed for the kill. A smile to his face, his groin tightened. He and Sarah would be the finest twosome there. His fingers played through the ruffles on the shirt.

Hamilton preened. "*Mmm*, big boy—" and grinned at his animal leer from the mirror. "'Spect I just might ought to show up in church. Give 'em a good look and something to talk about."

He patted the swell of chest, his flat stomach, thrust his hips forward. The velvet pants pulled tighter.

"Well, well..." A beaming Rundell stood in the doorway of his son's room, pride shining his face. "Looks as though I've sired the finest looking young buck in the whole parish. How's it fit?"

"Fits good." Hamilton brushed his hands along his thighs as he turned in the mirror. "'Specially since that last fitting." The hang of the coat swung straight from his sides and over his hips. "Yours get here yet?"

"Picked it up yesterday while I was in town waiting for the smithery to finish the new rims for the carriage. Glad we re-rimmed. Found a couple of spokes dry-rotted near clean to the hub. One good bumpy rut on those chug hole Brier Creek roads might've busted the axle. Wadn't riskin' wheel trouble. Changing wheels on a loaded buggy can be the very dickens, dangerous if the buggy slips, and it always seems to be raining when something like that happens. Sort'a surprised me how long it took to get the iron for the straps. Smithery said he had cotton lorries lined up waitin' for parts, said he had to get them out'a New Orleans. Foundries in Richmond way too busy."

"Lose a wheel, we'd likely have to borrow a Victoria or leave someone behind," Hamilton said. "You give any thought about taking the train to Charlestown? We could board in Hamburg across the river from Augusta."

"Rather be in a buggy with a face full of dust than all those cinders," Rundell said. "And that brings up another thing I intended mentioning if we were short a buggy. No one's staying behind. For a sure certainty not you and Sarah." He gave his son that look. "Whether you believe it or not, I was your age once. Andrew Greer has been a good friend for many years, and that's not gonna suffer 'cause you and Sarah want to get each other's clothes off."

"Papa—" Hamilton started.

Rundell held up his hand. "Don't interrupt, this needed sayin' for some time. Sarah's got a wild streak in her as wide as yours, and both of you come by it honest. I've enough of my own—still got plenty. Got no quibble about the heat in a man's blood. Because your mother's dead don't mean I am. Makes for an interestin' life between a man and a woman, bonds you together against the bad times. I know you and Sarah done shared each other, and that's a good thing when two people love each other. But I'll not shame Corinne and Andrew by having it flaunted for the whole parish to take note of."

"Papa, I never—"

"Let me finish," Rundell said with firmness. "I'm not talkin' Sarah down. She's the making of a fine woman, an' I'll be genuinely proud to have her as a daughter. She's enough fire to keep the likes of you tuckered out. A man needs that, but I mean to keep Andrew as my friend in the doin'. Guard your times when you and her are together. Respect her and yourself enough to make sure it stays private." As he started out of the room, Rundell stopped, and said, "And be good to each other. Love each other, like your mother and me, like Corinne an' Andrew. It's nobody's business. See you keep it that way."

Hamilton was more than a little embarrassed that his papa knew. He unbuttoned and shucked off his fancy duds, then yanked up on his underdrawers and into his work clothes and boots, and hurried out the back door. In the kitchen, as Rundell finished his chicory he watched his strong-minded son head toward the barns.

As Hamilton carried the toolbox up the ladder to fix the hayloft door, he wondered how in the world Papa found out about his and Sarah bein' together. The 20th was not much more'n two weeks away. One Sunday left before they'd be starting for Charlestown. He couldn't wait.

•

"Right this minute you husht sech talk," Bessie's anger flared. Feet planted, fists on broad hips, dishtowel in one hand. "Don't let me hear you talk 'bout Marse Andrew like that. Never 'spected hearin' such talk from you. You been suckin' on Jamestown Weed, an' gone addled in the head? You hearin' me, Samuel?"

"He ain't my master," Sam spoke defiantly.

"Don't give me no sass mouth." His manner riled Bessie. "You not the onliest one around I hear talkin' that trash. 'Cause a body tell you a thing, don't make it so. Words comin' out'a you' mouth like you some blue-black what had no proper raisin', run-nin' your mouth 'fore you kick your brain to start. You ain't dumb—quit talkin' dumb."

"Mama," Sam pleaded, "...the Greers be way better than most owners, but that don't make the leash no less tight."

"Ain't no leash, an' if'n it was, it ain't tight. You talkin' it tight like tellin' lies. Samuel, what got in you? You top coachman here," Bessie chided. "Drive Marse Andrew's, Mistress Cor-inth'a's carriage. 'Stead of field work, you dress up nice when they goes 'bout, work in the main house. Have say-so for which teams be use. You keep mouthin' off, other hands 'bout the Bends'll use your word to git you put down."

Sam's green eyes were turbulent, stormy. "That just be it, Mama." His handsome high-yellow features fixed with a haughty pride. "No matter we don't smell like field hands, we slaves, no better off than street trash, what ain't—"

Before she thought, Bessie slapped his words shushed. As quick, her fingers grabbed her mouth in shock, tears wellin' up. She had never laid a hand in anger to none'a her chirren. Not Sam, not Missy, Mister Hamilton, or feisty Benjamin.

"Ain't havin' you raise your voice to me, ain't hearin' you call fambly *street trash*. Mistress Corinth'a learn you writin'. You been raised to have a mind, I is proud of you, an' you nigh to bein' full-growed, but you ain't puttin' sass to me less you want lumps. You don't respect me, you got no respect for yourse'f." Her anger sof-tenin', she continued, "Marse Andrew never hurt you, an' he don't keep no overseer. Marse Andrew never mistreated nary one of his hands. Seen him buy mistreated hands to git 'em from those what does whup."

"We be owned like mules be owned."

"That better'n shiftless trash in town what belong no place with nothin' to put in their stomach. You, Benjamin an' Hamil-ton growed up together, I loves Ben, Missy an' Hamilton much as I loves you. Love be one thing, the more you gives, the more you gits. Powerful lot've folks done forgit that, an' look at the ugly it be causin'."

"Benjamin own me," Sam brooded.

"Benjamin don't own nobody. Marse Andrew didn't buy us

neither. I come with Mistress Corinth'a at her marriage to Marse Andrew. 'Sides, Marse Andrew an' Mistress Corinth'a been talkin' 'about givin' some hands their own plots to grow their own crops, raise their own meat."

"I hearen lots'a talk, but that all it ever be."

"Marse Andrew don't hold strong to slavin'."

"But we still slaves," Sam snapped. "Least up North they talkin' 'bout endin' it."

"White folk in a bad pinch. Marse Andrew go agin the law it come down on him, an' git you sold God know where away from me."

"What be worse than bein' owned?"

"They's lots worse. Greers and folk what don't hold slaves, like Mister Rundell, in the same pinch with no easy out and not much say how it be."

"Seems simple 'nough...quit slavin'."

"All this shoutin' make it no better. Some words be the same as what you mouthin'."

Sam smeared away a tear and turned toward his mother with his curly head drooped. "Mama, I ain't staying' chained."

"Ain't no chains I see."

"They's the worse kind. Tears me up you willin' to stay so." His face was ashen. "Folks here'bouts talkin' fight."

Bessie was dismayed by what come from her flesh and blood. "You call *free* livin' like a night-crawlin' city rat scurryin' for the next mouthful anywhere it can sniff? Free got more to it than highfalutin' blab. We gots lots to be thankful for, a roof when it rains, four walls when it cold, food so we ain't hungry."

The look in Sam's eyes give Bessie fear; she didn't know how spite got so planted in this willful son. Her words was blowin' in one ear an' out the other like leaves in a windstorm. Pullin' Sam to places dirty and wrong, places her Lord say don't go, learn him godless things to hurt others.

"Bends be your home, you birthed an' growed here. Home be what make us what we be. If'n you cain't be free in your home, no matter what nobody say, sure as Jesus be watchin', no conjurin' gonna make you free in no sin-hole cities." She continued with a firm jut of her chin, "Loose women wearin' frilly next to

nothin', flouncy pantaloons with lace garters, peddlin' their wares
for whatever gold come janglin' along."

"This ain't my home, an' it ain't yours. Nothin' here be ours,
we ain't even our own." Bein' property had been diggin' at Sam
worser each day.

"You cuts loose from where you growed, away from those
what loves you, a body git lost quick. That what blood-kin be," a
fearful dread fillin' her like never before.

Afeared Sam's grindin' determination could make him a
flown-the-coop fugitive. If he run, she know there be no he'p.
Most hands here'bouts wouldn't tell, but worser, a few would.
Sam might would listen to Hamilton, but that'd put Hamilton in
a terr'ble fix. Seemed ever'one was locked tight to how it was.
Politics was white folks doin', but they was truly makin' a mess of
it. Bessie was scared. She'd seen posses and their dogs.

That long, cloistered night she wore out her knees prayin',
"Sweet Jesus, Bessie got a true burden. You bless me with a
lovin' son. But Lord, that sweet son of mine, he sure 'nough done
growed into one mulish, thickheaded man. You never give Bessie
what I cain't tote, but this heart be terr'ble heavy full of dread an'
sure need consolin'."

•

Andrew Greer had the older of their Victoria four-wheeler
carriages modified for four passengers, adding heavier suspension
and leather upholstered seats. With its polished, black leather top
raised against the sun, it rode easier as it crunched along on the
graveled road toward Queensborough Towne. Dressed in his finest, the reins loose between his fingers, Sam kept the paired black
geldings to a matched, steady slow clop. As they rolled into town,
gentlemen along the streets lifted their hats to Corinthia and
Sarah. Bessie, all the while, kept an eye on the back of Sam's
head as he sat ramrod straight on his raised up-front driver's
dickey seat.

"Mother..." Sarah piqued. "I don't see why we had to get all
gussied up, just because you feel it necessary to put on fancy
airs?"

"Proper manners doesn't cost a British ferthing." With ever the slightest of nods to passersby, the Mistress of Wisteria Bend gave slight smiles and quietly said to Sarah, "We have a position to maintain, as well as setting proper examples."

The creaking, glistening carriage turned onto the crowded Saturday-go-to-town main street. With stern looks, Bessie made sure no insolent stragglers gave uppity looks their way. Near the market, they saw the pushed-and-shoved huddled bodies, dull-dispirited faces etched with bewilderment, bold pride in a few, waiting for the bidding to start. Rumors had spread of a slave ship having docked in Wilmington four days ago—bargain prices up for the highest bidder. Owners from Queensborough Towne and as far away as Marthasville, Savannah, and Selma were present. The faces looking back at Bessie made her pity their plundered homes. She'd heard of the raids in faraway Africa, didn't see how one soul could treat another sech a way. Bessie fixed her eyes straight ahead and mouthed a silent plea Sam would behave.

Early that morning, a fidgety Bessie had warned him, "Mistress Corinth'a an' Missy be callin' on the Whiteheads an' McClendons. This be auction day. I don't want no show-off mouth from you in front'a town trash."

"Mama, I ain't never shamed you, ain't shamed none at the Bends or Hollows. I wouldn't do that."

"Maybe, but sometime you makes me think that head a yours need a good purgative, when you talk like you a slobberin' fox gone crazy with the rabies."

From his carriage seat, Sam cut his eyes toward her. Bessie glared back, clutched her umbrella tighter as their carriage moved on.

"Bessie," Corinthia asked, "whatever is the matter?"

"Crowds git the horses 'citable. Glad when we be back home."

Corinthia leaned forward. "Sam, take that next street. These crowds are upsetting your mother, and I can't say I care much for them either."

"Yas'um..."

Sam fixed on the slack faces to be sold, noticed a few eyein' his fine clothes. Mama was wrong.

As Sam turned the carriage up the curving drive, and brought it to a slow creaking stop at the front of the Whitehead's town mansion, Sarah said, "Mother, must we do this?"

"Yes, we must. Your father is a business associate of Jonhathan Blynhest Whitehead. As your father's wife, much as it is to my distaste, I will support your father, and you would do well to learn such behavior. It makes things so much simpler."

"I think it's perfectly ridiculous."

"As well you might."

As the buggy creaked to a half, in a high-flown commotion of crinoline and taffeta, Abigail Bothwell Whitehead flurried down the wide steps to greet them with her gushy, drawn-out fluffy insincerity, "Lands sakes, I do de-clare..."

With years of practice, Corinthia remained thoroughly imperturbable, saying, "Abigail, you must forgive me," not about to allow the likes of a Whitehead having the social upper hand. In her lithe Virginia blur of vowels, she smoothed, "I'm so utterly mortified."

"Corinthia, whatever in the world do you mean?" Abigail bubbled. "Y'all come right on in. I've just put a fresh pot of tea to brewin'."

What an barefaced falsifier, she's never boiled her own water, Corinthia thought to herself, as she said, "We've been so dreadful busy, I should've called on you weeks ago. Time gets by so—a body hardly notices."

Like the proper young lady, a bored Sarah quietly sat in the drawing room, daintily sipped her tea. Thinking how they'd be here for hours with this chitchat folderal, and wishing she was out riding.

Bessie stood to one side, tryin' not to think of Sam. She remembered Mistress Corinth'a calling these uppity folks with no manners *merchants..*

"It's understandable you're being so busy," Abigail sighed. "There's simply no time to do all the things a body must do to get ready for the Saint Catherine's Christmas Ball." She placed her Wedgwood cup and saucer just so on the marble-top tea table.

"Of course," Corinthia fastened on a charming smile. "Charlestown is all the talk."

Abigail leaned close, intimate. "I spoke with Jonathan. He

wouldn't hear of taking time off, spending the season in Charlestown. Heaven knows it would've done him a world of good. I told him if the Greers and Ingrams are going, the very least we could certainly do is be in Charlestown to welcome our Queensborough friends." Her immaculate French maid hurried in with more tea and an array of sweets.

Corinthia sipped with her smile fixed in place...*Showy hanger-on.* Being invited to Charlestown's Saint Catherine's Ball the week of Christmas was all the talk, not only Georgia and South Carolina, but considerably beyond. Invitations had come through Andrew's cotton and tobacco friends. Corinthia wasn't about to countenance having anyone think the Whiteheads were more than business.

"I surely understand why you're so very excited," Corinthia said.

"I was so relieved the invitations arrived yesterday." Abigail Whitehead fairly beamed. "When your man dropped off your note telling me you would call, it put me all in a twitter. Our invitations hadn't arrived. I immediately sent Jonathan straight to the post office." She rolled her eyes in mock insipid pinched smile, and gloated, "I was so reassured when he came back with them." She could hardly contain herself—*the* perfect dig at uppity Corinthia Greer. "It will be so grand. Anyone who's anybody will be there."

Sarah's expression matched her mother's composure. Corinthia's attention never left Abigail. Sarah knew how venomous this artless woman could be.

Corinthia gathered her gloves, and rose. "I do have other calls to make, and with the roads being so crowded with drays and freight wagons, Andrew insists we be home before nightfall."

"Of course." Abigail stood as the doorman retrieved their capes.

"You must pay the Bends a visit during the holidays." Corinthia pulled on one glove. "We're planning a New Year's masque festive."

Corinthia's cordial invite belied its command summons. She'd been bested, and it did not set well. She knew full-well an invite demanded another gown, and Abigail was widely known for spending more money than her husband could afford. She certainly was not about to stretch Southern hospitality by having any Whitehead drop in whenever they pleased.

"Gracious sakes!" Abigail's favorite expression. "Another ball—we'll be de-lighted." This was a royal convocation not to be turned down, if she ever wanted to receive another. "The season is getting simply so crowded."

As their carriage pulled away, Corinthia gave an ever so slight nod, and sighed a relieved, "Mercy me—"

Sarah needled, "Mother, how could you invite them?"

"Abigail Bothwell is insufferable," Corinthia's words were smooth as whipped chocolate. "She has never known her place since the day she married Jonathan. To think she calls that clap-trap house a *mansion*."

Sarah spluttered, "She'll tell everyone you invited her."

Corinthia's eyebrows arched. "Are you quite sure you're not concerned with more than invitations?"

"I haven't the slightest idea what you mean."

Bessie hee-heed. "You gots lots'a learnin' ahead of you if'n you think you foolin' your mother. You got the *don't-likes* for Betsy Lou Whitehead 'cause she wants to get Mister Hamilton in the hayloft."

Sarah glared at Bessie, and huffed, "Papa says they're cut from same cloth as lawyers and politicians—just a different kind of goat."

"Why Sarah Cornelia Gresham Greer—how vulgar, like something off the wharves at Savannah." Corinthia brushed at her dress and smoothed her cape. "I get so provoked with myself, behaving so wretchedly shoddy. Abigail is so unsuitable. Nevertheless, one must uphold one's position. Let's all settle down. I've been looking forward to visiting with the McClendons for weeks."

The McClendons were old money, bankers, lawyers, land owners from Virginia with a modicum of gentility.

Corinthia said, "Even if the Whiteheads go to Charlestown, we don't have to be seen with them. We'll simply handle it."

4

Hamilton helped Rundell pack the mule for the hunt with Andrew and Ben. The two Greer men had gone ahead the day before.

Rundell mounted his horse and took the mule's halter. "Likely see you sometime tomorrow afternoon 'bout sundown. Depends on if we have to dress out any kills we make."

"Y'all have a good hunt," Hamilton said.

Andrew called back, "We find the game we want, we ought to be back about dark."

As early evening light began to fade, they set up a camp a considerable downwind distance from their hunt spots. Ben got a good fire started. Banked the fire so it'd have a good bed of coals. Gathered more firewood if they needed it, when they come back. Hurried to join where his Papa had set up their shooting spots among the stand of old pines. They heard a couple of deer, but nothing else showed. It was long after midnight by the time they got back to their camp, the heavy evening dew had set in. The fire felt good.

"Hope we have better luck before sunup," Andrew said. "Last chance we'll have to stock up on venison before leaving for Charlestown day after tomorrow."

Back at the house, Hamilton doubled up on chores that needed doing. By eventide he'd called it a full day, and he and Sarah huddled in front of the fire with the big wooden bread bowl of poss corn with plenty salty bacon rendren.

He pulled the popped corn from the fire, shook it into a bowl, and stoked another log into the flames. "While we're in Charlestown, one of your papa's hands is coming over to tend the fireplace, keep it stoked." The tradition of a cold hearth, holiday or otherwise, was simply not allowed in case a weary wayfarer needed a stopover respite and warm up.

Sarah lay across his chest. Her fingers toying with his open shirt, along his hairless chest, bronze-dark nipples and the work-hardened muscles she loved to touch.

He nibbled a couple of kernels, pulled her against him, and murmured, "I love you." His tongue teasing the rim of her ear, down the curve of her neck. "You have any idea how truly special you are to me?"

"*Ummm*...me too you," she nestled cozy closer. "You haven't said that in a long time." Her loose hair splayed against his skin.

"We'll have to be mindful while we're in Charlestown." His words floated in shadows of warm skin and good smells.

Sarah gave another, "*Umm...*"

She felt good being with him, each time better than the last. Her hand nestled into his warmth, traced his stomach, the pleasures his flesh gave to her, flesh and skin he'd learnt her to crave with all manner of delights he gave her.

She sat up. "Clothes get in the way." Hurriedly she discarded hers down to bare glowing skin. "Now you." Her skin bloomed soft, mellow, enticing. "I want to see all of you."

His nostrils flared. He lifted his hips, kicked off his boots, socks, heavy legging underwear. The genteel Southron that was Hamilton Ingram peeled gone in singular urgent motions of wadded clothes as he reached for her. Sarah was enthralled with her virile, bull of a man, her eyes and hands all over him, caressing, stroking the tender parts of his body where she knew it thrilled him to be touched, his suntanned neck and shoulders and arms dazzled in stark contrast to his milk white butt and thighs.

Sarah pressed him back and rolled on top. His power arrowed bolts of white sparks through her insides. This irresistible male animal singing little darted shivers through her made her yearn for his sweet dyings, wanted to cuddle inside his tender iron embrace. No matter any others, her bedroom fancifuls were of Hamilton's majestic naked body, golden and storming her night-dream fancies.

His engorged power drove rough and demanding against her, into her, the world around them becoming only the two of them. She clung against the feel of his lips scooping along her belly and searing her with the singular desire for more of him. His body strained with ravenous gluttony, his pupils becoming bottomless craters swallowed in his bronze dusky green eyes. The two of them unsated in indulged voracity, wildly raced through the night.

With a long drawn heave Hamilton groaned, "God... " and with incoherent mumblings, his dervish body shuddered.

Their breathing slowed in the tranquil afterglow, hearts bumping against bare skin. Her arms enclosed his broad, field-hardened shoulders. Her lazy tongue licked his skin, tantalized tastes of sweaty beads reflecting the dance of flames from the fire.

Passion was quenched for the moment. Crackling logs crumbled, white glowing embers sloughing to drab ash reds. Sarah pulled the quilt over them. She felt safe and warm cradled in his arms.

"Still love me?" came her soothing words.

"I suppose..." he mumbled. "Right now you've got me too tired to love."

They dozed, Hamilton satiated. Gently slipped his arm around this soft wonderful genteel creature, who could be so untamed. Never quite sure about her. Thoroughly mystified by what she might do next.

"You are so bad." Sarah buried into him.

"You make me that way, Sarah woman."

"And don't you ever forget it," she giggled.

"You are the most perplexing woman I ever met." He rolled onto his back. "You've a mouth right out of a sportin' house when we're like this. Boiling my blood, beggin' me to do more an' more." He nipped her a quick nibble-kiss on her ear.

"And how would you know about sportin' houses?" She nestled her hand across the slick heat of his belly.

He grunted, grabbed at her hand, saying, "Tales I've heard."

"I feel so good." She stretched, then teased, "Moccasin Hollow, whorehouse of Queensborough Towne. Wouldn't churchgoers split wide open if they could see us like this."

"While they run an' hide their own buggy-ridin' shenanigans. If they'd practice more of what we just did, there'd be a lot less loose tempers."

Both of them snickered, nuzzled one another. With long drowsy sighs Hamilton's eyes drifted shut, his work-solid arms around the woman he loved. In the sweet after-melting, he savored the smell of her, this voluptuous headlong thoroughly female woman that held his heart. Why he loved her was beyond the call of flesh to flesh. He could get that for the asking from any number of willing partners around these parts, not a few of which had husbands and children. He'd long ago quit trying to understand. Putting it into words didn't matter, it just felt good to be with her. Something of her vanquished more than the scalding eagerness of skin.

No boar stud run wild, Hamilton Ingram'd had his fair share of the parish fillies. Some of them way more lusty than he wanted to handle. A couple of times tearing at his britches, under his shirt, inside his pants, the horse trotting casually along, the buggy creaking and bouncing. Next morning he found his chest or back with long bloody nail tracks. A few roaring escapades had reached Rundell's ears—which he never spoke of. Benjamin shared tales of wild sowings in the quarters. Hamilton had nothing against such things, but he wanted no part of that. No seed of his grew in the belly of a bonded chattel. Moccasin Hollow was tied to and symbol of the Ingram name with Papa its steward. Heir to a legacy passed on by generations of fathers to sons, Hamilton's duty to that lineage and its traditions were important to him.

The moonless night enclosed the three men like a familiar blanket. Andrew rubbed his dry, chafed hands, then held them to the fire. "Ben, be sure those carcasses are hung good. Bears or wolves'll gnaw 'em down for sure."

"They're strung high," Ben called out, as he continued dressing out the last kill.

Rundell tossed on a couple fresh logs, sending dancing dots of sparks into the brisk December night. "Fire feels good."

Off in the swampy backlands, a great horned owl hooted into the empty night. Ruffled his feathers, as it turned big yellow eyes toward the fire, eyeing all manner of four-legged things skittering in the dim reflections. It had been a good hunt, two deer and three plump turkeys, bounties for the holiday jubilee. Wouldn't have to hunt after they got back from Charlestown.

Above the background babel of cricket-and-frog nightsounds, Andrew said, "Rundell, sure wish you could see clear to changing your mind. We could use your say-so when the convention comes to the vote. Folks listen to you."

"This push for secesh…" A deeply troubled Rundell said, "I cain't back what I don't see being the best move. I plain don't see a need for all the hurry."

"You cain't deny the agitation."

"No." Rundell spit into the fire. "Cain't deny that."

"Look what happened at Harper's Ferry last year. Look at Kansas. Lawrence was four years ago, an' they're still fightin'. Kansas is Missouri territory, Kansas ought to be open to us same as Missouri. Those New England agitator bigots bought and shipped weapons to John Brown. Deliberately stirred insurrection—law don't mean nuthin' to that gang."

"You'll get no arguen from me on that account," Rundell said.

"Before he died, Calhoun warned we were in trouble. South should'a got out ten years ago, when the odds weren't tipped agin us. That Christiana situation in Pennsylvania should'a made folks see the light. Federals made no move to enforce it or protect property, yet when the law's on their side, they want it enforced.

They mean to use tariffs to whittle us down. Force up interest rates on what we owe, make fortunes for themselves off our sweat."

"You're right about the money. It's way more to do with that than fancy words about property and state lines," Rundell said.

"Except for the territories, they want to deny Southern states their rights in the territories." Andrew gave a dogged tug on his plug of pigtail tobacco. "Rights they agreed to, then refuse to enforce. We made a whoppin' mistake with that 1850 compromise."

"That's been hashed over 'til it's ragged out." Rundell gave a weary sigh. "But Calhoun saw another threat standing hard by with secesh."

"That bein'?"

"We leave the union, leave congress, we've got no checks and balances, no constitutional guarantee of any kind. It's do or bust."

Rundell and Andrew bestraddled the tug between all-fired hurry and caution. Rundell couldn't shake childhood tales of old wounds he'd heard during the colonies' upheavals with the British. Neighbors against neighbors, farms and towns upriver from Charlestown and Savannah Towne plundered, lives lost, families ruined. Unleashing war hounds didn't take much. Keeping them aimed where you wanted was an entire difference.

"Andrew..." distress wrinkled Rundell's blue eyes, "this has been talked since before our kids were birthed. Now everybody seems to've dug in. We saw it with those Virginia knuckleheads ignoring Bobbie Lee. Lee's not one to get loud, but he didn't mince words neither. He said it flat out, *secesh is revolution.*"

"That's one more reason we ought to get on with it before Washington City puts more troops into Southern forts."

"It'll take a good deal more'n our taking a few forts or a couple of weekends of waving sabers and cavalry charges. Once that's in the wind, and blood's been spilt, Lord only knows where that could take us."

"Won't matter," Andrew assured. "Once we've on our own, they can do as they damn please."

"That's what I mean," Rundell said, just as dogmatic. "Suppose them doin' as they please don't turn out to be exactly what pleases us."

"Let 'em!" Andrew said confident. "Federal government was supposed to be a republic. That's changed, and so has any reason for payin' lip service to a high steppin' Federal City that ever'day shows this so-called Republic ain't worth a burnt fritter. Rule of the majority is a damn democracy—in a country this big, worse government possible. Gives a big bunch the power to run over the little fellows. We ought'a leave for the same reason we wanted away from royal governors an' Farmer George. Without private property guarantees, a Union is useless."

"Most would likely agree with you, but ever'body's holding to things they ain't gonna turn loose, while at the time devisin' how to make the other party do the bendin'."

Andrew slapped his knee with the flat of his hand. "North wants to control the government, use the South and keep us a part of the whole in the doin'. Secede—let the Devil take 'em all."

"Right there, Andrew, is the whole tight stick of it."

"They cain't make war on cotton, it'd cost more money than all the banks put together. Show 'em who's runnin' the show, let their damnable mercantile economy collapse."

"There's more'n one side to ruination." Rundell stared into the embers.

"Slavery isn't the issue," Andrew said unyielding.

"You're right," Rundell agreed. "But it's the one that riles folks the quickest."

The pine logs sputtered, hot sap bubbled, crackled, sending up a fireworks of sparks. The owl hooted, this time a little closer.

"We can take care of ourselves," Andrew said, convinced by his own words. "Won't matter what they say."

"Any time you tumble off a cliff it's a certainty something's about to hit bottom. Trouble is, most aren't seeing the edge of the cliff. North don't understand how truly serious things are." Rundell poked the fire with a stick. "Andrew, if we stay in the Union, we can make them take heed of the grievances."

Andrew squinted. "Staying to the Union won't cut it. They on top of us in half of that worthless Congress. Compromises don't work. They yelled about Calhoun's nullification, yet they act like it's okay for them to do the same damn thing long as they call it their *Christian duty*. Abolitionist states won't enforce the law. Our last check was a presidential veto with an equal vote in the Senate. With Lincoln in and Kansas gone, we're cornered. It's either get out or knuckle under, an' I ain't for knucklin'.''

"No one is," Rundell said, "but they cain't ruin the South without ruining themselves. Secesh will squeeze Unionists in a corner like they're doing us. Ever'one's sayin' how cotton's our ace. Me'n you've seen cotton prices drop way down. With cotton lands opening in Texas, more cotton hit the market, drops prices further. I'm givin' thought to maybe plantin' none. A good many farms here'bouts are pullin' up stakes, sellin' their land, headin' west. There's good land adjacent to the Hollows up for sale, but for my thoughts it's still overpriced. Most plantations borrow money to buy hands, borrow more to meet debts. Borrowin' on crops still in the ground is risky. No matter what raw cotton pays, in the long run slavin' and cotton cain't do it."

Andrew snorted, "You're talkin' building factories and mills."

"We send raw cotton to mills up north, to England, then use borrowed money to buy back yarn or finished goods. Bank loans and interest forces the plantin' of more cotton, borrowin' more, the debt keeps growing. With our own mills more money would stay here, and we'd rely less on happenin's beyond Georgia."

"Rundell, at harvest time you pay your part-time hires hard-earned gold two to three times as much as factory workers make. Besides dirtying up cities, their factories are just another kind of ownership, yet they got the gall to condemn us for the way we do it."

"Yep, I pay more, but not near what you expend in chattels," Rundell said. "I've never known you to sell either."

"That's Corinthia's doin'. She always made sure they're cared for."

"Lincoln said he'd compensate slave owners."

"Scheming words—that'd never get through Congress," Andrew argued. "Congress send Lincoln a bill without that, which gives him the excuse to claim he tried. Lincoln's nothing but a black Republican with a bag full of shyster tricks. But with us holding cotton as the ace, Northern banks cain't afford to let Lincoln unsettle things. Their loans go down, it'd cause the worse panic anyone ever seen. Once we're free of their bank schemes, they'll have to talk with us. Cotton is the...blood of our..." Andrew almost said *country*, "...of the cotton states. We raise plenty food, way more than the North. They cain't starve us out."

Rundell poked the fire. "Andrew, those German farms across the North produce some mighty fine crops. An' they got a number of heavy industry centers across those states."

"We don't need factories. Ship our beef, grain, pork, mules, tobacco, timber all over the world, use our raw material as commodities to buy anything—guns, powder, pig iron. An' we still got plenty timber to build ships."

"North has messed up ideas about us," Rundell quietly added. "An' our ideas are just as messed up concerning them. We've grown apart."

"I can't see we ever growed much together," Andrew growled.

"Takes time to train good soldiers."

"I declare, Rundell..." Andrew gave out with a horselaugh. "You know better'n most—we got no need to train men. Southron men been riding our whole lives, we got the best cavalry in the world."

"Cain't nobody dispute that. But tell me where we get the hands to do the planting and harvesting if most of us are off cavalryin'? North has factory workers who can go soldierin' with plenty others left to get in the crops, make uniforms and blankets, build wagons, run foundries for cannon, bullets, gun powder. I've traveled up there. They got more to do the doing than we have across the whole South, Texas included."

"Governor's gonna keep Georgia militia in Georgia. Make sure we can do both. Farms like our's will keep runnin' just fine. If I was away the Bends would keep right on. Anyhow, those citified dandies got no stomach for a fight. One good whup, they'll skedaddle, talk peace quicker'n you can bat your eye. They ain't gonna fight for something that don't concern them."

"Andrew, one minute you're say how determined Washington City is to down us, then how they'll let us go if we show them we mean to fight."

"They'll back off like they always do," Andrew said, satisfied.

"Not if they've backed as far as they mean to back!"

"Then we show 'em how serious we are."

Rundell said, "They got more men, more money, more guns, more of everything."

"Outnumbered don't mean nothin'. Georgia won't be alone. Tennessee and the Carolinas'll stand with us."

"How you think Carolinians gonna feel being dragged into a fight they're not too happy about?"

"Tar Heels won't stand for Federals invadin'." Andrew had figured it all. "Virginia neither. We stand together they's not enough Yankees between Canada and Mexico to hold the South."

"That makes good convention oratory." Rundell cocked his hat on the back of his head. "But it don't answer if they land at Savannah or Charlestown or Mobile—anywhere along our coasts. You're not talkin' about Georgia, it'll tug the whole South." He pulled off the end of the cigar, spit out the butt, deep in his heart knowing precious few clear whys and wheretos remained.

"South Carolina already asked states to send delegates to Montgomery to work out setting up our own government."

"With that hothead Barnwell Rhett right in the middle of it." Rundell hated this mad acceptance to a bust up. "Yancey and Ruffin're just a bad. Want their way no matter what. Not a spit difference between them and abolitionist Pharisees like Sumner and Chase. I'd like to be rid of the whole rabble-rousing lot. Damn politicians to perdition! Ever one of 'em are godless idolaters not caring about boilin' the whole country to pieces. Parker and devil Gerrit Smith included."

"A little radical doings defending our rights ain't so bad. North gutted the 1850 Missouri bill," Andrew said. "Secesh used to be a bad word. I remember my gran'pappy spitting words like *disunion* and *treason* when Massachusetts tried to secede, join the British during the 1812 fracas."

Rundell hunkered tighter against the sucking damp wind. Wasn't so much the wind what chilled shivers bone-deep into his marrow. Hoping against hope with time it'd somehow settle out, yet each day the blood heated hotter. Like others with no heart for a breakup, his and Andrew's souls and the hearts of their families were tied to this land. He tossed away the pulpy cigar butt, stuck his feet to the fire, and snugged the collar of his coat up tighter.

Against the woebegone rustle of the wind, Rundell said, "I fear nothing more than doing nothing. If Governor Brown calls delegates to a convention, I won't change my vote. I stick by Georgia no matter what, but I cain't add my voice for goin' somewhere I figure's worse'n the path we're facing."

•

"Your father's unhappy having to take the extra brougham." Corinthia fidgeted with the blankets. "Says we're packing more than we need." She carefully folded another lap coverlet. "Should something happen on the road, and we should end up stuck out in the middle of nowhere, I'll not have us come down with a raw throat or the earache. Bessie, you pack your remedies?"

"Satchel's done tied down in Mister Andrew's buggy," Bessie said as she folded her rabbit-lined pelisse cloak.

"Mother?" Sarah called from the top of the stairs, "Where's my blue cape?"

"I packed that one, Missy." Bessie stuck out her head from around the corner of the foyer. "You said to pack the blue one 'til we stops in Augusta."

Andrew, up and dressed hours ago in heavy shirt and britches, his great coat on, hat in hand, ready to get on the road, came through the library. "Bessie, they about ready? Horses been harnessed for more'n an hour."

"She your daughter, Marse Andrew," Bessie answered, shakin' her head, done-up in her favorite dark blue bandanna. "Sam's got the other carriage loaded an' snugged down."

In a swirl of color, Sarah hurried down the wide stairs and breathlessly asked her mother, "Where we meeting the Ingrams?"

"They're coming here," Corinthia said. "We'll leave soon as they arrive."

"That is if you women ever get your stuff to your liking and in the trunks," Andrew said.

Sarah lowered her voice and asked, "Mother, surely the

Whiteheads aren't traveling with us."

"Certainly not. Whyever in the world would you ask such a thing? Riding with us, the very idea."

Through the open windows they heard the yells an' hollerin' of kids, *"They comin'...they comin!."*

Beneath leafless arches of the deceptive coolness of a late autumn morning, the handsome silver-trimmed rig swung through the main gate. The big house peeked white through midmorning sunlight dappling the whole length of the long approach. Hamilton drove their matched high-stepping team, Rundell seated beside him. The steady clop of hooves crunched the gravel, the benign elegance of the open Victoria pendulating on its leather and iron springs. He steadied the reins between his fingers as children spilled through the trees, yellin', runnin' alongside. The spotted Appaloosa gray on the left snorted, ears flicked back in a keep-away warning.

"Settle down." Hamilton gave a light flick with the carriage quirt. The Appaloosa jerked its head, backed its ears again.

"Got'ny candy, Mister Ingram?" Children surrounded the carriage with clamoring noisy smiles, knowin' Rundell most times kept peppermints in his pocket. "Kin we ride...kin we ride?"

"Stay back from the horses," Hamilton warned. He snugged up the reins. Neither horse liked strangers around them. "He get jumpy, might throw you under the wheels."

"Hamilton!" Ben yelled with carefree lightheartedness matching the holiday to-do.

Galloping toward them in black riding gaiters and jodhpurs, Ben burst through the trees, astride his favorite roan mare, NellyB. Horse and rider, a single animal, kids scattered out of his way. Hamilton thought Ben sat a horse better than his papa, and it would've made Andrew proud if he'd been privy to Hamilton's thoughts. A flick of the reins on NellyB's neck, and, breathing hard, the mare pulled to a graceful trot next to the carriage.

Ben tipped his hat. "Morning, Mister Rundell, mighty fine morning."

The Ingram Appaloosa snorted, nostrils flared at the smell of the mare.

Rundell pulled his cigar out of his mouth. "Mornin', Ben."

"I'm taking NellyB as far as Augusta," Ben said. "Poppa says Christmastide in Charlestown is no place for me t'be ridin'. Said Augusta'd be bad enough. Least I talked him into letting me take her that far. Gonna try to get papa to let me take her to Charlestown." The excited teenager-nigh-onto-manhood was ready for fun. "Me'n NellyB been out since before sunup. Like to give her time to warm up before I take her out riding."

His mare nuzzled toward the Appaloosa. "Here now..." He gave her a flick on her hind quarters with his looped riding crop. "You be leavin' that alone. Hamilton, why don't you take one of your horses and not sit in a buggy all the way? We can board them both in Augusta."

"Around your mare, this spirited one I like riding would be sniffin' all the time," Hamilton chuckled. "Roads're already crowded, and to stay with the carriages, I'd have to hold him back to keep him at a trot. I'd just as soon be in the buggy." His Appaloosa snorted again. "This morning I've seen half-a-dozen Tobacco Rollers with overload four-in-hand teams clogging tobacco roads, and Whip Crackers snappin' those bull whips. Papa says those big six-foot wheeled freight wagons are ruttin' the roads something fierce. No telling what we'll find once we're closer to Augusta. I don't want the women in the carriages without one of us. I suppose crowds this time'a the season are to be expected."

Ben lifted out of the saddle. Feeling the weight shift, NellyB came to a halt. As Ben dismounted, Hamilton eased the shiny, modified double-Brougham Clarence carriage to a stop at the center of a gaggle of cornrows and braided bright ribbons. The carriage tipped slightly as Rundell swung his stocky frame out.

As Andrew came out onto the porch, he said, "If I know Corinthia and that daughter of mine, we won't be leaving here for at least another hour, maybe two."

"Not this morning!" A smiling Sarah tripped lightly down the front steps. "Morning, Papa Rundell. You ready for Augusta and big doings? We're even stayin' with the Howells for a day or two."

Her eyes aglitter, she kissed Hamilton's cheek, then pirouetted away in a dandied swirl of Balmoral crinoline and taffeta petticoats. Her sky blue pelisse overcoat-dress and cape flapped open, bows and laces fluttering aplenty.

"Good mornin' Rundell—Hamilton," Corinthia called from the porch steps, "Sarah, I need you to come help." As Sarah came up onto the porch, Corinthia murmured a stern, "Behave yourself."

"Oh, Mother! You can be so stuffy."

"Call it what you want," she said as the two went back inside. "Flirting out in front of god and everyone. "

Rundell smiled at this vivacious mother-to-be of his grandkids and said to Hamilton, "Sounds to me like Sarah's ready for a good time."

Hamilton flushed beet red. "She's always ready for a good time."

Corinthia came out onto the kaolin-white brick veranda, sighed and announced, "I think we're finally ready."

Rundell couldn't remember Sarah or Corinthia being ready on time for anything, and it was obvious Sarah had picked up a great many of her mother's habits. He kept his poker face and thought to himself, *Life sure ain't gonna be boring for that son of mine.*

"Randell, Hamilton..." an ebullient Corinthia greeted them. "How're you two Ingrams doing this fine morn?"

"Just fine, Corinne," Rundell answered, using his familiar name for her.

Hamilton said, "Morning, Mother Corinthia. "

Angling for high-time late-night doings, Ben said, "If the Howells have other guests, you'n me might have to stay overnight at the Cobb House."

"Ben," Andrew said, "Help your mother into the carriage."

Corinthia smoothed her Coburg bonnet, its maroon bow snug under her chin, and said, "Might have to shed this palatine cape if the weather turns warm. This lining is so heavy." As she brushed off a speck, her hands stopped, clutched, then did a mad shuffle through her reticule velvet handbag under the seat. "My word!" Her face went pale. "Oh dear!" she sputtered. "The invitations!" Horrified. "Andrew will never let me live it down if I have to unpack—turn the house upside down."

Rundell interrupted his conversation with Andrew and asked

her, "What now, dear?"

"The *invitations!*" she exclaimed in near panic. "I don't know what I did with them!"

Andrew gave Rundell a look. "I knew it was too good to be true." He called back to her, "Corinthia, it doesn't matter. They know we'll be attending."

"After Edwyna Irwin took time to send them, I would be positively embarrassed to show up without them." She made another frantic flurry through her handbag. "We simply must have them."

"Mama, you put them right here." Sarah opened the blue portmanteau. "You told me to be sure and remember."

"Oh yes, so I did." Corinthia patted her face with the sacheted, lace handkerchief.

"Let's get this show on the road," Andrew said. "Bessie? Everything ready?"

"Miss Corinth'a's stuff snugged down good right here, Marse Andrew. Yours, Mister Ben's and Missy's, too. Sam done made sure about the gear and harness." She threw a quick, sharp eye toward a sullen Sam.

Andrew sensed a tightness akin to brooding between Bessie and Sam, but he'd long ago made a habit of leaving that sort of trouble in the cabins. Bessie'd let him know if things needed his handling.

His hand at her elbow, Hamilton helped Sarah into the coach, their glances one of those quick moments between lovers. A social pilgrimage of the parish's first families, the grand trek was finally underway. Sunlight glittered off shiny spokes as they moved down the long approach and onto the rutted dusty road. This was the apex of the season. The celebrations would culminate after the turn of the new year, or, in some places, a week beyond that.

Sam drove Corinthia and Bessie in the first carriage, Sarah and her father in the second, Ben on NellyB, their third carriage loaded with all trunks. Hamilton and Rundell followed far enough back to stay out of the dust. By the time they rolled through St. Clair later in the afternoon, scattered clouds were gathering to the northwest, portents of a cool and perhaps wet evening.

"Pull up," Rundell said to Hamilton. He called out to Benjamin, "How about letting me sit NellyB for a spell? You ride here with Hamilton."

"My pleasure," and Benjamin swung off his horse.

Rundell mounted, and as he rode ahead to Andrew's carriage, Ben climbed up next to Hamilton. He loosened the buttons of his chesterfield top coat, wet circles damping the pits of his broadcloth shirt, the fuzz on his upper lip sparkled with sweat.

He said, "They'll talk politics the whole way to Augusta."

Hamilton shifted the reins to the inside rumps of the team, spit out the sweet gum twig he'd gnawed fuzzy on both ends, and tried to shelve his harbingers. "Ought to ease off politics."

"You got to hold tight to what's right though."

"Cain't argue with that," Hamilton said.

Ben sat quiet for the longest, then said, "Hamilton, can I ask you a question?"

"Ben, we're about near to bein' brothers as two men could get. You can ask anything—must be serious."

"It is." Ben hesitated, looked down, then straight-ahead, shuffled for words, then finally mumbled, "You got to promise not to laugh. Not to tell anyone, not Papa, not nobody."

"You in some kind of trouble?" Hamilton's look was serious. "Last time me and Franklyn was having a round of Papa's corn likker, Franklyn asked about you. I told him far's I'd heard, they wasn't nothing to the tales about you and that Queensborough preacher's daughter."

"Franklyn knows about that?" Ben gulped. "He didn't tell nobody at the Bends, did he?"

"He wouldn't do that. Besides, Franklyn's got a few skeletons of his own. But you know how it is, gossip is Queensborough's main pastime."

"Lord have mercy—" Ben started sweating heavier.

"Preacher's kids—you got to watch out for 'em, and that parson's daughter's sure not one to keep quiet about hitting the hay with Andrew Greer's son. When it comes to that kind of monkey business, there's not any secrets around here."

"No, I ain't in no trouble," Ben blurted. "Not like that, but that's what I want to ask. I might could be, and I cain't talk to

Papa. But you got to promise. The fellas are always bragging, they'd laugh at me if it got around that I asked about certain things."

"Oh, those kind of questions. Men always brag an' preen around one another. I've done my share once the swaggerin' starts. Okay." Recalling his own doubts, he said, "I promise, ask away."

"Well..." Words still didn't come.

"Before you say anything, I got to say something. If it's true you're still squiring Betsy Lou Whitehead around on the sly, you better not let your mother catch wind of it," Hamilton chuckled.

Ben gritted his teeth, and puffed up defensive. "You promised not to laugh!" The renowned Greer pride flared.

"Hold on there." Hamilton held up a hand, warding off this younger brother's-to-be scowl. "Don't get riled on me. I'm not laughing at you. You reminded me of some of the crazy things I did."

"You did?" Ben asked, bewildered.

"How clumsy I was. Fumbling and getting familiar with all that girl stuff."

"That's what I need to ask. Me'n Betsy Lou hadn't gone the whole way. We've messed around, done about ever'thing else, and gawdamighty, Hamilton..." Ben opened his mouth to a gust of exasperation. "She gets me all stirred up. Rubs all over me, teases me under my clothes, giggles when she gets me half-naked. Mind you, it feels good, but then sometimes she just quits. Don't want me to do nothin' else. Leaves me hurtin' and aches a long time."

Hamilton muzzled his smile. "I'm glad you said you and Betsy Lou hadn't gone whole hog."

"Why? You and Sarah have. That's the reason I knew you'd know."

"What!" Hamilton caught himself. "I swanne, little brother, you're full of surprises. What'd you want to ask about?"

"I never felt nothing like she makes me feel, and I don't know how to do nothing else. If it feels as good with others as it does with Betsy Lou," Ben gulped. "Damn Hamilton, I'm gonna do 'em all. Ever'day!"

"Yeh, it was meant to feel good for men and women, no matter what anyone claims."

"Women like it just as much?"

"Sometimes more. Don't Betsy Lou?"

"I reckon to tell you the truth, she sure enough does."

Hamilton flicked the Appaloosa's rump, slowed his gait, yanked down on his wide brim hat, and said, "But you got some lessons coming. You're gonna find gettin' down with just anyone 'cause they happen to be in the mood is a risky way to stir a passel of trouble for yourself."

"Not gonna work that way for me," Ben boasted.

"Works that way for you, for me, for any man. Without you meanin' for it to happen, it can mean trouble for those that care what happens to you."

Ben brushed the words aside, saying, "Papa once said using my hand was abusing myself, that it'd hurt me when I got to be a man."

"Won't hurt you. I promise."

"You and Sarah done it," Ben said straight-out. "Both of you naked together, not a stitch on either one of you. I mean all the way with you on top where she could have a baby. I followed you a couple of times you headed off swimmin'. Watched you and Sarah when you thought no one's around. The noises you make—like it's hurting."

"Damn, Ben!" Hamilton was caught totally off guard, coughed, choked off his words 'til he got a grip on his thoughts. "Don't ever let Sarah know you watched."

"She'd never tell Mama."

"It's not about your mother. When your sister gets a mad on, she's a holy terror. Never seen a woman who can git so riled. She find out you watched, she'd throw a fit—at both of us. Likely think you learned it from me."

"I promise I never told nobody, but how you go about keepin' Sarah from getting a baby? Betsy Lou'll be in Charlestown, and if we get alone, I'm gonna do her just like I seen you. Me an' Betsy Lou played with each other a lot, but I never done the things you done. She knows all about how she gets me, and she's not scared one little bit about nothin'."

With a soft chuckle Hamilton said, "She likely bedded more men than most, and knows more'n about doin' it than most men, including me'n you."

Hamilton knew Ben was trusting him with real personal man-woman doings. He also realized he might not know much more than Ben did.

"How long you and Betsy Lou messed around?"

"Comin' up on a year. Other afternoon she didn't make no bones about letting me know she meant for us to have lots of fun alone in Charlestown. Like it was something I had to do."

"She's a good example of women who don't care about nobody but themselves, an' you'd better never forget they're dangerous. There's good women about. Women who knows when a man loves her, cares how he feels. Betsy Lou's spoiled, and those kind are the ones you better watch out for. They want to be the center of attention, in bed, at parties, whoever they take a fancy with, and they're never too picky."

"Mama or Sarah can get awful upset, sometimes over nothing, like each wants their own way. Don't see how more'n one woman can stay under the same roof with another. Not fit to be around when they get that way."

Hamilton coaxed the team to the right, gave the timber wagon room to pass. After the two teams cleared he moved the Brougham back to the middle of the road.

"How you and Sarah manage to keep from getting her with a baby?"

"Bessie has remedies."

"You talked to Bessie Mae about what you an' Sarah do!"

"If it goes on at the Hollows or your papa's place, Bessie knows about it. The baby stuff—most times you leave it up to the woman, but that's sure not a good idea with Betsy Lou. Judge your times with a woman by keeping your eye on the time of the month. That don't always work, 'specially if you got a woman eager for a baby. All she needs to do is have you give it to her once, or even sneakier, have several give it to her at the right time, and claim it's yours."

"Betsy Lou's always sayin' how she wants to have kids."

"Ever ask yourself why she talks that way when she's around

you? Any man could give her a baby. What makes you think you're so special?"

"I thought on it a time or two," Ben's voice lowered.

"You better think on it a bunch more. What I'm gonna say won't sound nice, but you asked. One day you'll be master of Wisteria Bends. Think that might have anything to do with it?"

"Might have a lot to do with it."

"I expect it just might, and I'm glad you see it. Glad all of your brains ain't below your belt. There's fine upstandin' women out there. Your sister is one of them, but there's plenty of the other kind. It's not just females, there's more than a few bastards needin' a good horsewhippin, and you'd better learn to spot them. There's nothing like having a woman you can trust, and you're messing around with one of the craftiest wenches in the parish. I wouldn't trust anyone in that family any further than I could throw a buffalo, and certainly not Betsy Lou. With you hot and lathered-up, Betsy Lou types can screw up not only your life, but your family's as well." He paused, then asked, "How long you been watching me and Sarah?"

"Ever since you two started going off by yourselves. I couldn't figure why you'd rather be with my sister than fish or hunt."

Hamilton chucked, "Sometimes I wonder that myself."

"I followed you two. If Sarah ever found out, she'd whack me, or worse, tell Papa."

They rode a few more traffic-clogged miles in silence until Hamilton said, "Ben, be careful. Word's out on Betsy Whitehead. She'll bed anybody. A reg'lar roundheels, and not choosy which bronc she bucks with. Some of her pickings are men with families and wives. I don't hold high regards for a man that'll behave that way. Gettin' down with different men is more about the ruination of trust than it is about who does what to whom. Same for a man. Man gives his word to anybody, to a woman, another man, in business, in front of a reverend or otherwise, it's a measure of his backbone to see he keeps it. Wouldn't be worth much if it was easy. Betsy Lou'd marry anything in pants long as he can pay her spendthrift bills."

"Mama says money's all Abigail Whitehead ever thinks about."

"Don't give Betsy a chance to claim a baby is one you put in her belly. She likely wouldn't know who the daddy is, but you make a truly promising candidate. She says it's your baby, she's likely tryin' to reel you in for the raising of someone else's bastard and giving it the Greer name. Tell me that wouldn't be a catch for the likes of a no-account Whitehead."

"You sound like Papa," Ben snorted. "Mama would have a stroke."

"I cain't tell you not to mess around, not with the things I've done." He sucked in a quick take of air, then said, "All I say is, take care. If you're as grownup as you think, take a good look at things straight-on. Sometimes a gut feeling says things aren't the way they ought'a be. Don't ever ignore that. That's easier sayin' than doin' when things get rough...or steamy. What a man does don't just affect him. We can hurt without meanin' to, and there's times it might seem family is buttinskies, but mostly it's 'cause they care about us."

"You sound like our papas talkin' politics."

Hamilton's eyebrows went up. "Hadn't thought on it. But I reknen it's much the same. You'd better draw in the reins on that lusty barnyard pole of meat Besty Lou's leading you by."

"How you do that? It's all I think about, wantin' to do it all the time."

"Me too. In the mornings when you wake up, the want of some lovin' right there and ready. Cain't think of nothin' else." For one of the few times in his life Hamilton felt lost for words. "You bet it feels good. Boy dogs are supposed to get excited when a bitch in season lets us know she's interested. Sniffing the mares is fun, and the chase is part of it."

"Women sure are complicated."

"It's for sure I don't have 'em figured. Ben, make me a promise." Hamilton sighed. "Anytime something's bothering you, or you have questions, you'll come to me. I'm not sayin' I have all the answers. Probably never will, but we'll find them together."

"I'd like that. I'd like that a lot."

"Don't take this personal, but me'n Sarah are gonna have to find us a new place. Can't have my brother watching me lay with his sister. Somehow don't seem fittin'."

"What'll I do?" he protested, disappointed. "I like watching."

Just then Andrew galloped up, called out, "Pull up under those trees yonder. We'll rest the teams. Bessie's got picnic baskets ready. It'll be nightfall before we arrive to the Howells. I talked to Carlton last week, told him we'd likely be a whit late to dinner."

The carriages clustered under the shade trees, away from the clamor and dust of heavy draies, and everyone climbed out. Corinthia and Sarah fluffed and brushed their dresses and bonnets. Bessie soon had picnic blankets and cushions spread and everything was just so. Ben rubbed down NellyB, tethered her with a rope halter on the other side of a clump of pines away from the Ingram's snorting gray. Bessie eyed Sam as he put out the feed sacks, unhitched the teams, hobbled them to graze, but stayed with the horses.

Bessie had chided him, "I don't want no actin'-up an' mopin' around like some cow off its feed."

Under the trees a light breeze flowed as Hamilton tossed his coat over the buggy seat, and unbuttoned the snug cuffs of the balloon sleeves. Last night's harvest moon had given way to another lingering day of east Georgia mugganess. He brushed off his snug twill dark tan riding britches he most always wore tucked into suede and chammy black flat-heeled boots. He knocked off his boots, then double checked the buggy, leather traces, bits, doubletrees and carriage tongues. It never hurt to be certain with a loose wheel, hub or a rim that should've been hammered.

Hamilton's talk with Ben had set him thinking. Growing up on the vast acreage of the Hollows added to an independence he was seeing less and less of. Raised to make the best of life, Hamilton enjoyed each day. The idea of that changing vexed at him like a pesky mosquito. Since the 4th of July, he'd sensed the same unsettleness in Papa.

Patting the gray on the rump, he shrouded his inner Ingram shell tighter. He refused to sour it for anyone, or make Ben think it was something he said. The yen for a good slug of corn likker called to him. Sarah had got truly upset that time they were alone, and he too drunk to do anything. She'd stayed mad the whole week.

"Get a grip, " he muttered, "Greers're not one tad hotter than Ingrams." He couldn't quite believe he had thought such a thought. "You and Sarah have daughters, you just remember how it was, Big Boy Ingram."

Bessie had packed way more than they could eat. The carriages stayed in the shade for a goodly portion of the afternoon, while everyone lazed and munched minced beef dodger corncakes, cucumber sandwiches, and cracklin' bread fixin's with plum jelly. Bessie had packed her peppermint mince pie and Indian pudding, along with cool buttermilk and pitchers of Windsor Springs cold artesian water. When Sarah stripped off stockings and shoes and waded into the pebbly-bottomed clear-cold sparkling rush of Windsor Creek, it scandalized Corinthia.

"Sarah!" Corinthia said aghast. "Of all things, showing your bare ankles in front of menfolk."

"Oh, Mama, we're practically family," she said as she wadded and wiggled her toes in the pebbles. "It feels good."

"I reckon it do," Bessie vexed. "That still ain't a reason to do a thing 'cause it feel good. She shuffled to the water's edge with a folded cloth toward Sarah. "Dry them feet. Put your stockin's back on, an' act like you was brung up. Marse Rundell and Mister Hamilton ain't yet fambly."

"Oh, Bessie..." Sarah wiped her feet and slipped into her hose and buttoned her shoes.

"Now..." Bessie smiled. "You presentable."

"I was presentable with my feet in the water."

"You set your rules when you be mistress of your own home."

With a shrug of her head Sarah brushed her hair up beneath her bonnet then plopped on the pallet, loaded a plate with sandwiches, some sweet alumen pickles, and carried it to where Hamilton was fiddling with the buggies.

"You haven't touched hardly any of the fixin's," she said. "So I brought you some sandwiches and buttermilk."

"That was sweet of you." He gave a final tug to a leather strap. "Does look good...better wash my hands."

Sarah sensed a somberness as they walked toward the creek. "You certainly are quiet today."

Kneeling at the water, he rinsed his hands and arms, dried

them, and said, "I suppose..." He took a bite, chewed slow, then left the half-eaten sandwich unfinished. "Guess I'm a touch off my feed—sort of like the gray here."

"Get your things, we're packin' up," Rundell called to them.

Back on the road for the last leg into Augusta, Hamilton asked, "Who else you expect will be at the Howells?"

Rundell said, "James mentioned folks from Milledgeville might be taking dinner with them tonight. Don't know if they're staying over. Seems they're headed for Charlestown too. Georgia delegates been invited for the doings there."

"Delegates?"

"Governor Pickens called for a convention to deliberate secession ordinances, and invited representatives from other states, Texas, Alabama, and I think, Mississippi and Georgia."

"From what I heard at the feed store last week, there's not much deliberating left to be done."

"Richmond newspapers say Virginia's not pushing secesh," Rundell said. "James said that's one reason folks out'a Milledgeville are going to Charlestown. Maybe some cool heads can head off this damn tomfoolery."

"You think South Carolina means to pull out?"

"South Carolina seems dead set on it," Rundell sighed. "And I don't see much in the way of stopping her."

"Gonna cause a bust-up," Hamilton said.

5

M ister Hamilton," the immaculately liveried, and nigh-onto-being-bald butler said, "Your refill."

"Thank you, Jeffa." Hamilton guzzled a big swallow from his third chilled bourbon and branch water.

A relaxing woolly you-know-better'n-to-drink-more fuzz swam behind his eyes. In the secluded amber oil-lit darkness of the long porch he reared back in the rocker; voices and light spilled from the chandelier blaze of the drawing room through the French doors. It was good to be off the congested roads.

Benjamin broke Hamilton's rambling thoughts as he reached his empty glass toward Jeffa's waiting tray. "Think I'll have another one, too," he said, liquored words flowin' loose and easy. "Hamilton, what's eating at you? You been moody ever since we left home."

"I suppose—all of it, I guess. I dunno," with two big gulps he emptied his glass. "All this hullabaloo on the road, things I wanted to get done before we left. Lots going on."

"No point wartin' about it." Ben rocked back as Jeffa fetched full glasses. "It'll keep 'til we get home."

"How come you sounding so sudden grown-up?" He slurred as he rocked, took another swallow. "Neither of us as growed as we like to think."

Glasses were refilled again, two men enjoying the quiet, the smells of the low-land river. Like most men when they had nothing to say, they said nothing in the close familiar night, as pillowy river mists rolled in carrying the moldy smells of soggy bayou leaves; fog fading everything to smudged indistinct grays, while cobblestone walkways and curbstones, hitching rails and iron gates and fences sheened wet. Pixie shadows danced in the swaying tongues of oil torches, thick water drops clung to shiny magnolia leaves that looked black in the dusky heaviness. The manor house was clothed in its own fogbound cocoon.

Sarah moseyed out onto the veranda gallery, saw Hamilton's drooped eyes, and turned back to the laughter and clink of stems of champagne and gossip. Hours lengthened. The men started drifting into the all-male enclave of the men's library. Sippin', laughin' at bawdy jokes, talking politics among aroma-rich clouds of cigars, pipes and imported Turkish Oriental cigarettes, the smoke hanging as thick as the fog. From the veranda one could almost see the wet shrouds of Spanish moss hiding Cherokee ghosts wandering up from their Isondiga-Savanno River, its waters lapping just beyond the carriage house.

"I've had more'n enough," Hamilton's words garbled, glad Franklyn wasn't here egging him on.

Ben slouched in his chair, his glass hanging in loose fingers.

"C'mon," Hamilton said. Limber, wobbly-legged Ben tried to stand. A not-exactly steady Hamilton caught the glass as it slipped from Ben's fingers. "Bedrooms in the big house are full-up. We got the garçon guest house all to ourselves. Jeffa made us a roaring fire to knock off the evening damp."

Hamilton hefted Ben's arm over his shoulder, and together they stumbled down the wide steps to the curving bricked footpath. Alone in their cloistered world, they tottered across the gently sloping grounds that ended in the quiet wash of water at the river's edge. Their path made a checkerboard of slender elongated rectangles of light thrown from the upper windows of the main house. From the nearby stables a horse whinnied.

Ben recognized his horse. "NellyB," he mumbled into Hamilton's shoulder.

Hamilton lifted the latch, shoved, and the door swung in. The feather beds had been fluffed, coverlets turned back, and the fireplace crackling warm, stoked for a long misty night. Hamilton slumped Ben onto the nearest bed, struggled off Ben's boots and shirt, twisted off Ben's riding pants, and tumbled a sotted Ben into the feather mattress.

In the blur of whisky Hamilton dragged a chair to the fire, kicked off his boots, popped a button off his shirt, and scratched at an ankle where one boot had chafed. Wearing only his underdrawers, he proceeded to stagger toward the bleary heap of the second bed.

As he lifted his knee and leaned over into the feather bedding, the slide of warm fingers down his belly yanked Hamilton full moon-eyed goggle awake.

"Gawdamighty," He knew her touch, her smell. He whispered, "Sarah, you scared hell out'a me."

"I don't always do that," she murmured, as she kissed just below his belly button.

"Ben's right here..." he gulped. He wasn't nearly as drunk as he thought.

"Room's damp and chilly," her hands pulled at his underdrawers, twisting them down around his feet, all of the wonder of him there and ready for her. "Get in here with me, keep me warm."

"Cain't get out'a these damn things." He hopped on one foot, kicked. "...Tangled."

She giggled, "I can sure feel what their twisted on." Her hands were hot around that massive part of him.

"Woman," he hissed, "somewhere among your ancestors, I swear there's the blood of a trollop." He madly kicked away his clothes.

"If not, there is now, and it's your fault. You made me this way."

He hurried. Surrendered against the scald and swirl of skin on skin, her hands and thighs, smothering into her glorious gleaming breasts. Whisky and lust spinning his head in a dizzying cascade as he moved above her, hungered for her, no longer cared whether Ben was watching or asleep. Cared for nothing except his pounding combustible need. Sarah guided him, helping him lose himself in her bewitching arms. She grabbed him—liquor and sex usually didn't work. This time it sizzled away in a flurry of arms and legs.

"This is crazy," he mumbled with a full mouth.

"Yes..." Drawing all of him fully into her wonderful heat.

Toward the pale misty dawn of a night flown by, Sarah wrapped her blue cape tight against the cool damp and slipped out of the room. In the folds of their warm bed, Hamilton snored away into the smell of her on his body. Their world serene and tranquil except for the slight ripple of a curtain at the upstairs window of the main house.

Ben hadn't moved.

•

After Corinthia's last-minute shopping and a farewell dinner party the night before, they departed the Howells two days later. Ben wrangled Andrew into letting him take NellyB. Their caravan stopped for two overnights, and a bit before noon on the 20th they arrived on the outskirts of a jostled bustling Charlestown. Amid an increasing mass of carriages, drays, wagons in a hustling push and shove multitude worse than Augusta, the Palmetto City was bustin' its bounds.

Hamilton closed the distance between carriages. "I don't want us gettin' separated."

"Dawdlin' in these crowds ain't a fittin' place for man or beast," Bessie grumped. "City'll eat you up. Bends don't have sech conglom'rations."

A magnificent piece of horseflesh paced by, its highborn rider in a soft gray suit trimmed in black tipped his hat, and mouthed, "Ladies."

Corinthia gave him a cordial nod as Bessie grumbled, "Missy Sarah, you know better'n to give sech'a friendly face with strange men on the street."

With a *who-me* tilt of her head, Sarah kept right on with fluttering eyes and bright smiles. It was such fun.

"I do wish we'd started the trip a day or two sooner," Corinthia said. "With the ball tomorrow we've so much to be done."

"It's not much farther, couple of miles or so," Rundell said. "Glad the Irwin place is out this way from downtown and the docks. Wouldn't want to go through town in this."

Ben road up beside Rundell's buggy, above the babel and bustle, and yelled, "You see that Militia Company back yonder? I rode with them a bit. They're bivouacked outside town. They said Federals moved into Fort Sumter, an' the secesh convention is already meeting. One of their officers has a plantation outside Columbia, he said state volunteers been called up, an' hustled down here from all over. Governor wants the Militia standing by."

Hamilton couldn't remember ever being so alarmed. Like a bolt of lightening, it jolted through him, his heart thudded in his throat afraid for Sarah and Mother Greer.

"Any Federals inside the city?"

"A few at the arsenal."

Hamilton groused, "That's all we need...in the middle of a fracas with everyone carrying guns."

"Gracious sakes, how thoughtless," Corinthia murmured. "You'd think they'd have some consideration for the season."

"Ought'a be at the Bends," Bessie muttered.

By the time they rolled through the tall black iron main gates of Marlgrove, it was the middle of the rather warm afternoon. Flanked by tall white columns Cassius Irwin and his wife, Edwyna, waited to greet them as their coaches rolled up the curving drive. Footmen hurried to begin unloading.

"Rundell, Andrew..." Cassius' deep, sonorous voice rumbled through the Palmetto Palms and manicured expanse that was Marlgrove. "Glad to see y'all made it through this hubbub." He offered Corinthia his hand and helped her out.

"Corinthia!" Short, stocky Edwyna came down the steps to welcome them. "It's so very good to see your smiling face after such a long time." The two hugged.

"It's good to see you as well, Edwyna," Corinthia beamed. "I've so been looking forward to this. Seems we haven't seen one another in ages."

"I do hope it was a pleasant trip. And Sarah," Edwyna said. "You have become a lovely young lady since the last time I saw you." She kissed Sarah's cheek, as the Irwin daughters clustered around Sarah, all chattering at once. Everyone moved up the wide steps and inside, Edwyna arm in arm with Corinthia. "Corinthia, your favorite suite is all prepared for you. I'm sure you'll want to freshen up with bath and nap before supper."

"That would be absolutely divine." Corinthia was looking forward to the privacy. "I feel as though I have layers of dust all over."

"These crowds are simply unbelievable," Edwyna said. "We've never seen anything like them."

"Takes hours to get anywhere," Cassius added. "City's growing mighty big...too big for my likin'. Countryside used to be so peaceful—but not lately."

"This humidity..." Corinthia daubed her face and neck with her sachet kerchief. "We're so excited about tomorrow."

Edwyna said, "Everybody but everybody will be there."

As the heavier baggage and huge Saratoga trunks were being unloaded, Hamilton wheeled their carriage with the lighter valises up to one side of the big house where he helped Sam finish unloading. Then he made sure all the carriages were backed into their own detached large livery paddock stall sheds. He and Sam unhooked and unharnessed the teams, got them watered, rubbed down, and put out grain and hay.

As Hamilton came around the corner of the columned terrace, he caught his father's solemn expression and knew something was amiss. After what they'd seen and what the officer had told Ben, Hamilton knew what had upset his papa. Rundell quickly buried his displeasure to put on the face of the courteous guest.

After everyone got settled and freshened up, a steward knocked on the doors of each suite. "High tea, sour dough cucumber sandwiches and pan-dowdy spiced sugared apples are being served in the gallery wing solarium. If you prefer, we can see they're brought to your rooms."

"Oh my," Corinthia gushed, "Edwyna serves the most exquisite rosemarine sandwiches along with milk chocolate-flavored cheesecakes."

The great manor of Marlgrove Estate, country shire in its sea of land, blazed bright into the lowland, star-salted Carolina night. In the guest wings, trunks were opened, *oohs* and *aahs* as yards of crinolines and crepes, French silks, Virginian satins, English velvets spilled before covetous eyes, all the while with Bessie pickyin', keepin' her eye on the two house girls attendin' Mistress Corinth'a and Missy.

Dinner had lasted well beyond nightfall. A personal houseboy assigned for each guest, Marlgrove's abundance spilled freely, accompanied by an unending variety of liqueurs and fine wines. As the evening lengthened the Ingram and Greer men joined Cassius and his two sons in the enormous paneled library to the enjoyment of brandies and imported cognacs.

A time or two Hamilton noticed that same arrested look on his papa's face. Sometime later Rundell excused himself and strolled out onto the veranda. Hamilton followed and found Rundell puffing a glowing red tip to another cigar.

"Papa, what's wrong?"

"Am I that obvious?" He shook his head. "I thought I was puttin' on a right good face."

"I've known you too long not to take notice."

"From what I've seen and heard since we arrived, I venture we didn't pay enough mind to all this secesh hullabaloo. All this goin' on set me thinkin'. While we were at the Howells, Carlton and me busied ourselves considering different crops, less cotton and tobacco, maybe some grains, barley, some of that new strain of wheat. Carlton's stickin' with cotton, even opening some new fields, and it put me to thinking we could do the same with that fallow river bottom acreage. Good soil there."

"I didn't think you planned puttin' in cotton for another year or so."

"Wasn't thinkin' cotton, but it might be a good time to open those bottomlands. No need ever'body else rakin' in money, and us leave it to slide by. Cost next to nothing to clear it."

"Why do I have the feeling your thoughts aren't on what we're gonna plant?"

Rundell stared off. "Never figured it'd come like this, never thought I'd see the day."

"You mean what Ben said about Sumter and Pickens?"

"That and more," Rundell muttered.

"Could be just show." For a moment both listened to the distant clank and commotion of wagons. "We both know how politicians run off at the mouth."

"I reckon," a downcast Rundell said. "Banty roosters struttin', like a runaway team of horse with the bits set in their teeth, out'a control, takin' steps nobody knows how to undo. Yancey and Rhett, and Edmund Ruffin with the Virginia delegation, never struck me none'a them had intentions for cooling ruffled feathers." His words drifted gone on the night breeze, as though never spoken.

Rundell's words hammered at Hamilton. "You think we ought to forget about the ball, get the women back over the river and home?"

"Bears keepin' an eye to. With no Federals in the city I doubt there's much concern. Least not quite yet." Rundell snorted. "Corinthia would need a tonic if we pulled up stakes, and skedaddled, make her miss this big to-do. She's been plannin' this since the first of the summer." He smushed out his cigar butt, jabbing it harder and harder 'til the whole cigar crumbled.

"Gonna put a real tug to things if South Carolina pulls loose." Hamilton tried to reassure himself that he was reading too much into Papa's being upset.

"It'll rattle more than a few things. Only hope is to put a damper on South Carolina 'til tempers settle. Trouble is, I don't see nothing happenin' to down all the threatenin' talk."

The main house slumbered near to next day noon with only infrequent jangles of service bells, and muffled breakfast trays being hurried to bedrooms. Beyond the house there were outlying sounds of rigs being polished and harnesses being readied for the evening's grand procession. What was left of the day drowsed through the afternoon with sporadic comings and goings of dispatch riders.

Still in her nightgown, bare legs flashing, Sarah rushed across the hall and flung open the double doors into her mother's suite. Corinthia sat in bed munching buttered toast and fresh strawberries. One of the maids was ironing, while Bessie laid out their clothes.

"Mother, I can't find my hair ribbons."

"Missy Sarah, they right next to your leather key satchel basket where I puts 'em, an' what you mean runnin' around nigh nekked. Make a body think us country folk wadn't brought up no better."

"My hair's a mess," said Sarah fluffing curls and ringlets. "Bessie, it'll never stay under my bonnet."

"Jes cause Marse Andrew spoils you, you don't have no call for flouncy hair. You already done plenty a' that. I don't care how much you is up in the air about ribbons." Bessie shook out one of the gowns. "Anyhow, you brung twice what you ever need even if you changed ever time the clock dong."

Sarah ran her fingers along the folds of her pale green satin gown, recalling how it matched the dark green of Hamilton's suit. Tonight Charlestown society would get an eyeful of the first families of Wisteria Bend and Moccasin Hollow. She and Hamilton would set absolutely every heart pitterpatt atingle jealous.

With her gold and silver brocade gown in her arms, Sarah twirled the wicker dress form around and around on its rollers and stopped in front of the mirror. "I simply *must* look my best."

"Lookin' ain't the all of it. This here Marlgrove might look bigger'n anything 'round Queensborough, but you best not mix no tomfoolery in front of Charlestown folk."

"Mother," Sarah bubbled, "this gown is simply splendid."

"You and Hamilton will make such a fine looking couple."

Sarah sighed. Everything was just perfect.

•

In the washhouse the oval scoop of the wooden tub hardly held the splash of steamy water. It held even less of Hamilton's rangy long-muscled frame. He slung a bare leg over the rim and lathered again.

He sniffed the scented soap. "Sure beats our homemade lye. Last batch could've rawed the hide off a boar hog." He raised the other leg and scrubbed away road grime.

The water boy hollered out, "Ready for splashin'?"

"Pour slow." Hamilton stood, turning as the bucket was dumped. "Be sure and get the soap off my back."

"You walow'n an' soakin' longer womenfolk," the boy said, as he reached for more water. "Ever'body else right finished gittin' gussied."

Hamilton shut his eyes tight, ducked his head, and thought about the coming evening as water cascaded over his head, down his back, and gurgled through the slatted floorboards. He stepped out, grabbed a big towel and wrapped it around his waist. Then he grabbed a second towel to dry his hair as he hurried up the back stairs to his second-floor suite of rooms to begin the grand transformation into Country Dandy.

When he finished dressing, he came downstairs and waited in the parlor. He was glad there'd been a fair-to-middlin' frost, hoping tonight would be as cool. The ballrooms and anterooms would be crowded. With garden doors open the cool evening air would feel good.

Voices interrupted his thoughts and he looked up. Sarah and Mother Greer were coming down the spiraling stairs into the reception foyer.

For him it didn't matter what Sarah did or didn't wear. To him she was always his beauty, but this moment caught his breath. It quickened his whole body all under. He beheld the most breathtaking revelation ever, her face and shoulders mellow in the diffused glow from tiered chandeliers and tall bronze candelabra. Her eyes were lightly shadowed against the bloom of dark red lips and lightly rouged cheeks. The swell of her emerald gown highlighted the subtle shadows and curves of her figure as it fell from a long willowy neck and off her shoulders. Her hair, a golden fleece woven with sparkling rhinestones, seemed to Hamilton like stars in a crystal bespeckled night. Her gloved hand lightly trailed along the polished bannister.

Their eyes locked, and Sarah smiled. She thought he was grand, but she always thought that, no matter how he was dressed—or not.

A mesmerized Hamilton spotted the tiny, folded booklet dangling inconspicuously from her wrist, deciding then and there she wouldn't need that to jot down her evening progress and promised promenades. Rooted to the spot, he tallied the whole of this wondrous creature flowing toward him.

An eminently pleased Corinthia was ever so proud.

He stepped toward Sarah, offered his arm. "Who is this fair damsel in need of an escort?" Exhilaration cleaved his heart with peacock covetousness. "You look lovely tonight."

"My, how charming. My personal Sir Galahad."

He smiled. "As good as you look, you need a Galahad to protect you."

With a pert tip of her sassy nose, she said, "My apologies, Sir Knight, but you have me at a disadvantage. Your face is quite familiar. I'm sure we must've been introduced, but at the moment your name escapes me."

"I am your most dutiful admirer." He raised her hand to his lips, kissed the back of it, his upper lip glistening with passionate beads of sweat. "At your service," his emerald eyes burning only for her, as they moved into the grand ballroom with its milling guests.

Nodding to their assemblage, Sarah whispered for his ears only, "And precisely what sort of services do you provide?" She flashed him a wicked merry conviviality.

"All manner of services." His eyes skidded down her neck, down the soft milky skin of her plunging décolleté.

Under her breath she muttered, "However, you remind me of someone I once saw all sweaty, working the fields, and perhaps infinitely tasty."

He whispered, "You never cease to amaze me."

Another smile, more nods, teasingly squeezed her hold on his arm, as an anxious Bessie came to them. "Carriages be ready. Sam drivin' you two, an' takin' extra care on them roads."

Andrew escorted Corinthia, and Hamilton with Sarah as they made their way onto the verandas to their carriages polished black as a South Carolina bayou ebony night.

A white-gloved footman held the carriage door open. Hamilton assisting Sarah, he said, "Sam, how you tonight?"

"Doin' fine, Hamilton, jes fine."

Hamilton climbed in, and behind him the coach steps folded

up, the plumed coaches with their occupants preened to strut their high-stepping fantastics. As the coaches rolled into the night, rows of flickering torches danced gargantuan leafy shadows across the ivory columns of Marlgrove.

•

The Master of the Ball stepped forward and announced, "From our fair sister state of Georgia, Mister Hamilton Bothington Graeme Ingram, Esquier of Moccasin Hollow and his betrothed, Miss Sarah Cornelia Gresham Greer of Wisteria Bend."

For months Mistress of Gossip Edwyna had made certain *the* word spread far and wide beyond Marlgrove. Hamilton and Sarah came forward, amid a flutter of muttered *oohs* and *aahs*.

Murmurs rippled, "Such a handsome couple."

As eyes ogled and goggled at these two honored guests of the Irwins, the lilt of a Virginia Reel picked up. Guests cleared the floor as Hamilton escorted his lovely lady to the middle of the ballroom.

Floating in the elegant grace of his arms, Sarah said to him, "At this moment, you own the world."

"You are all the world I need."

In this lighthearted mood, Hamilton enjoyed the swirl and gaiety of dancing with Sarah, time rushing by with her in his arms, his eyes never leaving her, neither wanting this fairy-tale evening to end.

Following a number of polkas, two-steps, change-of-partners, which some were calling the square dance, and a Viennese waltz, the musicians took a short break. Couples drifted about, clustered groups sipped holiday refreshments and chatted with acquaintances not seen since last year's gala. Moments later, slower strains of music once more picked up.

Sarah daubed at her forehead and throat with a pleated ruche of linen. "It's so very warm." She fanned her dainty kerchief across the rise of her glowing bosom. "Catch my breath."

"Come, it's cooler on the veranda," Hamilton said, leading her out. "I'll get us some champagne." He wiped his forehead, then stuffed the handkerchief back under one buttoned cuff.

He returned shortly with bubbly stems of iced cider and amber champagne. "Try this, it tastes right good."

As she sipped and fanned, he leaned closer 'til her hair brushed his lips, and with a slight smile said in her ear, "Your favorite Betsy Whitehead was lurking about the champagne fountain, and about spilled her plate of spiced duck shoving her way toward me."

Sarah stiffened. "That brazen lonesome goose has been craning her neck all evening, trying to catch your eye."

Resting one arm on the granite balustrade, Hamilton said, "She asked if you weren't feeling well."

"She could care less."

The music grew louder, as he whispered, "Can't fault her for chasing the best looking man here tonight."

"Hamilton Ingram, there's times you can be so—" her eyes smoldered a deep ocean blue. "I don't find that remark in the least amusing—even with the remote possibility that it's true," her flashing eyes smiled at him. "You are such a rascal. We both know what that mare is after."

At her remark, Hamilton sputtered, dribbled champagne, and said, "You shouldn't talk that way about your future sister-in-law."

"Gibraltar will cleave right down its very middle before that ever happens," Sarah emptied her glass.

"Don't be too sure. She asked why Ben wasn't here."

"Aren't you just full of yourself tonight. So what if talk I've heard about my brother and that trollop is true. Tonight's just for you'n me." Slipped her arm through his, "Let's walk."

"I'll never figure women."

"Most men never do."

"Your mother would have a fit if she heard some of the things you say."

"Of course, if I said them in mixed company. But for a country boy raised on a farm with a barnyard of little pigs, calves, puppies and kittens and all manner of babies you sure are right about one thing. You don't understand women hardly a'tall. Papa is a healthy man, and Mother keeps him that way—the same way

I keep you happy."

"I like that," he squeezed her closer. "Don't change."

He wasn't about to let on Ben had told him how he was anglin' to bed Betsy Lou this very night. He smiled at the thought of Betsy ending up family. Wisteria Bend would truly have some feisty family fireworks. He reached into his vest pocket and tugged out his gold watch and chain.

With a flick of his thumb, the engraved cover flipped open, "Half-passed eleven, still early. I've not seen Ben or your father."

"Ben was with Mama. She mentioned Papa had some business to settle, but I expected them long before this. I haven't seen Papa Rundell either." She pushed away. "You don't suppose something happened—you don't suppose there's been an accident?"

"Don't start jumpin' the gun, gettin' all flustered." Hamilton was more puzzled than worried.

In the middle of a waltz the halt of the violins got everyone's attention. From the platform, fiddle and bow clasped in one hand, the crusty, whiskered little Virginia Reel caller said, "A moment please." He waited for the buzz of voices to quieten. Then motioning with his bow, he excitedly called out, "Ladies and Gentlemen, gather round," his voice rose. "I've been requested to make a momentous announcement. One that makes this particularly happy time of the year even more so." The curious crowd rippled as he patiently once more waited for the murmurs to settle. Then he continued, "We gathered heah tonight for the highlight festivities of this holiday season. Now the occasion becomes doubly meaningful." Hamilton and Sarah moved inside with the others. In his mix of Charlestonian and Geechee drawl, the man continued, "Several distinguished guests have just arrived from Marlgrove Plantation," his gaze swept back and forth across the ballroom. Voices tittered, expectant. "As soon as they have freshened up, Colonel and Missus Cassius Irwin will join us shortly." The word *Colonel* jolted Hamilton and muffled voices grew louder as the caller continued. "Colonel Irwin has brought us long awaited news. Please, there'll be plenty time for celebratin' when..." A slight commotion interrupted him. Glancing toward the alcove he nodded, then puffed up as much as his thin frame would allow and announced. "Ladies and Gentlemen!" his squeaky voice shouted. "It is a great privilege to announce the sovereign Republic of the Palmetto State of South Carolina once more takes the lead—the Union is dissolved!"

A near unanimous gasp was followed by a brief silence, then a thundering bedlam of whoops and hollers.

Hamilton was stupefied, his chest tightened. "My God..." The words ripped through a thunderstruck Hamilton like the slash of a saber. He and Sarah were lost in a swell of shouts and tossed hats. Somewhere in the back of his mind he recalled Alex Stephens' warning.

The wiry caller raised his arms once more for order. "South Carolina chooses her own path." More catcalls and clapping. "Let us toast the Palmetto Republic of our forebearers. To the gentleman and his lady that brought us these long-delayed good tidings," his arm swept to the pillared entrance two steps above the grand salon floor, "I present Colonel Cassius Irwin of Marlgrove and his lovely wife, Missus Edwyna Brothington Irwin."

Boisterous acclaim followed the Master and Mistress of Marlgrove as they made their way toward the platform, Cassius Irwin in the uniform of a Colonel in the South Carolina Militia. Behind them Ben escorted one of the Irwin daughters. Hamilton spotted a stern-faced Rundell in the darkened archway where the Irwins had entered. The contrast between Rundell's and Cassius's expressions was like that of a thunder-sparked night and bright spring day.

Cassius Irwin mounted the podium. "Thank you, thank you all for such a fervent reception." He nodded to the guests, waited for the tumult to die off. "However, I'm only the bearer of such momentous tidings. Honor is due the delegates meeting in our fair city, who early today gave accordant unanimity for separation." More hurrahs shivered the domed ballroom. "We are also pleased to welcome compatriots whom most of you know. From the other side of the river it is my pleasure to present honorary volunteer to the ranks of Marlgrove Militia, Colonel Andrew Greer of Wisteria Bend, his most gracious wife, Missus Andrew Greer, Corinthia Gresham Greer, sponsor of the Marlgrove Militia, and their son, Corporal Benjamin Greer."

As Hamilton watched the Greers make their way to the podium, he couldn't take his eyes off Andrew's uniform with its brilliant cavalry stripes and polished gold swirl on the sleeves, the encrusted sword at his waist.

"Doesn't Papa look grand," Sarah stood on her tiptoes for a better look-see."

Andrew waited for the renewed furor to die away, then said, "This is indeed an important day for South Carolina, and we are proud to take this small part in it. As did our forefathers, South Carolina once again pledges itself to vouchsafe independence for the citizens of this renowned Republic among sister Republics."

The charged mood in the ballroom turned buoyantly dreamlike as Rundell moved next to Hamilton. Stern looks passing between them, Hamilton sensed a thing indefinable beyond the high sounding words. The air was somehow heavier, like overcooked brown sugar taffy, with chandeliers and torches throwing off a deeper yellowish haziness. From across the city came the muffled unremitting tempest thundered from thousands of throats, as the word spread through the night, embracing an unimaginable end to this unpredictable year. With Cassius Irwin's announcement Saint Catherine's Ball become more carnival than holiday.

In the wee hours of the following morning Marlgrove was a mix of euphoria and letdown. So as not to disturb anyone, Hamilton quietly packed. He had their carriage loaded, tied down and ready before the sun broke the dawn. Then he joined Sarah on the breakfast porch, just the two of them. With no appetite, he picked at his untouched breakfast.

Sarah tried to assuage his mood. "There was nothing anyone could've done."

"Somehow that don't make it feel any better." He nibbled at a piece of toast. "Perhaps, if more had spoken out sooner..?"

She tenderly laid her hand on his arm. "Maybe, if you stayed the rest of the week. Gave it some time."

"My sour face doesn't need to be mopin' around, putting a damper on everyone's good times. It's best Papa and I leave soon as we've made suitable good-bys. Last evening was lots of fun, we were having a such a good time. Plain as the nose on anyone's face this was comin', and the saddest part is it didn't have to be like this." He reached out and lightly brushed her check with the back of his fingers. "Lots t'be done at home before winter sets in. Quicker I get to it, the quicker it's done."

Just then Rundell came in and poured himself a cup of coffee, ignored the steaming eggs and grits on the sideboard. He pulled out a chair and sat down next to Sarah. His expression not much different from Hamilton's.

Slowly he stirred thick cream into his coffee. "Tarried long enough in the comin'. Good men did too little lettin' this take us where most didn't want to go."

Sarah said, "Mother wasn't too happy when Daddy told her he'd likely be leaving for Milledgeville soon as we return."

"Didn't take long for a part of it to land on Georgia's door-step." Hamilton was more than a little troubled.

"I could tell your seein' Papa in his uniform upset you."

Hamilton, silent for the longest, finally spoke. "It's not so much that as what it could mean for everyone. Talk's always been mostly about other places, somewhere else. Seeing Papa Andrew and Mister Cassius in those uniforms made me see how what seemed far-off can be right under one's nose. It bothered me havin' it this close, being so blind to it without my seein' it. Makes me wonder what else we hadn't paid any mind enough to."

6

The junket homeward seemed longer than the going, Hamilton and Rundell taking turns catnapping while the other drove. They pushed themselves, pushed the team, didn't overnight, holiday cheer plumb gone. Although rainy and chilly, they kept moving the whole way. It rained hard the miles after leaving Windsor Springs, the penetrating December dampness boring bone-deep. Except for occasional gusts the buggy's foldup roof kept off the worst. By the time they rolled in late on the 24th, Rundell had a raspy throat and a slight cough.

After they unloaded, both huddled in front of a roaring fire. "Good slug of Bessie's remedies'll loosen your chest," Hamilton said.

"...And a good hot toddy."

Rundell was never one to complain, yet a week later he was still coughing. Hamilton could tell he was feelin' poorly. "You feeling any better?"

Rundell swallowed a choking cough. "...A touch better."

•

Instead of a raucous shivaree, Hamilton let it be known he'd rather have them come out to his papa's place and have a good hunt. It was a mix of both. He and his rowdy friends were plumb tuckered from their uproar'ous get-together with more on the get-together than the hunt. They made their way back to the Hollows for a game supper and a hot fire.

After several toasts, through an alcoholic haze Hamilton proposed one more, "Happy New Year everyone."

Steins and mugs were raised, emptied, refilled. Spiced cider, bourbon, hot cinnamon wine, homemade whisky corn likker swilled away well into the night. With no other big to-dos planned to usher in the New Year, it was a night for lettin' loose and getting roarin' soused. Even Corinthia's post-Christmas parties had been subdued.

Andrew drew a deep puff on a fresh cigar, blew a cloud of smoke that drifted above them. "Well Hamilton...what you think of Lincoln's fancy promises about peace, now that he lied about not sendin' reinforcements to Sumter?"

"My estimation is he evacuated the shore forts so he could hold Sumter." Hamilton didn't quibble. "It could still settle out, no other state's joined South Carolina."

"They will...Mississippi an' Alabama any day now."

"Lincoln's got time on his side," Hamilton said. "He can wait out South Carolina."

"We'll see after the holidays." Andrew puffed another cloud of smoke, blew two, three, then a fourth smoke ring.

"I hear you're forming a company of volunteers."

"Governor and I been talkin'. Have 'em ready in case the governor sends out a call. You ought'a join. The way you handle a horse, you'd make a fine cavalry officer."

Rundell cut a quick glance at his son, then said, "Andrew, Georgians will need food. Grain needs planting, harvesting, hauling—farm work needs hands."

"This concerns all of us," Andrew said, liquor loosening his tongue. "Lincoln promised to evacuate Sumter. If he don't, South

Carolina means to take it. You can see the need of that."

"I don't see any reason for the rush," Hamilton said. "Has nothing to do with backing away from a fight, but I never made a point of startin' one neither."

"South Carolina's not picking a fight." Andrew was insistent.

"Maybe not, but doin's in Charlestown are shaping up with neither side cutting the other much leeway."

"...And leaving us no choice."

Hamilton stood. "Get anyone a refill?"

"One for me," Ben called.

"Me too." Andrew reached up his mug.

•

Sam was hell-bent determined. "I mean it, Mama." His eyes steady on her across their supper table. "If Georgia go the same as South Carolina, I'm set t'leave."

"Lordy, Lord, Samuel." His intendin's tearin' at her heart strings, she said, "You don't got to do this."

"Yes, Mama. I do."

Bessie couldn't accept this kind of talk, an' how it would hurt ever'one. "I knows your feelin's, but this cain't turn out no ways 'cept terr'ble."

"Mama..." Sam's head drooped. He stiffened. "What we is was here 'fore I was born, 'fore you was born, but it eats at me all the time seein' how you live with it. I cain't, not with what's goin' on."

"There be worse. I never lied to you, Samuel, there for sure be worse." Her hands wrung tight in her stark white apron. "Things maybe settle down, maybe work out if you give 'em a chance."

"They hardly be no way out. You likely right about worse bein' out there, but that don't make what's here no better."

"What you 'spect me to tell Marse Andrew once you gone?"

"I know you have love for the Greers. So do I. In lots'a ways we is family."

"We be family 'cause Marse Andrew kept his promise you'd never be sold from me. Now, you undoin' things by runnin' 'cause you cain't tough it out."

"Ain't a matter of toughin'," Sam bristled. "I don't see it bein' Marse Andrew's word to sell or keep me or let me go where I want."

"It the law."

"Reknen it is," Sam sighed. "But fam'ly don't always agree, an' fam'ly don't call one another Marse and Mistress neither. Just say the truth, Mama. Say the truth like you taught me to do."

She stared at this son, felt things changin' from where they ought'a be. "It shame me fierce."

"You shamed yourse'f more'n they could."

"That far 'nough," a stern Bessie said. "Bein' with the Greers got no shame to it. I raise me a son I be proud is mine, an' all the time you growin' up, you know you was safe at the Bends. Marse Andrew never mad when he learn you learned letters." She shook her head firmly. "Don't tell me Mistress Corinth'a lookin' out for us don't count for nothin'."

"After Marse Andrew pass on, his promise to us carry no weight, not at the Bends, not with nobody outside." Sam grew sullen. "We can be bought an' sold like mules, then thrown out like wore out boots."

"Never seen Marse Andrew sell a one 'cause they aged." Bessie gave another firm shake of her head. "Anyone tell you different be puttin' a lie on you. When the day come you see how wrong you be, I pray the good Lord it don't be somethin' what cain't be undone."

•

More shocks rumbled across the land the first two weeks into the new year.

"This *Augusta Constitutionalist* newspaper rag is supportin' those talking Yankee politics," Rundell snapped to another page of the paper. "One day those Northern democrats will wake up and see they've been sold a sack of barnyard manure." He flipped to the next page. "*Hmmm*, seems Lincoln don't like Crittenden's compromise. Aside from bein' a politician, Lincoln's like every other lawyer I ever known...cain't believe nothing they say."

Hamilton reached for another slice of the pork roast. "He

never struck me as being different from other radicals raising a ruckus, not the compromising type."

Rundell kept reading, "Mississippi and Florida followed South Carolina, and it don't appear William Yancey and the Alabamians are far behind."

"If Tennessee votes to go out, Georgia'll be surrounded by stand-alone states."

"I doubt there's enough levelheadedness to stay the momentum with the tug gettin' harder to resist. For what it's worth I think Georgia'll go with the gulf states, and be worse in the doing. Seems Ben Franklin was right thinkin' we couldn't keep our grand republic. He'd be sad to behold knowing his prediction has come to this sort of fruition."

"Some claim it was never worth much."

"Pity everything's swung to excess," Rundell said, disgusted more than angry. "Windbag braggadocio done took the saddle. Voice a conviction other than cuttin' loose, it's looked upon as disloyalty. Called such in public. Hotheads makin' honor an excuse, and the same's stirring up North. No longer just the conniving abolitionists, ever'one's tearing at the old. I don't envy Andrew bein' in Milledgeville next week."

"Sarah said her papa's away from home more often than not."

"He's gonna be away a lot more." Rundell let the paper slide to the floor. "Think I'll turn in...been a long day."

As Hamilton cleared the table, he thought how all the doings, including harvesting an' hauling, were whyttelin' more and more into his and Sarah's time. He hadn't been over to the Bends in more'n a week.

Last time he buggied into town to fetch barrels of flour and bags of salt, he mentioned that prices were up some from last time as he paid.

"Costs are going steady up," the feedstore clerk said. "Price of a bale dropped again."

Least, Hamilton had mended several sections of grazing fences, got the new one put up around the feedlot, and got shingles split for patchin' the cotton shed roof. Helped birth the new calves earlier in the week, rubbed 'em good 'til the cows started lickin' 'em dry. In what little daylight was left before supper today, he'd finally got the firewood cut and stacked. He headed to bed. He was bushed.

•

"Just 'cause a goodly chunk of our neighbor states up an' pulled loose don't mean Georgia ought to join the stampede," Alex Stephens said. "While we're in Congress, Lincoln's bound by the law. We pull out, there's no brakes on what he aims doin'."

One of the last voices against turning loose, his failure hall-marked the dwindling restraints. By the first day of February, Texas and Louisiana had made it a Gulf Coast clean sweep.

Later that week, Andrew returned home and found himself confronting the mess churning around Sam. "I come back to get ready for the trip to Montgomery day after tomorrow, and find Sam's been gone three days." He tried to stay calm.

Corinthia had a long face and teary-eyes. It was one of the rare times she'd had a situation she couldn't spare from Andrew. She had known how this would upset him.

"Bessie," Andrew was thunderstruck, "how long you known about this?"

"Since 'bout 'fore Christmastide." Her voice caught, hurt by Sam, an' hurt as deep for hurtin' those she cared about.

"Christmas!" Andrew flabbergasted. "Why didn't you come to me?"

"Marse Andrew, I truly wanted to," she sniffled. Wiped her nose. "...I couldn't."

"Where'd he go? Who helped him?"

"Sam wouldn't let nobody he'p."

"You telling me he told nobody in the cabins?"

"Tell nobody nuthin'. Didn't want no one to have to lie or ketch the blame."

"It's alright for Sam not to tell no one, but it was alright for you to lie to me!" he stormed.

"Andrew!" Corinthia gasped.

Bessie's face contorted at the reproach, seein' how the hurt was on him, but she'd never been accused of passin' lies. "Marse

Andrew, I never lied."

"You're cuttin' a mighty hair-thin mislead between falsehoods and not tellin'."

She daubed her eyes, pulled up proud, and asked, "Who Bessie gonna tell? You be off Lord knows where with no word when you be home. Bessie facin' with a young'un what meant to have his way, wadn't givin' an ear to no caution. Who I tell? Mistress Corinth'a? What she do? Hog-tie Sam in the barns, then worry herse'f sick? He listen to no caution. He just bust loose, an' gone," Twistin' her dish towel, she sniffled and chewed her lips. She'd never spoke to his face like this. "Jesus is my witness, Samuel jes up an' went. Didn't tell me when he go."

"But you knew he was gonna run!"

"Marse Andrew—"

"Andrew." Corinthia's expression pained.

"Stay out of this," Andrew snapped, confused, confounded.

"Don't raise your voice to me, Andrew Cornelius Greer." A miseried Corinthia didn't waver. "I most assuredly will not stay out of this." She put her arms around Bessie's shoulders and pulled Bessie into her. "Bessie's right. With your not being here, anything she might've done would've only made things worse."

Bessie wiped at her tears, afeard what might be acomin'. "I kept the hope I could talk him from doin' this foolish. If I tell Mistress Corinth'a, it put her in the middle of this mess. I wadn't doin' that."

"God!" Andrew paced, turned, paced more, his face perplexed with a disconcerted frustration more than rage. Came toward the two women, stopped, and said, "Bessie, you know what it means if Sam crosses the state line? If authorities find out?"

"Samuel didn't take nuthin', didn't take nuthin'."

"That may be, but far as they'll concern themselves he took hisself...he's part of the Bends." His voice was rising. "He cross out from the state, it'll be out of my hands to keep him from being declared fugitive!" He hadn't meant to shout, but he did.

"Oh, Marse Andrew, don't let 'em do that to my boy. Be like turnin' young Benjamin over to the law for him doin' somethin' you know he had to do even if you didn't side with the doin'."

"Sam's nigh to bein' a man. A man's responsible for his actions."

"They put the dawgs on him!" Bessie choked back a sob, fearin' terr'ble dreads for her flesh. "Or shoot my boy!"

Mother and master barbed between impossibles, both caught in the rigid chattel house that was squeezing tighter, squeezing love and caring and anything what got in the way.

Andrew stepped out onto the front veranda and called out to his field boss, Sam's cousin, "Luke, you growed up with Sam. I want this hushed up. Hushed thorough, and kept inside Wisteria Bends. It'll get worse for Sam if the sheriff comes askin' questions and puts out a reward. If others got the same idea, or worse, if they sell out Sam for the reward. The word spread, Sam'll be in hot water."

"I make sure it stay quiet," Luke said. "Bessie have my hide if'n I don't see it happen."

"And I'll have what's left of you after she gets finished."

"You be out'a luck, won't be no pieces left to pick. Bessie tear me up, I let somethin' happen to Sam."

"No one goes off the property for no reason, not to town, not anywhere. I want this handled quiet."

"Please, Marse Andrew." Bessie breaking the unbreakable rule to ask, "Mister Ben, Mister Hamilton growed up with Samuel. Send them after him, they won't shoot my Samuel. Don't let them loose the dawgs."

"Dogs're better than bullets."

"One come with the other." A great dread rose inside Bessie.

"Quicker he's back, the better." Andrew ground his jaw. "In all my days, I never in my life had such commotion with one of my hands."

Greer business was Greer business, nobody else's. Without seeing as such, the fissured Union was already ripping clean to the heart of the once-tranquil world of Saint George Parish.

•

Whether clear-headedness or politics or something in between, a twilight moment of sanity somehow managed to straggle along.

Hamilton let the Augusta paper slump to his lap. "Papa, you think President Buchanan's refusing to use the firing on the *Merchant Star* as an act of war will let things cool down?"

"Nope." Rundell kicked off his boots. "Whole thing just makes blockheads on both sides that much more determined. Like a bunch of infernal school yard bullies playing the blindman's buff, same as the surrender of the Augusta arsenal last January. Each inchin' creep don't seem to amount to much, each side daring the other to step over the line, not lookin' where each inch is takin' things, and damn fewer of them carin'. It'll work to a point 'til it's time to put up or turn tail. That's when there's gonna be hell to pay."

"Virginia's holding on secesh, voted against it." Hamilton turned the page. "Says here Robert Toombs met that Texas Senator Wigfall on the Senator's stopover in Augusta. Toombs is raisin' a ruckus, sayin' South Carolina's got no choice, how no state stands sovereign with a hostile force blocking its port. How Sumter has to yield."

"He's a fiery one alright. Charlestown forts are squeezing everyone. Forcing Jeff Davis' new cabinet at Montgomery to deal with the situation. Neither side left the other much wiggle room with self-righteous Lincoln taking the high ground." Rundell sneered, "Self-righteous is a dangerous thing in any man. Doubly so in a politician, an' 'specially with a President...Jeff Davis as well as Lincoln."

"South Carolina looks to mean business."

"The hitch of it is Lincoln sees a powder keg he figured was a bluff. He's seein' it a mite late, and the dangerous part is he don't see the fuse bein' as short as it is." Rundell wiggled his toes. "Those do-gooders and power grabbers who bought Lincoln his election, are pullin' his strings, and they want their payback. The whole bunch is blind as cross-eyed bats. Whether they believed it or not, they convinced him secesh talk was all deception. How South Carolina didn't mean what she said. Now he sees otherwise with both sides fumbling with a hornet's nest and our butts crammed right in there with him. A fight looks to be about what some fools have hankered for all along."

As Hamilton pulled on his boots, he said, "I got that last corn field seeded."

It was shaping into being a ragged spring.

●

Hamilton finished a day of hard ploughing, grabbed a bar of lye soap, towel, a pair of clean pants, and headed for the creek. The cold water felt good. He scrubbed good, soaped up all under, took a couple of headers underwater to shed any soap, dried good, and slipped on clean pants. He got home, finished dressing, and saddled up. As the horse slow-gate cantered on the Hollow's cutoff toward the Bends, Hamilton mulled the changes he'd seen in his father. Nothing he could put his finger to. Papa had sweated his whole life to keep the Hollows pay as-you-go. Money was snugging tighter, and he knew for certain Papa wasn't about to borrow. Thought on it the whole way until he found himself riding under the arch of the Bend's main gate.

He tied his horse to the side hitch rail and strolled in through the French windows from the garden. In the parlor he found Sarah and her mother crocheting, the light streaming through Sarah's hair.

Corinthia looked up from the sofa. "Hamilton, how nice to see you."

Sarah continued with her needles, as she said, "Hadn't seen much of you lately."

"Been busy."

Ben came through the foyer hall, a cup of coffee and chicory in his hand, and Bessie right behing him with high tea coffee cakes and cucumbers.

"Hey, Hamilton..." Ben said.

"Been a while."

"Time somehow gets gone."

Hamilton caught the quick look from Sarah. He hadn't stayed away deliberately, but he'd somehow made time for that sotted weekend. Him and Frank at Queensborough Towne's sportin' house, the next two, three days a blur, vaguely remembered some faces, a couple of married ones. Kept remembering Betsy Lou

Whitehead's face twisted in the satin sheets with Frank. Come sunup, he could hardly make his feet work, but managed to stay on his horse.

He went to Bessie and asked, "Heard from Sam?"

Bessie shook her head. "Nary a twit."

Hamilton was almost glad there'd been no word. Least Sam hadn't been dragged back in chains, or in a shroud like a sack of flour tossed across a mule.

Bessie set about with the saucers, tea cups and linen napkins. "Each day comes, goes, still no word." She choked off more words.

"You want some of us should go look for him?"

"Be a heap better'n some sheriff. Sam maybe listen to you, but no one knows where to look." Her chin quivered.

"Hamilton?" Ben called out. "When you'n this sister of mine gonna set the wedding date?"

"Benjamin!" Sarah flared and flung down her needles. "Mother, when is that blabbermouth brother of mine going to learn to use the manners he's been taught!" She trounced up the stairs, not all that upset Ben had tugged it out into the open.

"Ben," Corinthia half scolded. "Why do you agitate your sister so? My apologies, Hamilton."

Hamilton said, "Me'n Sarah talked maybe April or May for the promisings with a wedding sometime in the fall."

Corinthia caught her breath, as though Hamilton's remark hadn't taken her off guard. "Sarah hadn't mentioned anything about that."

"I suspect she was waiting until I talked with Papa Andrew," Hamilton said. "With all that's going on things somehow been shoved aside. We've been right busy opening portions of that upper scrubland."

Andrew came in, brushing at his sleeve. "Hamilton, good to see you."

"Papa Andrew..." Hamilton greeted.

"Just got in myself, right brisk out there."

Hamilton said, "I expect there'll be a few more frosts before spring sets in to stay. Ben's just asked me about mine and Sarah's engagement."

Corinthia had seen the unpredictable side of this son-in-law to-be, but not this impulsiveness.

"Been wondering why you two were takin' so long." Andrew clapped him on the back. "So, you young'uns finally decided?"

Corinthia kept her smile in place, but she'd had enough. The audacity of men, do the planning, then whenever they pleased, drop it in a woman's lap to make it happen.

"Sarah and I have been waiting on the weather to settle," she said with an agreeable smile to Andrew, a look to Hamilton. "We were thinking of an outdoor gathering, a garden wedding, at least a garden reception."

Andrew lifted the decanter. "I'd say it was time for a toast."

As Andrew handed her a small snifter of brandy, Corinthia smiled ever so much more pleasant. She raised her glass, took a slight sip, then excused herself. Sarah didn't come down the rest of the evening. The men were left to themselves.

•

Rundell scooted the chair closer to the supper table, hungry after a tiresome day in town. "Got some of the new seed cotton and four more cows. They'll be here early part of next week."

Hamilton said, "Be a good build-up to the herd."

"Plus three hands who say they'll be here to help with planting. We'll see how good their word is about stayin' once we put money in their pockets." He got up from the table. "Come take a look at the mules I found."

In the barn Hamilton checked their withers. "Looks to be a fine set, strong pasterns." Reached down, lifted a front foot. "Broad hooves, good fetlocks. Not many good mules around. You have to go up from what you wanted to pay?"

"An ole horse trader like me?" Rundell grinned. "Started the bid low. By the time it got down to the wire, price was right about where I figured it ought'a be. When Andrew sees these, he'll turn pea-green. He's been wantin' a pair like this since last year."

"We set the date for the promisings. Greers will announce it for the afternoon, wedding will be in November."

"Be nice having Sarah for a daughter." Rundell grinned big.

"There's not a finer lady in the whole of Georgia, well 'cept Corinne, maybe. You set up any groomsmen?"

"Figured to let you do that. Beings we ain't set the date for tying the knot, my best man's got to have something to do."

"Come." Rundell slapped his son on the shoulder. "Let's open a bottle of that good wine, celebrate my good fortune and yours." As they toasted, Rundell said, "Word around town is Andrew about finished puttin' together that company of Queensborough Cavalry on authority from the governor."

"He mentioned it while we were in Charlestown, but he's never said much else about it since. Where'd you hear about it?"

"Feed store," Rundell said.

"I don't like that kind of talk. You figure Georgia'll be needing volunteers?"

"Things are belly to belly snug in Charlestown. Jeff Davis took over the situation there, and for my money it's way passed time he ought've done it. If those Palmetto hotheads were left to their doings, they'd already started shootin'."

"There's still a chance it won't come to that."

"...Damn little."

"Lincoln's shoved South Carolina to the wall. Sayin' how they can come back in the Union if they lay down their arms."

"Won't be no suckin' up to that," Rundell growled, his eyes glinting through swirls of tobacco smoke. "One way or another Lincoln means to have done with it, break secesh, use it as an excuse to do to whatever he wants. Never cottoned to the likes of him. He don't speak straight, uses two-edged words, wants to make the South look bad while makin' like he's talkin' for peace. No, sirree." Rundell chewed off his cigar, spit it out. "Black Republicans mean to take the South, then use it up."

"He send in troops, he'll lose Virginia," Hamilton said. "Whole upper South'll bolt along with lots of folks that wanted to stay Union. Kentucky claims she means to stay neutral, but I wouldn't be surprised to see her tear loose."

"Got us a mess. Maryland and Delaware will go if Virginia leaves," Rundell said. "Gonna be hell to pay, and there ain't gonna be none of this Kaintuck neutral ground."

"If Virginia holds for the Union, that'll wedge out Maryland,

Delaware, maybe North Carolina and Tennessee. If Tennessee stays Union, Federals on the Ohio River could come through to Chattanooga, knock out the railroads on to Marthasville."

"Could get rough for some states," Rundell said. "East Tennessee mountain folk are the same mind as those up in the North Georgia mountains. Could be no fight a'tall if Lincoln can bring about splits inside states. With Federals stirring around Sumter and the harbor, won't take them no time to do the same at Savannah, Mobile, and New Orleans. But if Lincoln's as blind as I think and pushes the wrong place at the wrong time, it has all the makin's of an ugly brother against brother fracas—same as we ended up with in the rebellion against the Brits."

"Papa, you make it sound like we're already facing a fight."

"We are. The shootin' just hadn't started. That's what most folks don't see when something like this gets stirred. Revolutions take place in the heart long before anyone loads a gun, and by then it don't matter what's talked or printed. We're down to the doin', and Georgia's up to her neck in this whether she's ready or not. Take a dead man not to see how the facts stack. There could be a fearful lot lost neither side's lookin' to. We'll give Georgia all the support the Hollows can muster, but this secesh is strung out from South Carolina to Texas. If it dogs down into a long fight, that's a lot of borders to defend."

7

It was near high noon, and Hamilton had been ploughing since sunup. He decided the mules weren't the only thing needin' a break. As he was unhitching, he caught the sound of a lone rider yelling at the top of his lungs and coming his way. He adjusted his hat against the sun and recognized Ben on NellyB, tearing across the field in full gallop, NellyB's hooves slinging dirt clods high in the air behind them. The hogs, rooting the fresh turned clods for Guinea grass roots, leftover peanuts and potatoes, squealed and scattered.

"We did it! We did it!" an excited Ben yelled at the top of his lungs. *"We did it!"* He yanked NellyB to a skidding, stiff-legged halt. "Beauregard took Sumter!" Out of the saddle and breathing hard, his fist clenched a wrinkled front page of the *Charleston Courier*. "Lincoln asked Virginia for troops, called what Carolina done sedition. Like Carolinians got no say to it. Virginia called for volunteers, arming her state militia, claims any Federal invasion of a state violates the constitution. Georgia governor is

calling up Georgia's Militia—Papa's signing up more volunteers for the Queensborough Cavalry. Yankies'll back off once they see we're ready to fight. If me'n you don't hurry it'll be over an' done with before we have to be home for spring planting." He shook the newspaper like it was a call to a fun-time fancy dress shindy. "We get to take our own horses. I'll take NellyB."

Hamilton shook his head. "Ever'one sure seems eager to jump in and fight."

Hamilton thought back to his and Papa's trip up to Philadelphia to pick up the new water turbine for their sawmill. He'd never seen so many puffing chimneys, kilns, furnaces, more railroads, steam engines, switchyards and roundhouses in one city than in the whole of Georgia and South Carolina put together. Rundell had hurried back home to make sure the sawmill was coming along. Hamilton journeyed with the crated turbine by steamer ship to Savannah. During the voyage he saw ships enough to cargo a whole year of Georgia's cotton bales all at once.

He reached for the paper in Ben's hand. Stared at the bold black headlines, and thought of Calhoun's warning more'n ten years ago. "Could be way more to Sumter than us ridin' there for a weekend of horses and sabers."

Ben saw only glory, his exuberance leaving Hamilton with all manner of mixed feelings. Ever since their Charlestown trip, Hamilton had watched a deep-seated fret auger at Papa's de-Worthe gentle blue eyes. Lately those eyes, which met each day with so much life and the fun of living, had become careworn. These headlines wouldn't help.

"Don't just stand there sprouting roots, say something." Sweat trickled down Ben's face.

Hamilton hobbled the mule, leaned the plow over in the furrow, then fixed Ben with a straight look. "You already know my answer. I agree with Papa. I don't think it's the way Georgia ought to be headed either."

"You're not joining up?" Ben didn't hide his disappointment.

"The kind of fight this could turn into won't be all about ridin' and shootin'. Georgia's gonna need food, maybe more than she ever produced."

"Georgia grows more'n enough food an' then some." Ben dropped NellyB's bridle to let her graze. "Sure wish you'd change your mind." He aimlessly kicked a dirt clod. "I was lookin' forward to you'n me having adventures."

Hamilton chuckled. "Come sit a spell."

They trudged across the ploughed rows toward the gully and the clump of water oaks by the springs. "I stuck a jug of cider jack in the spring this morning before I hitched up. More'n I can drink, more'n I should drink or the rest of the afternoon's ploughin' likely'll be crooked as a dog's hind leg."

"That'd sure hit the spot. Day's got right warm. Been riding hard."

They sat under the shade, close as any brothers, sipping the amber squeezin's. Ben said, "Mama tell you about all the plans for yours and Sarah's wedding?"

"No." Hamilton gave a belly laugh. "But I had no doubts Sarah and your mother were working on them."

"They're planning big doin's."

"Mother Greer never waited on no one to get ready in her life—except possibly your pa, and from what little I've seen, I'd wager he's done most of the waitin'." Hamilton feeling the barest coming-ons of the hard cider on an empty stomach, licked cider tartness off his lips, brushed a hand through his hair. "Your mama's a good woman, Ben Greer." He propped his arms across his knees, "You already know I care for your mom and dad, as much as I do my own papa. Your papa's fortunate having a fine woman like your mother to wife, and I've never seen your mama fail to get anything she sets out for. Sarah's the same." He took another swig. "...Good woman." Then handing the jug to Ben, said, "Here, finish it. I'm gettin' fuzzy-headed. Mules will have better sense than me."

Ben took a couple of quick slugs and stood up, brushing grass off his britches. "Got to get back." He took another quick draw on the cider, swished it around, and swallowed. In one motion he grabbed saddle and reins in one hand, and swung himself into the saddle.

NellyB snorted as Ben said, "You and your dad coming for supper Friday?"

The sun behind Ben, Hamilton squinted into the bright halo of Ben's head and shoulders. "Papa talked about it. Far as I know we'll be there, less something comes up."

•

Chilly evenings gave way to a full-fledged April spring, green sprouts poking up everywhere, and come the first week of May, Arkansas slipped away from the Union. Easter came and went with Andrew away most of the month.

Ben had never bucked his papa, but he was upset. "What you mean, I stay here?" He was raring to sit the saddle, side by side with his papa.

"Benjamin—" Andrew had known Ben wouldn't like his decision. "This place needs you. I need you in charge here. Nobody knows this place any better'n you. Besides, Sarah has Hamilton, and with my being away, your mother'll have considerable need of you."

A disheartened Ben was pissed, but knew Papa was depending on him, knew there was plenty to be kept on an even keel. April and May crops were coming up right well. After Andrew left Ben buckled down, made sure things kept moving smooth.

At the Hollows, as the first early crops came on, the need for extra hands increased. The day Rundell was in Queensborough to hire workers, the town seemed more crowded than ever. To him it looked to be mostly family men. He recognized a few faces, who'd had comfortable small spreads. He talked with several who'd left their farms. Hired the few he figured he'd need. Come second plantin' time most showed up. The afternoon the last of the second plantings were seeded, Rundell paid the men.

"Glad that's done," Rundell said as he and Hamilton grabbed soap and towels and headed for the creek for a good scrub. "Now we need a good slow rain."

"Never seems like enough time to get done all what needs doing," said Hamilton.

Rundell nodded his head. "Farming comes in spurts. One thing at a time is all a body can do."

Corinthia was vexed one afternoon as she set to redoing the invitations for the betrothal announcements. "We simply must get the socials over before June. After early June, the middle of the summer is entirely too warm." She'd considered having the invitations to the engagement party printed, but changed her mind. "They wanted to charge an outrageous amount for such a simple task. We'll do them by hand. Instead of mailing folded invitations, I'm thinking of having glued envelopes made. I've heard they're quite elegant." She had already threatened everyone with dire consequences if anyone dared change the dates.

Taking care with the elegant cursive lettering, Sarah said, "If we had the wedding in the fall like we talked, that would give us lots more time."

"Sarah Greer, I do declare. Sometimes I believe you don't look two steps in front of you. Fall is well on to harvest time, and you know how busy it gets. Not only will the autumn rainy season be coming on, but your father never knows if he'll be called away at the last minute. I know lard-oil lighting would be easier, but candles are so much nicer, and we haven't near enough hard candles. There's mutton tallow, camphor, beeswax and alum to obtain, and we've yet to secure creditable daguerreotype services. We simply must have photographs. With a firm nod, Corinthia sighed. "All this runnin' about takes time, and certainly doesn't make it easy to plan something like this."

"Why not just set the engagement?" Sarah slowly placed her penhold with its pen point in the inkwell, rose from her writing desk, and ambled to the tall windows. "God willing and the creeks don't rise, pray for good weather. I'm sure things will work out fine."

"Sweet child of mine—" without raising her head Corinthia continued writing, "—as if your father's comings and goings in Milledgeville weren't enough, now he's involved with the Queensborough Cavalry's move to Richmond." She rolled her eyes. "We hardly ever see him." Corinthia had never thought of herself as one among thousands of wives left to the home front. But she was.

"Papa's sure to be home for Christmas," Sarah continued. "He knows I couldn't bear the thought of him not being here for my wedding."

Corinthia didn't respond, the pen in her nimble fingers paused. Careful not to smudge the note, she placed it precisely next to the boxwood inkwell she kept on her Queen Anne desk. For the longest her eyes remained fixed on the paper in front of her.

Sarah finished printing, then checked the next name on the list. "We could..." and looked up.

Corinthia was staring at her, the room very still, her expression almost severe. Sarah felt an anxiousness, like those times she'd wakened from a scary dream, or was jolted from sleep by the crash of a thunderstorm rattling her bedroom windows.

"Mother?" Sarah's voice faltered. "Whatever in the world is wrong?"

"I never intended mentioning this."

"Mention what?" The invitations forgotten. Has something happened to Papa?"

"Nothing has happened to your father, but perhaps this is as good a time as any. Until now I saw no reason to address what seemed unnecessary." Her hushed seriousness was clarion enough that this was no idle mother-daughter chitchat.

"Discuss what?" Puzzlement crowded in at Sarah.

"I will speak of this once. Then I most definitely do not wish to ever hear it mentioned again." Corinthia's wide amber-brown eyes were as black as the blackest night. Usually soft-spoken, her voice sounded a bit brittle. "Your father's involved with this..." She hesitated, "...this situation. One we may all have to confront. He's never happy being away from us, and certainly not during the busy hay or harvest seasons with new sections needing his attention."

Deep down Sarah's stomach quivered. She'd never seen her mother quite like this. Her mother never discussed Papa's doings.

"You've always seen things the way you wished them to be, which, I might add, has brought much joy to your father and me." Corinthia's voice continued, unwavering, "Much of your father's present obligations are out of his hands as well as ours.

No matter, your father is part of it, which makes us part of it as well. Sometimes good men can become frightfully possessed, amusing themselves with the flighty types."

"Types like Betsy Lou Whitehead."

Corinthia gave a singular nod and continued, "Most have the propriety to keep such trifled dalliances discreet. Away from home and away from family. When men are ready to settle down and raise a family, they want a woman with a good head and an understanding heart. Men look for a solid woman they can depend on, one with the makings of a good mother to his children. A woman with any sense knows the boy in the man often fancies being drawn to what they've wanted from the first. She also knows that any man worth his salt always lives with that boy inside him. Sometimes that boy gets the man into more trouble than he ever saw coming."

Sarah frowned. "You can't possibly be talking about Papa."

"No, I'm talking about you and Hamilton, your father and brother, about any man and woman that care for one another. It's fallen to Ben to see the Bends is run like your father would wish. We must do whatever is necessary to make his concerns less burdensome. When your father is home, everything is to be exactly as it was." Sarah's mother spoke with steely words, and steelier expression. "I will countenance nothing less. Do you understand?"

"Yes," answered Sarah, certain her mother knew all the things she and Benjamin whispered to each other about Papa's escapades.

This grand lady, her husband's social centerpiece, smiled with that knowing smile mothers and wives have, and said, "You can be proud of Hamilton. Hamilton is a fine young man. Perchance with a bit too much of the single-mindedness Ingram men seem to possess, but which when properly conveyed can be altogether quite charming. He's been raised proper. Which I can't say for some of the other sons about the parish. Hamilton grasped the shaping of this dreadful contention clearly long before your father, which I'm not so certain your brother has yet managed to do. Benjamin still believes perseverance can triumph over any adversity. Most times it can—but not always. It's an admirable trait, as long as it's approached with a good dose of reality. Your father adores his darling daughter. Spoiling you has given him considerable pleasure, which, I might add, I've indulged more than I should've."

"Mother—"

"You *are* spoiled. You and I both know it. However, times being what they are, you no longer have the luxury of such behavior. Hamilton may come to depend a great deal on you. Ingrams are noted for not taking lightly the obligation of duty and responsibility. He's ready to take you to wife, a wife who'll be there for him and the children he'll give her—no matter what you two must face."

"I do love him, so very much."

"I'm sure you do, almost as much as he loves you. Sometimes love isn't enough."

"Mother, I've never seen you so serious."

"These are times for being serious, and there's no better time than the present for us to understand exactly what we must do."

"I've never known you to speak like this."

"I've seldom had reason to. Men often like to toy with frivolous women full of fluff and nothing, and I must say, there are women who do the same. But..." Corinthia looked at her daughter. "There are times when considerably more is not only called for, but indispensable."

"Mother, you're frightening me."

"It's not my wish to do so, but if it gives you thought about certain things, perhaps it's just as well. Little-girl wiles can be engagingly amusing, and yours often work exceedingly well with your father. However, my sweet daughter, they have no place with a man like Hamilton. You don't know men half as well as you think. With Hamilton, you have a man who is deeply devoted to you, but, like his father, he is a man of many facets. Some of which I've never seen in Hamilton, and only a few times in Rundell. Certain aspects of Ingram behavior I prefer to never witness again. I assure you, one does not wish to provoke either of them. They rile immeasurably slow, but once angered, they've an uncontrollable fury that drives fear into people. The old wives' tale about women being the true romantics is rubbish. Women are pragmatic, men are dreamers, and a good man can be peculiarly naive, exceedingly tenderhearted, inordinately enduring—but seldom weak. Your papa and your brother are no exception, and I love them both the more for it. Like a firm handshake or their word, their honor once pledged is a soul-deep bond reaching clean to their gizzard. More important to them than life itself. Once he sets his mind, Hamilton is much more that way than Rundell, and in many ways that's understandable."

"There's been a time or two I've known Hamilton to be stubborn, but that doesn't seem so bad in a man."

"No, being single-minded isn't bad. You are willful, but in another way. There are times." Corinthia's engaging softness turned pensive. "It's not unusual for young folk to refuse compromise on principles. They consider death, as though it's meant for someone else, 'specially where honor becomes duty. Men often wear such feelings on their sleeve. Ingrams are well known for taking it a bit further, their passions are felt deeply, but held private. With Hamilton it's even more so, which makes his heart that much more vulnerable. Once such a heart is wounded, what's left is a husk which can never be mended. As Hamilton's wife, your family's happiness depends on preventing that ever happening."

A shiver settled about Sarah. "Mother, what's truly bothering you?"

Corinthia paled as she rose from her writing table and stepped to the tall window framed by brocade and lace curtains. "Your father will have some peace of mind knowing you're with Hamilton."

"Mother, you talk as though we'll not be more than a good buggy ride down the Trace."

"We may be facing far more unpleasantness than a father missing his daughter's engagement social." One hand pushed aside the lace panel as she gazed out across the vast tree shaded sprawl that had been her home for most of her life. "I simply can't shake the feeling…" Her words stopped.

With a hesitant, far-somewhere-else gaze, her hand slowly dropped away from the drapes and came to rest uncertainly at her throat as Corinthia recovered her composure.

She looked at this lovely daughter, smiled her reassuring smile, and said, "The good Lord never gives us more than we can bear."

Sarah said, "Ben and I used to giggled about how much it seemed you weren't aware of what was going on around you. I suppose we—"

Corinthia interrupted, "Let that be a lesson how wrong one's perceptions can be. Time has a way of taking care of those things one can do nothing to change...not always, but most times. Pay no mind to idle gossip. When possible, a wife who loves her husband and family heads off problems before they become problems. Do that and you need never worry a smidgen about your husband or the father of your children." She winsomely picked at a thread on her dress, inattentively brushed it aside. "Bessie and I often were amused by you and your brother carrying on with what you thought were your little secrets. Believing you were getting away with things, your giggling and laughter flowing free as the wind. It does one's soul good to hear such gaiety from those one loves. I've always liked to think one of Jehovah's great gifts was laughter that came from the angels. It always lightened my days to know you two were so close. Hamilton as well."

"You're worried, aren't you?"

"About all of those I love." Holding her daughter's look for the longest, her words drifted as she kept her dismayed thoughts to herself.

Sarah had never before appreciated how her mother's face seemed to bear such a stately composure.

Breaking the solitude, Corinthia said, "Your father has worked hard, and we've been more than fortunate. I suppose one could fault us for having indulged you and your brother." She spoke hardly above a whisper as she shifted her gaze momentarily out through the tall graceful window, then back to her daughter. "This bewildering strife has left me intensely uneasy, for your father, for you, for all of us. Although my place is here, I can't put away thoughts of other mothers and daughters weeping for sons and loved ones and husbands they may never hold again. It's the same dread I felt when you had whooping cough. That whole dreadful night Bessie and I sat up praying for you to draw the next breath, just one more breath." Corinthia straightened, forced that pleasant smile again that said *all is well.* "Enough of this." A delicate fingertip quickly wiped at the corner of one eye. "We shall not speak of this any further."

Sarah saw a quick sad quiver at the corner of her mother's mouth. It unsettled her. In her whole life there'd never been anything her parents couldn't handle. In that stilled blink of an eye, the little girl in Sarah Greer did considerable growing up. Tenacious Greer blood was telling.

Corinthia brushed back the hair from the sweet face of this daughter. "When you become a mother, you'll realize parents must love their children enough to let them make mistakes, let them find their own way."

"We'll let Papa decide on the date."

"That would please him very much."

"We can send out the engagement announcements, and we'll have the wedding any time your father feels he can make it."

This daughter's abrupt change might've surprised anyone else. Not Corinthia. She'd seen it before. Gresham-Greer blood fueling a will strong enough to match any Ingram, a perfect mating for well-blooded grandchildren.

•

By late spring and early summer, the Confederacy gained two more states, North Carolina and Tennessee were out of the Union. Missouri never got out, but she copied bloody Kansas, and Confederate defenses on the upper Mississippi crumbled. Maryland and Delaware didn't make it out either. Neither did all of Virginia, and Kentucky proved Rundell wrong. She declared neutral, which neither camp cared about. The stakes were edging higher, getting meaner. Unemployment fell. Plantations and bustling cities profited from a better than average run of prosperity.

NellyB and Benjamin galloped full tilt to the Hollows, waving the wind-tattered newspaper with the news. "Got a letter from Papa! Beauregard whupped 'em good at Manassas Junction. Whole Yankie bunch run pell-mell all the way back into Washington City. Just like Papa said, one good thrashing an' those Bluebellies trampled all over one another to get away. Newspapers calling it the *big skedaddle*. Bunch of me'n my friends sang Dixie when I read 'em Papa's letter. Papa wrote they could see the unfinished capitol dome from their horses on the Potomac. Sure wish I'd been there, bet there was a heck of a celebration in Richmond. Papa figured they could'a marched right on into Washington City. Says that's being planned, and once they do, we'll clean their whole bunch out from Maryland. Fly the Stars and Bars over the Baltimore capital. Delaware'll join us, and Lincoln can go climb a tree. Not much fightin' left to be done," Ben hooted, slapped his thigh. "Papa always said buy Confederate bonds. With all that Texas land there'll be all the cotton we want, white fields clean to the Pacific with factories in England waiting to buy all our cotton."

"Ben, you ever notice how land beyond Texas was talked about? East Texas maybe, but further west there's less water."

"Irrigate..." said Ben jubilatin' like a fire-breathing revivalist.

The invitations to the engagement party were sent, Corinthia was more in a dither the closer it got.

•

Betsy Whitehead got her invite to Corinthia's engagement party for Sarah and Hamilton. Gyrating in little girlie circles in her gauche new gown, she squealed, "Isn't it just too wonderful! Our gallant sailors brought it through the New Orleans blockade all the way from Paris. I hear it's not even in the latest edition of *Godey's Lady's Book*." Gushing her Georgia drawl, "...All for just for little ole me."

She zealously relished flaunting her boon. She'd finally made it. Mama talked it all over Queensborough Towne, rubbing it in the faces of the cherished inner snob circle of the whole of Saint George Parish's dandied upper crust old bags stuck in last year's stodgy fashions.

"Peahen showoffs, both of them," one matron whispered to another.

From another, "No breeding whatsoever."

111

A third, "One would expect someone from a good family like her father to have had better sense than to marry so utterly beneath himself."

"That dress must've cost a fortune," another joined in.

"Everything does nowadays," one added.

"Inexcusable in times such as these."

At the Bends, Sarah was having last-minute doings to her hair and bodice. "Mama, surely you could've found a way to not invite the Whiteheads."

"Your brother can be ever so thoughtless," Corinthia said with an austere mien. "And I simply do not wish to discuss it further."

Sarah giggled.

"And stop twittering about it," her mother snapped. "I don't think it's the least bit amusing. I can't imagine why Benjamin would take up with Betsy Lou Whitehead."

"I can," Sarah snickered again.

"Don't be so uncommonly vulgar." Corinthia snapped.

That evening Corinthia and Sarah descended the stairs into the sea of upturned faces. In his unobtrusive turned-back cuffed waistcoat and riding pants, leather gloves in one hand, Hamilton waited with Ben at the foot of the stairs. To Sarah he looked grand. She most definitely was not leaving him alone with Betsy Whitehead on the loose.

"Mother Greer..." Hamilton greeted.

Ben escorted his mother as Hamilton offered Sarah his arm and whispered, "Glad you finally came down to rescue me from some of your...ah..." He cleared his throat. "...guests." He gave her a wicked leer as they moved out into the crowded gardens with their guests, cordial nods here and there, including Betsy Whitehead and her mother.

With her sociable smile in place Sarah snugged a firm grip on his arm and said for his ear only, "It's not you who needs rescuing. Betsy Whitehead has her eyes on landing that untamed brother of mine."

"No chance of that happening," Hamilton said.

"I wouldn't be too sure." Sarah nodded to familiar acquaintances. "You know as well as I how Ben can be. What a disaster to have her in the family," she said and tried to push the utterly horrible thought clean out of her mind.

"Your mother would never condone a Whitehead coming close to ever being Mistress of the Bends...not in ten lifetimes. Ben get too frisky, your papa'll lay down the law."

"Hamilton Ingram you talk like men have any sense a'tall when they come across some anxious filly in heat."

With pretend shock, he said, "Listen to you, my sweet innocent bride-to-be."

"Innocent, my foot..." She flashed him *that* look. "That has nothing to do with it. You talk as though women have no mind of our own. Betsy Whitehead most certainly does. Although I admit it usually concerns one thing, money, and she doesn't care what anyone thinks or says."

"Oh, you women got a mind of your own alright." His eyes glittered and he chuckled his earthy gentle roll. "I never doubted that for an instant ever since you taught me a thing or two."

Sarah gave out her lilting effervescence soft laughter, as she said, "Listen to the likes of you."

They moved about, the center of attention, accepting their expected place as though they belonged exactly where they were.

One of Queensborough's bankers gave Hamilton a pat on the back, and said, "Congratulations my boy."

"You two make such a fine looking couple," the banker's wife chimed.

Corinthia's imperturbable graces worked a successful evening that everyone would talk about for weeks. She and Ben waved as the last guests' buggies pulled out of the porte-cochère carriage entrance, tall, fluted brass torchères blazing along the curved drive until the last coach turned onto Moccasin Trace. The Bends seemed emptier than usual.

The entire evening Hamilton had curbed his ill-at-ease feelings and made himself the gracious guest of honor, accepting good wishes and felicitations. It wasn't so much Papa Andrew's not being here, or when he might be able to be home, as it was a vague harbinger that crunched at him over the last weeks.

"You've been bothered about something the whole evening." Sarah had sensed his affable discontent. "Is my favorite beau getting a bridegroom's cold feet?"

"It's nothing."

"Was something bothering you tonight?"

"No." Hamilton shook his head.

"You *do* have the prenuptial jitters." She hugged him.

With a strained brittleness to his words, he said, "We'll have the wedding before fall weather sets in."

Corinthia's soft voice countered, "Hamilton..." Her tea cup and saucer never bobbled in her slim fingers. "Surely you can see there's simply not enough time. Such hurried arrangements would be so—so unseemly."

Sarah was somewhat dismayed at the look on his face. "We've all had a full day."

"There's no point delaying 'til next year," Hamilton said, and he walked out onto the veranda.

He knew he'd said it badly and timed it worse, as though he was being blind stubborn. These were loved ones he ought to be making things easy for. There'd been no call to just blurt it out.

Corinthia watched him leave and said, "Sarah, I've never seen Hamilton so abrupt."

Sarah was nonplussed as well. "Mama, I truly see no reason why we couldn't go ahead with the wedding. Most of the details are already settled."

Without replying, Corinthia looked at this unpredictable daughter, who lately seemed to be full of one surprise after another.

Hamilton walked along the porch toward the open French doors of the library. Inside, Rundell was enjoying his usual after-party cigar and sipping a jigger of the warm relaxation of home-grown whisky.

"Andrew'll be sorry he didn't make this party." Rundell exhaled a smoky side-stream cloud. "I heard what you just said to Corinthia and Sarah. Sometimes you can have a prickle cocklebur way with your words that sort'a put folks on edge."

"Sorta did come out wrong." Hamilton moseyed to the fireplace. "But I meant it."

"Any reason you felt you had to blurt it like that?"

"Seemed like a good time. Times being what they are. Putting things off don't seem like a good idea."

"I agree, things being unsettled and all, but rushing things isn't always a good idea either. 'Specially when it upset Corinne or Sarah. They've enough on their minds, and they for sure want Andrew to be part of it. Matter of fact, if it was me, I sure wouldn't want to miss it."

"There's no reason we can't plan, have things set, so when Papa Andrew can make it, we'll be set to go."

"It's not that simple. Sarah is Andrew's only daughter. A father feels different about a daughter." Rundell smiled at the look on Hamilton's face. "Oh, we fathers are particularly proud of our rascal sons, maybe a bit too much. Maybe because our sons are a lot like us. But daughters are different."

Hamilton filled a tumbler with bourbon, took a hefty gulp, took another, swished it between his teeth, and said, "I'll drink to that." He hitched up his britches, sat down, leaned back in the high-backed stuffed chair with its cherry wood arm trimmings.

"The wedding is one thing. You give any thought to the honeymoon?"

Hamilton stood as Sarah, her mother, and Ben came in. "Sarah mentioned New Orleans," he said, glancing at Sarah.

Sarah's eyes sparkled. "New Orleans would be absolutely splendid."

"A couple of weeks..." He caught the gleam in her eye. "Longer if we want."

"That would be such fun," Sarah said.

"We'd thought of going by river steamer. On the way back take a coastal wheeler out of New Orleans to Mobile, then home from there." Hamilton slipped his arm around Sarah. "Papa can handle things while we're gone. Might be good to let him know how much work I'm worth."

Rundell sucked several puffs from his cigar, smiled at Sarah, then at Hamilton. "Here we go, this son of mine bragging about all the work he does."

Sarah hugged Rundell, put her arm around his shoulders. "Guess it won't be long before I'm calling you Papa Rundell."

"About time, too, Sarah girl." Her calling him Papa made Rundell beam. "Be nice having a daughter around, 'specially one such as you. Don't know why you two put it off so long." With the notorious Ingram charm, he said, "Now Corinne, don't you think that'd be a fine plan?"

"I declare..." Corinthia reconciled to the inevitable. "There's no way around you men. What'd you two Ingrams do, decide this ahead of time?"

Rundell snuffed out his cigar, walked over to her, and said, "Corinne, don't go gettin' flustered." and kissed her lightly on the cheek. "Like you women say about men taking a woman for granted, it never hurts letting a woman know not to get too settled about a man. Keeps her on her toes."

"Rundell deWorthe Ingram." A coquette gaze of pure, serene granite peeked from Corinthia's eyes. "Of the two of you, I don't know which Ingram is the biggest scoundrel. You or your strapping son."

"Chip off the ole block." Rundell, as he fired up another cigar, blew smoke. "Blood always tells." With a big grin, proud he'd fathered such a son. "You always said so." Corinthia blushed.

"Alright!" Ben yahooed, roaring ready for a big time party. "We'll give the bachelor doings at the Hollows!"

"Benjamin Greer!" Corinthia assumed the manner that was brusquely austere. "Have the manners to at least wait until the groom asks his father."

"Excuse me," Ben said, hardly pausing as he asked, "Mister Rundell, it okay?"

"Benjamin!" Corinthia rolled her eyes, muttering, "What ever in the world am I to do with that boy?"

"Wouldn't have it any other way, Ben," Rundell beamed. "It's good to see our young folks so happy. We'll have us a real shindy."

Sarah threw an irritated look at her brother, then piped up with a sunny, "You better enjoy this party Mister Hamilton Ingram. Be the last time something wild like that will go on at the Hollows once I'm mistress." Her eyes were atwinkle, but every word serious.

"I don't know about that. Seems I remember you enjoying a good party." Hamilton hugged her. "Somehow I can't see that being a problem."

"Mistress Sarah Ingram of Moccasin Hollows." Rundell turned nostalgic. "Now that has a special nice sound to it."

Hamilton could tell from the look on his father's face that he was thinking of the wife and mother they'd missed all these years. His papa never talked about the loss, but a few times Hamilton had found Rundell in the library, wistfully staring at the painted miniature in his hand.

"Yessirree," Rundell continued, "extra special good having a woman back to the Hollows. 'Specially one like this daughter-in-law to-be."

The Bends moved into high gear, war-talk about happenings somewhere else. All of Saint George Parish set to talkin', Andrew Greer's daughter was getting married.

8

A mildish spring with early growin' weather and plenty rain yielded good second and third plantings. Whitney gins combed wagon loads of the white fluff into bales. It seemed of little concern around the parish that bales were stacked high alongside tobacco and rice on the wharves of Augusta, Savannah, Macon and ports along the Gulf of Mexico. Most planters were in high spirits, profits better than ever, higher for blockade-runners. A goodly number of imported goods were getting through, taking lifeblood bales on return trips out.

One evening, Ben and Hamilton were stoking their daily cigar. As Ben paged through the latest daily paper, he sneered, "Blockaders callin' our cotton contraband, so they can steal it. And they're invading Kentucky was about what I'd expect of them. They don't give a damn about Kentucky's neutrality."

"I'll lay odds equal numbers of Kentucky troops are wearing Union blue and butternut." Hamilton coughed out some tobacco, then spit. "Kentucky is gonna get as stirred up as Kansas and Missouri. Glad Georgia's not that close to those borders."

"There's been riots in Baltimore." Ben flipped another page.

"Corn and grain I sent to the Moccasin Creek flour mill last week cost more'n double what it was the last time we milled our flour barrels full."

"Even Galphin's Mill is chargin' more," Ben said. "Gettin' ridiculous. Papa said inflation's eating up our paper money. He bought more bonds—says it's better than worthless paper."

"Freight rates gone sky-high cause of the waiting list for railroad rollin' stock with more wagons on the road than ever. That last haul of cotton out of Millen Junction was the longest pull of freight cars I've ever saw. Flatcars piled so high a good wind could tip 'em over."

"Take the Canal Road next time," Ben suggested. "It's miles longer, but it wasn't so crowded the last time."

"It'll get just as full once the mills and grinders for Augusta's powder works gets up and running," Hamilton said. "Never saw so many people there the day they had that big send-off parade down Broad Street for those cavalry units. Cavalry was boardin' their horses at the rail depot. Saw a few faces from the parish that've gone bust, free hands and farmers flocking to Augusta. Shipping cotton from Millen sounds more'n more like a better idea. Augusta's waterfront docks were stacked with so many bales I could'a walked on top of them from Lover's Lane on East Boundary upriver to Hawk's Gully. A riverboat captain who runs his double-ender between Augusta and Savannah told me Savannah had more cotton than they knew where to put it, and that there'd been shooting around some of the coastal islands."

"A rail spur from here to Millen would let us ship direct out'a there to wherever there were runners takin' cargo. Papa talked with the railroad people about adding one. They told him Tredegar Iron Works was running full out with the military havin' top priority. Things'll look up once the Selma foundry gets workin'."

"Georgia's rail system'd be in better shape if we'd do something about the different gauge tracks, having to move freight from Hamburg across the river to Augusta's south terminal or the Georgia Railroad line to Marthasville. No point havin' that kind'a tangle in times like these."

"I see the governor took steps to keep Richmond from takin'

Georgia men from foundries and gun works," Ben said. "Seems Alabama and North Carolina are looking at doing the same."

Hamilton said, "I suspect Davis don't cotton to the governor's actions, states havin' the last say. Sure one way to keep Richmond from gettin' as highhanded as Washington City."

Neither the Hollows nor the Bends had time for politics or war next to the big doings of a daughter's wedding. Larders were full. Things had never been better.

•

More seemed to need doin' all at once. Way before the cockcrow beginning of early forenoon, Bessie had been fussin' an' fluffin' over Sarah's wedding dress taking shape elegant and fine in the sewing room. She pinned one more seam, got up off her knees.

Stepped back, and looked at the vision in satin, laces and knuckled linens. "Missy, this be the prettiest dress these eyes did ever see."

"Oh, Bessie..." Sarah said with a burst of jittery tears. "It is— it's lovely." She hugged Bessie and laid her head on the soft warm bosom. "It's beautiful."

"Chil', you quits this or we'll both be all weepy." Bessie tucked at the pleats, straightenin' 'til it hung perfect.

"I'm so happy." Sarah daubed her eyes.

"I be happy for you." Bessie's love was unconditional, her heart makin' no distinction between her Sam or Missy or Ben or Hamilton. She kissed Sarah's cheek, as her hushed heart gave an ache for Sam. "Aside from the fact that you takin' Hamilton out'a circulation, you marrying him gonna mighty upset other gals your snarin' one of the best in these parts. An' none too soon— Hamilton be a true prized, full-blooded man. You be sure an' keep him pleased, keep him out'a circulation. Bessie knows you can do 'xactly that."

"Bessie, I love him so."

Sarah was all aglow. As she twirled out of Bessie's arms with a giddy headiness, thoughts of their honeymoon pulled her belly tight way-down deep in her stomach.

A weary Corinthia came into the sewing room in a hurried flutter, stopped, and muttered, "I do declare..." Her eyes fixed on the wedding dress. "Bessie, you've done an absolutely magnificent job."

Bessie grinned, her face and eyes one big smile.

•

Parish harvests produced an overflow bounty, adding to an already market glut. In the early weeks of November prices began to tumble, shuddering through the money clips of the parish. The mounds of white bales massed higher, docks stacked beyond excess, more than anyone could remember, more than anyone could handle, more than blockaders could get out.

Early daylight fading the night. While finishing up breakfast, Rundell read through the *Charleston Courier*.

Hamilton finished off his buttermilk. "Looks like we came near losing Savannah." He sliced another short wedge of roasted bacon.

"Reckon Federals were after cotton on the islands," Rundell said. "Northern mills got to be low on cotton. Feds're confiscatin' as much as they could put their hands to. I doubt they got much cotton on those outer banks rice lowlands, but there's aplenty in Savannah just waiting to get took. If they'd pushed inland rumors say they could'a broken the Charleston-Savannah rail line, that we couldn't've held 'em. They take Fort Pulaski and block Savannah, it'll bottleneck Augusta shippin'."

"Glad we're not stuck with cotton we can't get to market."

"A Millen rail spur don't much matter now or not," Rundell said.

"It'd mean a back track for Augusta freight to Mobile or Montgomery to New Orleans, and if New Orleans is choked off it could push shipping west as far as Brownsville."

"That's a lot of railroadin'. Further we ship, the more it costs. I'm surprised they didn't come on down the coast after they took Fort Walker. They had to know coastal warehouses are chock-a-block." Rundell finished his chicory, folded the paper, tossed it into the kindling lightwood bin.

"I hear cotton drays loads are bein' smuggled through the lines to agents working both side, gettin' paid in gold."

"Gold is a mighty temptation," Rundell said. "'Specially if a body's faced with a bunch of hungry kids."

Hamilton poured the leftover bacon lardy into the holding crock for soap makings. He set the dishes to soak, as Rundell stoked the kitchen stove, make sure it kept hot 'til supper.

Rundell jabbed the coals. "Could wring the hothead necks for letting this whole brouhaha get so infernal out'a hand. No matter those preachy New Englander mouths, it's mostly over money. Might'a been one time we should'a left it to the bankers." He poked the coals harder.

"Savannah roads to Augusta are full of refugees crowding west after the word got around on Forts Walker and Port Royal. Guess they expected Federal troops to move inland."

"We sure 'nough have our fair share of thick-headed generals," Rundell avowed. "And it's not all one-sided. Lots of our battlefield successes been equal thick-headedness on both sides. Holding them offshore islands with warships off the mouth of the river, keeps Savannah harbor plugged tight." Rundell gave a hard yank to a boot, shoved his foot in the second. "There's nothing much stopping them coming upriver after Augusta except the Savanno is crooked as a dog's hind leg, and full of chancy shallows. A river pilot could scheme a boatload of Federals into gettin' stuck in range of Confed sharpshooters, and make it truly ugly. Your grandpa used to tell about the time Colonials lost Augusta to the Redcoats, and moved the provisional capital to Old Heard's Fort, mostly just a stockade from Indian days. How the state opened up after that scuffle got settled. Capital moved from Louisville to Milledgeville. We're lucky the capital's not Augusta. With the powder works there, it'd make a powerful temptation. War or not, a city that close to us is not something I hanker to."

"Using the river to attack Augusta all the way from Savanna Town would leave Union lines flanked thin with our troops along both sides of the river."

"With canon on those bluffs below Augusta, they face the same problem the British had," Rundell said. "They might pull reinforcements from Savannah, strong enough to make it up river, get at Augusta, but attackin' a city that far behind enemy lines is one thing. Makin' it stick is another. They'd have none of their naval support, but their riverboat keel depths isn't their only hindrance. With Bobby E. Lee loose up in Virginia they don't have enough men to hold seaports like Savannah, and march on Augusta at the same time without thinning down their harbor garrisons. Aside from leaving them with unprotected supply lines, there's a sizable number of our infantry and marines around Augusta and Savannah. They'd likely stir up a pikforkes and grubben hoe hornet's nest they couldn't handle. Governor was smart doin' what he did, keeping Georgia militia handy."

Hamilton said, "When I was aboard that steamer out of Philadelphia bringin' our new turbine home, I saw deep draft frigates big enough to stand up to about anything. Their longboats could supply most any coast areas, and from offshore they could shell harbors, but they're way too heavy to come up shallow rocky rivers like the Savannah. Runners from places like Wilmington are shallow-draft enough to get over the bars—still making right regular runs. In stories I've heard about the revolution, I never gave much thought to what families faced with the British prowling the Carolinas, holding Savannah and Augusta. Rankles me Federals meddlin' in what's none of their business, shoving guns in our face, threatenin' families."

To Hamilton the notion of hostiles marching in and around Queensborough seemed unbelievable—of Sarah and Papa, ever'thing, ever'one he growed up with. Lots of things had bothered him; that week in Charlestown about topped it off. But a conquering horde...couldn't happen, not in Georgia. The thought of a dusty pall of tents and horses and shell and shot tightening around Savannah seemed a lot closer than some creek up in Virginia called Bull Run.

"Might be a good time to buy land." Rundell's words broke Hamilton's train of thought. Rundell continued, "Better'n holdin' paper. Gives us planting room if we see good use for it, army needs beef and pork. Gold won't buy nothing if there's nothing to be sold."

"You still considering buying another pair of mules?" Hamilton said. "They'd come in handy gettin' the ground ready for spring and for harrowin' an' plantin'."

"I'm havin' second thoughts. Prices done jumped way high from what mules are worth."

"I don't see prices comin' down anytime soon," Hamilton said.

Rundell looked out the kitchen window across the field. "I was thinking how to work this year's hiring of extra hands. Lots'a folks need work. With money being no good, our surplus crops put us in a good barter position. Helps everyone, allows us to increase planted acres, raise more beef and hogs, store away more surplus to barter, at the same time support those soldiers Andrew's with. There's lots me'n Andrew stand side by side on— King Lincoln's minions marching against a state, bringin' tyranny to its people is one of them. He's like Julius Caesar, doin' anything he wants, thieving tribute, callin' it contraband—too damn highhanded for my likin's."

Hamilton said, "More dispossessed crowdin' Augusta each passing day."

"Gonna get worse. Rail junctions were the comin' thing before this, even more important now. Wagons and barges can't move near the tonnage of soldiers and ordnance to where it's needed as quick as rails can." Rundell sighed, then asked, "You an' Sarah got y'all's New Orleans trip set?"

"It was." Hamilton poured another cup of chicory. "Until word came warships had been seen poking around the delta south of Jackson and Phillipe."

"Seems we're havin' problems keeping hold on the upper Mississippi. Missouri and Arkansas already none too steady. We're in trouble if they get a good fist on either end of the Mississippi. Texas beef comes across that river. Anyone with half a brain can see they're building for a push against New Orleans, and I don't see much keeping them out except for them not ready to do it. Those Delta forts, Jackson and Phillipe, won't stop them, and a move up the Delta is one jaw squeezin' the river closed to us."

"I'm thinking instead of New Orleans, maybe Mobile." Hamilton took a swallow, licked his lips. "Sarah had her heart set on New Orleans, but I won't risk her being in the middle of something like that. Be okay if it was just me, but I'm not comfortable with her along."

"Wouldn't feel too easy myself." Rundell bit off the end of a cigar, rammed it unlit between clenched teeth, and out of the side of his mouth. "You talk to Ben about the doin's here tomorrow night?"

"Ben said he has it took care of. Looks like Papa Andrew might not can make it. It's been nigh onto eight weeks since Ben's heard anything."

"Last time me'n Andrew talked was right before he honchoed the Saint George cavalry to Augusta to board the train." Rundell lit his cigar. "First of them to leave been called to replace Carolina regiments ordered west for that Wilson's Creek scuffle up in Missouri."

"Appears Lee wasn't able to hold upcountry of western Virginia. Cain't believe they threatened the coastal railroad right at Savannah's front door."

"Few more raids like that, and we might be facing some hard choices of our own." Rundell flicked his cigar ash against the side of the fireplace. "Savannah's not that far from Augusta and Millen for an army comin' inland from the coast."

"If it's as bad in Missouri as they say, that lays Kentucky's border wide open."

Rundell said, "Kentucky can scream neutral all she wants, neither side is finished making her bleed."

"Sure has gotten way out of hand."

Rundell stared out the window. "Yeh...sure has."

•

Ben made double-sure the word got around to Hamilton's friends still in the parish. Andrew managed to make it home for Hamilton's party, but just barely. Good-times and home brew flowed, boisterous ribald yarns rehashed, told and retold in the smoke-filled greatroom. Ben was belly-whoopin' over some joke with Hamilton and Franklyn as more guests rode up.

Andrew refilled his glass and said, "Ben, you had enough."

Over the crackle of the roaring fireplace and the commotion of the bachelor jubilee, Ben didn't hear his papa.

"Andrew, leave 'em have a good time. Those what cain't stay in the saddle we'll make a spot in one of the beds, shovel 'em in, let 'em sleep it off." A touch of melancholy painted Rundell's words. "Could be one of the last times Ben and Hamilton see some of them..." He didn't finish what both were thinking.

"Probably better if he stays the night...better for me, too," Andrew slurred. "Feeling this more'n I thought. Must'a been some of your makin's."

"Sure is. Saved the good stuff for this shindig." Rundell sipped. "Last spring's early corn tasseled out fine, corn and barley had good yields. Made up a good batch of Irish usquebaugh squeezin's."

"My Grannie Greer used to call whisky by that Scottish name. I hadn't heard it called *uisca beatha* in a long time."

"Good corn likker makes a man right proud, if I do say so. Personally my preference is barley mash."

Andrew's face was drawn. "Tired as all get out." He took another big gulp.

"Things rough in Richmond?" Rundell'd never seen Andrew look so tuckered, noticed more gray to his beard.

"No longer a fashionable city. Bawdy, violent, dirty...worse ever day. Ever'thing needin' done, nobody doing nothin' about it." Andrew bottom-upped his Julep tumbler, then sucked a long puff on his cigar, stretched his legs to the fire. "I thought I had a bad opine about politicians being around those hardheads in Milledgeville, but the things goin' on in Richmond would make a preacher pound *hell fire an' damnation* from the pulpit." Deep lines puffed around his eyes as he nodded a bleary head. "I feel sorry for Jeff Davis. The man's aged ten years since the last time I saw him, but he's my kind of stubborn cuss, and one working son of a gun." He refilled his whisky, gave a weary sigh. "Never thought I'd see the likes of such bikeren an' frettin'. Bends is too marrow deep in my bones for me bein' in a citified office, shoving papers across a desk. I'll take bein' in the field with the men any day. Least I can look to their needs, even if I cain't do much about it. Running a plantation, you see something needin' doing, you take steps it gets done."

"I feel the same about farmin', watching things grow."

"I brought you a souvenir I picked up at Bull Run." An exhausted Andrew stumbled and sloshed his whisky as he got up. He went to his slicker out on the hall coat tree and fetched out the brown, rumpled paper-wrapped package from his oilskin satchel. "Come here in the library."

He pulled a chair up next to the small table, turned up the lamp, laid the parcel on the table. Carefully he spread open the paper wrappings, unfolded the cloth-wrapped bundle to reveal the gleaming polished weapon, and handed it to Rundell.

Rundell cradled it under the lamplight for a closer look. "A handsome piece, splendid workmanship." He hefted it. "Good balance."

"Standard Union issue," Andrew said. "Colt Model 1860, eight-inch barrel, six shot, single action. Federals pay twenty-five dollars a piece. Picked it up after the Bull Run battle. Figured you'd appreciate a fine piece like this."

"Our foundries can't produce anything like this." Rundell sighted along the sights.

"Rundell..." Andrew hesitated, pursed his lips. "I want to ask you to do something."

Rundell caught a guardedness to Andrew's voice, something he'd never heard before. "What you need?"

"Georgia's got high stakes in this. Governor and Alex Stephens are doin' ever'thing they can to protect Georgia. Cain't say I go along with Brown putting his plans on Georgia being able to make a successful stand, but I'll not go against it." He took a long pull on his cigar. "Looks as though I'll be reassigned, expecting orders any day. I'm not doing justice to the men by being away so much. The governor's agreed to my turning the latest volunteer group for Queensborough Cavalry over to the state. He'll appoint a new Commander, hold them in reserve in the state, keep the men closer to their homes, families. Howell Cobb got himself a Brigadier General's commission. He and I plan spending time in Virginia resupplying, refittin' the units, bring them up to strength for a Federal push that looks to be shapin' up south of the Potomac. Davis may have one of us go take a look-see to problems in Kentucky and Tennessee."

"Good idea to look in on Kentucky and Tennessee," Rundell

said. "Western Confederacy is as important as Virginia and the lower South. Beef from Texas is worth its weight in gold with the Shenandoah so torn up. Men cain't fight without food."

Andrew said, "Least ammunition and powder supplies are gettin' some better with Selma beginning to ship, but the railroads are in bad shape. Need repairs and replacement cars, steam engines about wore out. Food surpluses not gettin' from where it's grown to where it's needed. South's big. Bein' so spread out is one problem Jeff Davis has never got a grip on. We got to put more men under arms or some of our weak spots ain't gonna hold."

Rundell buried his surprise. Andrew's words allowing all the shot and shell was tuggin' its own tug in different ways and different places.

"Andrew, we got good farmers and good fighters who know how to hunt and shoot, but the doubts always been lurking if we got enough to do both."

"We planned for a short skirmish. It's way beyond that and uglier." Andrew stared into the fire, his words what he never considered possible. His eyes locked to the yellows and orange curls of smoke. "He doesn't know it yet, but I got Ben's discharge from the Regiment. Once I tell him he'll pitch a fit, an' I don't want him thinking I don't believe he's man enough to handle it."

"You havin' problems with your hands?"

"Nothing like that, but there's been a steady bit of pilferin'. Our properties cover right big pieces of land with plenty places scoundrels can take cover, hide during the day or scout and watch the house. With Sarah marrying away from the Bends, I'm not comfortable with Corinthia bein' alone without me or Ben around."

"Ben'll settle in. Hamilton's got a lot of the same in him," Rundell said. "We'll look in now and then. He an' Hamilton bein' brother-close, they'll stead one another, keep Sarah and Corinne in touch."

"I told Corinthia I'd speak with you. I don't like asking you to keep an eye out, but I feel a heap better knowin' you're here for Corinthia, and it'll make her feel better. She's not happy my bein' gone longer'n any of us figured."

Like heavy curls of snuffed candle smoke swirling in a still dim room, the soft spiraling darkness narrowed tighter around the two of them as Andrew said, "My hands can handle what needs caring for, and I won't hear of your ignoring your place. You got enough to keep you busy. I'm giving Sarah three slaves."

"Andrew, you know how I feel about chattels," Rundell said, discomforted. "And even stronger about having them at the Hollows."

"If it bothers you, I'll hold off. There's no choice except to buckle down with what's at hand. Ben thinks he's more growed than he is."

"So does Hamilton," Rundell chuckled. "Full-time running the Bends'll put Ben right quick enough. Ben need help, Hamilton'll let me know. You and Corinne raised two good kids. You got a fine son and a good daughter, Andrew. You got no worry on neither account."

"Corinthia wants Bessie to come with Sarah."

Rundell started to object, but Andrew held up his hand. "I know...but I've spoiled Sarah. Besides, I don't care what papers say at the courthouse, Bessie's not truly chattel to none'a us. She's near as close as Sarah's own mother, helped birth her, been with her ever since. I asked her how she'd feel about movin' to the Hollows with Sarah. She grinned, got all excited."

"...And one of the best cooks in the parish."

"You're right about that." Andrew patted a slight paunch. "Don't let on to Sarah I told you, but she's been having Bessie help her learn to cook some of the special dishes Hamilton likes. Bessie's been angling me to let her bring some kitchen help with her to the Hollows."

"It's bad. Isn't it, Andrew?"

"Bad enough."

Rundell said, "You're expecting to be away from home for a long spell, aren't you?"

"Long as needed, and it looks to be that might be quite a spell."

Rundell knew there was no need to tell Andrew not to worry. Each could read it in the other.

The rowdy bachelors celebrating carried on through the night. Come morning, some rode off with tight grips on saddlebow pommels to keep from falling off. Others needed help into their buggies, leaving the horses to plod their way homeward to their barn stalls. Hamilton had a good time without getting stumbling soused. Ben got drunk. A drumming head and bilious stomach followed him most all next day.

The Bends was in full gusto on the wedding day, and Corinthia kept a calm at the eye of confusion, making sure everything went entirely as it should.

Bessie helped Sarah get dressed. "You be beautiful." Her soothin' throaty voice like a warm glass of milk. "This time the morrow, you no longer be my Missy. You be Mistress of Moccasin Hollow."

"*Mistress* sounds strange coming from you."

"Be strange my ears hear me callin' you *Mistress*, when you always been *Missy*," Bessie answered, pleating and tuckin' the tucker chemisette just so. "But you sure look the full-growed Mistress—a grand bride for fine Hamilton Ingram. He be so proud. You an' him make fine chirren."

"Bessie, how you do go on."

"Be true. Your mama lookin' forward to bein' around her gran'chirren."

"If it was up to Mama, we'd already give her grandkids."

"Lawsy, Missy, your new husband git you with chil' soon 'nough." She gave Sarah an earthy leer. "Onct he see you in this weddin' gown, you likely be with child 'fore your honeymoon be ended." Both giggled. "You chirren all special to me," her stomach shook as she giggled. "Be fun you an' Bessie makin' up names."

"You an' me will just make us a little secret this very minute. I'm kind'a used to you callin' me *Missy*, like it's a special name you have just for me. Bessie..." Sarah cupped Bessie's warm fingers with both her hands. "There's times I've been simply terrible, but I never meant it to hurt you."

"Chirren sometimes be that way. Bessie know you didn't

mean it."

"Forgive me?" Sarah hugged her.

"Chil', bein' mean ain't in you. You be cranky at times when you feel poorly, but you never been mean. You strong-headed like your mama, with a equal dose from your papa. So is my Sam..." Her words stopped.

"You heard from him?" Sarah asked.

"Nary a whisper. I wishes..." Her words choked. "Lordy, I pray he safe amid all this uproar."

"Bessie, I'm glad you're coming with me. I know that sounds selfish. I don't mean it that way. I do feel bad for Papa. He was unsure leaving Mama without you to keep the house girls in line."

"That be the further'st problem," Bessie giggled. "That mama of yours never put up with that a tad longer'n a flick of a hummin'bird's tail. She take 'em to task in a heartbeat, snap the dawdlers right up straight if they don't step to. Mistress Corinth'a got that sized down a long time 'fore you was ever poke your head up at the Bends. Folks what think your mama be addled fluff an' frill got pig sweat twixt their ears for brains. Them what knows her even from 'fore your papa took her to wife, knows Mister Ragon Gresham's first-born daughter took after that Scotland clan of Ragon coal miners. They never held with that upcountry kind'a Car'lina Buncombe. If there a hint'a trouble, be the girls what ketch it."

"Mama Bessie, I love you." Sarah gave her a tender, sweet kiss. "You are so very dear to me, to all of us."

"I's the same 'cept for the whelpin', tried learnin' that lightnin'-struck son of mine how powerful love be." Bessie licked her lips, fighting worried tears if Sam be safe. "When love be pulled away it hurtful no matter the reason. Even with his willful doin' Sam didn't mean to hurt. Too many folks too dumb to see love got nothin' to do with skin. Love got no reasonin' . I never know words what can say how it truly feel. No matter who say what, this terri'ble fightin' mostly 'bout spilt milk of kindness. Lettin' wickedness agin the Lord take over. Slave or free, white or black be for godly sure the least of it."

Bessie's love was clearer than most. Clearer than Sam's,

clearer than fire and brimstone, clearer than abolitionists or secesh. She knowed it was gonna take a heap of the Lord an' a lot
of givin' to get through what looked sure 'nough to be was on the
way.

9

With Corinthia's accomplished touch, the afternoon wedding went off without a hitch—a splendid affair under a warm, speckled-leafed, unblemished pale sky with fussing mockingbirds chasing redbirds and jays in and out among the limbs and red clustered seeds of the dogwoods. The day ended with a settling sun gilded with flaxen canary-rimmed thunderheads tacking way off to the west. Tears sparkled down a smilin' Bessie's cheeks, while Corinthia daubed her eyes, making sure not to smear her powder and rouge. Aristocratic cavalier Andrew was a resplendent figure in his new tailored uniform, gold braid flashing with his promotion, as he escorted Sarah toward her waiting betrothed. Corinthia, who had pinched and saved, had been on needles and pins whether the material would make it through the blockade in time to surprise her husband with his finest uniform ready for the wedding.

A none-too-happy Ben was in uniform for the last time. He had groused to Hamilton, "Special courier yesterday brought the governor's executive order renaming the Queensborough cavalry the Saint George Regiment. Also had my discharge with it."

After the exchanged of vows the reception was gay and light-hearted. One could almost believe the picture was truly a *happy ever after* fairy tale with no wicked witch.

While horseback riding the afternoon before, Hamilton told Sarah, "I've changed our New Orleans honeymoon."

A startled Sarah pulled her mount to a stop. "Without discussing it with me?"

"Most of the rail travel as well," he added.

"I must say, you're most definitely full of surprises, aren't you?"

"I wanted to surprise you with something just as exciting. I know your heart was set on New Orleans. I was looking forward to it as well, an' I didn't tell you any sooner because I wanted this time to be happy for you, and your father. He don't get home often, and I didn't want anything blighting it for him. Be mad if you want. It's done."

"How gallant of you." Her horse snorted, impatient, as she gave a nudge with her spurs. When he caught up with her, she remembered things her mama had told her, and said, "We wouldn't have been in the crowd of we'd've accepted the offer of our own private parlor car all the way to Macon."

"Wasn't the car that was the problem so much as the trains. Military having priority, it's way too uncertain for my liking. Rail timetables don't exist, and the hotel and ladies' cars often get sidetracked if there's unexpected precedence-freight."

"Hamilton..." Sarah felt left out more than anything.

He reached across, took her reins. "Whoa up, horses."

Firm but gentle he took her hand in his and said, "It's my duty to see you're safe as I can make you. There's been fightin' down-river below New Orleans. If it was just me...if something happened to you because of anything I ever did—"

"My, my," she teased at him to lighten the dark mood shadowing his face. "As though a woman can't take care of things herself."

"When shot an' shell get to flyin' thick and heavy, nobody has control. If we went to New Orleans, I'd pace clean through to the floor sills worryin' about you being caught in the middle of something like that."

With a sharp glance at him, she said, "Papa asked you to do it, didn't he?"

"I've had the carriage checked and recovered. Overland'll take longer. We'll skirt around Milledgeville, avoid those crowds, take our time on the back roads to Macon, and it wasn't your papa who talked to me. It was your mother. She was genuinely concerned for both of us, but it was my doing."

Sarah rolled her eyes, resigned to his dogged insistence. "I should have known."

"We'll board the side-wheeler in Macon."

"A steamboat...how romantic." Truly excited.

"From Macon we'll go downriver to the coast, catch a coastal steamer for the run into Mobile."

Sarah gave out a gay laugh. "Being on a boat with you, all that time to ourselves, just the two of us. Sounds like fun."

"It'll make for a leisure trip. Besides," his hand tightened on hers, "who needs New Orleans? You're excitement enough for me."

He had decided not to mention how his papa was more than a little troubled with the mention of Mobile. "You keep an eye peeled," Rundell had said with a stern look. "I hear blockaders been spotted off Pensacola around Santa Rosa Island. That most steamers out of Apalachicola come an' go after dark in order to make the passage through Santa Rosa Sound and Choctawhatchee Bay before dawn."

"Makes sense," Hamilton said. "Keels on most blockaders are too deep for them to maneuver in those narrow coastal channels."

"Runnin' at night..." Rundell shook his head. "Needs a pilot that knows the bars."

Listening to Rundell and Hamilton, Sarah fought being so spoiled. With what was going on in her world, her pesky vexations seemed so childish. She never questioned why she loved this wonderful man. She just did. She couldn't help herself. She knew his love for her drove his protectiveness. She found it somewhat charmingly delightful, but she wasn't about to let on to him one little bit, that she liked it very much. Regardless of being a tad nettled, all she had to do was take one look at any part of him to feel herself swallowed by this soon-to-be husband's bottomless eyes and the promises swimming there.

"You worry far too much about me. A night cruise, eluding pesky Yankies interferin' with our honeymoon." She gave her horse an exuberant flick of the reins. "it all sounds very exciting," and cantered ahead of him.

Hamilton spurred his horse and caught up with her. "I reckon Yankies don't stand up much against you."

By their late afternoon return, Bessie had about finished packing. Sarah kept two trunks back for last minute things. By early next morning, Hamilton saw to the loading of the last of the trunks they were taking. Sarah puttered, packing, unpacking, repacking, a trinket here, a pair of gloves, another this, and picked through several other pairs of shoes.

Exasperated, hands on her hips, Bessie said, "Missy Sarah, quits this empty-headed dallyin'. Here you is Missus Hamilton Ingram, an' here you keep your new husband waitin'."

"Isn't it beautiful?" She carefully held the *something old* antique lavallière that Corinthia had given her the morning of the wedding when Sarah was getting dressed.

"Mama said Grandmother gave it to her on her wedding day."

"It be beautiful. Mistress Corinth'a wanted you to have it."

In her dressing room mirror, Sarah took care to pin it just so on the lavender satin lapel bodice of her dark purple jacket. Its rubies and amethyst glinted with a flash and glitter sparkle. Her fingers caressed the ornate glow of its rose gold surface just as Corinthia entered.

Sarah quickly glanced around the room. "I do hope I haven't forgotten anything."

Bessie gushed, "Sarah Greer Ingram, git yourself to the buggy. Mister Hamilton waitin', never saw a man so patience."

"He gets it from Rundell." Corinthia smiled with a mother's knowing understanding.

"Mistress Corinth'a, tell this daughter of your'n to git a move on."

Sarah kissed her mother. "I love the brooch."

"Your grandmother would've wanted you to have it, just as my grandmother passed it to me. It was given to your great-grandma by a member of the Duchesse de La Vallière's family." Corinthia's face was aglow. "From what I was once told, it was a token of an unrequited love—one the Vallières found necessarily unacceptable. It is said the stones held such meaning for the Duchesse that she commissioned this special mounting for them. It must have been quite a compelling love. It's said the stones of the lavallière still shelter the love the two had for one another...an enchanting tale of a special kind of haunting. Unchanged, it's been passed down in our family from mother to daughter ever since, a marvelously romantic heritage of unrequited romance for my granddaughter."

"Your jewel box be hainted...got spirits about it." Bessie shied away from gittin' near the brooch.

"You and Hamilton most certainly will have daughters," a radiant Corinthia chuckled. "Perhaps providence will allow me the good fortunate to see one of them wear it at her wedding."

"There be a porch full of guests waitin' to give you two love-birds a proper send-off," Bessie said, following behind the last of the rounded top Saratoga trunks. "Feel a heap better if you took one of the houseboys, Josiah or his brother Nathaniel to travel with you two, leastwise to Macon," as she started down the steps with Sarah and Corinthia.

Hamilton stopped her, kissed her cheek, and said, "You hear from Sam, you tell him not to do anything dumber'n he already pulled. Tell him if he needs anything come find me or Papa."

"Bless you." Bessie hugged him, kissed his cheek like she'd done since he was a spindly towhead. "You take good care a you'n Missy. Soon as you two leave out, Nathaniel goin' to the Hollows with me for a spell. He'p me'n Mistress Corinth'a get the Bends back in order. I make sure Mister Rundell be looked after, an' have the house ready when for you an' Missy's comin' home."

Hamilton took the steps down two at a time, helped Sarah in, hurried around, and climbed up. He flicked the reins, and with everyone waving, they drove away.

Bessie watched long after the carriage had disappeared up the

Trace. Then she turned to Josiah's older brother, Nathaniel. "You got our belongin's trunked on the wagon? Be no time 'fore we leavin'."

She bustled through the kitchen breezeway from the main house, climbed the servant's stairs to the second floor, and entered Corinthia's rooms. "Mistress Corinth'a, you be here? I set to leave for the Hollows."

Wisteria Bends was the only home Bessie knew, this day changing it all. She swallowed at the lump in her throat.

"In here." Corinthia sat dabbing moist eyes. "I suppose I'm being silly. It's not as though we're not right on one another's doorstep. We simply must promise one another to never let too much water pass under the bridge before one of us pays a callin' on the other."

"Lordy mercy." Bessie smiled. "Been some time since us two sat at the kitchen table an' talked away our pesterin's."

"Yes, and you'n me will see that clearly does not continue." Corinthia kissed her again.

"Take a heap of stoppin' to keep Bessie from the Bends. Be my home, too. 'Sides, you be in an' out from the Hollows more'n ever. Mister Hamilton and his papa live too long without a woman, likely git plumb weary havin' us underfoot. Anyhow." eyes earthy asparkle with a lusty hee-hee. "You be comin' to see all them grandbabies Missy and Mister Hamilton gonna be makin'."

"Mercy me, Bessie," Corinthia chuckled. "How you do go on." Her warm smile broadened. "...But you're absolutely correct."

Bessie's cheerful face faded, and she nervously rolled her lips, a tiny muscle quivering her chin. "I got somethin' terr'ble personal t'ask." Her hands twisted, tormented, clenching and unclenching.

Bessie was more upset than Corinthia had ever seen her. "About Sam?" She laid her hand on Bessie's arm and felt the barest of shivers.

"Lordy, it keep me awake nights. Sam got no idea I is movin', no notion how to git word to him." Bessie was crossing an unspoken barrier the only way she knew. "Heard nary a single word from Sam, or what become of him."

"It's worried me as well, and knowing how troubled you were, I refused to bring it up. From now on if it gets to botherin', you bring it right to me."

As she'd watched the troublesome war grow worse, Corinthia had kept her fearsome trepidations to herself. Distressed with each new dawn, her place was here, doing all she could for Andrew; and as he was drawn farther from them, she was not wanting to see the grim lists posted in Queensborough. With no news of Sam, she knew the dread and anxiousness Bessie felt. The long dark nights were worse, fearing all manner of calamities for their loved ones. Trying to push away her guilt when she prayed the horrid prayer that if Andrew was to be taken from her, that he be killed outright instead of suffering a lingering mortal decline. She had uttered hardly a single word against his undertakings, but her life with Andrew and their children no longer seemed quite so taken-for-granted unalterable.

Both women facing bleak apparitions, Corinthia's arms held tight around Bessie's troubled soul as a flood of tears quietly broke loose in the crook of Corinthia's shoulder. Neither quite understood the blight across their homeland.

Bessie wiped her eyes. "I's so scared for Sam..."

"Yes, I try to think of Andrew being safe and warm." Corinthia forced a smile. "In these times we must believe someone is looking over those we love."

Bessie sniffled. "Hearin' such awful things, I dread for Samuel."

"Yes." Corinthia thought of her wedding day, which seemed some far yesteryear away. "We mothers will put our heads together and think of something."

"I tried to git Sam to go to Marse Andrew, or talk with Hamilton. He wouldn't, said it'd make 'em part of his doin'. I know it hurt Marse Andrew. What Sam done was wrong."

"I'm not so sure."

The words astonished Bessie. "Mistress Corinthia, it agin the law!"

"Sam's a good son. He's no more wrong-headed than I've seen Benjamin at times, and perhaps he did the only thing he felt he could do." With a weary sigh Corinthia said, "Bessie, the lives you and I grew up with and took for granted is changed. Our world has changed, although Andrew finds it somewhat difficult to accept. Men don't like change, least of all ones they feel they've no control over. Sam's doing was part of that. I don't know what's to come."

"Miss Corinth'a, this fightin' ain't Sam's doin'." Bessie's hands twined in her lye soap, scrubbed-white travelin' apron.

"This appalling conflict must end." Corinthia had tried to keep her dreads private. "There's enough blame for ever'one to share. Pussyfootin' politicians not looking where all the bluster was heading us, we mothers and wives for keeping quiet, with no one quite knowing how it all came about."

"There be talk of terrible fightin' way north from here."

Corinthia blanched. "We take each day as it comes." Resilent determination strugged with bone-deep emotions. "And pray our loved ones come back to us safe. Hands here know where you are. Sam'll get the word."

"He got a fugitive warrant reward on him, some might hanker the money more'n he'pin' Sam."

"Andrew doesn't hold with the law handling his private matters such as this sorry business. He was so distressed it got so unspeakably out of hand."

•

It was late night by the time Hamilton and Sarah rolled into Macon. A cold drizzle pelting the roof of their gold striped olive green phaeton, the wheels squishing muddy grooves in the rough mire of the corduroy dugway roads, the two of them were cozy and dry inside.

"Sure glad we strung new thoroughbraces underneath," Hamilton said. "Roads worse than I expected."

"The streets are crowded." Sarah peeked through the leather pulldowns at the hustle-bustle outside. "You'd think by this time of night everyone would be in bed."

"We aren't," he snugged her against him, caressing her under their wool buggy wraps. "But we soon will be."

"I'll bet Augusta isn't this crowded." She was eager for his arms, his embrace, his touch. "You are worse than bad, right out here in public."

"And you love it." His hands slipped under her chemise.

"As if you don't." She giggled against his neck.

"Let 'em watch." His lips smothered her beneath the rim of her bonnet.

"You stop this right out here in front of God an' ever'one." She tried to straighten her cashmere shawl, which he'd twisted under her fur collar. "You just wait 'til we get settled in our rooms."

Hamilton gave her a lusty chuckle in her ear and a quick kiss. "I don't plan on getting settled. In fact, I plan unsettling just about ever'thing you have."

He turned into the drive. The shadowy reflections from the gaslights gave his grin a devilish saturnine look as he pulled the team to a slow stop under the porte-cochère. He stepped out and helped Sarah out as a porter hurried out to meet them.

The doorman said, "We been looking for you two newlyweds. With this nasty weather and roads congested with army Dougherty wagons, we figured you might'a stopped 'twixt here and this side of Queensborough."

"We thought about it," Hamilton said, unstrapping their luggage. "But we weren't sure what if the paddle-wheeler might be due to depart early." He lifted down Sarah's overnight leather valise, then pointed. "Only those two trunks go to our rooms. And don't unhitch—since we're leaving tomorrow, soon as this rain slackens; the other trunks can go to the wharf. We'll board the horse and carriage here until we return."

"I wouldn't leave no luggage at the wharves t'night," the porter stopped him. "It's best we store it here. No telling when they'll load passenger cargo, and with so many strangers about, filching is gettin' right common."

Hammilton buttoned his heavy-fitted overcoat against the chill. "Very well."

Hamilton checked with the concierge to make sure everything for the morrow's sailing was settled, yet he couldn't shake the words about thieving. He wasn't accustomed to that sort of low-down behavior, and he found himself wondering what else might no longer safe. By the time he got to their upstairs suite, the fireplace was cozy warm, both trunks opened and their travelin' clothes laid out for the morrow. In her new blue satin robe, Sarah sat warming herself by the fire, brushing her hair.

"Trunks are taken care of." He decided not to mention the warning. "And our carriage will be waiting for us on our way back." He looked at the full closets. "How come all our clothes are out?"

"Our maid unpacked my trousseau portmanteau. She said she didn't want to see all my nice honeymoon things get creased and wrinkled."

"Looks like you brought everything you have, Missus Hamilton Ingram."

"She has an absolutely glorious bath prepared for me." Sarah gave him an impish smile, let her robe fall enticingly, teasingly open, as she continued brushing.

"Too bad the tub isn't big enough for two."

"Depends on how you stack things."

His eyes fixed on the soft dance of yellows and reds from the fire gilding her breasts, tracing the skin of her neck and belly with saffron flaxen golds.

"You are wanton..." He swept her into his arms. "Turning a gentleman's head."

"Maybe you're right, maybe I ought to put both of us in the tub."

"The bath can wait."

His words muffled in her hair, as he nuzzled her neck. "All manner of wicked things could happen to a lady dressed in something as fetching as this."

"Tonight I want no gentle man. I want my wild stallion. Do wicked things to me."

Fingered the silken ribbons, he said, "Is that why you got me alone up here in your silken bedchamber?"

"Of course. I like having you around, 'specially with all the special services you provide."

One powerful arm slid to her waist, yanked her against him. "Your boudoir door unlocked for any man who might chance to wander in."

He kissed her, his nostrils flared, kissed her harder than she'd ever been kissed before, felt the power of his mouth bruising her lips, felt himself impatient, excited between them.

She mumbled, "Seems the best-looking one just did."

His eyes boiling directly into hers, as he buried his face in the clean smell of her, his tongue trailing along her bare skin.

"*Umm...*" she softly hummed at each stroke of his lips.

Her robe slipped off one shoulder. He jerked at its entangled folds, flung it aside to reveal the never-ending spice and sweet promises of her thrills, and carried her to the bed. In the dimness of the room lit only by the fire, the only sounds were their rapacious plundering not-so-muffled tumultuous lovemaking.

Entwined, the night melted on, never quite sleeping, the clamor and hubbub of the outside world closed away. Their cloistered hideaway was a dreamy bliss of having each to the other all to themselves. The fire burned into ashen embers, with the chill of the room mellowed by their own wildfires.

A sated Hamilton rolled onto his back, arms and legs sprawled wide. He inhaled the smell of their bodies. "I love you, wondrous creature." It was barely a whisper.

Sarah stroked her hand along his chest, felt his heart beating slow and firm against her bare breasts. She couldn't get enough of him. Her light strokes barely touching, they moved together once more, flesh and desire, tender and rough, carnal and attentive all mixed in the same tumultuous interludes.

"My beautiful husband with his beautiful body..." she whispered with short quick breaths.

In the subdued bedroom Sarah whimpered softly into the side of his neck as he playfully nipped along her belly. Her nails raked the work-hardened muscles of his back, dragging groans from him, and her lips branded wet streaks across the salty sweetness of his sweaty chest. She pulled him down into her, his glittering eyes feasting on her body, each dallying their honeyed dreams on and on through the dwindling night. They lazed 'til late midmorning, covers askew, with Sarah in the curve of his arms.

The whole night long the clank and rumble of CSA ordnance wagons had never slacked off as they snaked through the narrow alleys and streets to and from the rail yards; lead and salt, soldiers and horses, cannon and powder, bales of cotton headed to the wharves, some to be loaded as shipboard barricades.

A light rap interrupted their coziness as the door opened, and their maid gave them a cheerful, "Good midmorning." She rolled in the laden serving cart, breakfast-lunch being delivered late, as Hamilton had requested. She glanced with a covetous smile at the disheveled twosome and the strewn blankets and bedclothes. Then with lively quickness she set out chafing dishes, silverware and place settings, and laid out two dressing gowns. Next, she hurried into the adjoining sitting rooms, then to the bath, snickered at the watery disarray, and prepared a hot bath.

Returning she asked, "Will there be anything else?"

"Nothing," Hamilton replied. "Thank you."

With pillows behind his head, a naked Hamilton watched Sarah slip into a sheer dressing gown and retrieve a plate of cold cuts and fresh fruit. As she fed him one slice at a time, he licked her fingers with each bite. With carefree, childish laughter, they tumbled the bed tray over.

"Hamilton!" Sarah squealed, juice splashing her belly.

"I'll take care of that," he said, as his tongue followed the sugary juice between her breasts and into her bellybutton.

Afterwards they bathed one another in the great enamel tub. "A bathtub for two is way better than skinny dipping." He splashed her, making another soapy mess.

There was a firm knock on the door. A soapy Hamilton grabbed a robe, opened the door, exchanged a few words, closed the door, and said, "Missus Ingram, our carriage awaits." He quickly dressed and pecked his lips to her shiny wet nose. "I'll leave you to your toilette while I find out what's goin' on with our steamer."

As he started for the door, Sarah threw him a kiss. "Don't be too long, I'll be terribly lonely while you're away."

In the muggy morning bright sun Hamilton made his way through the fragrance of steamy horse manure, leaky turpentine kegs, open bales of mildewed cotton, and the rankness of where dockhands and vagrants had relieved themselves. The docks were one milling multitude of shirtless, cussin' teamsters off-loading cargo from wagons onto several steamers, while a company of uniforms boarded through one forward gangway. Hamilton back-tracked the buggy through the rail yards, away from the heaviest traffic, and hitched the team to a sturdy post, so they'd have no runaway buggy if the horses got spooked. Then he located the Portmaster behind an open Dutch door office.

"Any idea when the steamer's leaving?"

"Don't know what the holdup is." Eyes peered at him over the gold rims of his spectacles. "You might check with the captain. He runs a right tight ship. We're already behind the timetables with all them army stores due out'a here for Marthasville and the powder works in Augusta. Should'a been done gone from here yestermornin'."

By the time Hamilton returned, Sarah had almost finished packing. "I declare, I don't know how Bessie got all this in, these valises are stuffed."

"Bessie's long been packing for you and Mother Greer." Grinning, he buckled the straps tight on one. "That's how."

"You stop that laughing this very minute." Her eyes flashed. "You wouldn't think this was so one bit funny if you had to make it all fit."

He put his arms around her. "You could stop packing. We'll stay right here tonight in our passion den. Give the bed another workout, mayhaps catch another steamer tomorrow, or the day after."

"*Owww...*" her eyes glittered, moving close against him. "Aren't you the charming rascal. Laughing at me, then turning a woman's head with your silver tongue."

"Yes, but I'm your rascal, and I'm quite sure something would turn up for us to do in this fair city." He kissed the side of her neck. "Very likely without even leaving your bedchamber, or even your bed." His tongue nuzzled, insistent. "Turning more than your head does seem a delightful suggestion."

She pretend-struggled against him, chuckled deep in her throat, softly saying, "Don't you ever get enough?"

"You keep distracting me."

"You never needed that sort of distracting."

The knock at the door intruded. Hamilton smiled, stepped

toward the door and reached for the latch as she straightened her traveling coat, smoothed its velvet trim, and brushed back a stray hair.

He spoke with the gruff-looking man and then told Sarah, "Our Chattahoochee paddle-wheeler is about ready. Guess we'll have to break in a new bed."

Their trunks were hustled out, put on a dray, and headed off to the dock. Sarah checked around the room and under the bed to make sure she hadn't overlooked anything.

"Cities got a ponderous hell-bent disorder about it," Hamilton said as they buggied toward the waterfront. "Folks rushing around, shanties and lean-tos sprawled among fine old buildings. Waterfront's Market Row buried in cotton bales, cracker wagons, braying teams with trash that looks as though they haven't—"

Just then in front of them, one horse in a four-in-hand team harnessed to a dray reared. Hamilton saw the horse-drawn army caisson rushing through, braced himself, took a firm grip on the reins. The driver lashed his twenty-two-foot whip to get out of the way, but couldn't avoid the grinding crunch as wheels tangled, leather thoroughbraces and harnesses snapped, spokes cracked, drivers cussed.

"Hang on." Hamilton said to Sarah.

She clutched his arm as he began backing their coach, maneuvering toward the narrow alleyway. Once he had room to turn, he gave a light flick of his buggy whip to the rump of his lead horse, swung the buggy across railroad tracks, and through the alley, coming out with the docks directly ahead.

Like Queensborough's squabble with the Millen Junction rail spur, the fire and thunder hustle-bustle business loosed at Fort Sumter had changed this quiet town. What wouldn't change wouldn't last long. His jaws set, Hamilton worked toward a hitching post alongside the huge cotton barn.

"We'll walk from here," he pointed. "That second side-wheeler is ours. We'll take our hand valises, leave the heavier pieces. Once I get you out of this mess, I'll come back for our trunks."

"I can stay with the buggy, make sure the trunks are alright."

"I'm not leavin' you by yourself in this ruckus," he blurted. "I don't give a damn about any clothes."

"The portmanteau has my best dresses."

"Horse get spooked in this multitude, you might not can get clear with these drays." He handed her the carrying case. "Can you carry the two small valises?"

"Yes."

"I'll get two of the bigger bags."

"Maybe a private parlor car would've made it easier."

"I doubt it." His words were brittle. "A parlor coach has to be hooked to a train. Even with the governor offering Papa Andrew the use of his private car, military schedules don't exist. We could've ended up on a siding 'til the next train was ready."

With two valises Sarah stayed close to Hamilton as they hopped tracks around piles of gravel and horse droppings, piles of rails, cotton bales, tumbled discarded crates, jostling animals, lumbering hulks, and gruff sweaty bodies. Finally they reached the gangway ramped from dockside. The forward cargo deck double-stacked with cotton bales for protection gave Hamilton an uneasy feeling.

"Ah—" First Officer Klannahan called out from the deck above, "Mister Ingram, bring your Missus right aboard." He hurried down. "We weren't sure you two made it. Congratulations on your recent nuptials." He introduced himself. The two shook hands, as a steward took the valise and bags. "You two will be our only passengers," he explained, walking with them to the rail. "Thing's will settle down once we cast off. Missus Ingram, next time you see your father, tell Andrew Greer I send my regards. We met over cigars in Savannah."

"I certainly shall," Sarah said, making sure flower and ribbon trimmed hat was just so.

"I'd better fetch the other pieces of luggage from our buggy." Hamilton indicated the cotton shed on the far side of the tracks, their shiny leather-roofed buggy lost in the swirls of dust.

"No need," the officer said. "One of our deck hands will have your belongings to your cabins. Stokers have our boilers full-fired, steams up, we'll be shoving off soon."

Hamilton said, "I have to return our horse and buggy to the hotel livery."

"Dock hands see to that." He signaled one of the crew. "This is Steward Clayton, your personal steward. He'll show you and the Missus to your cabins. With our sailing delayed, we'll serve dinner somewhat late. That'll give you and the Missus time to freshen up, and there's plenty hot water if you'd like a bath."

With a quick impish glance at Hamilton she said, "That would feel so good.

"This way, ma'am." The Steward went ahead of them.

He took the passageway toward the bow, opened the door into their secluded staterooms, then the louvered windows and French doors onto a private veranda. A slight breeze carried only a scant smell from the streets.

"If you need anything, just tug the bell-cord," he said, and closed the door as he left.

Hamilton, relieved to be out of the confusion, found himself missing the solitude of home. There was a knock on their door. Their trunks were brought in just as a shrill blast of steam whistles split the air and a steady chugging thrum picked up under their feet.

Hamilton came up behind Sarah and slipped his arms around her. "Sounds as though we're getting underway."

"Let's watch."

Swarthy billows belched from the twin stacks, and settled out over the river. Dockside mooring lines cast off from the bollards splashed the water, dragging alongside, and the gangplank hoisted, swung inboard. Twin paddle wheels sloshed several lazy rotations, stopped, churned slow in reverse, stopped again. The Harbor Pilot let her drift away from the dock. As she took to the river, the current swung the bow of the graceful workhorse steamer midchannel, and the city slipped astern. A white egret winged its way over the syrupy water, settled downriver ahead of them, as tall cypress trees seemed to wade along the banks of lush undergrowth. The boat's throaty whistle cut loose several short and one long farewell toots, as the paddle wheels picked up a steady rhythm.

"The whistle travels on the water," Hamilton said. "You can hear it for miles."

"It sounds so forlorn."

"Even more at night. Tonight you'll be able to hear the engines through our pillows."

"I hope it rains one night while we're aboard." She gave an infectious come-hither look. "We'll leave the doors open to the veranda, pull the blankets around us, listen to the splashes of the paddle wheels and the patter of rain."

Hamilton loosened his cravat, "I doubt we'll do much listening to the rain."

With the occasional clump of footsteps and muffled laughter of soldiers, the boat picked up a steady speed. Politics and turmoil seemed worlds away.

They skipped their evening meal and drew the curtains. The rhythm of the engines lulled them into their own solitude as the countryside slipping by. They sipped muscadine wine, got wickedly naked, and pulled blankets and satin coverlets from the bed to snuggle in front of the grated firebox that drove away the damp river chill. During the night a slight drizzle turned to cold rain.

Hamilton woke late, rolled close to her, and licked the delicate hollow of her neck. "I'm famished."

"My goodness gracious…" she teased. "I can't imagine why." She gave him a wicked look. "It's common knowledge you've idled away this entire morning with some wanton creature."

Hamilton growled. Flung away the covers. His naked skin glowing rose-gold in the soft lights as he above her, straddled her. Sarah reached for him, murmuring little nothings, as he pressed down onto her. He was even hungrier by the time they finished.

Two days later at Chattahoochee, as a salty crew of grousing men transferred cargo, they boarded the sleek low-hulled sternwheeler for a short run into Florida's inland waters.

Her sea-crusted captain introduced himself, then added "This ole lady has been through quite a bit." He patted a handrail. "Having you young folks aboard brightens things right up. It's been some time since she's hosted callers. I'd be honored if you two would join me for dinner. Our cook is preparing something special just for the two of you."

"How very nice," Sarah said.

"It would be our pleasure," Hamilton replied.

"We will dine shortly after dusk," he said. "The galley will be secured before we leave port. We'll make the run into Pensacola Bay before sunup while there's not too much light, then a quick dash into Mobile. Weather's fouling some, might kick up a slight blow. We'll stay close to the coast, keep it smoother. Not to worry, I've weathered worse in these Gulf waters. It won't get much beyond some whitecaps, clouds ain't blowing from the right direction for a heavy storm. *Flamingo* here is a good ship. She'll get her belly to Mobile. What with the Atlanta to Montgomery rails so crowded, they need our cargo. I'll have the cabin boy fetch you when we get set for supping."

As they strolled abaft Hamilton said, "Blockaders been pesterin' much?"

"Some, not enough to matter. Last few weeks we've had sightin's outside the approaches to Mobile Bay and around Santa Rosa Island. Nuthin' this coastal crew cain't handle this fine ole lady—good, strong keel runs at a five feet depth when loaded. Can hold a steady fifteen knots. Open full sails, she'll make seventeen if there's a fair wind and she's stroked right. She needs a patch here an' there, but she cuts through shallow shoals like she knows where the reefs are." His palm slapped her mainmast. "One of the best little steamers pridefully flyin' our Stars and Bars. She'll outrun most anything, show those deep keeled patrollers a few tricks. She's teased a couple of them into narrow channels, where they couldn't come about." He grinned. "She glides right over the shallows while they rip open their bottoms."

"She armed?" Hamilton asked.

"Wouldn't do no good. We couldn't outgun them big gunships." The captain shook his head. "Other than bales stacked and roped to her sides, she's not armored. If we mounted guns for a run outside the shoals, say for instance Bermuda or Havana, cannons and added ballast would cut her speed and cargo tonnage we carry, besides givin' blockaders a leg-up. Put her at risk. She's got speed and handles well, that's her grace. Slips in and out of inlets, hides in bayous, key is to not let the big cruisers corner us. It'd mean her finish." He hooked his thumbs in his paisley vest. "We've been spotted a time or two. Give her full sails, let out our jibs, tie down the safety valve…" He caught his sea-dog vulgarity before it spilled out in the presence of this grand lady.

"Give her all she's got, leave 'em sucking wind. Bar none...along the Gulf, Wilmington or Liverpool, she's got the best crew I ever sailed. Each time we make a clean run, it's just that much more for Gen'l Lee and our men in gray."

Sarah gazed at the sweaty backs in the chilly sea breeze and said, "The brave men of General Lee's army owe much to these gallant sailors alone out on the sea."

"I'll pass on your obliging words," the captain beamed. "The crew will esteem your caring."

"By all means."

Her eyes swept along the decks of the Flamingo, her rough unshaven crew with the same fierce pride that burned in Hamilton and her papa. She thought of their unbeatable thousands across their South who'd beat back the Indians, Redcoats and Spaniards, and they'd turn back these invaders. Consternation pinched at her, these were someone's loved ones like Hamilton or Ben, or Papa Rundell and her father. Seeing them as they pulled and tugged and cussed and manhandled their boat—death stole into her thoughts. She didn't like thinking of water-soaked bloated bodies bobbing gently in the ocean swells, or rolling languidly on a sandy beach, crabs picking and pulling at the corpses. The wretched horror of such a death fluttered her heart, a soft gasp escaping her lips.

Hamilton noticed and steadied her with his arm. "You look so pale."

"Perhaps I'll rest for a spell."

A simple late supper was well prepared. Afterwards, they took a meandering stroll around the deck. Rising lowland mists wrapped the unlit small port town as it slid away behind them into what was left of the fading light.

"Best my favorite wife gets out of this damp sea air, wouldn't want you catching a chill." As they walked toward their cabin, Hamilton looked toward shore. With no street lamps or torches showing the town seemed abandoned.

The late meal and slow gentle swells rocked them to sleep in each other's arms. Sound asleep, Hamilton was yanked wide-awake by a fist pummeling on their door. He sat up, his brain muddled 'til he remembered where he was.

Sarah mumbled, "What's that racket?" and she clutched the bed clothes around her neck.

"I'm comin'!" Hamilton rolled out of bed. The cabin's damp chill goose-bumped his bare butt, as he slipped into his britches and opened the passageway door.

"captain's apologies..." the man said, as several crew hurried passed behind him. "You an' the Missus best get dressed as warm as possible. We run up blockaders patrolling the channel approaches east of Pensacola. Two others with her, one frigate is comin' hard. captain wants you dressed should things get out of hand."

An anger surged in Hamilton as Sarah called out, "Hamilton, what is it?"

"Union warships. Get dressed, the warmest you have."

Sarah was out of bed in a flash. Both layered the warmest they'd brought. Sarah put on her short Persian lamb jacket, stuffing sleeves and waistbands not made for slipping over and doubling-up, to be as ready as they could be against the cold wet unknown. Hamilton disliked the prospect of leaving the Flamingo for a bobbing lifeboat in windblown seas that were getting rougher by the hour. In case they were shelled, he decided the bridge was farthest from the engine boilers. With cargo mostly for the army there was a good chance there was powder aboard. If a shell found it...

As they entered the bridge, the captain ordered, "Hard over, bring her into the wind."

Answering the helmsman's head, full steam churned, unfurled sails luffed full, and the Flamingo shuddered up through her decks, as she began to swing alee. Coming around, dead ahead the curls of beach foam marked low dunes and sand spits off their starboard bow.

The captain lowered his brass spyglass. "My apologies for having to disturb you," he said to Hamilton. With full steam and sail for now we have speed on their lead ship. They'll try to angle us off from the inlet this side of Santa Rosa, but I mean to give 'em no chance of that. Too shallow in there for them to clear the reef. Once we get lee to the shoals." He raised his glass. "Lead frigate is gaining." He shook his head. "First time we've picked up anything this close in."

Sarah walked to the bridge railing and fixed her eyes toward the tall white sails of the onrushing juggernaut. Her father's enemy, Hamilton's enemy, her enemy. Until this moment the battles had been some place far away. Tall and sleek in the distance, coming toward them, a deadly beauty in the mad fury of men's devotion to destruction and death.

Hamilton asked the captain, "Will they try to board us?"

His jaw set. "When we don't heave to, she'll try to force us to ground. Failing that they'll use their guns."

The thought of this pirate flag bearing down on them, their seafarers clamoring over the side, stabbed Hamilton into a heated white-hot hate of Yankies...good ones, bad ones, any of them.

"They're not boardin' us," the captain said. "We'll scuttle first. No Yankee's puttin' a foul foot on my ship, as long as—"

The distant muzzle flash was followed by a muffled *boom* rolling across the water. Hamilton sheltered Sarah in his arms. The shot smacked the water off their port bow, sending up a tall blossoming white plume tall and falling back in a graceful slow splash.

"A warning shot for us to heave to," the captain frowned. "Allows 'em to adjust their range." With a growing concern, he eyed Sarah. "Missus Ingram..." he said, "To avoid exposing you to harm, I am prepared to yield to—"

"You will do no such thing!" Sarah bristled. Her head turned toward this full-sailed invader. "These philistines are in our waters, attacking us!" Sarah's blood was up.

"Sarah, the captain's right," Hamilton said

"No, I say!" Sarah whirled to face both men. "We will not yield to those, those barbarians!" Greer fiery rage showed in full vigor. Her fists clenched. "You said you could make a run for it! Our armies need your cargo. If there's a chance..." She glowered toward the oncoming menace.

Hamilton saw not the pampered daughter of a rich plantation father, but a wind-whipped chalk-faced New World Jeanne d'Arc girded for battle, blazing with indignation, exchanging armoured horse for ship and English for Yankee, and loved her the more for it.

153

He nodded to the captain. "We run for it."

Her lips tightened, her chin quivered. "I know how Papa felt when he said he hated runnin'."

"...To fight another day," Hamilton hugged her tighter.

Cannons roared, two shots bestriding their vessel. Others followed. One smashed dangerously abeam, close amidships. The next one struck, smashing deck and hawsers, men screamed, the *Flamingo* shuddered, but her speed didn't slacken. As a grim-faced Sarah started toward a wounded deck hand, Hamilton grabbed her.

She struggled. "Let me go, they're hurt."

"Not in the middle of this," he held her firm. "Others could be hurt trying to protect you."

The *Flamingo* changed heading, her captain gingerly feeling his way between sandbar fingerlets toward the sanctuary of the pursued. More shells sent high waterspouts astern.

"Shallowin' fast!" a bow sounder shouted. " Bars dead-ahead!"

"We might just skin it." The captain leaned over the rail, studied the changing colors of the murky waters sliding beneath them. He spit a thick tobacc plug toward the other ship. "We'll leave them Yankees cussin' our canvass. If we had more lead, I'd tease her into followin', run her up on one of these shoals. Then we'd see who did the boardin'."

"Skipper!" the sounder cried out. "We turned too early, we ain't westward 'nough—ain't the deep channel."

"Take her in!" the captain bellowed. "That gunboat's closin'—no time to come about. Tides on the rise, we might catch enough water." He threw a fierce look to Hamilton. "You an' the Missus find a good support and belt yourself snug. Could be rough."

The sounder lookout yelled, "She's gonna bottom!"

"Steady the helm." The captain eyed the soundings, the bottom coming up fast. "Better us slicing her open to the sea than let them shiver her to splinters with shot."

Hamilton felt the first gravelly ripple, followed by the slight tugging break in the *Flamingo's* rhythm. She held her point, seemed to regain speed, then bottomed hard. She shuddered, heeled over without her speed slackening, deck planking groaned, her masts creaked, as the scrappy *Flamingo* drove against the grind of sand and coral, shoveling her way through the sea floor, objecting mightily to being sailed without enough water. The mainmast split, riggings snarled. The bowsprit snapped, fell away, but mainmast held. Her list increased, then settled back. A sail cracked loose, snarled aport the riggings, and upturned faces expected a shower of spars and canvas. Momentum skidded her into deeper water, the *Flamingo* groaned, then righted herself, as their pursuers hoved to and curled back to sea. The indomitable *Flamingo* eluded them—one more time.

"Sound for damages!" bos'n yelled down the hole to the stokers.

"She's sluggish answering her wheel," the helmsman yelled out.

"Captain," stoker's head poked up from below, "boilers are okay, but she's making a fair amount water. Pumps can keep ahead of it if we make for port."

"Bear for the yard across from Santa Rosa, and steer clear of those batteries on Fort Pickens. Fort McRae'll keep 'em busy," the captain yelled, his eyes on the shallowing bars sweeping alongside. "Bilges flood toward the fireboxes. We'll kill the fires, dump the boiler."

"Can she make it?" Hamilton asked.

"She'll make Santa Rosa before daylight. She'll be riding a tad low in the water by the time we heave to, but she'll make."

In the distance, its squat mud and brick outlines of Fort Pickens looked ridiculously small as they slipped by. Knowing what he did about New Orleans, Hamilton was angry with himself for having agreed to Mobile.

A scramble of deckhands, the thump and grate of the boat against the wharf, bollards and hawsers were made snug, and they were docked. With a scurry of activity yard repairs got underway. Cargo was off-loaded, her open seams okom caulked, bilges pumped dry, coal and wood reprovisioned, and sugar came aboard. They slipped to sea that night at high tide, docking in Mobile before dawn.

Hamilton and Sarah woke to the slothful loll of water against the *Flamingo's* sides, their valises and steamer trunks already waiting dockside.

As they were having a late breakfast, the captain came to their table. "May I join you?"

"Please..." Sarah motioned him to sit. "I haven't had English tea in quite some time, and I must say I'm enjoying it thoroughly."

He smiled, nodded. "A token from one of my colleagues in Bermuda. However, before I sit, this old seafarer would like to propose a toast." He poured a cup of strong East Indian tea and raised the cup. "To Missus Ingram and the fair ladies of our South. Your valor under fire prevented the families of this crew suffering the loss of their loved ones to capture, or worse." With none of his blarney, this Irishman spoke straight from the heart, "I salute your devotion in this most unpleasant war. Without the women of the South this Southern nation could not stand."

"Captain, you are a romantic," Sarah said, smiling. "How kind of you on behalf of these brave men."

"I would like to continue enjoying your company, but my other lady, the *Flamingo* requires my attention." He stood. "Please excuse me."

"It's been our pleasure," Sarah said.

Under the brisk cool bright sunshine sailor's fair-weather azure sky they finished their breakfast, Sarah enjoying a last cup of the delicious tea. Returning to their cabin, Sarah freshened up, then the two of them made their way toward the gangway to go ashore.

The captain waited in a fresh starched collar and his weathered bridge coat. He extended his arm to Sarah, saying, "With your husband's permission I'd esteem it an honor to escort you to your carriage."

"How very considerate of you." With a rosy smile she lowered her ribbon-trimmed silk parasol and took the captain's arm. "I must say my husband and I have had quite an exciting time."

At the bottom of the gangway, Hamilton shook the captain's hand. "A memorable adventure, my wife and I wish you and your crew fair winds and clear sailing."

The captain helped Sarah into the carriage. "The same with

you and the Missus." He raised Sarah's hand, lightly kissed the back of it, stepped back, and saluted them as the carriage moved off.

Hamilton looked at Sarah. "An exciting time?"

"Perfectly delightful." She waved to several of the crew. Giggle softly, and in words only Hamilton could hear, she said, "You looked absolutely terrified."

"I was angry."

"Well I was scared to death enough for both of us."

"You sure didn't show it."

"I wasn't about to let anyone know," she said.

"You could've fooled me."

"Good." She slipped her arm through his. "Don't ever forget it."

The ride to their hotel took hardly no time. The grand lobby bustled with bodies from as far west as the Pecos River in Texas. Tall polished malachite marbles gleamed in the prismed reflections from huge chandeliers. Before they'd settled into their suite, their maids had their trunks unpacked and their clothes arranged in the tall black walnut armoire.

Sarah slipped off her hat, tossed it on the bed. With arms spread wide she capriciously pirouetted across the bright, high-ceiling room toward the sunny balcony. Then she spotted the be-ribboned envelope propped beneath the enormous glazed jardinière of red and white roses, yellow gladiola, blue and pink hydrangeas, cattails and swamp lilies.

"They're beautiful. Did you arrange for them?"

"No, but it's a nice thought."

"Who knows we're here?" She picked up the pale off-white eggshell tint of the envelope. "Gracious me..." she stopped. "It's engraved...an Imperial Crest."

Hamilton looked at the Coat of Arms. "A Habsburg Coat."

"My word..." Sarah broke the seal, and read, "...A reception and ball...tomorrow night for Her Majesty Marie Carlotte Amelie, Empress of Mexico." She grabbed at her gown. "There's no way I could possibly be ready." She gave him a look. "Did you know about this?"

"No..." He took off his coat and sat down beside her. "But

Macon's *Daily Telegraph* paper in lobby had headlines about Maximilian's wife traveling through the South."

"I've nothing suitable to wear."

"Lord have mercy, woman." He swung the doors of the armoire wide. "Any of these gowns would make you the most stunning, desirable lady there, the envy of the ball. Wear this off-white one with the Belgian lace. Empress Marie Carlotte is Belgium, and with Bessie's nimble fingers having done the work, it'll fit you perfect."

"My, my, Mister Silver-Tongued Ingram, how you do go on." Sarah fluffed out the gown. "It's so wrinkled. I can't present myself in audience to the sister-in-law of the Austrian Emperor looking as though I'd been stuffed in a pantry. I'd rather stay away than have her ladies-in-waiting telling half the courts in Europe how Georgians have no taste. Whatever in the world would folks back home think?"

"Consider what folks back home would say should you ignore such an invitation? Its being here, engraved with our names, isn't by accident. I'm sure the social graces of Mobile know Colonel Andrew Greer's daughter is here on her honeymoon, and took steps to insure the invitation being extended. Besides, this may be considerably more than a command performance."

"What do you mean?"

"Empress Carlotte is visiting Mobile and Gulfport on her way to Richmond to meet with Jefferson Davis. Gossip in the lobby has Davis in Gulfport for a few days. His being in Gulfport and this invitation is no coincidence. I'd say more than likely it's your father's skillful hand in this. If Maximilian extends recognition to the Confederacy, Austria likely will follow. The Mexican emperor has problems. If things work well, both parties could benefit. Lincoln don't look kindly to French troops across the Rio Grande in Mexico. He's supplying Benito Juárez with weapons, egging a revolution along the Texas border. That was one thing Papa Andrew was upset about when he was home for our wedding. If Matamoras falls to Juárez, the Confederacy loses the Brownsville port, but with French and Austrian support, Matamoras will stay open to the Confederacy. Lincoln and Davis both walkin' tight ropes. Lincoln'll do anything to prevent British recognition, even eating crow like he did in '61 with that Trent business. Queen Victoria calls our struggle an internal affair few years back, but it's said most of her cabinet is pro-South. Aside from our independence giving England a chance, so to speak, of puttin' we upstart Colonials in our place, England's true interest is keeping the Federals from havin' a bigger say-so navy than the Redcoats. I lay odds England don't recognize the Richmond government. Business is too good twixt the North and England, and gold talks loud, 'specially with Princes and bankers. Davis will pry against the North any way he can to keep 'em off-balance. We've no choice, we must accept."

Hamilton had mentioned nothing to Sarah how the shelling of the Flamingo had made *the struggle* a whole bunch personal for him, seeing Saint George Parish as vulnerable. The blindman's blunder of Fort Sumter had geared everything toward pillage and destruction, gunboats, railroads, factories, forts, armies, disease, desertions—a grand smash up. They had to win.

10

The ball was dazzling resplendent, aristocratic pomp and circumstances not seen in Mobile for some time. The gentry of the South mixing with Old World blue-bloods. Staid New Orleans, aloof Richmond, nor haughty Charlestown could've glittered brighter.

In the receiving line, just before they were presented, Sarah held tight to Hamilton's arm and murmured, "She's quite a beauty."

They were announced: "The Ingrams of Saint George Parish."

Sarah gave a deep curtsy and said, "Your Majesty..."

The Empress Carlotte said, "Yes..." imperially serene, gracious, sedate. With a slight anxiety, she continued, "The new bride. As lovely as you were described. And her handsome charming husband. His Majesty sends his regards to your father."

The evening progressed serene and uneventful, yet to Hamilton it seemed tinged with a macabre displacement. Perhaps only the raven haired, ambitious but unnaturally reticent consort of Emperor Maximilian, Madonna Carlota sensed some lamentable twilight closing about her husband. Sounds of Vienna Woods, the merry strains of the Blue Danube and Old Wien, Virginia reels and polkas waltzed above the night, while others in their countries were dying with each passing hour.

·

The wanderlust weather in Mobile couldn't have been better. Sultry gulf breezes coaxed back an autumn not quite finished. Hamilton and Sarah turned lazy into a sublime art, indulging their fancies, catering to whims, and sightseeing 'til they were weary of seeing sights.

One afternoon, as they leisurely strolled barefoot in the warm sand on a secluded beach, Sarah said, "Reminds me of wading the creeks back home, except this water is warmer, and crawdads are a lot more skittish than these skitterin' beach crabs."

The next morning, after a prolonged languid morning of lovemaking, Sarah nestled against Hamilton and whispered, "I love being here with you, but I want to go home."

"I'm glad." He gave the end of her nose a gentle nip. "Me, too."

Excitement or not, after the close call of their gunship ambush, Hamilton was taking no chances. He changed their return plans and posted a letter to Rundell about the change. From Mobile to Montgomery they traveled overland by carriage, took the train through the rolling Alabama upcountry of small towns and villages toward Atlanta, with their last leg on the Georgia Railroad into crowded Augusta. When they rolled into the Augusta station, Josiah was waiting.

He tied down what trunks the buggy would hold. "Tomorrow I'll bring the wagon an' fetch the others," he said, and they were off.

An impatient Bessie had about wore out the carpet in the front parlor of the Hollows, trompin' back and forth by the front windows.

Spotting their buggy turning up from the Trace, she whooped

a holler, "Lawsy, yes, they finally git home where a body ought t'be at." Hurrying out to wait at the bottom of the wide steps, she called back down the dogtrot hall, "Josiah here with Missy an' Hamilton."

Sarah stepped down from the buggy, and Bessie flung her arms around her. "I is so glad seein' you two. You two have a good time?"

"Sure did, but it's good to be home."

"I wants to hear all about your goin's, an' what you saw."

"We had a splendid time." As they unpacked, Sarah and Bessie never quit talking. Sarah pulled out the small wooden box she'd special packed and handed it to Bessie. "I found these just for you."

Bessie carefully untied the ribbon, fingers trembling as she folded back the shiny wrapping paper so as not to tear it, and raised the delicately hand-carved lid.

"Missy, they beautiful." Her eyes grew big and round at the shiny earbobs. She kissed Sarah, and tried them on. "Put 'em on ever' mornin'."

Hamilton jumped back into things needing doing, starting with him and Papa harrowing and turning the fields. Their special order of fertilizer had arrived the day before he and Sarah got home. Nathaniel and Josiah had started their cabins. Got them framed, walls boarded and whitewashed, roofs caulked and nigh dried in. Bessie bustlin' with pride with her own spic-and-span room. Swept ever' mornin', spotless curtains, table cloths and hand-sewed bedspread.

In March Andrew was gone almost the whole month. As summer came on he was with Howell Cobb firming up plans to join the Army of Northern Virginia. Rundell hurt his back clearing stumps and got laid up a spell. Hamilton was glad to have Nathaniel and his brother.

Rundell's back kept bothering him, and Bessie never quit fussing over him. "Mister Rundell, be no wundor you ain't abed all the time." She said to Hamilton, "Back ought to hurt the way he won't rest it none. He won't poultice it, won't listen how he ought not agitate it haulin' and pullin' with them mules. I swears, men sometimes ain't good for nuthin' 'cept pesterin' women."

Home the second week of July, Andrew straightaway paid Rundell a visit. "Hear you been laid up a spell."

"Seen better days. Cain't seem to get rid of this back ache." Rundell noticed how Andrew had aged, the ruddy complexion sullied with deep lines and dark circles under his eyes. "Had no chance to get over to the Bends lately—you're all-time gone."

"Gone a right bit, I admit. I'm right proud of Ben. He's doing a fine job with me away so much."

"We been hearing things from Virginia and out west."

"Taking longer'n we figured, a great number of unforeseen vicissitudes…" Andrew buried the rest of his words then perked up as he added, "Lee's an outstanding officer, has an uncanny sense of when to be where, and sure not afraid of a fight. Whupped 'em good during the seven days when they tried to sneak his flank into Richmond from the south." Sucked hard on his cigar, blew smoke. "Stopped 'em less than five miles from the city."

"Hadn't any idea they got that close."

"Too bad about Memphis. " Andrew looked away. "And Shiloh cost us Corinth's rail junctions. Could'a been different if we'd gotten troops there beforehand. Ought to've had them there all the time. Don't need havin' tracks tore up, already got more traffic than most lines can handle." Bit off his cigar stub, spit it out. "We got good soldiers, but we need more." Blue smoke spiraled around his head. "Once Bragg gets on Buell's rear in Tennessee, we'll retake Memphis, go down to Vicksburg, open the river all the way to New Orleans. Jackson's readying to move up the Shenandoah. Stonewall uses cavalry like he plays poker. Does the impossible, bumfuzzles the Federals, they got no match for him," His words died off. "I miss being home, restful and quiet, seems another lifetime ago."

They visited on 'til the sun sank. Andrew took dinner with them, then left. His leave was over at the end of the following week, and he'd be off to Virginia with Cobb. The day before he left, Sarah told him she was pregnant. It was a matched race as to who was the most excited. Grandpa-to-be Andrew or Bessie and Grandma-to-be Corinthia in Sarah's bedroom hovering and flutterin' about the expectant mother.

"Dear me..." Corinthia patted her neck with a sachet hanky. "My first gran'child."

"Mistress Corinth'a you be actin' like you was already a grandmama. 'Sides, you always sayin' how you couldn't wait to hold your first gran'kid."

Sarah turned sideways to the mirror, pressed her hands across her belly that hadn't begun to show.

"Birthin' another chil' from my body tain't work I wants more of," Bessie heeheed a toothy grin. "Don't mind a man plowin' me, but plantin' a seed fer growin'?" Her stomach jiggled with laughter as she shook her head. "Nawsuh, done lost more babies than either'a you two'll ever whelp. Glad your belly be ripe 'nough t'grow young Hamilton's seed."

"Bessie, you do carry on," Corinthia said. "Greer women always raise healthy kids."

Sarah pulled at the fit of her bodice over her blouse. "It seems too tight."

"Breasts gittin' ready to suckle that baby," Bessie grinned. "Get a tad tighter once that lusty Ingram git to nudgin' an' pullin' on 'em."

Hamilton came into the room, armpits and back sweat-soaked. "Mother Greer..." He kissed her cheek. "How're you this fine day? Josiah told me your carriage was here." He sat on the bed and softly stroked Sarah's cheek. "You feeling alright?" His hand moved ever so gentle under her chin.

"Of course." Sarah looked to her mother. "You'd think I was sick or something the way he frets."

"Special..." Hamilton said. "Not sick, real special." This expectant father was ever so tender to a lover-wife who had become extraordinary wonderful in his world, the mother of his first-born.

"Daughter..." Corinthia chuckled. "You might as well get used to this man acting like that. Your father was the same when I was carrying you and your brother. Always puttering about, like I was fragile and gonna break, stopped his field work two, three times in an afternoon to come and check on me."

"That be God's truth," Bessie giggled, happy anytime when those she loved were happy.

•

With plenty rain and warm days, growing season busted loose, things sproutin' everywhere. Cotton, the hardy new Virginian tobacco, fertilizer pushing yields higher than Hamilton ever seen. Hogs and cattle fattening good for the coming first-frost butcherings—larders, corn cribs, and smokehouses not big enough. Looked as though they might need to build new ones. The whole of Georgia glutted, blooming its bounty on a fat land.

"Got more to market than ever," said Ben takin' pride in his first year running things. He and Hamilton leaned on the top rail of the fence behind the Bend's two main barns. "Been a good year."

"Ought to've used fertilizer before now." Hamilton chewed on one of Rundell's cigars. "Doubled the yields without bleedin' the soil poor."

"You're right. You ought to see our cotton, and I won't have to leave sections to fallow. Even less acres would still bring in the same weight. Georgia can use all the cotton we grow."

"I'm picking early," Hamilton said. "Move the early cotton through Augusta before shipping gluts up and good runners are gone out from Savannah."

"You talk like blockaders are gonna rush up river, grab our cotton if we don't get rid of it."

"Not concerned about them getting up river. Concern is if runners can't get in or out from the harbours."

As they walked up onto the west porch, Ben stopped, gazed off across the white fields. "Shipping'll be no problem. We can always move cotton out of Wilmington or through Atlanta to Macon. Same route you an' Sarah took to Mobile, ship it out of Gulfport or Pensacola. Yankies cain't watch all the ports."

Listening to Ben, Hamilton could see the father in the son. "Ben, you taken a look lately at the rail yards and wharves in Augusta? A good portion of last year's bales are still stacked higher'n your head with this year's harvest yet to be picked. They're leaving the older, moldier bales on top to keep the others from going bad. I didn't pay much mind to Union ships off the coast either, not 'til me'n Sarah ended up in the middle of that runnin' cannonade. Rails are pushed to the limit, loads are bigger, carrying all they can and falling further behind ever day. Freight gets shipped when the rolling stock is available, added to that is the army takes first call. Cain't have it no other way, but that don't unsnarl the docks and holding houses. They're full up, everything waitin' on runners, the ship losses way up, insurance rates shot clean through the roof, most owners sailing cargo without it."

"Then we move it like we used to—with cracker wagons."

"You consider how it don't matter how much cotton you grow if you can't move it? Even heavy drayage wagons are hard to come by."

Hamilton could see there was no point to pressing it. Even with wages and prices pinching higher, he'd managed to scrimp and barter enough for extra hands he needed for harvests. He was seeing more farmers leaving their land, going into the town, with Confederate conscripters waiting in the wings to snatch up those the governor couldn't keep out of their hands. In the last couple of months the two farms down the Trace from the Hollows had been abandoned.

"Ben, if you get short of wagons you're welcome to what we have."

"Appreciate that." Ben gave a weary sigh. "They'll likely come in handy these next few weeks."

Days later Ben began moving his cotton to the Queensborough gins. Mountains of white grew glutted, more pouring in each day, the overabundant legs of King Cotton's kingdom getting wobbly.

At supper one evening after Hamilton returned from town, he said, "Papa, I'm thinking we'd be better off cutting back on cotton. There's so much around, it don't even barter well. I cain't see takin' worthless paper money for hard work. We've got next year's seed crops're in the barrels, smokehouses are full."

"Been thinkin' the same." Rundell walked over to the sideboard, reached inside, brought out his long-dead wife's jewelry chest, and raised the lid. He untied the crinkled ribbon from around the paper wrapping and brought out the shiny gold piece, together with a dried crumpled rose. "Ever see one of those?" he asked as he handed it to Hamilton.

"Been a while...a Portuguese Johannes?"

Rundell nodded. "Only one I ever had. Worth a heap more than its Confederate eight-dollar value, and I'll wager you double to triple that in less than six more months." A wistful softness came over his face. "I wrapped it in this piece of netting and tied it with a rose. Gave it to your mother on our wedding day as a keepsake promise just between me'n her. She treasured it our whole life together. Stuck it in her jewel box, told me she'd have my head if I ever touched it. That she wanted to pass it on to her first grandchild, and I mean to have exactly that happen."

The first week in September wasn't forgotten by many as prices on store-bought goods struck harder, jumping sky-higher than ever. The ten-dollar bill with Jefferson Davis and an artillery piece had just about pushed the worthless fiver out of sight. Word trickled through the parish about a resounding victory at the second battle of Manassas, how Jackson had stolen a ride on Union forces and taken their Manassas Junction supply depot. Word also came about Lee's advising his president that *peace should be aggressively pursued.*

A wail of death also swept the parish. Burton McClendon's only son, nineteen-year-old Hezikiah McClendon, became one of a rising number of the dead. His was one of the few bodies identified. Others disappeared into mass graves or were left to rot in scorched thickets and cratered fields. Rundell's wariness becoming prophetic. Upheaval was tottering the old into a breach become unbridgeable. Woeful faces around the parish were hearing a different call, one for unlimited victory instead of long-gone weekend cheers of a scuffle *over-by-Christmas.* What few had foresaw, even fewer knew what to do about it.

•

Hamilton hovered about Sarah, forever in Bessie's way, 'specially the day of the wake.

"You feel up to riding all the way into town?" he asked.

"We got no choice, Hamilton." Sarah adjusted her black cape around her shoulders, snugged it close. "We've known Hek and the McClendons our whole lives. Besides, quit frettin' so. I'm not sick, I'm having a baby. Course..." she pecked a kiss on his cheek, "Having a baby of your's might be an affliction of sorts."

Bessie called out from the parlor, "Covered dish fixin's are packed in the buggy."

"The baby's fine." Sarah straightened Hamilton's collar, then patted her belly. "Growing like a weed, kicking like a mule." Her face was deliciously bawdy. "Comes by it honest, considering the way you planted it."

Hamilton couldn't shake his restlessness. Like boyhood re-memberings of nighthorses and the bogeyman carrying a satchel of hungry goblins spooked loose in the dark, lurking and ready to gulp the unsuspecting, he couldn't quite put a finger to it neither.

He slid his arms around her. "Woman, I love you."

She cozied up to him. "It's nice to hear you say it, Mister Daddy Ingram."

Bessie gathered buggy quilts and lap blankets to ward off any sundown chills. She'd seen that look on Hamilton's face, an' it be skeeren her with the chilblains. Knowed she had ought'a divine fresh chicken entrails, stave off evil haints seekin' that chil' in Missy's belly. Buryin's an' funerals always choked her with miseries and the sech. Bessie clung tighter to Sweet Jesus, and kept banjo-eyed candle vigils in the dark of her room, sometimes rattled the bones with magic rituals. Never told a soul, less they blame her for the voodoo. With death come asniffin' close, she didn't take to thinkin' on Sam, not with dyin afoot. Bessie didn't like feeling the haints afflictin' her loved ones.

Bessie eyed Hamilton, her brows knitting a frown, as she said, "We ready."

It was a solemn ride into town. Even the sun seemed not quite so bright in its cloudless sky. As their buggy pulled up among other buggies on the long side of the McClendon lawn, they spotted Ben in his black suit, a black veiled Corinthia on his arm. Bessie placed their covered dishes to the sideboard, as Sarah asked her mother if she'd heard anything from Papa.

"No," she answered with a strained look, as though she'd read her daughter's mind. "But I do wish we'd some news of him. Most likely he's not had time to write." Neither spoke of it further.

Long faces from around the parish paid their respects as Hamilton grasped Burton McClendon's hand tight. "My condolences, Mister McClendon. Hezikiah was a friend of mine."

"Yes."

Burton McClendon, with a hard-shell, forlorn face, stared at Hamilton with a knowing heaviness that the last of the male line of cultured McClendons had been severed.

"Corinthia, Sarah, " Burton softly spoke. "Thank you for bein' here." Tears pooled his red eyes. "Benjamin..." he nodded.

"How's your Missus?" Sarah asked.

"She's abed," Burton said. "Her sister's come to stay with her."

Guests moved into the parlor where young McClendon's open coffin was consecrated, draped above it the Stars and Bars of the flag he'd died for. Sarah bit her lip. Corinthia's feelings clamped tight. Hezikiah was buried under his favorite Weeping Willow, near the gazebo and his fishing path to the creek. Military honors were extended by an officer of the Army of Northern Virginia and the Queensborough Honor Guard. As the sun crept behind a murky overcast, a mournful muffled dirge could be heard throughout Queensborough. Hezikiah McClendon's war was finished.

Hamilton caught Bessie's eye, gently whispering to Sarah, "It's time we left," and they made their goodbys.

Hamilton was even more agitated by the time they got home, and for sure didn't want Sarah pestered by his moodiness. He saw to it that she was settled, unloaded the buggy, and got the team watered and fed.

"Send Josiah if you need me," he told Bessie. He didn't have to tell her where he'd be.

Under a scattered overcast he saddled his horse, mounted and eased into a comfortable canter, crossed the pasture, through scant undergrowth, and the stand of dogwoods to come out beneath bare willow branches on the river bank. The sodden smell of dead leaves filled the air. He got off, dropped the reins, let the horse graze, and walked to the edge of the Tsalaki Cherokee's Ogeechee River where Ingram domain stopped and Georgia kept going. He stared into the gentle swirls of placid waters. In his retreat, like the swift flow of water, he wanted the world to pass on by, for the water to carry his problems slow and sure away to the sea. He ambled up the slow rise to the teetering old willow tree he'd adopted as his own when he was five. Here he could still be ten-years old and full of carefree wonder in a boundless world, where Papa could fix anything.

His papa lived by the motto, "Handle a problem, or forget it."

Hamilton didn't put up with troublings without trying to do something about them. If he couldn't, he shelved them to the back of his thoughts. Ingrams usually led long lives partly by shedding concerns one way or another. This quiet sanctuary had always served him well, yet the portentous of things too big to be shed seemed to make everything a whole bunch less tranquil.

"Dammit, Ingram," he growled at himself, "Get a hold on yourself. You weren't that close to Hek."

Yet Hek was part of it, not so much the funeral or the buryin', but the loss of an unfulfilled life and the squander of others just like Hek. Anger flooded full back, the same he'd felt as shells fell around the *Flamingo*. Fury tightening his muscles, he flung a rock out into the river and watched it plunk, its undulating ripples like far off crash and booms of war, affecting people and smashing lives not involved in this deranged bloody slaughter.

With a slow clop-clop his horse plodded homeward. Once there, Hamilton pulled off the saddle, put out grain in the feed-box, and rubbed the horse down. Stacked grain sacks and piddled around the barn until after dark. He went in the house through the back mud room, kicked off his soiled boots, padded baresocked into the parlor, and plopped down in front of the warmth of the fire. He'd always thought of North and South like he thought of up or down, east or west, just another direction. The *Flamingo* episode fissured Hamilton's views. Hezikiah's death finished the change. North become home to rogues in blue aiming to shackle his land to suit themselves. His mind fixed to places that were once names beyond Georgia, now no longer quite so faraway. Names for blood and death where armies grappled for railroads or harbors, not caring about the devastation and burned-out despair they left behind. He thought of other Hezikiahs, of Sarah, their child, their lands, Ingram land, things and places he'd taken for granted. What-ifs stirring at him, he didn't like the way white-hot *things* akin to hate were rooting inside him or the shadows being cast about those he loved.

•

The postmaster handed Hamilton the grimy envelope. "Could hardly read the scribbled address. I figured the *Wistria Bents* scrawled at the bottom and the *Mama Bessie* right above it, it might be meant for the Greers. Thought maybe you might want to drop it off on your way home. Hadn't seen Benjamin in town in some time."

Looking at the carefully printed *Mama Bessie*, Hamilton said, "Ben's been right busy, I'll see it gets there."

He turned the envelope over, found nothing else, folded and stuck the letter in an inside pocket. As he rode back to the Hollows, his hand slipped over the pocket with its letter, making sure it was safe, wondering what it had been through after it left Sam, and where he was.

Soon as he was home, he took it to Bessie. "This was at the post office for you." He handed the crumpled envelope to Bessie.

"It from Sam!" her outburst heard all over the house. "I can tell from how he writ my name." She pointed to her name, her hands trembling. "...Too 'cited to git it open." Reached it to Sarah, "Missy, you read it," not about to let her poor letters slowup hearin' Sam's words.

"I'm so happy Sam wrote you," Sarah beamed.

"Told you he would, if'n he got the chance."

"Yes, and Sam's a scoundrel for keepin' you on needles and pins."

"Hurry, Missy." Bessie's eyes were glued to the crinkled paper her Sam had touched. Wringing her hands. "Suspense killin' me," flustered like she'd never been flustered in her whole life.

Sarah struggled with the erasures and penciled scribblings.

> to my lovn Mama. after i left i walkd an rid fer nigh to a munth for i git to a city nobody with you ever saw. never hear what it called. warn't no problim

to git betwixt camps of confed and yank lines. stayd goin north threw kentuck two ohio. jined the union army...

At a scratch-out Sarah had a hard time making out the words.

...cross a kentuck river where they give me a uniform. i git awful hunger. some food ain't fit to eat. cold at night in kentuck mountains. we got word we fixin to march to Tennssee. i know you mad on me leavin home an cain't understand my havin two git. i love you Mama an tell those what keers i git lonely an miss bein home. bents allway be home. mayhaps one day i kin stay home. taint lik i thought it bee. i speck warants still out on me. best i stay gone so sheriff want trouble you cause of me. tells ben an sarah an hamieltn an mistress corintha i ask on them an pray they be well an not sick. your lovin son samuel.

"Lawsy..." Bessie's watery eyes tight shut, her tears slowly rollin'. "I prayed hard on these achin' old knees, Lord stay with that mule-headed son, an' Jesus answered. Answered my boy be so far alright. Let him don't get shot, an' bring him safe back."

Sarah hugged her arms around Bessie's shoulders. "I'm sure Sam'll be alright."

Sarah pushed away images of her father in the same clouds of smoke and shot Bessie feared for Sam.

"Missy Sarah..." Bessie sniffled. "In the nights sometimes I gits so bothered. Sam so stronged, an' they be terr'ble lots of killin'."

•

Faraway on a hill overlooking the Antietam River, a weary, powder-smudged Andrew Greer sat slumped beneath the raggedy limbs of a shell-ripped tree. Two horses had been shot from under him in a searing artillery hell, where valor hadn't salvaged their offensive into Yankeedom. Andrew wasn't squeamish, but for this day he'd seen enough maimed, brutalized carnage to last a dozen lifetimes. Fearing more battering of the shredded Army of Northern Virginia, Lee was marshalling for a move homeward toward Virginia.

11

Winter come early and mean, and turned sleet and snow flurries nastier by the time Hamilton and Sarah celebrated their first anniversary in November. Corinthia snuggled her heavy wool cape tight under her chin, as she carefully stepped her way up the icy front stoops of the Hollows. She'd made the trip to help Bessie get things set for Thanksgiving. Outside the parlor hallway door she slipped off her the cape, and shook off the flakes of beaded snow and sleet.

She'd settled the matter weeks earlier, saying to Sarah, "Of course we're having Thanksgiving at the Hollows. I won't hear of you getting out in a buggy in this dreadful weather."

"That be a fact!" Bessie said, as she took Corinthia's cape, and spread it in front of the blazing Yule log. As she reached for the fireplace poker, she muttered, "I declare..." and jabbed the chunks of red and white embers. "Even in her condition, that daughter of your's be as mindful as ever, actin' like she able to do anythin' she takes a want about."

"You two just stop it this very minute," Sarah snapped.

"Ever'one's hovering about me. It's enough to make a body swear off having babies—going on like a body was afflicted."

"Yes, and how're you this fine, snowy mornin'?" Corinthia smiled sedately, giving Sarah that *none of this* look. Her smile broadened. "Your father sends his regards to us. He asked about you and his first grandchil', told how much he was looking forward to being home during the holidays, and if we'd heard anything from Sam."

Bessie pulled the frazzled letter from her apron. "Sam proud showin' how you learnt him letters." She folded the precious paper, secreted it inside her bodice inexpressible, riskin' no chance it git lost.

Hamilton said, "Weather's down near freezin." He and Ben cozied themselves in front of the fire. "Dampness cuts straight to the bone, gonna drop colder tonight."

Hamilton leaned forward, elbows propped on his knees, hands spread to the fire. Ben got up holding the filigreed copper holder with its crystal cup, refilled it with steamy spiced wine, and sat back down with his feet kicked up to the fire. Both men were enjoying the comfort of hearth and family.

A stooped Rundell hobbled in. "How's ever'body?"

"Rundell..." Corinthia greeted.

"Corinne, nice seein' your lovely face."

Bessie brought him a steaming brandy toddy. "Mister Rundell, Bessie special stirred this for you with them cinnamon sticks you likes. And your pewter pitcher of hot mulled wine is 'bout ready for the table. Johnnycake pone 'bout ready to pop out'a the oven, an' we'll sit to supper."

"Here, Mister Rundell..." Ben scooted his chair aside nearer the fireside. "Have my chair. Your back any better?"

"Coming along, not as achy. Sure not havin' it stop me joining everyone come to visit. The smell of that wine callin' me clean across the breezeway."

Over good food and a plentiful stock of homemade scuppernong brandy, the meal lingered into late evening. Everyone ate too much, except Sarah.

Bessie said, "She bird fed."

"I wasn't hungry. Feel fuller than usual," Sarah pressed her stomach. "I'm not about to fatten up like a bloated cow. I'm big enough already."

"You not eatin' like you ought'a." Bessie looked at Hamilton. "Pecks at her food like some baby robin redbreast. With that young'un of yours in her belly, she ought to be eatin' for two."

The bite of the wind died off during supper, leaving a cold drizzle to soften sounds beyond the house to a soggy bitter Georgia night. With hugs and kisses Ben and Corinthia made ready to leave.

"Mistress Corinth'a, you wrap this heavy lap robe good and snug. They's a meanness to this night air."

Corinthia hugged Bessie. "I'll do exactly that."

"I'll see you out," Hamilton said waiting, his hand on the door latch.

"Don't come out to bid us off," she said, and kissed her daughter. "Stay in here where it's warm, this weather is simply dreadful."

As soon as Mother Corinthia was seated and wrapped, Hamilton shut the door of their double brougham and waved as the night swallowed them in the muffled crunches of hooves and carriage wheels on the gravel.

He hurried back inside and pulled Sarah into the shelter of his arm. "Was good to have them over. You feeling okay, Mother?"

"If you don't quit asking me if I'm alright, I think I'll scream," Sarah snatched away, her outburst grouching away the pleasant evening. "Everyone fidgets over me like I was some kind of invalid."

The look from Rundell didn't escape Sarah. Bessie stopped in midstride, her arms full of dishes. She shook her head, and moved off toward the kitchen.

In the kitchen, she said to Josiah, "Missy in a mood tonight."

"Weather puttin' the ague to Mister Rundell," he nodded. "Bunions on my big toe achin' fierce."

As Bessie came back in the parlor, Hamilton was saying, "Sarah, what in tarnation is the matter?"

"I'm tired, I'm going to bed." She idly plucked at loose threads from the quilt in her lap and tugged the quilt up around her neck and chin.

"Missy, you catch chilblains climbin' twixt them cold blankets. I ain't got your bed warmer twixt the feather bed and down comforter."

"I don't care about any bed warmer," she grumped, gathering up the quilt.

"You care when you come down with the whoopin' chest. You got another life what ain't yours."

"I don't need anyone to tuck me in." She rushed passed Hamilton.

The hurt on his papa's face exploded Hamilton's Irish de-Worthe white-heat ire, startling everyone as he shouted, "Sarah!"

"Mister Hamilton!" Bessie gasped. She'd never heard him raise his voice.

"Sarah, I know you're tired, but that's no excuse for bein' rude."

Without looking back she stomped into their bedroom, saying to him as he followed, "I'm fat and big and ugly." She untied her chemise.

As he helped her slip into her nightdress, he gently laid his hand on her swollen belly, "I don't think you're one bit fat or ugly."

"You're just saying that," she sniffled, then lowered her face in the crook of his shoulder, big tears dribbling wet streaks down his tan, roundabout shirt.

"You silly, sweet girl..." Hamilton said with concern. "I think you are the most beautiful *mia domina* mother-to-be in the whole world."

"I bet you say that to all the mothers you made pregnant," she sniffled as Bessie hurried in with the bed warmer.

"Not all of them," he joked softly. "I forgot to ask some of them their name."

"Now you're making fun of me." She sniffled. "I'm so tired all the time." She wiped her nose. "I'm sorry, I didn't mean what I said." She wiped away a lonesome tear. "I'll apologize. Make sure Papa Rundell knows I'm sorry."

"That would make him feel better." Hamilton rubbed her neck and back.

"Missy, you talk like a field hand the older you gets. Now

move out'a the way, let Bessie warm you a spot 'fore you catch your death. Got to keep you fit to suckle that spankin' new mouth you bringin' on the way." Bessie fluffed the feather bed. "There, scoot right on in, it nice and homey warm." She looked at Hamilton. "Your cup of hot chocolate steamin' by the fire."

"Thank you," he said, as Sarah slid in, and he tucked the covers up around her.

Rundell already abed, Hamilton sat down by the fire, sipped the chocolate, sprawled his legs to the glowing crackling logs. Josiah's shadow danced about the room as he carried in another hulk of a log and wrestled it to place, with a flurry of red-white shimmers curling up the chimney. Hamilton took another slow swallow, his eyes fixed on the changing patterns of yellows and oranges.

As Josiah started out, Hamilton muttered, "Night, Josiah."

"Night."

Hamilton was alone with his curtained thoughts, the long night-shadows growing still in the crackling sound of the fire. Hours later he entered their chilly bedroom, his footfalls creaking the wide heart of pine floorboards. A single candle burned low at his side of the bed. Sarah lay on her back, smothered in the downy rolls of the featherbed, breathing regular, shallow. He kicked off his boots and slipped out of his trousers and long drawers, the chill stinging his bare butt. He hated sleeping in anything, in the middle of the night everything twisted in all sorts of troublesome places. Sarah mumbled as he shinnied beneath the goose-down comforter and scooted next to her. Her warmth felt good.

From a sleeping-alone bachelor he'd gotten used to having her against him. The times he'd worked late and she'd been restless, he'd slept in one of the guest bedrooms, finding himself uncomfortable without her smelling familiar good next to him. Her closeness relaxed him, they'd liked falling asleep in the spoon of one another. Careful as he reached his arm across her swollen breasts, lately so tender she didn't want them touched. In her half-sleep she turned toward him, her breathing quiet, safe in their cuddled drowsiness. The mound of the bellied child in her stomach bumped soft and protected against his flat work-hard stomach. He'd helped pull calves and watched sows bring their piglets, but the wonder of his growing baby awed him. He laid his open palm on her stomach, her belly button a bare ripple on the curved mound. With a light stroke, he lovingly brushed the bump and push of a little rounded heel or elbow or knee curled in its tight cocoon as it pushed against its crowded confines to get out. He found himself craving to hold it.

Sarah gave a meager groan. He jerked his hand away as her hand moved along his side, coming to rest amid the short curly tufts of hair above his belly button. A fine bead of sweat coated her upper lip. In half-sleep she shoved the quilts away from their shoulders, cuddling closer into the heat of him. Her touch trailed with a cold and thrill mix that goose bumped his skin. His arms encircled her, the intruding Baby Ingram cupped between them. She raised a thigh, resting it on top of his. The pressure off her stomach and back seemed to let her breathe easier. He felt the press of one breast and nipple swollen ready for their baby. His hips snugged against her, his body eager.

She murmured, opened her eyes and reached for him.

"Back still aching?" he asked. Their lips barely touching, he kissed the tip of her nose.

"More than usual," she muttered. "I can't help feeling guilty about how I hurt Papa Ingram."

"It's been a long day," his lips lingered against her.

"I hope it's a boy, just like you," she whispered. "I don't know what I'll do with a stubborn Ingram towhead of yours running around, but I want a bunch of—" A rush of pain cut off her words. She took a breath. "This baby of yours is raising cane," caught her breath again. "He's getting too big to stay cramped up inside me."

Hamilton's work-roughened hands helped her onto her side to take the pressure off her stomach. Covers fell away as he moved behind her. His long sinewy muscled shoulders and arms rubbed tender, firm, massaging, kneading the tight deepness of her sore back.

She murmured, "That feels so good," her eyelids drooped. "Aches aren't deep down like they were." She curled inside the moist circle of his body.

179

He whispered, "I think we fuss just so we can make up."

In their twosome darkness she smiled into her pillow, flinched at the sudden catch that pulled through her stomach. "The way this baby kicks, it has to be yours."

"That the only reason you know he's mine?"

"Well..." she teased. "I'm pretty sure it's yours."

"Seems I've bedded a lusty mother for my first born." He flattened his hand, felt the child moving, sharing their growing baby. "I love you," he mumbled.

"Me too you." Her hand moved along his belly. "I don't know why I get so fretful." She nestled closer. "We haven't made love in so long, and we used to do it all the time."

"I stopped bedding you to wife because I was afraid I'd hurt you. You've been so uncomfortable, and I didn't want to cause any problems for you, or the child."

Shadows frolicking across their faces, Sarah murmured, "You won't hurt your big strong baby. Not as good as you planted your seed."

Her words gave him a quick intake of breath. "The doin' wasn't all mine," he muttered. "God, Sarah..." He kicked the comforter to the floor.

She shifted sidesaddle, the cold dampness washing her satiny nakedness, pulling him toward her, yielding to him.

He hesitated. "Jesus, Sarah..." A throbbing craving behind his eyes, consuming him. "I want you, more'n anything. Our baby, I'm afraid, I couldn't stand it if..."

She felt him swollen, slipped her hand between them, his breath choked by his need, with a tantalizing slowness he let her lead his drive into this long-denied delight. His eagerness beyond his control, their breaths coming in little spurts, his body convulsed, filling her with a scalding wonder. His hands craving, molding her glorious curves, coaxing famished little whimpers from her, their eyes so close they were blurry black pools in the lone flickers from the candle.

Sarah gave a momentary grimace. "*Umm...*" her arms clasped him to her, as though she might wake and find it had been a deliciously wonderful phantasm.

The night became an unbroken tempo of timeless embraces

only lovers relish. A limp Hamilton cradled against her in dissipated sleep, when she felt the first tightening twinge. She frowned, and lay very still, hardly daring to take a breath until it eased. There was nothing more, and she was soon asleep.

The deep pains started next morning, and did not go away. Sarah held her stomach, her breakfast untouched.

"I think I'll go rest a bit, maybe that will help." She pushed away from the table and slowly stiffened into the kitchen chair against the pullin' throbs.

Bessie not likin' what she was hearin'. "I'll fetch up some bonnyclabber. Whey's good for your stomach. Spoonful of curds'll settle your stomach in a heartbeat."

"I don't want anything."

Rainy drizzle pattered the dogtrot roof as Hamilton steadied Sarah toward her bedroom. Bessie knowed the signs, and was in the kitchen, an armload of lye-boiled cotton compresses an' strippin's ready to set a boiling. The cramps continued the whole long night, sometimes easing up, sometimes worse.

They waited a whole day and into the following morning, when Hamilton said to Bessie, "I'll go for the doctor."

"Nawsuh, you stick in close. Josiah an' Nathaniel done left with the surrey an' your fastest team 'fore daybreak. Wanted them to go 'stead of you. 'Sides, Bessie might needin' he'p, with yellow jack fever runnin' about, they's no tellin' what they have to go into to fetch him. When they git back, they not to set foot inside the house. Don't want the yellow jack brung to Missy. They won't tarry, I put the fear to 'em both, and Bessie got plenty calomel ready."

"We're not giving her calomel."

"Mister Hamilton, we gots to rid her of the poisons."

"Use another purgative. She's not taking calomel," his agitation mounting with each moan from Sarah.

In the drab half-light each steady tock of the pendulum clock in the parlor hammered his ears with fearful unremitting remorse by what he'd done to her, to them, to their baby, unable to escape the bleak specter of tomorrows if he lost her. He shouldn't have laid with her, not with her time so near. A cry of pain from the bedroom daggered anguish through Hamilton like the rough

181

thrust of a spear point. As she hurried out of the bedroom, her arms loaded with bloody sheets, Bessie threw him a disquieted look.

Slumped at the kitchen table, he stared into nowhere, seeing only his weakness, his fault for not caring enough to leave her be, not man enough to master himself. Then, in a daze he paced into the library, sagged fireside, his distress fixed on the dancing flames. Time seemed to stand still, the logs glowing grayish embers in the chill, when a rumble of thunder and the heavy patter of rain brought him to his senses, and the library door opened.

"I needs you." Bessie's voice was stern. "Missy bleedin' bad. They's no more waitin' for no doctor. She crampin' heavy, not keepin' still, makin' the bleedin' worse. You might have to hold her if she keep strugglin'."

He hurried with Bessie into their bedroom, barked his shin on a bedside stool. His heart fell through the floor when he clutched the feeble grasp of Sarah's hand. The light of the oil lamp shaded a macabre grayness to her face and washed him with the same mournful pall he'd had at the McClendon funeral.

"Hamilton..." Her one weak fluttery word.

The faint shallow sound of her sighing his name struck a haymaker blow to his gut. He'd always met life head-on, death a horseman he accepted. His mother only a name to him, not someone he loved more than life itself, he sensed the loss his papa must've felt when his mother passed.

"My baby..." Sarah's cried out a mournful wail, tried to sit up.

"Missy Sarah, you got to be still." The bedclothes splotched with scarlet.

"I don't want to lose my baby!"

With fear-filled eyes, he cupped her hands with his. "The doctor'll be here soon," he whispered, silently praying to take her pain into him, his body willing his strength into her.

Bessie shot him a bleak look, Sarah's low moans stabbing the stillness. Then she seemed to rest, grew quieter, as he brushed sweaty strands off her forehead.

"Press this to her lips." Bessie handed him a clean wet cloth. "She need water, but daren't let her drink. Might start her cramps agin. She throwed up last time I give it to her."

As he gently moistened her fever-cracked lips, Sarah licked, mumbled, "*Umm...*" continuing to lick the dampened cloth.

With the full gush of bright red blood, Bessie knew her doin's warn't enough. "It comin'." The fight was done lost. "Nuthin' left to do 'cept be extra hands. Only the Lord he'p this poor baby now."

Sarah gave out a keening whimper, "I don't want to lose my baby!"

The weakness of her voice terrified Hamilton, her skin a pasty bluish, her breathing fast and shallow, eyes rolling up, opening, closing. The dry skin of her face pulled feverish tight against her cheekbones. She gave a piercing cry penetrating the rooms, a maimed creature-sound gulping for life.

As though she had nothing more to give, her pathetic knell stopped with a thundering silence. Their baby boy never breathed. Bessie swaddled the tiny bundle, lovingly tied it in its clean shroud ready for the burying. Sarah slept.

"Most bleedin' stopped. Missy be strong. If she don't come down with the birthin' fever, likely she come through alright."

Was less than an hour later Josiah and Nathaniel come with the doctor. After staying with Sarah for some time, he came out and said, "Bessie, you did a good job keeping the bleeding down. When it comes on like this, I've seen mothers bleed to death." Looking at Hamilton. "Without Bessie you might'a lost both. Her kidneys might'a shut down, and we'd lost her to uraemia. I don't think that'll be a problem, but we best not ignore it. If I'd been here I couldn't've done anything more to save the baby." He closed his bag, patted Hamilton's shoulder. "You best get some rest yourself, at least your wife's sleepin'. I'll leave my last bottle of laudanum—medicine's gettin' hard to come by. Keep a sharp eye on the whites of her eyes 'til we know for sure all the poison is out of her system."

Hamilton said, "Her eyes start yellowin' up, I'll get the word to you."

The next worryful days were a blur to Hamilton. His own fault he near lost Sarah, every tick of the clock branded a doleful remorse deeper into him. Nothing, not the land, or life itself meant anything without her. He sometimes found himself riding Ingram land far from the house, or sitting on the soggy bank of the creek staring into nothing. He worked to forget, resettin' fence posts that weren't a bit wobbly, restretching fences that didn't need tightening, clambering on steep barn roofs, patching and replacing shingles that could've been put off another month or two.

Nigh to a week Sarah hung between red-eyed, peaked despondency and sleeping most of the day. Baby Ingram was buried in the family plot with its own small, Georgia granite headstone:

Gone to be with God
b-d the 21ˢᵗ day of November 1862

Ben, Corinthia and hunched-over Granddaddy Rundell stood with Hamilton as dirt clods plopped hollow sounds on the tiny pine lid of Josiah's handmade, wee coffin. From the window of her bedroom, Sarah watched until the first spade of dirt was thrown in, then loosed the curtain and turned away as the small coffin was covered. Emotions stormed over a grievous Hamilton, tears he couldn't stop welling up. Corinthia pulled his head onto her shoulder, as tortured sobs shook his body.

A few days after the burying, Josiah and Nathaniel cut the Christmas tree. Once brought inside, the fresh-cut smell filled the rooms with its pick-me-up cedar scent.

"Bushiest one we could find," Josiah said, nailing the stand, making sure it stood straight.

Sarah shuffled into the parlor as Bessie was saying, "Stand it kitty-corner aside from the settee by the winder. It'll catch light, be away from the fire so's not to dry out, git so crackly."

The next day Ben and Mother Corinthia came over for the decorating and brought Corinthia's special holiday sweets Sarah liked. When Sarah smiled for the first time in days, it gave Hamilton a lift. He made a silent resolve to do whatever it took to cheer the sorrows out of her.

"We heard from your father." Corinthia was particularly excited as she shed her coat, gloves and hat. "He'll be home for Christmas. His letter's here somewhere," she said as she rummaged through her handbag. "I knew you'd want to read it." A

184

frown danced above her eyes. "I laid it out this morning, told Ben he'd have to go back if I forgot it." She dug into the other side-pocket. "Here it is." She smiled as she unfolded the well-creased paper and handing it to Sarah. "It's dated the 10th, almost four weeks ago, tomorrow. He's probably on the road by now. Read it for everyone."

"*My dearest Corinthia and loved ones—*" Sarah perked up. "*I've only a few moments for writing. I miss all of you very much. The army's back in Virginia in camp here at Fredericksburg. I am packed to leave on the fourteenth to be with you for Christmas. Kiss Sarah for me, and tell her and Hamilton to plan a big Christmas, and...*" Sarah's face paled stony white. "*...And to take care of my little grandchild if it gets there before I arrive.*"

"I wrote him it was about Sarah's time." Corinthia's eyes were as unflinchingly steady as the room was noiseless. "Our letters must've crossed."

Sarah turned the paper over, and continued, "*Holiday leaves will end before it gets long into January. Winter's a mite fiercer up here than there, where I wish I was with all of you. Some of the men aren't coming back after their leave is over. They're considerably worried about their families. Jeb Stuart wants to keep our numbers up. General Lee depends a great deal on fine men like Jeb Stuart and Stonewall. The ranks idolize Lee. No finer man nowhere. Any man would be proud to serve with him.*" Sarah paused, then continued, "*My dear wife, I miss you a great deal. I have a surprise for you—something you've wanted for some time, and right off the latest runner into Wilmington.* He signed it, *Your loving husband and father,* and underneath, *Fredericksburg 12-13-62/Staff Officer APHill's 3rd Corps.*"

"Gosh—" Ben puffed out his chest. "Papa's with A. P. Hill."

Sarah handed the letter to her mother. "You any idea what he's gotten you?"

"You know your father." Corinthia's cheeks and neck blushed rosy. "Some flashy trinket that caught his fancy."

She caressed both sides of the paper. Then with loving touches, folded it, and gently tucked it in the very same pocket of her purse. Bessie broke the stillness as she came out carrying a big platter of stuffed, baked apples candied with blackstrap and brandy. She hurried back to the kitchen, and returned with a second large silver tray of gingerbread, sweet chipped beef and mutton basted with mint jellies, and peanut fudge brittle and honeysoaked poss corn balls.

Before the evening finished, there were groaning bellies and sweet tooths overfed with candies, thick Indian pudding, cookies, cakes, pies, the bounties of both the Hollows and the Bends, finished off with brandy and rum flips, hot chocolate flavored with a little more than the usual chicory and spiced hot wine. Hamilton was pleased to see Sarah eating like he hadn't seen her eat in weeks.

"*Umhmm...*" Bessie was all smiles. "Eatin' like a pig, jes what she need." And she hurried away toward the pantry for Mister Rundell's favorite special sweetmeat spread she'd made.

Ben and Corinthia stayed the night. It turned cold and dreary, and by morning more snow had sifted the grounds with a blanket of fairyland white, with a feeble overcast sun beginning a slight thaw. Through frosted windowpanes there were rabbit and deer tracks, and at the corner of the nearest barn a red-tailed fox sniffed near the chicken house. Fireplace logs were banked high and hot by the time everyone was roused to breakfast with the smell of frying sausage, bacon and steaming corn grits with cracklin' flapjacks. Hamilton was more pleased seeing Sarah enjoying the company. Mother Greer and Ben lingered.

"We got plenty room and plenty food," Hamilton said. "Stay longer."

"Ben needs to get back." Corinthia kissed his cheek. "I want to get the house decorated a bit more for Andrew."

Josiah helped Corinthia slip into her heavy buggy cloak. She pulled on her wool knit gloves, and snugged her hood. With her lap blanket over her arm, she and Sarah were goodby-chatting when Bessie stepped just inside the door behind them and caught Hamilton's eye. Puzzled at the look on her face, he threw a bullet-quick glance toward Sarah and Mother Greer, then back to Bessie.

He quietly eased his way toward Bessie. "Bessie, what's the matter?"

Without a word she turned, left the room, stopped in the hallway, and waited. Soon as Hamilton followed, she closed the door behind him and nodded toward the dark silhouette of a man framed by the white glare from outside.

"He a officer. Come from the Bends, axed if a Missus Andrew Greer be here." Her saucer-big eyes peered over Hamilton's shoulder at the man. "Man like him don't come with good news. I fear it be Sam." Shook her head. "Don't like it nary a bit. Want me t'git Mistress Corinth'a?"

"No..." Hamilton answered firm. "I'll see what he wants. Make sure Sarah stays with her mother." Bessie nodded and left. Hamilton approached the tall figure and extended his hand. "Excuse our manners. I'm Hamilton Ingram, Missus Andrew Greer's son-in-law. Colonel Greer's wife is inside."

"Colonel Martingael, at your service," he said as they shook hands. "On special assignment for General James Ewell Brown Stuart."

The officer's ungloved grip was calloused and rough from long hours in the saddle. In the chill of the dogtrot hallway the snowflakes hardly melted into the coarse wool cape thrown over one shoulder, frayed seams and shiny rub-spots discernible on the worn uniform.

Hamilton was concerned. "Might I inquire as to the nature of your business?" This wasn't about Sam. "My wife is convalescing from the recent loss of our child."

The officer reached inside his tunic, brought out a folded paper, handed it to Hamilton, came to handsome attention, and said, "The government of The Confederate States of America wishes to extend its sincere condolences. Colonel Greer, a staff officer with A. P. Hill's Third Corps, fell in battle at Fredericksburg."

Hamilton's heart sank. "Dear God..." Unyielding Ingram control snapped into place. "You serve with him?"

"I didn't have the pleasure. The men under his command spoke highly of Colonel Greer. Marye's Heights where Colonel Greer fell was a mean fight...took a fearful toll."

Hamilton hesitated. It was Sarah's first truly bright day. He didn't want it to end, but there was no way to keep it from her.

"This way, colonel. There's a warm fire in here." He showed the officer into the library. "Being out in this weather, I'm sure you'd like to warm up. We've plenty food if you care to partake."

"I appreciate your being so hospitable." Removing his hat, he followed Hamilton into the library. "I haven't had a good meal since before boarding the train in Charleston for Hamburg. Quartermaster there packed me a saddle pouch bit of venison jerky."

"There's brandy." Hamilton brought the decanter and snifteren, set it on the small round end table next to the fireside chair, poured a healthy portion. "There's hot toddy if you prefer something stronger."

"That would warm me right up, but I'd best not, thank you. I've other visits about the parish to make."

Hamilton added a couple more split logs, poked at the library fire grate, the log blazing bright, steeling himself for what was to be. He'd heard gruesome tales of gut-shots or shattered gangrenous limbs, of men screaming away their final hours, as their life bled away or blood poisoning festered. Dying alone in some overrun forgotten ravine, or facing the roar of approaching flames in a blazing thicket.

Bessie, a frozen statue at the hallway door, the tray of food gripped in hands, had gone numb, trying to swallow the shock an' face Missy or Mistress Corinth'a without tears spillin' from her eyes.

"Did Colonel Greer suffer?" Hamilton asked.

"It was artillery," Martingael poured a second generous slug of brandy, took it in one swallow. "Colonel Greer was out front, leading his men. I doubt he ever felt it." He emptied the snifter, and poured another.

A blizzard of emotion churned at Hamilton, knowing this would sweep away the holiday.

He looked at Bessie. "You alright?"

"Lets me be a bit," she said as she placed the tray next to Martingael. "Nothin' to do now 'cept prayers." She wiped at her sniffles.

Hamilton turned to Martingael. "Excuse me, I'll fetch Colonel Greer's son."

He stopped outside the parlor doors that loomed like granite barriers he didn't want to go through into what he knew had to be. With a heavy heart he hung back for that dwindling moment, peels of gay laughter strumming merriment on the other side. Death taking no holiday, lightness and felicity was not to be. With a knot in his stomach, he opened the door. Ben and Rundell had their heads back, belly laughing. Sarah chuckled a blithe gayness, then burst into uncontrolled giggles.

"Oh my, Rundell, how perfectly unruly." Corinthia cried with laughter and gasped for breath at the same time, trying to maintain a ladylike demeanor. "You are perfectly incorrigible," and she burst with laughter once more.

Ben glanced toward Hamilton who motioned to him. His laughter dulled, as he caught the look on Hamilton's face.

As Ben came out, Hamilton closed the door behind them. "Ben, there's an officer here from Virginia." He didn't know any way to soften it. "It's your father. He was killed at Fredericksburg."

Ben blinked, felt rooted clean into the floor. His body shuddered, he swallowed, swallowed again.

The color of his face melted to the hue of mud-spattered snowy slush. Hamilton laid a hand on Ben's shoulder and gently asked, "You okay?"

Ben coughed, muttered a slack whispered, "Yeh..."

The two entered the library, and Hamilton said, "Colonel Martingael, this is Benjamin Greer, Colonel Greer's son."

"My condolences on your loss. As I told Mister Ingram here, your father was a fine officer, and will be sorely missed."

"Ben, I'll get your mother." Hamilton said to Bessie, "You stay with Sarah and Papa. When I fetch Mother Greer, they'll know something is wrong."

"I right behind you, stay right with her."

Everyone was still laughing as Hamilton and Bessie entered. Corinthia smiled, as Hamilton came up, and said, "Mother Greer, you need to come with me."

Rundell looked at his son, his gut telling him what the look on his son's face meant.

"Hamilton, what is it?" Still smiling, Corinthia rose. "You're pale as my grandmother's ghost."

Her smiled faded. Corinthia had seen death in too many faces to not know the look. It could only be about the one person that wasn't here.

"Hamilton?" Sarah stood, looked around. "Where's Ben?"

Corinthia stood, gripped his hand with an iron fastness, her eyes never wavering. Ben met them at the door, took his mother's arm, and closed the door behind them. Hamilton stepped back into the parlor with Sarah, leaving son and widow with as much dignity as the living could put to the waste of another life. There would be time enough for sharing the grief. Bessie stood behind Sarah. Next to Rundell, Sarah's face remained a standstill mask, her eyes glued to Hamilton.

"Sarah…" Hamilton said, as he went to her. "Sit down."

"It's Papa isn't it? How bad is he hurt?" Her heart pounded.

Hamilton swallowed hard. "He isn't hurt," he said, putting his arms around her. "He cain't ever be hurt again. He was killed at Fredericksburg."

The room plunged into the austere stillness that comes with such loss, the dancing color of the fire the only movement. Hand to her throat, Sarah gave a soft low whimper. Quietly shaking her head slowly back and forth, then resting it in the crook of his shoulder, she wanted desperately to deny his words, make them not true.

"Oh, Mama," she murmured. "Papa was so looking forward to being home for Christmas."

Bessie said, "Chil', I is so sorry."

Rundell hobbled over and laid his hand to her shoulder. "Sarah, there's no words to say how I feel." Then he muttered into the frosty gloom, "Such a waste…"

Rundell shuffled out of the room into the darkness, his head trembling, his grief too personal. He couldn't imagine indestructible Andrew gone. Their arguments hadn't stopped Andrew from plunging into the gale wrenching everything loose, his friend now one more name on a growing long list.

Sarah straightened, emotions harnessed. "I must go to Mama."

12

When Andrew Cornelius Greer's body had been layed out, readied for the bereavement and mourning, Bessie said, "Mister Hamilton, I ought'a be to the Bends, Mistress Corinth'a gonna need all the he'p she can have. I sure wadn't lookin' on Marse Andrew's remains bein' fixed out so folks could view. Josiah take me, an' bring the buggy back."

"I'll take you right now," Hamilton said. "Come back, fetch Sarah when she's feelin' up to it, likely late this afternoon or before the wake tomorrow."

He buggied her over, paid Mother Greer a quick visit, then hurried back to the Hollows. He and Sarah buggied over early next frosty morning. Bessie met them on the front stoops, a solitary figure in black, her white starched collar gleaming as bright as the tall rows of stark white columns.

Bessie said, "Sure glad you two here."

"How's Mama doin'?" Sarah handed Bessie her thick buggy cape.

"Handlin' this piteous day like the lady she be," Bessie answered, her eyes red and puffy.

Sarah and Hamilton went immediately to Corinthia's rooms, and a teary-cheeked mother caressed her quietly sobbing daughter. His heart full, Hamilton left them to the privacy of their grief. He stayed out of the parlor where Papa Andrew rested. Instead, he ambled out onto the upper porch, took the side steps down, and walked the grounds in solitude, his breath making steamy puffs in the brisk morning chill. The only sound was a mockingbird's clean, clarion call. He looked back toward the grand columns, glaring brilliant white through the remaining wintry-singed leaves clinging bravely to almost leafless limbs.

Straddling a fence, he crossed a patchwork of fields stretching as far as he could see, sunlight glinting off frost-glazed tufts of golden rod, sumac, clumps of scrub oak and scraggly sweetgum trees scattered across the unplowed sections. The weeded fields struck Hamilton as uncommonly out of place for Sarah's childhood home. At the Hollows, he'd ploughed under several crops, turned under the clover and beans for fertilizer. His next year's crops would cut the amount of feed grain they'd need to buy by more than half, and still fat-up their beef and hogs with plenty left for the mules and horses.

Ben call out, "Hamilton—"

Startled, Hamilton squinted against the sun to see him. "Mornin', Ben, I just left Sarah with your mother. You doin' okay?"

"Yesterday, when they laid Papa in the parlor, was rough. Mama insisted he be in the room with the tree, wanted him part of this Christmas."

The two fell silent, too much to say and no words to say it. It didn't seem like Christmas.

Andrew Greer was buried on the last day of 1862. It seemed the whole parish attended, along with an Honor Guard from President Davis and another from Governor Brown. It wasn't anything Hamilton could put his finger on, but with Papa Andrew's death something of the brightness of the Bends seemed to fade.

Other things hurried out the battered old year and heralded in the new one aborning. Far up in Tennessee on the same day Andrew was laid to rest, Braxton Bragg beat back the persistent Bluecoats at Murfreesboro, but not so far back as they had been. The following day Lincoln issued a proclamation, a politician's double talk that sealed compromise in its own crypt and downed moderation. The house was divided even more.

At home in Crawfordville, Vice-President Stephens read Lincoln's words. "Be no peace..." he muttered. "They mean to subjugate us."

His whole life Hamilton never thought of northern people as different, but he felt that changing. Their invadin' armies made slavery a godly cause, using words to thieve and plunder. John Brown abolitionists had carried on about how South Carolina was tearing apart the Union, ignoring how Massachusetts was the first secesh state wanting to leave the Confederation of States, rejoin her ties with Crown and Mother England. He could see this fight was becomin' another French revolution, ripping and tearing and killin' whatever it touched just for the meanness of the doin'. Papa Andrew had been right. Greed wanted to keep Southrons out of Texas lands. It wadn't about the Union, it was about who was going to be boss. The collision would stop only when one side was fully reduced. He couldn't see neither side recoverin', the dying not for any high and mighty sounding reasons.

Hamilton's heart was double-heavy. Change come years before Papa Andrew met his destiny, but too many like him just hadn't seen it.

Mid-February brought another dreary mean-fought mangled year, Papa Andrew's words about the South coming out on top in a month or so of good whuppin's only wishful memories in this worse kind of family spite and grudge.

•

Everyone gathered at the Bends for the reading of Andrew's Last Will and Testament. On the back porch with their cigars, Hamilton and Ben waited for the lawyers.

Hamilton blew a mouthful of smoke. "Rosecrans took us pretty bad at Stone's River."

"Davis ought'a get reinforcements up to Tennessee. Don't ap-

193

pear like Tennessee's important to him."

"Lee might not can spare the men."

Ben tried to blow a cloud of swirling blue smoke bigger than Hamilton. "Leaves his plantations in Mississippi hangin' in the wind if Federals make a move on the Mississippi."

"Bull Run right quick showed anyone that looked how the fight was gonna be a railroad war. That's what Chattanooga's all about—supplies, men, animals—all moved by rail. With Union reinforcements in Nashville, if Confederates cain't get what help they need from Tennessee, holding Chattanooga looks mighty iffy. Georgia could be in more of a fix than I like to think. Rail lines between Chattanooga and Atlanta make a temptin' target."

"Yankies set foot in Georgia, they won't get very far." Ben's war cry was as fierce as his papa's.

"Won't get far?" Hamilton blew a puff of smoke. "Ben, what in tarnation you call Savannah? Bluecoats are doing what folks said they couldn't do. Blockades strangling us, and the only part of the Mississippi we got is between Yazoo and Vicksburg. Which ain't much considering where we started. If Vicksburg falls, we forfeit Texas beef."

"Texas can take care of itself, just like Tennessee ought to do."

"We need Texas."

"Bring beef out through Bolivar and Sabine Pass or Brownsville and Mexico." Ben spit out the soggy cigar butt. "Run it into Mobile or Charlestown, or Wilmington, send it to Lee that way. It'd take a load off Montgomery rails if we brought it in by ship anyhow."

"Confederacy is still alive 'cause Lee's army is holdin' them out'a Richmond, but Virginia's not the whole picture. Lee's back door's gettin' shaky. Something confound his army, the Army of the Potomac get loose, it could move through the Carolinas, come down on us. Without Vicksburg and the Mississippi, the South cain't do it."

"You sayin' we're whipped?" Ben blustered.

"Lee's army needs food. Without it they cain't fight. You cain't drive cattle from Texas to Virginia and have them arrive in good condition. With salt scarce for curing and packin', uncured beef shipped from Texas would rot before it got to Lee."

"They got farm stock in Virginia, the Carolinas, the Shenandoah," Ben said.

"Not if raids in the Shenandoah continue. Gulf's full of Federals out of Key West. Savannah and Charlestown plugged right tight. Mobile and Wilmington cain't run in enough, we've not retaken one harbor since Sumter. Without Tennessee, Alabama, Mississippi, and Georgia is about all that's left of our coasts."

"What else can we do?" Ben lashed out. "Quit?"

"It's not a matter of quittin'."

"They'd turn the South upside down. I won't sit an' let them tromp over us, steal anything they take a likin' to, and God knows what else. You won't neither."

"There's a lot done tore to smid'rins."

"Better to tear down everything ourselves, back to where the Almighty gave it to us. Lincoln lied before he was elected, and still is. Like most Yankie-lovers Lincoln don't like darkies, don't want 'em up North. Yankie desertions are up on account of it."

"We got our fair share of deserters."

"...Fathers worried about families," Ben grumbled. "I go along with freeing hands slow, but all at once would be a true mess. We've lived our whole lives around slaves or children of slaves. They're no different from me or you."

"You say the fight is to keep the South from being turned upside down. What you think this war's doin'? Wounded from the Shenandoah say the valley is a wasteland, homes and crops burnt, cattle and hogs stolen, slaughtered, nothing planted, nothing growing."

"Come spring," Ben was unrelenting, "Lee'll take the fight to them, tear up their farms, their towns, make them wish they'd left us alone like we wanted."

"Lee tried that at Antietam and tore up the Virginian army." Hamilton spit bits of tobacc. "He couldn't do it then, what makes you think he can do it now?"

"We're fighting for our homes. They want to gobble us up, take what we worked for 'stead of workin' for it themselves. Lee's not the only army we got."

"Hamilton, Benjamin..." The lawyer stuck his head out the

French doors. "We're ready."

After everyone assembled in the library along with a nervous Bessie, the lawyer began, "Andrew specifically requested Bessie be present."

After reading the usual legalese he got to the bequests to beloveds.

"...And therefore to my only son, Benjamin Cornelius Greer, I leave all holdings and improvement on and to the original crown grant and lands thereunto added and known as Wisteria Bends with all appurtenances and attachments to be held as he sees fit. To be the residence for the rest of the natural life of my cherished and beloved wife, Sarah Corinthia Gresham Greer. To my beloved daughter, Sarah Cornelia Gresham Greer Ingram, I bequeath to her by title fee simple her favorite section of land along the Ogeechee River known as Moccasin Springs, up to and including the road that forms its boundary known to all parties hereabouts as Moccasin Trace, so that she, as lawful wife of Hamilton Bothington Graeme Ingram, and at a time of her choosing, bring it into ownership with like sections unto that Real Property held by her lawful husband, Hamilton Bothington Graeme Ingram. Thereunto adding to the land grants of the Trace originally titled and known as Moccasin Hollow."

He paused, glanced at each of them, waited, then said, "Andrew specifically wanted the section where Moccasin Trace leaves the main road to be kept together. He reached for the codicil. "Now, to this amendment to the will Andrew added concerning Bessie. He was quite unequivocal about his wants."

He continued reading:

"Therefore let the following be known and set to record in the County Seat, Parish of St. George, Township of Queensborough, Sovereign State of Georgia. Know unto all hereunto and forevermore that the faithful bonded servant, loved by us and known as Elizabeth Mathilda, better known as Bessie Mae, is henceforth and on the confirmation of my death manumitted and set free for the duration of her natural life. Furthermore..."

•

"Sweet Lord!" Bessie's shout rattled the lawyer's pretentious decorum. Her weepy-eyed, soft smile met Corinthia's.

"Furthermore, that all flesh of her flesh, specifically known as Samuel, her son, is likewise manumitted and set free for the duration of his natural life and the lives of all his offspring. All and any bonds and warrants against his person as fugitive from Wisteria Bends in the sovereign State of Georgia are nullified and void. Let all by this presence under the law know, all offenses stemming from his servitude and departure from Wisteria Bend are pardoned and done away with forever. Notification of this action is to be made known to all authorities civil and military."

Bessie rushed to Corinthia. "Sam washed free in the blood of Marse Andrew." She threw her arms tight around her mistress. "You promise you try to he'p Sam. You give my Sam his life, he free." Quite tears of gladness flowed.

A sad smile on her face, Corinthia held this black mother, so dear to her. "Andrew wanted to do this for you."

Across gory battlefields, one life might not've seemed to matter. To Bessie it was her whole world. For this brief moment two mothers and a husband and father's death had made a difference. Sarah daubed her eyes. Hamilton cleared his throat. The lawyer coughed. Andrew's loss was a little less sad...other dyings had achieved far less.

"You always do what need doin', nobody make me believe nothin' else. Samuel never see what I tried tellin' him, what be here all the time."

Corinthia said, "It would be good to see him."

Trying to maintain propriety, the lawyer took time to sniff a thumb of snuff, wipe the remains of the brown powder on a linen handkerchief, then shuffled to another page and continued.

"Furthermore, to provide for the well-being of Bessie and her descendants, a cabin is to be built with enough land set aside to be hers until such time as she or her heir or heirs wish to dispose of such property by selling it at fair market value back to the current owner of Wisteria Bend."

Bessie blinked fast, hand across her mouth, tryin' to grasp if the words meant what she heard.

"I write Sam this very day t'git hisself home," she said as she mopped her eyes. "That he don't have to run from the law, how Mistress Corinth'a saw to it bein' fixed."

The lawyer sighed, folded the papers, laid them on the desk. "There was an addendum to the son. I was instructed to turn it over to him, and have done so. It concerned Andrew's wish that all Wisteria Bend chattel be manumitted and given papers." He fixed steely eyes on Corinthia. "Somehow I sense your fine hand in this."

Corinthia nodded. "Perhaps a bit."

"Nonetheless," he said. "Andrew wanted Benjamin's signature to be the one put to such documents."

Before the lawyer made his out of the house, toward his buggy, Bessie was pesterin' Sarah to help her write her letter to Sam.

"Bessie, there's no return address on your letter from Sam. We don't know where to send it."

"Don't see no problem. Sends it to the head of Mister Lincoln's army." Her voice was firm. "He best know where my Sam be. If the army boss don't keep track of who be where, how he do much good at armyin'?"

"Bessie, there's thousands of men in the army."

"Tain't thousands like Sam, less from Georgia." It was plain simple to her. "Ought be no problem, he cain't find Sam, I sure 'nough can."

Sarah wrote the letter. Three days later Josiah drove her and Bessie to the Queensborough's post office.

"Miss Sarah," the elderly Postmaster looked at the address. "This address might cause some difficulty, not to mention gettin' through all the fightin'."

"Don't matter." To Bessie it was simple. "How long 'fore Sam gits it? Tell 'em it from his mama, to pass it on to Sam. Sooner he know, sooner he be home." She wasn't sittin' still to no problems for Sam's letter.

As the postmaster gave Sarah the stamps, she said, "Cost of stamps has gone sky high."

Later that week, Ben rode out with an excited Bessie to pick land for her homesite cabin. Winter rains were becoming less chilly, and tufts of springtime green poked up everywhere.

•

"Wild onions are up." Rundell poured the pitcher of tainted milk into the slops bucket for the mash for the hogs. "...Tastes sour."

"Bluejohn onions," Hamilton said. "We'll pen the cows in the barnyard, feed 'em there, or we won't have milk fit to drink. Got word the fertilizer we ordered finally arrived."

"Cain't believe it took nigh onto three months."

"Ever'thing's gettin' harder to come by."

When he buggied into Queensborough to fetch the fertilizer from the freight house, Hamilton asked the stationmaster, "You happen to know anyone looking to hire on for farm work?"

"Extra hands are hard finding now'days, folks are havin' to go where work pays better, aside from that they got to keep an eye out for conscripters pokin' around, drafting stragglers. Those not holding protected jobs risk a good chance of gettin' hauled off, stuck in a uniform. Day before yesterday two deserters got arrested selling exemption cards."

Once home, Hamilton unloaded the sacks, stacked them in the corner of the barley and grain storeroom. What he'd seen, heard in town gnawed at him. He bagged his tools, saddled up. Turning his thoughts to farming, he rode the south sections where he checked the east-line hedge and fencerows and the gateposts that needed resetting. He slipped off the horse's bridle and bit, put on a rope halter and let the mare graze while he reset posts. When he lost daylight, he packed up, headed to the house.

At the stand of scrub oaks, he swung the horse toward the Trace where it forked with the dirt road that ran back of their barns. He hadn't intended taking the cutoff to the river, but when his mare jumped the spring-fed ditch, it snapped him out of his preoccupation. He let her have her head, and at his riverbank fishing spot, she stopped. He climbed out of the saddle, walked down to the edge of the soggy bank. The swift mirror surface looked deceptive, but he'd seen it flood out of its banks, washing out bridges and gristmill water wheels.

He felt little solitude. Each day came some word of the war, 'specially in town where he'd seen the gaunt faces of families, grandparents, and wives fearfully reading the daily casualty tallies. He'd never dealt with feeling exposed, but he couldn't shake a growing unease. He was brought up to see a problem and take care of it. This was out of his hands, and so was Papa's not mending well. Rundell seldom left the house.

Couple of evenings earlier, Hamilton had told Rundell, "Papa, I'm cutting back some spring plantings. We'll raise enough fodder and grain for the horses, fill out a head or two of beef enough for our needs, couple of hogs for killin', and still have oats and feed corn for barter. No cotton, considerable lot of last season's crops are still piled in parish storehouses and cotton barns."

"Extra grain'll cut down need to buy sacked feed," Rundell had agreed.

He'd almost lost Sarah. After what the doctor found with her kidneys, his only resolve was to protect her from anything, from himself. Day after day his heart wanted to tell Sarah how guilty he felt, causing the loss of their baby. More confused than when he was a kid at thirteen. His words muddled, or worse, choked off between what he felt and couldn't put words around. Sweaty memories of sweet nights and glistening skin afternooners become bittersweet each time he caught himself looking at her, being close to her, her wonderful smell. Cold sticky sweat washed over him, afraid of what could happen if he got her with child again, and this time lost them both. A wall muzzled a silence between them. Tossing and turning through wordless dragging nights, awake and near her, listening to her breathe, his silence meaning one thing to her, another to him. Wanton thoughts of other women dammed with goodly portions of Papa's home-brew. Wanting her so bad, the hours dragging toward the relief of coming daylight, and breakfast left untouched.

"You've gotten so grumpy," Sarah said one morning.

"Tired..." he grumbled. "Lots'a of stuff on my mind." He pushed his feelings deeper down inside.

He felt ashamed remembering Papa once saying, "Man's not much of a man if he don't go face to face with an obstacle."

•

Hamilton tightened down on himself. Spent more and more time in the fields. Managed to find more'n more fix-ups around the place, that he'd kept putting off.

One day Ben rode over with a bucket of fresh dug squirmin' crawlers. Climbed down, and said, "Take a break. Besides, we cain't let these go to waste.

As they baited their poles, fixed the bobbers, and settled the lines, Ben asked, "You not plantin' no cotton?"

"Cotton prices bein' what they are don't pay for the seed. Richmond saying we need more, but more is pushing market prices down."

A dejected Ben said nothing more about cotton as he threaded another fat worm on his hook. "You still not been with Sarah man to wife since you lost the baby?"

Hamilton slumped against the trunk of the Willow, eyes closed, muttered a soft, "God."

"Man ought not go without, don't know how you sleep at night. I'd be so cranky nobody'd stay around me. Not natural for a man to live that way. Let me pick out a young one I hadn't signed the papers on yet."

Hamilton ignored Ben's offer. "Cranky's about the size of it."

"Sarah always needed a firm hand. Strong headedness runs in the family."

"Strong headedness runs in both our bloods," Hamilton said. "I hear there's been more trouble with runaways here'bouts. You had any?"

"Not so many since the word got around about Papa's will. Anyhow...I'd just as soon they'd get gone instead of sticking around, agitatin' freedom talk coming out of the cabins. Get nothing out of that kind anyhow. Still, I don't like what's in the wind." Fatigue added years to Ben's face. "Hamilton, things aren't right. The bonds Papa put gold in won't mature until five years after the war. Cain't run the Bends without hands, and there's damn little money for hiring." Ben shook his head. "Prices are drivin' us to ruin."

"Our dads saw what was coming clearer than anyone knew," Hamilton said.

"The older ones and most others I've given papers want to stay near their kin, keep their families together."

Hamilton felt a tug on his fishin' line, gave a short quick jerk to set the bent-wire hook, missed. "Federals thumped us a right hefty bloody noses in several places." He pulled his line up, put on another squirming worm, flicked it back toward a shady spot. "I don't see much room for things gettin' better, and I don't cotton to waitin', doing nothing."

Ben frowned. "Such as?"

"Maybe not much…maybe raise extra hogs, store up what extra salt we can to cure extra hams. I've already had spare barrels of flour milled before grindin' prices go higher. A body don't wait for rain to make sure the roof won't leak."

"Hamilton, you talk like we'll wake up in the mornin' with Bluebellies campin' in Queensborough's town square. Dammit Hamilton," Ben grumbled, "I'm not just lettin' 'em run over me, not in my own place, my own house."

"You and what army's gonna stop them?" Hamilton jiggled his line, spit. "If you'n me had all the Minié balls in France, we couldn't shoot fast enough to nail them all. You give serious thought to what could happen if it comes down to shoot or don't shoot? Mother Greer's lost your father, who's to console her if you get hung and her home burnt? You think about that?"

"I'll get her where it's safe, send her to Augusta or Millen."

"I swear, Ben, you sure enough got the Greer stubborn streak. Things could be where there's no safe place. Suppose she don't want to leave her home where she and Papa Andrew lived. You've swallowed too many cigar butts if you think anyone can force her to do it. You better take a hard look at that train before you jump in front of it. It'll run over you without even knowing it hit anything. You so stiff-necked, you gonna play right into their hands, hand them an excuse to put a bullet in you or a rope around your neck?"

"I got to do what I got to do!" Ben blustered.

"That's pretty much how this fracas got started. Federals are looking to be doin' most of the shoving and us the backin'. Dying is the easy part, and there's plenty'a them ready to oblige you. Your problems'll be over. Livin'll be the touch slice, an' you'n me got lots to think about besides ourselves."

Ben said nothing for a bit, then, "Why don't ya'll come for supper on Saturday, stay the night? How's your Papa getting along?"

"At times he feels right good, the other day he chopped firewood, slopped the hogs, put out hay in the stalls. Then there's days he just stares off to nowhere, don't say nothin' the whole day. Saturday sounds good, get Sarah out of the house."

The week came and went. Hamilton finished turning most of the fields he intended planting. More and more farmers and merchants were feeling the squeeze between war needs and prices. A fractiousness burrowed between him and Sarah, taking root in the bedroom where there'd never been problems. In bedew-specked daybreaks or day's ends, their bed was neither compassionate nor passionate. Love was left vulnerable with no gentleness to dull the edge of brooding rebuffs and saber-slash words carried through endless nights and morrows. The loneliness grew between them, two strangers in a house become barren.

Friday night before going to the Bends next day, a tired Hamilton soaked the achy calf he'd bruised fixing the wagon tongue. In the big wooden tub brim full of the hottest steaming water. He was tired, his whole body plumb tuckered out. With sunbright cold windy weather holding through the last several days, he along with Nathaniel and Josiah had finished the harrowing. Working the earth, making things grow pleasured Hamilton. As his bath water cooled, Josiah dumped in more.

By the time he climbed out of the tub, his fingers and toes were wrinkled. He grabbed the towel, shivering as he dried, shucked into clean underdrawers, put on his brown wristed shirt and wool pants. Next to the fire, he slipped on knitted knee socks and the new leather boots the Queensborough cobeler had made from cowhides he'd had tanned. He felt good, looked good. Would've done some Friday night howling, if it'd been howling times.

After Sarah nibbled her supper, she sat by the fire and cro- cheted. Hamilton lazed across from her on the love-seat sofa with his second snifter of brandy, soon switching to his customary corn squeezin's 'til he fell asleep. In the prickly Saturday dawn, he woke, scratched his head as Josiah stoked the fire logs.

Brushing her hair, Sarah watched through the bedroom win- dow as he trudged toward the barn, brought out the team, hitched and made ready the carriage. Sarah flung herself across her bed, buried her face, and had a good cry.

In the kitchen Bessie muttered to Josiah, "Hollows full of chills worse than a ice storm, them two's tight feelin's torment me. Hear 'em toss an' turn the whole night, no mumblin's, no talkin', don't speak a word to one 'nother the whole day."

As they boarded the buggy, Bessie said, "Don't worries about Mister Rundell. His favorite porridge done stirrin' on the stove. An' Missy, tells Mistress Corinth'a an' that rascal Benjamin I axed 'bout em."

"We'll be back tomorrow," Hamilton said.

Before noon they swung through the main gate of the Bends just as Ben came riding up. After all-round hugs and howdy-dos, Sarah and her mother hurried off in a buzz of gossip. Following a relaxing lunch, Ben saddled horses. He and Hamilton walked their mounts down one of the wagon traces, then mounted and rode the sprawling glens of Greer lands in the warm of early af- ternoon.

"Decided to do the same you're doin'." Ben pointed to several unseeded sections. "Cut back on cotton."

Hamilton shifted in the saddle, looked across the lane at other acreage covered in an ocean of white. "You'll have plenty."

"Gonna use the extra for barter instead of sellin'."

"Better than worthless paper." Hamilton shifted in the saddle. "I been givin' thought to what I noticed during our trip along the Alabama coast. Coastal water traffic moves cargo right good. Au- gusta does a good deal of bargainin' through the cotton exchange. Farmers here'bouts with surpluses could do the same, not only with cotton, but other farm stock. We pool harvests and livestock, swap among ourselves, muster our own drivers and wagons. Be more reliable than these crowded railroad traffic, and take some of the sting out of this gawdawful inflation, move our surplus to ports, might get lucky catch some runners, export a bit more than we are now."

Ben reached inside a shirt pocket. "This letter came a week ago." He pulled out a crumpled envelope and handed it to Hamilton. "Been six months since Fredericksburg. It's addressed to Mama. It was torn and open when it came. I hadn't told her about my having it. Looks to have been carried for some time with some scratch-outs Papa made. Use your judgment whether you tell Sarah. Stained in the corner." Neither said what the dark stain looked to be. "Considering its date, it may have been with him when he was killed. Could've been mailed by one of the grave details. Some of the handwrittin' on the outside isn't Papa's."

Hamilton sort of smoothed the crinkled pages of Andrew Greer's graceful cursive pen.

22nd December 1862
Fredericksburg Virginia

To my Dearest Wife Corinthia,

There is a feeling about me on this twilight evening I cannot put aside. I heard a mockingbird singing in a nearby lilac bush. I so wish we could grow lilacs around our home, their deep purple blossoms add such a refreshing springtime fragrance. However, the men in our command from the ~~Shenn~~ Shenandoah Valley tell me unseasonable summers are far too warm for lilacs.

A feeling impels me to take up pen and write to you. Should necessity disrupt my finishing, I will keep it with me until I've put to paper what I wish. I have felt very near to you this entire day. A terrible fight is shaping up hereabouts with Federals continuing to press our beleaguered soldiers. Virginia has given more than most ever dreamed necessary. In the coming days these ragged gallant men from across this beloved land will be asked to give even more. We could have no better than Robt. Lee. He is all that is good, an embodiment of the principles so dear in this nightmare loosed upon us.

Moccasin Trace

My dear Corinthia, let your heart rest easy. These fine boys are the best I've ever seen. It is an honor to officer them, though it seems the harder we fight the more afflictions we encounter. Fathers can be prideful having sired such sons, as I am of Benjamin's shouldering the difficulties of my absence. Our men will never rest until our way of life is free of these wretched assaults. Most of us believed we could have done with independence in a short span of time. I fear that is not to be, and possibly never was. Perhaps it was a fearful oversight to believe it could ever have been so. It appears their well-provisioned intent is to press their advantages upon our fair land, as they ravage farms and homes with no thought as to the innocents betwixt our feuding armies. I conceive no recourse but to continue this appalling struggle begun with such lofty hopes. With blood and suffering enough most would welcome a compromise, brothers and fathers on opposite sides, the reasons no longer matter. Short skirmishes or hours of cannonading only prepare the fields of death for loathsome robbers and looters scavenging from the dead. More piteous are our living taking necessities from the dead to cover their feet or near bare backs. I shudder at my part in allowing this to come about. Both sides have much to regret in our foolhardy sanction into this madness. At least my heart can rest knowing our children's children will never grasp the suffering we have engendered. Once the struggle ends nothing will be solved or worth the having.

Virginia, our Mother Commonwealth, has become a charnel house, its people astray in the wreckage, seemingly abandoned by a peace loving God. It has come to that in Virginia, New Orleans and much of Tennessee. Oh, that this war would cease. Alas, it appears it is not to be. Even I would not accept peace beneath the unconditional foot of the avaricious plundering Huns who sundered the fabric of Union. They wish us to accept life at the whim of their swords.

As our royal forbearers disunited the ties between Mother England and once loyal colonies, while I draw a breath of God's free air, I shall never rest until such rights are secure. Our proud union is gone forever. One forged by blood and cannon is conquest and destruction. If we be unable to stem the tide, no matter what else, these two dominions, North and South, can never be the same.

You have been the best wife any man could wish, a dear and true partner, pillar to my often uncertain behavior. My devotion to you knows no end—I pledge you undying honor, devotion and respect. Remember

206

these words to our children and grandchildren should Providence say nay to my return. To Sarah and Hamilton and Benjamin I plight my life and honor. Dearest Wife, we have been truly blessed with much that is worth this struggle. We have had each other. Some never know such love and the sweet respite it brings.

This too shall pass, and in passing I pray it leaves untouched those for whom I hold great love. Of course you will remain stouthearted, your heart is much more heroic than mine. We have borne worse. We must be brave, lesser folk look to us to set demeanor and conduct.

Plan a big Christmas. I pray God's grace warrants I may join with you in its celebration.

Your loving husband
Andrew Greer

Hamilton choked back the lump in his throat and reached the letter back to Ben. "Keep this safe, Benjamin. I don't want Sarah to see it right now, but there's much in there Mother Greer should have. Even more, it's a piece of Papa Andrew's heart, a rare treasure for you and Sarah. Mother Greer will cherish it close to her heart, but now's not a good time."

"I been keepin' newspapers out of the house, makin' excuses how it's likely paper shortages. Mama's not been to church or to town in some time. I don't think she's heard about Jackson's death or about Chancellorsville. I feel I'm deceiving her, and she'd likely be upset at my doin', but she's had more than her share of hard times."

His horse snorted. Hamilton looked at the animal, as he said, "Hard to believe Stonewall is gone. Me and Sarah don't talk about the war." He didn't tell Ben they hardly spoke at all.

13

As summer got into hot July, Lee pushed into Pennsylvania to snap the railroads at Harrisburg, isolate Washington, force an evacuation, and bust Maryland loose. Nobody had a notion how shoes and provisions in Gettysburg would suck up a tangle that took and took and took. Three days of slaughter an' maiming for ground that changed hands again and again. Lee left with little choice except get the mangled army back to Virginia before it was cornered, or worse. Vicksburg fell days after Gettysburg, slamming the Mississippi shut.

The next trip he made to the mill in town to have some flour ground, Hamilton picked a midweek early morning to avoid a crowd of buggies and teams. He wasn't paying no mind no mind until he overheard one armchair backbencher sitting in front of the feed store contend. "I warrant you there'd been no Gettysburg fight if Lee'd had Jackson."

He saw a copy of the pro-Southern *Mesilla Arizona Times* newspaper, which had editorialized calamity:

•

Large Union armies from Vicksburg are swinging toward Chattanooga with its Memphis and Charleston Railroad to Atlanta. A noose readied to snug tight around the heartland of Georgia…

•

To Hamilton, places like Richmond and Vicksburg once seemed a long way off. The same with Chattanooga and Atlanta, but not quite so far as they once seemed. Each day he saw Georgia giving more of the gristle of war to its warriors—food, powder, cannons, guns. In the quiet evenings, Hamilton could almost make himself believe he could hear distant cannon roars.

Hamilton and Ben found themselves cleaning guns, stocking up on hard-to-come-by ball and shot loads, extra powder.

•

Right before Sharpsburg, Sam decided. He took *Greer* for his last name. After the carnage that was Sharpsburg, Sam Greer was detached from the McClellan command. Bessie's letter with only *Samuel* on the outside, got even more tattered, as it followed him. The word never reaching him, how Marse Andrew broke his own code, never put the word out that Sam had run.

It was a big army, getting bigger every day. He and a bunch of other contraband transferred to the Vicksburg siege. Lincoln's army had made him free, still it took time before Sam shed the fear of being hunted, dragged back to Queensborough in chains. Mama said Jesus promised Jubilation Day. He was seein' freedmen and runaways flockin' to the camps in numbers bigger'n Sam knowed to count. Travelin' at first thrilled Sam. He learnt how much bigger the country was even than Georgia, and he wanted Mama to see. To show her all the wonders.

Sam learnt to shoot and kill, took risks he shouldn't ought'a, put up with slurs and put-downs worse than anything he ever faced at home. He was doing his part for those still held. He knew how stubborn folks was back home, far as he could see warn't no other way 'cept fight it out.

Meanness was never a thing his mama held with. To Bessie her chirren a blessin' not to be tainted with Lucifer's wiles. Sam never forgot his mama's teachin's. Sam hadn't paid much mind to Union clamor and hammerings to *Crush the South.* Around the campfires, they was always officers and rowdies talkin' big how they were gonna tear up homes and towns of those that started all this..

He tried not to listen, as they boasted, "Hammered Sumter good this time around." But Sam couldn't forget their words, when they laughed and said things like, "Throwing those new fangle incendiaries into the houses of those traitors'll show them what they're going to get for firing on the flag. Before this is over, that's how this is gonna be."

Somewhere after the trenches of Vicksburg, Sam found himself looking to the very things he'd run from. High-livin' city-slicker dandies meting out suffering to others, buyin' an' sellin' substitutes. Sam was comin' to find he wadn't coddlin' much to this *crush* mean-spiritedness. Balked at takin' pleasure in other's misery, proclaimin' Godliness and brotherly love, while pocketin' blood money from the hell they laughed about. The Hell they brewed was lookin' to be gittin' scareful close to where he was born—and Mama. Each day Sam came more and more to not likin' the wrongs he was seein'.

Sam still marched along with Moses-Deliverer Lincoln's soldiers, tearin' an' wreckin' an' deliverin' fearful carnage against the slave Pharaohs that was Antietam. Antietam wasn't his first battlefield, and it wasn't so much the dismembered, splintered arms, legs and spilled guts that shivered Sam something fearful. Things upside down, the Jubilation, side by side with thievin', brought him Mama's disapprovin' eyes, knowin' he was helpin' take from those what did the work. Same as stealin', it afflicted Sam.

Between smoke and thunder, at quiet campfires under a tree, washin' in a creek or sleepin' in a field tent when he had one, Sam come to think on Mama an' Hamilton, of Ben an' Sarah and happier times. The Greers never was mean. Like an agitating cocklebur, again and again, he saw soldiers make fun of those

210

what come to them to be free, an' it began augured doubts into Sam what he was about.

One day in camp, a scruffy-bearded chaplain blurted, "You uppity niggers do what you're told."

It hit Sam like he'd been slapped. Back home nobody talked to him like that, never called him that. Christian Good-Bookers just like slavers in Queensborough's market. Sam tried hard to believe he was helpin' drive down evil, but what he kept seein' said his was just another hand in a different killin' version of John Law, with no care to the outcome. Long as they did army chores, none'a them cared about the morrows His fear growed hearing more talk about the Federals from Savannah Town comin' up-river to Augusta, to grab its cotton an' powder works. He'd watched Uncle Billie Sherman-types with their flankin' plans. If they two-pronged out from Savannah Town, an' swung south of Augusta, raids could come through the parish with Mama caught in the middle.

After Vicksburg, Sam began to see the dark side of Jubilee, *contraband* beggin' for ever'thing, food, shelter, protection. None'a them free, they just different masters. Slave hands were for cookin' an' washin' an' doin'. Sam feard for Mama. Vengeful hellhounds plagued his imaginings. Union foragers comin' across Mama trudgin' among the unnumbered. Least at the Bends, he wasn't considered a throwaway. As he cleaned his rifle, Sam saw that runnin' had cost more'n he ever counted. With Mama in the way, could cost more.

Federals pricked a hornet's nest in early August when Chatta-nooga went down. Rebs turned the Vicksburg tables, meted out plenty killin', drove the occupiers back into trenches inside the city, and put the city to siege. Sam's company done a fair share of fightin' to hold of the bled-white, scrawny-bearded dogged Johnny Rebs tryin' to follow up their Chickamauga victory.

After one skirmish, as he and a cook walked the battle field, the cook said, "Saw worse at Vicksburg."

Sam agreed as he stepped over another sunken-eyed corpse in a tattered coat Mama wouldn't used for rags.

Union'd pretty much knocked the stopper out'a the Confed jug. Rebs were barefoot or had rotten shoes, the wounded pitiful worse off than the dead. Sam couldn't dodge what was riding the storm of cannon booms. Prayed against the dread of comin' across Hamilton or Ben's body. Somewhere along the way, Sam lost his hate.

After a time in camp around Chattanooga, rumor and war-monger talk grew thick and thicker. "Getting ready to go down on Atlanta."

"Naw, it'll be Knoxville. Then we'll cross east Tennesse mountains, come up behind General Bobbie Lee, and catch him between our armies."

"Tear on down through South Carolina," an officer blustered. "Burn ever goddamn plantation to the ground, hang everyone in the whole turncoat state."

A desperate discouragement came to Sam. If this army headed to South Carolina, to Seceshville Charlestown, then Augusta, on to Georgia's capital, it'd go straight through Queensborough. It would be like Chattanooga, where he first began to question. He couldn't fire on home folks, and Hamilton and Ben would for sure fight. Mister Rundell and Marse Andrew, likely Josiah too, they'd all fight. Sam shuddered. If Mama saw harm comin' to Mistress Corinth'a or Sarah, Mama'd be right in it. If it went bad for the Feds, Marse Andrew likely still claim him as a runaway.

Nobody set him this task. Was his own free doing, an' he knowed this Jubilation Army wasn't his friend, no matter how loud wrinkled-faced Lincoln talked. Lincoln's words had no handshake-trust to them. Lincoln run too. Run from Kaintuck, the same as Sam, but Lincoln never went home. Must'a not cared about home, which was a whole bunch different than Sam felt.

He'd heard Marse Andrew say, "Don't trust a man with a weak handshake. Got no backbone."

'Membered Mama sayin', "Those what don't care none for chattels ain't like Marse Andrew. He's manful face to face, never behind his back."

Sam'd heard Bluecoats talkin', callin' the likes of him *pesky*. He prayed it'd soon be over.

Sam got his prayers answer, except not the way he wanted. Day after day he watched Chattanooga get crammed fuller and fuller with supplies from everyplace—munitions, powder, caisson, cannon, shells, wagons, tents. More men arrivin' ever'day, along with word Jeff Davis was visitin' Chickamauga. Somethin' big was gearin' up. Some companys got sent way west to Texas. Hearsy again had it they was getting ready to take Knoxville, and from there to Virginia.

Sam had seen more burnt chimneys, than Queensborough got houses. He was on watch duty the night some Georgia stragglers come through Union picket lines, and one hungry one said, "Chickamauga Confeds bracin' for an attack. Lots ain't hankeren to tangle with Federals bent on takin' the Chattanooga-Atlanta railroad."

By the end of November, Missionary Ridge forced Braxton Bragg back to a town named Dalton. Sam had heard of Dalton. Standin' on a hill, he knew home couldn't be much beyond the sunrise from a vengeful army cravin' retribution. And Sam knew what he had to do.

•

Come the end of August, Hamilton and Ben happened to make a provisions run into Augusta at the same time Longstreet's corps was changing trains onto the Georgia Railroad, heading for Atlanta and Chickamauga. They found themselves in snarling, confused jostles, clouds of smelly dust and braying mules. Longstreet's corps unloaded their supplies onto rundown wagons, some of the wheels with no rims.

"Guess Knoxville Junction has been occupied. Must be why Longstreet's having to come through Augusta to get up to Tennessee," Hamilton said, as they waited for a string of boxcars to clear the crossing. "Should'a made our trip another day. This is worse than Macon. Rolling stock looks wore out handlin' these kind'a loads. Papers claim Davis is gonna do what Lee's wanting, restrict the rails for military use 'til things get put back straight."

"Don't matter much, since we're already using wagons," Ben said. "Saw Franklyn the other day. He's home on furlough. He told me Lee's talking how Richmond ought to barter cotton we're holdin' with the Bluebellies for supplies for his army."

213

"Last issue of the *Richmond Examiner* I got hold of reported we won't get the ships from England. Navy could've used those Laird Rams." Hamilton shook his head. "Looks to be the longer this goes on, the more we're alone."

"It's all coming apart, ain't it?"

"Hard to believe the difference these few years have made. Like things we took for granted never was," Hamilton said, watching the push an' shove of men and animals. "You tell Mother Greer 'bout your papa's letter?"

"Not yet. You tell Sarah?"

"No."

They headed homeward with what powder, salt, flour and rice was for the havin'. As they stopped in Queensborough to barter some more, Hamilton said, "Perishables hadn't gotten to the hoarding stage, but prices sure are goin' up."

Back on the Trace, Ben said, "I filed another set of papers last week. Did what you asked, made sure Josiah and Nat were included. Told 'em I needed 'em, but couldn't pay. Those that wanted to stay didn't want paid in paper script, asked if I'd pay in goods. Told 'em we'd share what we had." Pulling the wagons behind the barns, Ben and Hamilton began unloading. "There's not enough men to keep a sheriff's posse on the hunt, and I cain't chase after ever one that runs." Ben hefted a second heavy croker sack. "Sam's runnin' still sticks in my craw."

"It's too bad how Lincoln's freedom talk's become nothin' but hoodwink conniving," Hamilton said.

"Least we don't call it somethin' it ain't. I hear there's hoards trail behind the Union army, some being took care of, some not."

After stacking the sacks into the new feedhouse, Ben yanked the deadbolt shut and snapped the padlock. "Never thought I'd see the day when such as that would be needed around the Bends."

"Did the same at the Hollows. Deserters, scalawag Southerners, properties no longer respected, private premises is like an invite to pilfer."

Ben's jaw set in a ramrod jut. "Bein' short-handed, I'm not sure we'll get harvests in before the rains."

"Some of my hires didn't show neither."

"I'm glad Papa isn't here to see what's happening," Ben said, recalling the closest he ever heard his papa grumble how things were changing, Andrew saying, *"Lately running a plantation takes more cotton to buy more hands to plant more cotton with bank notes comin' due all the time. Damn eastern tariff mongers with their money schemes. Things cain't go on like it's goin'."*

"Without Josiah and Nat, lots of my crops would rot where they stand." Hamilton sighed. "With the army needin' food, seems we can't move enough of the plenty in one area to where it's needed. A good bit rots in warehouses and freight sidings."

"Sure could use the money Papa put in those bonds. Cashin' in early means I lose money."

"Better to get what you can, so you can use it. Confederate paper's not good for anything but mattress stuffing, and not very good stuffin' at that. I'm seeing more corndodger families from farms that showed plentiful crops a year ago, out preening moldy cotton boles from old fields. Cardin' the cotton wool to get rid of the seeds, spin cloth to sell or to patch what few clothes they got." Hamilton stared out across their lands. "This war's gnawin' on Georgia. Capital at Milledgeville to the west, the rail hub between Macon, Chattanooga and Atlanta north of there, powder works in Augusta, Federals in Savannah, Millen Junction on our east, and us smack in the middle."

"No worry about Augusta," Ben insisted. "There's floating batteries along the Savanno River and the ironclad steamer *CSS Georgia* with four guns. I met her captain, a Lieutenant Gwathmey, a fine officer, who..." Ben caught the look on Hamilton's face. "What?"

"We need ironclads we can't build fast enough."

•

Things got tighter. The Horseman-of-Hunger ranging the land, shanty squatters and hollowed-eyed starving Rebs with broken dreams in towns and countryside, surviving on ash-pone, collard and polk greens. Drifters traipsing from nowhere to nowhere across a land where privilege once flourished. Deserters, draft-dodgers, the battered and displaced hunkering in shady tangles by creeks, under bridges, in abandoned barns and houses, begging at whatever back door didn't shoo 'em away. Skulkers and bummers made carrying weapons a given and made nights less pleasant. Small farms were easy pickings. The Hollows and Bends didn't turn the hungry away, but they kept a watchful eye.

One hot afternoon, Bessie put out a steaming crock of dried black eyed peas and corn bread on the makeshift table set up in the dogtrot hall, and warned Nat and Josiah, "Keep a eye on that bunch onct they done eatin'. See which way they heads, an' keep them rifles primed."

That night Sarah found the pistol placed by her bed, and Hamilton said, "Anytime you're out and about, I want you to have it with you."

Later in the week Ben asked, "Hamilton, you think Lincoln be re-elected?"

"He will less we throw a Bull Run defeat into 'em, open the Mississippi to us, give the Northern peace party a chance. I don't see that happ'ning. I doubt anything'll stop Lincoln. Even if somethin' did, I cain't see it making much difference. Northern Democrats might be just as disagreeable."

"North Carolina's making compromise noises, talkin' peace."

"Those not talking it, I'll guarantee are thinkin' it," Hamilton said. "Except ever'body has different ideas how it ought'a come. Davis best listen while he's got enough left to talk peace with. Fire-eaters got too much at stake to belly up. War's changed. It's not what it started out to be. Republicans dead-set against compromise will get rid of too-moderate Mister Lincoln. To keep his head above water, Lincoln's got to shove hard. Trouble is our shovin' back is getting less bothersome for them."

The South didn't throw a big shove into the North. Lincoln stayed in the White House, and that December brought a flood of reconstruction out of Washington City. Utterances grievous to Southern ears hardened staunch-to-the-core moderates. They buckled down, belts tightened another skinny notch, and steadfast grit set in. The war hammered on.

"No amnesty..." Ben incensed. "Uppity bunch of jackasses passing judgment on the likes of men like Lee!"

Hamilton felt as strong. "Warmongers never been noted for

good sense."

"They want us to bootlick, make freed men boss, give 'em the vote, but damn well don't want 'em up North. They can occupy all they want, garrison our ports and the Mississippi River for the next hundred years. Won't do no good. Look how they treat folks in New Orleans. I'll see those pious bigoted bastards in hell, gut-shoot the first one that puts a foot on my land!"

"Whatever's comin' ain't gonna be long coming," Hamilton said. "And your gettin' shot won't help Mother Greer."

"Mama visits Papa's grave ever day." Ben spit a brown thick stream, then chomped hard on the pestered tobacco plug. "Sarah seems to have settled a bit since you two got hitched."

"With Christmas comin' on, I'm hoping it'll cheer her some."

Christmas holidays didn't seem all that cheery. For the first time since she wed Andrew Greer, Corinthia didn't hold her Christmas Ball, and Rundell took down with a wheezin' chest cold that nigh turned into pneumonia. It settled to his lungs, lingered with a fearful cough that racked his chest. He never completely got rid of it, but by January the howl of a freezing winter no longer threatened to lay him in the ground. He stayed bundled in front of a roaring fire or smothered under mountains of quilts with Bessie's mustard poultices.

The mint tea she used for settlin' biliousness and loosen catarrh, along with good English tea had long vanished to once-upon-a-time somewhere else. She replaced them with summertime dried mint mixed with sassafras to settle Rundell's sickly stomach and break some of the rattle in his chest. He managed to sip vinegar water, and Bessie's boiled chicken-bone broth steamed heat into his frail frame. His color picked up some, but the cough hung on. Bitter, damp February howled down from the North Georgia mountains, stabbing through cracks and crevices, shivering man and beast.

"I keep the fireplace stoked hot," Bessie consoled Sarah. "Make sure Mister Rundell keep warm. You go gits your rest."

Sarah hugged Bessie. "I've depended on you so long, always knowing you was there if I needed you. What would I do without you?"

"You'd make do, that what you'd do." Bessie hugged her

back. "You stronger than you think. Lord don't give us nuthin' we cain't handle. Ofttimes we never knows less things comes what calls on that."

"There must have been times when I hurt you and didn't even know. I love you, Elizabeth Mathilda."

"Lordy chil'..." Bessie stammered. "That be the first time I ever hear you call my full, Christian name."

"What last name did Ben put on your papers?"

"Greer, told him I wanted it Greer." Bessie pulled the paper out of her apron, unfolded it. "Keeps it with me all the time. See right there." she pointed. "I learnt to read where it say 'Greer'."

"Daddy wanted you to have papers."

"Your papa was strict in his ways with a powerful heart like most good men." She kissed Sarah's forehead. "Now you husht 'bout bein' spoilt. Chirren always pokin' at grown-ups. Love can tell love. Sam done his share of the same, an' he a lovin' son. So is Hamilton and that rascallion Benjamin. Sit down." she pulled out a chair, scooted it closer. "Bessie gonna do butt in, woman talk. I loves you an' Hamilton, but you two puttin bone-deep worries to Bessie."

"Oh, Bessie." Sarah's eyes puddled, a tear dribbling down her cheek.

"Wipe them tears gone. Ain't no time for little girl snifflin'. Nothing wrong with eyeballs full of water 'cept it won't he'p. You a woman with a woman problem. I seen lusty bucks wanderin' wench to wench in the cabins, not carin' onct they done. Ain't stayin' shut-mouth on the side, watch it happen with folks I love, not as long as Bessie got a mouth. You an' Hamilton got to git out'a this mulish mood, an' you got to be the one do the doin'. An' so we not cross-hearin' one 'nother, I's talkin' on you not havin' that fine husband in your bed in your arms."

"Bessie!" Sarah startled.

"Don't Bessie me, I ain't finished. He a good man, an' God give woman sweetness to take the edge off a man's hanker'ns. Make him want you like I watched you do before you two got the marriage. Watched him be so tuckered out when you got finished all he can do is snore, hardly work next day. Best way under the sun to keep a man."

"Bessie, you never..."

"Hesh...I ain't finished," she said, her bandanna-wrapped head cocked one side. "Hamilton got the grit of a mule, sometimes too much for his own good. Men be like that, an' it don't hurt fer a man to have it, but ain't natural a man to go without a woman t'stoke his fires. Hamilton ain't tetched no wench since you lost that baby. I got ears at the Bends an' in town. A man good lookin' like Hamilton Ingram could'a bedded any what gots the wants for a fine buck like him. Could'a shamed hisself, shamed his name, his family, shamed you, but he ain't strayed onct. He too upstandin' for that, an' it say a heap 'bout his Ingram backbone. You a fool riskin' it more. I know plenty light-skinned ones that would take on a buck like Hamilton, enjoy the poundin' he'd give 'em, an' not hesitate one flyspeck 'bout a prissy wife to the main house what wadn't providin' none of what they was ridin'. You an' me both know men here'bouts what don't care 'bout their pledged woman. Tain't that way with Hamilton. He a God-given full-blooded man. He give his word, but you cain't have no reason 'spectin' him to stay true you keep crowdin' him away. The right hussy looker come along, you'll have a heap more cryin' to do. You a kicked-in-the-head fool you let that come about. Hamilton be made for a woman, an chil', you better set that Greer mind of yours an' see the wench what does the takin' be you." She reached and hugged Sarah tight. "You hearin' me?"

Sarah mumbled into Bessie's soft warm shoulder. "It's like he don't want to touch me."

"I don't care none 'bout sech goose-chatter. You a woman, he a man who likes mighty hot female flesh. You didn't have no problem gittin' to him 'tween here and the Bends, or overnight at the Howells in Augusta on the way to that dress up ball in Charlestown. I stand by the winder, made sure nobody bothered you. I see when you an' Hamilton sneak down to Hamilton and Benjamin's sleepin' quarters. Didn't matter none that Benjamin be in the same room."

"Bessie!" Sarah gaped-mouth at what she thought were secrets.

"Don't Bessie-me no malarkey. An' stop play-actin' like you

got no idee what I means. Bessie keeps quiet long as you two ain't each hurtin' the other. Tonight I make sure nobody bothers neither of you. He a man. You know how to get him riled, you got hot Greer and Gresham bloods. Git to the doin'. Lord knows they's 'nough trouble brewin' outside these walls without more hurts inside. Prayin' do the soul good, but right now, Jesus be mightily busy with the hell Lucifer done stirred."

"It didn't use to be this way," said Sarah, sorrowful.

"That a fact, an' it don't have to be. Folks git along mo'betta if they listen with their hearts. Hamilton hurtin' as bad as you 'bout that lost baby, afeared he was gonna lose you both, an' 'bout did." She gave Sarah a stern look softened with a tender smile. "They be hot cocoa steamin' ready on the kitchen stove. T'night be good for you two t'git on with talkin', an' Lord knows, you two got plenty talk to git done."

Sarah's eyes got big and round, her stomach fluttering. She nervously chewed her lip. With a quick look at Bessie, Sarah turned, her footsteps quickening down the dark, chilly hallway, her belly full of diddery butterflies. Outside the closed door the hesitant Sarah paused, the sliver of light underneath the double parlor doors beckoning, her wet palm trembling on the brass handle.

She pushed down the handle and stepped inside. Hamilton, leaning by the fire with a near empty brandy snifteren in his hand, drained his brandy, and poured a refill.

His aloof separateness was a void between them, his barricaded heart unnerving Sarah as she moved toward the fireplace. With Bessie's warnings burning her brain, her clammy fingers clenched in white-knuckled fists. She moved next to him, warmed her hands to the fire, rubbed them, then spread them again. The howl of the wind through sounded mild compared to what she sensed from this imperious male.

Her voice trembled, "Guess we'll have another hard freeze tonight."

He muttered, "I suppose," and took a couple of long gulps.

"Bessie made some hot cocoa with real sugar. She must've been saving what little we had left. Tastes right good on cold nights like this. I'll get us some." She hurried away.

On her way to the kitchen, she caught the slight movement of Bessie's bedroom door easing shut. Aquiver like a new bride as she rushed to the kitchen, the moment took her thoughts to women who'd lost their husbands, sons, lovers. It made her fearful and angry for the wasted times neither she nor Hamilton could call back.

"Dear God..." her heart whispered, *"Please don't let anything happen to this man."*

In the parlor, Hamilton was befuddled as the liquor loosened him. He stared at this last bottle, been a good while since they'd been able to get imported brandy. Didn't matter, good squeezings was better'n French fancy stuff any day. He opened the decanter and poured. Through the fuzz of the brandy, he wondered which drove his hunger, drink or woman. Down deep he knew it was both. His bleary eyes focused on the ginger liquid in his hand. Something was different about Sarah tonight, or was it the brandy? He leaned into the heat of the fire. It had to be the booze. His thoughts rummaged up visions of her tumbling with him through hay lofts and the smells of crushed clover. Instead of savoring the rarefied taste, he chugged down gulps to force shut the cracks in his armor. He drained the goblet.

As she turned to leave the kitchen, she saw hanging behind the kitchen door the print challis dress where Bessie had left it ironed and powdered with fresh sachet. Bessie knew Hamilton liked seeing Missy dressed up, fluffy around her neck, ruffly along the hem with puffed sleeves just below her elbows. Sarah quickly slipped into it, picked up the hand-carved hickory tray with its cups and saucers, and hurried down the hall. Balancing the tray with one hand, she nudged the door open with her shoulder and stepped through, swung the parlor door shut with her hip, and settled the tray to the side table by the fire.

His head buzzed with brandy-loosed barbarous desire. The looks she kept giving him, the faint aroma that followed her raced through his foggy brain. Hamilton's nostrils flared, yet he couldn't forget their baby was dead because of him.

"Be careful, it's hot," she warned, reaching him the steaming cup on its saucer. "Bessie made some black walnut cookies." She bit into one, her lips curling around it slow, her wide blue eyes searching his. "Try one. They're so good." She patted the sofa next to her.

Almost without thinking he settled beside her, took a cookie, nibbled, sipped the sweet, strong chocolate, just the way Bessie knew they both liked. Sarah blew out the candles, making the room cozy, the fire dancing a carrousel of shadows about them.

"Bessie got Papa Rundell settled." She ran her tongue over the rim of her cup, slid off the sofa to kneel on the braided hook rug in front of the hearth and set her saucer on the floor. "She gave him some tonic to make sure his cough doesn't wake him during the night and his chest don't tighten up."

She curled her legs underneath, leaned back against the sofa, her shoulder barely grazing his knee. Her touch scorched his leg like a red hot branding-iron, his upper lip beaded with sweat, setting his blood aboiling. He couldn't swallow, couldn't breathe, couldn't move, couldn't do nuthin'.

She raised her cup, her pinkie finger poised as she sipped. "You've hardly touched your's."

He took a quick swallow. "Taste good."

"Sit with me by the fire." she patted the floor. "We haven't done that in a long time."

"Lots on my mind."

She spread her palms to the heat. "It feels good."

A shiver tingled deep inside her belly. Part of it was fear that this quiet moment was only the fire and the brandy, that he'd once more turn away from her.

He slid down beside her. He hadn't intended putting his arm around her shoulder, something he did when they sat close. He almost jerked it away as her head rested, ever so softly, on his shoulder. He wanted to hold her, comfort her. Instead the cold phantom wraith of their dead child rose from its grave, sucking the air from him like a gurgled death rattle.

She felt his body tense, his arm dropping away.

He stood, as though recoiling from her. Self-control about useless, he crammed his feelings away from this beguiling creature. His cup and saucer clattered, sugary cocoa slurrying across wide pine boards.

Sarah was startled. "Hamilton..."

His face stoney, he said, "This..." he faltered "...can't happen."

"What's the matter?" She was confused. "We never talk. We've grown so apart..."

"I don't want to talk about it." He struggled to harness jumbled feelings.

His mulishness was nothing new to Sarah, but she'd never seen him so withdrawn. Hurt at his brusque dismissal of her, she recalled Bessie's warning and swallowed hurtful words she could have never called back. She thought of Ben, silently promising to wring his neck if he tempted Hamilton with any of those wild ones he often squired about.

"Hamilton," she implored, "we can't go on like this."

With a cornered animal look, his words came out almost a moan, "Like what?"

"How we no longer live like man and wife." Her voice rose in spite of herself, and she couldn't stop. "How we live under the same roof, sit at the same table, pass in the hall, as though the other isn't there." She struggled with bitter hurt, didn't know what else to do except say the truth. "You haven't touched me since the baby. I suppose I'm no longer as appealing as those fancy ladies in town."

He was dumbstruck.

The instant her words came out of her mouth, Sarah wanted to bite off her tongue. She knew it was the worst thing she could've possibly said, striking at the vulnerable part of him. Her silly mouth had made a complete mess of the whole evening. His face blanched with a pained blank wintry stare, his hazel eyes turning a firestorm incandescent bronze.

"I've never..." he stammered. "I shouldn't have..." He fell mute.

Sarah's hand flew over her mouth as she fled the room and slammed the parlor door behind her. A china bud vase jarred off the shelf. As though in slow motion, he watched it shatter in starburst jagged fragments across the floor—the evening gone dreadfully wrong.

She rushed into Bessie's arms, buried misty eyes on Bessie's shoulder, while a sorrowful Bessie hugged her. "Oh chil..."

"I never felt so unwanted in my life."

"If you two chirren don't try the patience of Job." Bessie patted her back. "I watch you handle any man ever set foot on the Bends. From that rascal Papa of yours right down to Hamilton, an' here you fly off the handle with the one man what truly matters. You like ever woman what don't have much say when it comes to the man we love."

"Bessie, he shuts me out like closin' some kind'a door. Won't let me or nobody through. Like he don't want me anymore, like he blames me for losing our baby."

"Finishin' the pain in your hearts 'bout that poor little dead chil' gonna take a heap of understandin'." Bessie hugged her more. "Warn't no fault to it, jes happened. When it come to pride an' guilt, men be only boys with bigger britches. Been bred in 'em. Look what it done to Sam, an' how it tearin' at this country. A wife can be proud, too, proud she a good mother, raised good chirren in a good home. That her man be happy to see her when he come home from the fields the end of the day. Mistress Corinth'a plumb the best I ever see at the doin' of that. You think your papa be a saint?" Her belly shook with a quiet laugh. "Ain't no man that. Ain't no man like that. You gotta put your mind to havin' a man do the givin' without his lookin' the fool. Even if a man act a fool, a good wife make it 'pear some other way. You two ain't doin' much to help the other. Don't tell Bessie you never see Mistress Corinth'a in action." Bessie pushed back, looked hard at Sarah. "Time or two more like you an' Hamilton just had a go, an' you lost your man. Once Hamilton Ingram buck, you ain't got no more chances. No breakin' a Ingram stallion, not no full blood thoroughbred like he be." Bessie frowned at the change she saw on Sarah's face. "Sarah girl, what you cookin' twixt them purty ears of yours?"

"I'm thinkin'..." Sarah wiped her nose.

"Oh, Lordy me...what?"

"Never you mind."

"Oh, Lordy me."

Sarah schemed like a cornered petticoat spy. Hamilton cloistered himself inside a world of work, eat, sleep. His grumped *yeh* or *thank you* as though she were talking to a wall. She kept up small chitchat at breakfast, lighthearted bits and pieces by the fire at night. Bessie givin' her that *don't-nary-let-up* looks.

Downhearted and more than a bit frightened, she once blurted to Bessie, "Am I so awful to look at?"

One evening she sat knitting by the fire. Besotted with white lightning, droopy-eyelids Hamilton was in his usual vigil by the fire, when his empty glass tumbled to the rug. Sarah put down her knitting, picked up the glass, set it to the side table. She then shucked off the dirt-clodded boots, propped up his feet, pulled a down comforter around him so he wouldn't catch a chill if he slept his usual insensible vigil by the fire. She looked down at this troubled man, thought of how many times he had excited her beyond belief. Then she tucked the comforter, blew out the candle, and started to leave the room.

He pulled at the comforter, and through closed lids grunted, mumbled a near incoherent, "I love you..."

The garbled liquor-slurred, hardly-perceptible-thunderclap three words stopped Sarah dead still. Her mouth agape, dumbfounded, she wasn't sure she heard them, yet utterly certain she had, words that meant the world to her, that her heart ached to hear again, words she hadn't heard from him in what seemed a lifetime. With heart pounding, she fervently prayed it wasn't the liquor talking.

She knelt in front of him, whispered, "Hamilton, Hamilton..."

He coughed, gave a low groan, his eyes fluttered, then he slumped into a deeper sleep and didn't answer. A tear quietly trickled down Sarah's cheek as she hurried out of the parlor to the bedroom he seldom occupied. There in the room, she flung herself across the bed and sobbed. The whole long night in troubled sleep she heard over and over those same three little words that meant so much.

Next morning Bessie found an unshaven hungover Hamilton wadded on the sofa with the comforter cradled in his arms. She called from the kitchen, "Hot water be ready for his shave. Have him fixed up in no time."

Sarah started to say to let him sleep, but instead kept silent. He hardly touched breakfast, and was just as quick out of the house and gone with Nat and Josiah. Sarah and Bessie got on with house doin's in a joyless, empty Hollows.

In the warmer than usual, shirt sleeve day Hamilton hacked at the tangled undergrowth of honeysuckle and poison ivy twisted in the rocks of the fence row. Even though preoccupied he turned the stones careful under each for the coils of a rattler or the multi-colored shy coral snake. It was a whit too chilly at night for any corals to be out, but cramming fingers where critters might be was one way to get snake bit. Under one rock he spotted the bright red hourglass satin-black belly of a sluggish Black Widow. He brushed it aside, tumbled another stone into place.

"Don't care what the doctor said," he muttered to himself.

Dug and tore at the weeds and vines with a frenzy, remembering the awful dread he'd lost them both. Wanted to tell her, wanted to say right out how sorry he felt. Each day his hurt eat at him, beating him into tongue-tied numbness, not knowing how or where to begin. Used to be he could say what needed saying, but for the most important thing in his life, he couldn't.

He worked late, Josiah and Nat at his side. Pushed himself 'til he was tired enough to sometimes fall asleep without a drink. No matter which meal, across the table he always found that terrible accusing look in Sarah's eyes. And each morning from her window, a troubled Bessie watched him, his shoulders drooped, disappear toward the barns.

14

One dreary, cold Saturday toward spring, Hamilton made his monthly supply run into bustling Queensborough. He made his regular stops at the General Mercantile & Feed and loading docks, bartering grain and cured beef for salt, pepper, a few spices, the rest of the seed corn he wanted, and a bright piece of gingham that caught his eyes. After loading the surrey, his long strides took him toward the tavern. One drink became two, then three. Kept right on 'til he'd nursed away nigh the whole bottle and started on a second. The tavern fulfilled with oblivious faces, and he forgot the gingham. Forgot the time, forgot supper as well. It was dark by the time he staggered back to the buggy, and the horses plodded slowly homeward.

"Thank God he's only drunk," Sarah said, aggravated he hadn't cared for the fret and worry he'd put them through. "He smells like a dirty spittoon, looks worse. I'm half a mind to dump him in the barn, let him sleep it off with the hogs and goats." She turned down the bed covers, as Josiah and Nat helped a stumbling Hamilton inside. "Worryin' the very daylights out of every-one. He could've been waylaid by bushwhackers, left hurt in a ditch on some dark road. All the while he's getting stupefied drunk, not caring a smidgin."

Sarah stripped off his soiled clothes, yanked off his boots, lifted his legs onto the bed, and pulled an old blanket over him...one foot was sticking out, his big toe poking through a hole in his sock. She stomped out of the bedroom, not knowing which she was with this besotted husband—glad he was safe, or dis-gusted, or both. At least through the reek of cigars and liquor, she hadn't smelled any fancy lady's cheap parfum.

She and Bessie stacked and put up the provisions, scooping cornmeal and precious spices into tins to keep them fresh and safe from the weevils and borers. The brown paper package was left unnoticed by Josiah on the hallway settee. Later Bessie spotted an edge of the bright gingham pokin' through a tear in the wrapping. Knowing it was for Missy, she started to take it to Sarah, then stopped. She rewrapped it tidy, put it in the pantry, an went on to the parlor. There she gathered the whisky decanters and hid them in the pantry, behind the barrels.

That evening, after making sure Sarah was with Mister Run-dell, Bessie hurried to Hamilton and said, "Brings your hungover achin' head, an' comes with me."

His head throbbing, Hamilton stammered, "What...?" He hadn't heard her use that tone since he was ten year old barefoot tyke, and she caught him licking the honey jug lids and snitchin' jawfuls of honeycomb.

"Don't bat your eyes an' gimme no what-talk like you don't know what I say." She gave him her *you heard me* eye. "Git your hind-end in my kitchen, an' do it jiffy quick. I had 'nough of you an' Missy's pussyfootin'."

Hamilton followed, knew she was fixing to scold, could tell by the measured steps of her broad hips. He remembered times he and Ben had gotten into mischief. Through the fog of his throb-bing head it hit him how much of their lives pivoted around Bessie.

At the kitchen door she threw quick glances up and down the dogtrot hall, made sure no one was in earshot, and said, "Here."

Closing the door, she reached him the cloth. "This was with the sacks you brung from town. With that liquor in your belly you forgot to give it to Missy."

Hamilton fingered one corner. "First time there's been cloth on store shelves in more'n a year."

"You must'a paid a terrible lot."

"Sarah hadn't had a store-bought dress in a long time." He shuffled his feet and dropped his hand away. "You give it to her."

"No." Bessie's hands flew to her hips. "No sech thing." Her stubborn was as hard as his. "You brung it. You do the givin'."

"What?" Hamilton had never heard her so staunch.

"You go blind deaf? I say no!" She didn't budge. "It your present, you do the givin'."

"Better to leave it where you found it."

"Ain't doin' that neither."

"What's eating you all of a sudden?"

"You is, an' tain't all of a sudden. You ain't leaving Missy's package with Elizabeth Mae, makin' me part of what gone way beyond serious. You go buy somethin' for someone you loves, then leave it lay. Ought not be sech twixt a lovin' man an' wife."

"I'll put it—"

"No you ain't."

"I don't want to," Hamilton said, agitated.

"Don't care what you wants. You gooder at finaglin' than Ben, but you ain't gooder than Bessie be at spottin' it. You brung her a surprise, then go wormin' away from it. You gonna do what you intended. I declare, even when you is wrong, onct you Ingrams set your mind, I never seen men so bullish twixt the ears."

He could smell his nervous sweat. "I don't want—"

"Ain't 'bout what you want." For a stout woman Bessie moved quick, right up in his face. "I prayed my knees sore over you two chirren. You actin' like you need a good belt strappin'." She shoved the bundle into his hands. "Lucifer be damned 'fore I don't try ever trick I knows. Now git your scrawny butt an' present to Missy like you wanted in the first place. An' another thing, Marse Andrew give me papers with a place what's mine. 'Fore I watch you two tear each other's love to tatters, Bessie leave the Hollows, plant me some corn, beans, have me a settin' hen with baby chicks, eggs, sit in my cabin, listen to the birds chirp, an' never put a toe back inside this house. Tain't no place in Jehovah's heaven for such doin's. Bessie'll know if'n you give it to her or don't. Git to it."

Slump-shouldered, the walk down the windblown dogtrot seemed the longest he'd ever made. His stomach in knots, he stopped in front of the parlor door, his fist clenched about the bundle. Was Sarah on the other side? Why'd it seem so hard? *How do I ask her to forgive me for the awful thing I did?*

His throat tightened, and Hamilton bolted. He grabbed his heavy coat off the clothes halltree, rammed his arms through the sleeve, charged out the front door to the barn, and flung the saddle on his mare. She broke into a full gallop, he didn't care where, the wind stinging the wetness streaming from his eyes. Anguish, bittersweet self-rejection, nasty bottomless fear, denial and guilt searing hotter than a blacksmith's white-heat forge. A low-hung branch saber-slashed his face, the pain snatched at him. He jerked up on the reins, the mare slung dirt clods, skidding to a stiff-legged slosh in ankle-deep bayou backwaters. He swung out of the saddle, boots mired ankle deep in mud, icy ooze soaking into his wool socks. He'd never run from a problem, never quit on anything, faced his own doing of it. He climbed up the soggy creek bank, squatted against a tree, chin drooped to his chest, and gut-wrenching sobs wracked him. He didn't know how long he stayed by the creek, but when he grabbed the saddle horn and hoisted his wrung-out frame to remount, it was a different Hamilton Ingram that climbed back into the saddle.

•

Sarah and Bessie were finishing up in the kitchen, hanging the dishtowels to dry, when they heard Hamilton come in, closed the door into the parlor.

The determined Greer look on Sarah's face surprised Bessie for only an instant, and she said, "I make sure nobody interrupt you." She'd seen that look before.

As Sarah eased open the door, Hamilton stopped pacing back and forth in front of the fire. They looked at one another, no word breaking the crackle of the fire. She'd never seen him look so whipped, the short distance between them reaching wider than the Cherokee's Isondiga-Savanno River at full flood.

His throat choked, he gave a nervous lick to his lips, his face twisted, and he stuttered, slowly mumbled, "I want so bad for us to try and start over."

Hoping against hope, her heart lodged in her throat, thudding so hard she was sure anyone could hear. The pit of her stomach was spinning. She'd wanted so long to know he cared, and murmured a faltering, "Oh, Hamilton..."

This man was her whole life. She so wanted to soothe his aching, tormented, vulnerable heart, take away his pain and still her pain. But she was fearful she would be rejected again—they'd bungled their love so terribly. She reached for the muted core of their love, knowing she was the only one who could mend his heart. She had to say something. If he tried and it came twisted, their last chance would be gone forever.

Her lips trembled remembering their wonderful sunshine days, and she softly spoke his name, "Hamilton..."

Her head buzzing woozily, her heart fluttered. "We can never forget our lost baby, but you must quit punishing yourself. It has happened to others. It wasn't your doin'." She forced herself to keep talking, afraid if she stopped she'd never say what had to be. "It wasn't what either of us did," her chin quivered. "We've grown so apart. We hardly speak," her words rushing faster. "If we keep going like we're going, this affliction will stand so big between us it'll take our love, make it into something terrible, tarnish the rest of our lives we could have together. I don't want that. I don't think you do either. I want you to love me like you used to do. You thrill me every time I see you. I want to be held by you like you once did, know you again, never lose you. Times I've wanted to come to you, wanted you to tell me it's okay, but you'd turn away. I want to be wild and crazy with you, get excited anytime I think of you and those incredible things we had. Knowing it's time you were due in from the field, or times you came to the Bends for a picnic or go swimming. I want to laugh and cry with you, thrill one another 'til nothing else or no one else matters. These last months when you turned away, it pained me so awful I didn't want another day to come and bring more of it."

The blistering intensity of those Ingram amber-bronze eyes fixed on her, eyes that had always entranced her, and they glared a fearsome spike into her until he lowered his eyes, his shoulders slumped, his head drooped. Slowly he raised his head and plunged across the room toward Sarah, startling her. She stumbled back a step from this oncoming beast-creature until his arms swept around her, crushed her to him, and knotted tight fist in the loose soft waves of her hair.

"God...oh God," he moaned. "What have we done to each other? I've wanted you so much. Wanted to tell you how much I love you. Afraid if I didn't stay away...if I touched you...knowing it would be my fault if you were with child. How if I lost you. I don't know what I'd do. Thinking of the future without you...I can't think of—" He clutched her to him, as though he might wake, and this moment would have been a dream. "I never meant to hurt you."

She shivered in a warm gush of feeling that filled her whole body, and stopped his words with a gentle brush of her lips amid a flood of tears from both. Her dreadful lonely apartness swept away by the tender power of his embrace, her heart blooming new thrills by what she feared was lost, still wonderfully vibrantly alive.

"No more words," he muttered.

His kiss was long, barely touching, passionate, as though they didn't need to breath, as though he'd never kissed before. Their kisses starved, tender, crushingly sweet, so hard it was painful, their passions more powerful than life or death.

"Hamilton..." she murmured against him.

"I thought you never wanted me to touch you ever again."

"Right after the baby came, I didn't." She held him, cleaving to the magnificent power of his touch, arms that once crushed thrills through her.

"You're the only woman I ever..."

Her fingers pressed his lips silent. "Kiss me for the first time," she whispered, seeking all of this magnificent man.

With his finger he tenderly lifted her chin, sucked away her breath with another long insatiable kiss. Knotting her hair with his hands, he nuzzled her neck and ears with long breaths of her smell. Her touches smashed through his months of denial like a roaring flood. He felt young all over again, as though he'd stepped skinny-dip water-sheened naked out of the creek, watching this mysterious woman rising from the water like a glistening angel with a bedewed halo. He wanted her, wanted her to possess him. Hands, hurts, his body, their souls, cravings loosed to run wild with the soothing embrace of each to the other. The parlor became a bordello of disarrayed scattered clothes, lonely days and nights forgotten in a marathon renewing. He swept her into his arms, to their bedroom, thudded the door shut with one foot, holding one another tight and tighter, as he flung away the bedclothes.

In her room Bessie heard their muffled commotions. "Thank you sweet Jesus," she muttered with a broad contented grin.

Dawn's first creep brightened the overnight snowfall. In their dim room Hamilton snored like an overworked lumberjack, his arm flung across her, one hand cradled across her golden breasts. A glowing Sarah slept fast, cuddled safe and sound, her newfound lover spent into her, fairy tales of babies tripping through her dreaminess. She felt a wonder with this wild splendid man fathering her another child. Arms and legs askew, both slept sounder than either had in many long nights.

When dreary snowflake gray skies dulled toward dusklight, and they hadn't come out of their bedroom, Bessie tiptoed in with a tray of cold cuts and homemade cheese. The two barely stirred. She made sure to be extra quiet, eased the door shut behind her..Seein' these two at peace give her good feelings.

In the kitchen Josiah said, "Hamilton said we got gate posts to set."

"You git on with it. It be Mister Hamilton's posts. He be there, when he git there."

•

One afternoon an excited hatless Hamilton galloped up to the porch where she sat, and hollered out, "Mother Greer!" He hollered louder, "Mother Greer! You're gonna he a Grandma. I gotta tell Ben," and leaped off the porch, into the saddle, galloped off in a cloud of dust and dirt clods.

Out of her rocker with knitting in hand, an ecstatic grandma-to-be Corinthia called out, "Lullilia, have my driver hitch the buggy." She hurried toward her rooms. "If Benjamin comes, in tell him I've gone to the Hollows."

Halfway to the Hollows Ben galloped up to them, and Corinthia said, "I'm so excited," then urged her driver, "Do hurry."

"Mistress Corinth'a, them ditches along here is deep," her driver cautioned. "Dangerous any faster on this bumpity road."

Already back home, proud Papa Hamilton was on the porch with his arm around Sarah's shoulder when Corinthia's buggy rolled to a stop. Sarah skipped down the steps, Corinthia bustled out; mother and mother-to-be hugged.

"Are you sure?" Corinthia said, fluttery.

"Yes, and soon as I told Hamilton, he tore off straightaway to tell y'all." She gave a bubbly giggle. "An' frettin' over me already."

"Let's walk." They hugged again. "It's such a grand day." The two went off in a rustle of long skirts.

Arm in arm mother and daughter strolled the grassy lane flanked by the great oaks with waxy leaf buds beginning to open. Sarah wore her new, bright gingham dress she and Bessie had fitted an' stitched perfect. Spring was coming on hard.

"Drink lots of water," Corinthia said. "Keeps your kidneys flushed."

"Isn't it wonderful, and I never felt better," Sarah said. Then solemn, she asked, "How's things at the house? We don't see Ben much, and when I do he looks so tired."

"He's got lots on his mind. I never hear a single complaint from him, but one can't help noticin' the fencerows and fields. So much needs looking after. The house and outbuildings not only could use a spruce-up of whitewash, the roofs need looking after. The place simply looks somewhat unsightly." Her eyes softened with a touch of the despondent. "Your father put his whole life into the Bends." Shaking her head slightly. "It's tearing Ben apart tryin' to hold it together."

"Knowing he's to be a father again, I don't think it'd matter if the roof fell on Hamilton."

Corinthia chuckled. "How's Rundell doin'?"

"Holdin' his own. He'll be so glad to see you."

Ahead of them, two horses trotted out of the tree line, Hamilton and Ben coming toward them. Corinthia's lace-trimmed kerchief fluttered as she waved. Hamilton's sit of his horse reminded her of the grand opening of the Queensborough Hunt season, stately times harkening from a lifetime ago. A high-spirited Hamilton brought his mount up in a graceful, unbroken Canterbury gallop and swung out of the saddle.

"This is one fine day." He kissed Corinthia's cheek and said to Sarah, "You shouldn't be tiring yourself out like this."

Sarah look at her mother and raised her eyebrows. "See what I mean?"

"*Pshaw.*" Corinthia was pleased to see them so cheerful. "You two simply must come to supper this very evening, Rundell, too. We haven't had anyone pay us a visit in way too long. It'll be nice having everyone together, and do everyone a world of good. Bessie can ride back with me and Sarah. It seems ages since Bessie and I've had a good heart-to-heart talk."

"I'll get a shawl," Sarah said, as they turned toward the house.

As Sarah hurried inside, Hamilton called out, "A coat and blankets for the carriage."

Josiah and Nat bundled up Rundell and brought him over to the Bends for a late supper, the table overflowing with its usual bounty. As Bessie headed for the kitchen, Corinthia followed.

"I declare, Mistress Corinth'a, here you be cookin' for you and young Ben," Bessie said perplexed. "Don't su'prise me none that no-count Selmina run away."

"So many lost souls are clinging to most anything they've been promised."

"That a fact. Like Samuel, most lookin' in the wrong places." Bessie reached into the oven, pulled out the bubbling, syrupy blackberry cobbler.

In the dining room Sarah hummed a cheery tune as she put out dessert bowls, saucers, custard spoons. Corinthia came from the kitchen with Bessie's steaming cobbler smothered with thick whipped cream and honey.

Ben and Hamilton were talking as they came in, Ben saying, "Never seen a woman so happy just 'cause she was expecting. Where'd you pick up that ditty you're hummin' anyhow?"

"In church," Sarah said. "As well you might know if you'd come along once in a while. It's a nautical song, dedicated to captain Semmes and the gallant crew of the Alabama. One of the crew was in church last Sunday, and the choir sang it for him, as a tribute to the sacrifices they're making for us."

Hamilton said, "The *Alabama's* taken more shipping than any of our privateers."

"Starving folks..." Sarah's anger aboard the *Flamingo* rushed back, her face and neck flushing a rosy pink.

"To open Mobile and Wilmington, we'll have to sink a considerable number of blockaders," Hamilton said.

"Wish we'd sink all their wicked ships," Sarah snapped.

"Never thought I'd see our ports an' harbors bottled up." Ben sounded like his papa. "But they ain't took Sumter or Charlestown."

"Don't look as though they'll get it any ways soon either," Hamilton said, "but they're keeping the harbor corked tight. Privateering's costly. Both sides costing the other a lot, but damn sure costing us more'n we can replace. Couple of runners lost outside Sumter last month. One got through the blockade, then grounded on the shoals. Union gunboats tried to take her for prize. Sharpshooters along the shore drove 'em off. No one could get to her. The crew got off, watched her burn to the water line."

"You two have some more cobbler," Sarah said. "I declare, the two of you talk about the situation as much as..." she stopped, turned paled, and the room went dead silent with the keen-felt absence of Andrew.

"As bad as Andrew an' me used to." Rundell broke the tension, straightened his head as best he could. "Sure do miss that ol' scoundrel. I bet my last pair of boots he's found someone else to contend with."

Ben said, "But you two never got mad on one another."

"Yep." Rundell had a faraway look. "Sure do miss him."

"Papa thought highly of you, and likely would agree with you on lots of stuff before he—"

"Before he left that last time for Virginia?" Rundell's mind was going through the good times, the good cigars. "Andrew was a fine man. Stubborn as a mule, but you could depend on him through thick and thin."

"Of course, Papa Ingram," Sarah cheerfully teased, "Neither you or this son of yours have a stubborn bone in your body."

"Wouldn't want a friend no other way." Rundell smiled at this daughter-in-law as beautiful as her mother.

It was a subdued exceedingly pleasant evening of good food and fond recollections. They stayed the night since the ride between their places had enough isolated wooded stretches to not be safe in the daytime, much less after dark. If a body was alone the roads were getting as bad. Hamilton had already armed Josiah and Nat. Corinthia, a deadeye with her over-and-under Derringer, kept it loaded and handy. Ben let it be known he was doing the same with some of his hands, which riled talk already stirring.

In Queensborough one cigar-totin' store owner ranted, "Lee's talking puttin' slaves in uniform!"

"That's not the worst of it," another carped. "Ben Greer's done put lead and powder in slave hands. Stirrin' rebellion same as John Brown."

"You know the Greers better'n to say something like that," a third maintained.

"Hear the Ingrams're doin' the same."

"Niggers got as much to protect as any others, farms an' plantations are in a bad way, lots'a folks starvin'."

Word spread. Most troublemakers gave Ingram and Greer property a wide birth. But not all.

Some days later, Hamilton, Josiah and Nat had gone to the fields. Sarah, belly barely beginning to show, was with Bessie in the cellar, gathering jars and cleaning out the crocks for fall canning, when the first popping sounds were heard.

Bessie's head jerked around. "Them gun shots."

A stooped-over Sarah looked up. "What?"

"Gun shots." Bessie put down the box of jars and headed toward the cellar door. "From the direction where the men be. We gittin' upstairs, an' gittin' now."

Sarah's heart pounded as they came up out of the cellar and looked in the direction of more shots.

"Come on." Bessie hurried into the pantry, where she reached down the powder horn from the top shelf, then the rifle and pistols. "Git 'em ready with all that shootin'. 'Til we know different, we make sure two-legged low-downs don't sneak to the house."

Sarah rushed to the window and murmured, "Hamilton..." She feared for him, for their child, for all of them. "Surely you don't suppose it's Federals?"

"Might be better if'n it is, 'stead of what else be skulkin' in them woods. Stay away from the winder, an' finish rammin' this powder."

Sarah poured the ball and powder firm, rammed it, pulled the rammer out, and whispered, "Bessie listen...birds stopped singing."

"Except that cawin' crow seein' somethin' what don't belong."

Sarah took another quick peek. "There's several horses, but I don't see any riders. Mules are still hitched. I don't see anyone at the plow, but there's men on among the trees."

"You watch the front door." Bessie snugged the pistol in her apron pocket. "I cover the back. Anybody tries comin' through the dogtrot door or through the parlor, we back into here, keep 'em from circlin' us."

"What about Papa Rundell?" Sarah's stomach was queasy.

"He keep his rifle ready. Anyone bust in his room be dead 'fore they twitch a hair."

With a crash, the kitchen door flew open. Sarah brought her rifle up and fired, the shot splintering door and jamb. The sound thundered through the house. Bessie's rifle steadied dead-on.

The silhouetted head and shoulders ducked into a hunch and Hamilton yelled, "Sarah!" His hand smeared at stinging blood-speckled splinters of wood along his cheek.

Hamilton!" Sarah flung down her weapon and rushed to him. "Oh God—I near shot you. Are you hurt?" She daubed away the polka-dots of blood on his neck. "We heard shooting, saw riders on horses. I was scared, afraid you might've been..." Her heart pounded. "How you expect me to tell our son, that I shot dead his father?"

He hugged her trembling body close. "I'm alright."

"You best be alright," Bessie flared. "Bustin' in here, skeeren us half to death."

He said, "I didn't know giving you two guns would near get me killed."

Rundell busted in, rifle ready. "What happened!"

"My fault for rushing in," Hamilton said.

"That the truth. Nobody with sense be so milk cow chicken-dumb witless to bust in like you did."

"We're not sure how many there were." Hamilton wiped the blood smears. "I was afraid those shootin' at us were distractions...others making for the house. Couldn't holler-out, anybody sneakin' up would've shot first. They snuck up while we were working the mules. We got two of 'em, but not before they shot Josiah. It's a clean in-out through the shoulder, no bones broke. We'll fetch him. He was bleedin' right good. We got the heavy bleedin' stopped, left him with the mules." He started toward the door, stopped, and turned. "How you know you carrying a boy?"

With a sassy smirk she said, "Never you mind."

Bessie said, "Get your scrawny behinds back down yonder, an' hurry with Josiah. We have bandages tore and water bilin'."

He kissed Sarah and hurried away. The two women waiting ready on the back porch, as they brought Josiah.

"Put him flat down here," said Bessie, spreading the blanket.

"Josiah hold still while I have a look-see," Hamilton said. Then he asked Nat, "How's the mules?"

"One's leg-shot, likely need to be put down."

"What about their horses?"

"Scraggly critters." Josiah winced. "None'a them could pull a cart or a plow. One has *CSA* stamped on the saddle blanket with old blood."

"Deserters." Hamilton's jaw clenched. "We'll take the horses in town to Miller, sell 'em. Notify the sheriff about this."

Sarah said, "You think there's more about?"

"There's more."

Bessie mumbled, "Lordy mercy..." and knotted another bandage around Josiah's shoulder.

"If what they say is true up around Atlanta, I expect it'll get worse." Hamilton tried to look calm for Sarah's sake. "Sheriff don't have the men to chase after stragglers. We might need to form a county *comitat* posse, protect our own. This bunch camped in those woods down by the creek. Josiah stumbled on them when he went for water. Hadn't been for me and Nat, they'd likely killed him just to take whatever he had. At least six of em, likely eyein' us for several days. From now on, I want everyone within reach of a loaded gun. Nat, make sure you keep plenty shot and powder handy."

Nat said, "Still got most of what you gave us, 'cept for that wild hog we kilt."

Bessie gave a determined shake of her head. "Got my pistol in my apron. Missy, too." She gave Josiah's wrappin's one last snug. "Anybody poke round here, don't give Bessie a right answer, git a belly full'a shot. None'a you men best come up on this house after dark without givin' a *hello in the house* less you want to be the next one gettin' patched. From now on we draw winder blinds at sundown, have no lurkin' an' peekin' on our inside doin's."

"I don't want either of you women on the road or in town without me or Nat or Josiah with you," Hamilton said. "Nat, take my fastest horse. Hightail it to the Bends. Stay on the back lanes, let Ben and Mother Greer know what happened, that everyone's okay, and for them to keep a sharp eye. You come on any trespassers, you ride like the wind straight back here. They give chase, give us two shots, and keep ridin'. We'll circle round in your direction. If it's a diversion, that'll put us behind them, give us a chance to give 'em a surprise of our own."

It didn't take long for the shoot-out at the Hollows to get around. It sent fresh jitters throughout the parish, folks giving whispering looks at any hollow-eyed stranger. Law and order tattering more unloose in a world gone lunatic, survival coming down to eyeball personal. Hamilton sensed a deeper isolation. Nobody had to tell him if things kept sliding, they were on their own.

15

O ne evening, after finishing plowing his fields for their second planting, Hamilton had a good wash in the creek. After supper, Hamilton sat in the front porch swing with a week old copy of the *Augusta Constitutionalist*, "Editorials touted how battles around Kennesaw would see a slaughter of the invaders. Word is they're diggin' more trenches up around Kennesaw Mountain, north of the Chattahoochee to stop that scruffy Billy Sherman. That Forrest can't stop Sherman, Lee's sure enough got his hands full with Grant. Says here the governor is faced with too much to do, and too little to do it with. That we're already trenchin' the Dalton to New Hope Church roads. Says he's asked President Davis for reinforcements. Plain for anyone to see, there's no letting up. Richmond's about used up." As he turned another page, he noticed Sarah biting her lip as she wiped at a wayward tear, let the paper slump to his lap. Instantly solicitous, he asked, "What's the matter? You okay?"

"I'm alright." She leaned her head against the back of the cane-backed rocker. "Ben dropped by right after noontime today. He wanted to make sure we knew of the funeral in Augusta for Bishop Polk. The Bishop was killed at Pine Mountain. Kennesaw must've been dreadful." Her lips squeezed thin. "*The Alabama* lost, all those men, now this..."

"Come..." He patted the cushions next to him. "Come sit with me." His arm went around her, comforted her. "*Alabama* sank some place off the coast of France."

"Such a long way from home...I wonder if that young sailor in church that Sunday, the one we sang for, Hamilton," she whispered softly, "It seems so appallingly pointless."

The paper forgotten, Hamilton let his gaze move across the fields and pastures of this land so much a part of his soul. He gently stroked her hair. "Nobody figured it would get so bad. Long before lawless Kansas, anyone with half a brain could see where bluster and swagger was leading us. Most folks didn't want this. It's like the whole country went crazy...cruel words and hardhearted doings...as if they wanted to fight." They kept swinging, holding one another, counting lightning bugs into the evening.

The sassy end of spring lingered with June cooler than usual. The humidity stayed low.

After one pleasant evening under the spawling big oaks, he said, "Mosquitoes aren't so bad. Those hard freezes must've killed off most of them."

"Give 'em time, they'll carry us away before dog days get far along, then we'll have..." her words caught. She pressed a hand to the stitch in her swollen stomach.

He kissed her forehead. "Kicking?" He gently placed his hand atop hers, letting the swing slowly sway in the firefly evening.

"More'n more." she shifted to ease the discomfort. "You Ingrams are strong as oxen."

Hamilton and Sarah and their hefty rowdy baby stirring in her belly celebrated their second wedding anniversary in mid-November. With the tally of dead and wounded around Atlanta, refugees were squeezing on any trains for Macon or anywhere away from Marthasville. Hamilton didn't need the passed-down word to heed the constant increase of wagons and pile-high carts of sorrowful possessions on the rutted roads around Queensborough. As the weeks wore on, Sarah was showing bigger an' bigger. The sluggish warm days and nights made Hamilton yearn for Indian Summer. Without thinking about it, he often cocked a vigilant eye in the direction of rail lines south and east, knowing Railroad Sherman was covetous for those same roads of railroad ties.

•

"...and to give thanks for all the blessings bestowed," Ben finished the prayer, "Amen." He found this Fourth of July dinner on the ground was pleasant but not quite so spirited as so many others.

As everyone stirred and the babble of talk and clink on silverware began around the long, makeshift tables, Hamilton helped himself to the potato salad, passed it to Ben. "You read Jeff Davis' speech?"

"And right to the point." Ben lifted the silver cover off the steaming chafing dish.

"With Atlanta's rail hub gone, Lee's munitions'll be cut off from Selma." Hamilton ladled thick, creamy gibelet flour gravy from the terrine over Sarah's johnnycake biscuits.

"Selma can ship to Texas and Arkansas. Powder works in Augusta can handle what Lee needs." Ben plopped a second helping of middlings and potatoes on his plate. "Pushin' Yankies out of Atlanta won't be a problem if the rumor's true about Johnston being replaced by Hood."

"Hood got a lot of men killed," Hamilton said. "Rivers, including the Chattahoochee won't stop bridge-builder Sherman. And the Georgia Railroad out of Atlanta goes straight to Augusta. Knock out Augusta powder works, Sherman's on the backdoor to Wilmington with Lee not having the powder he needs. Fightin'll stop."

"Augusta's shored solid against that," Ben said. "Bragg can move men down from North Carolina, stop Sherman making toward Augusta."

Hamilton didn't tell anyone how it wasn't keeping Sherman

out of Augusta that troubled him near so much as how Sherman might take a notion to get in. Bragg's forces might have the rails into Augusta screened all he wanted, but on his trips to Augusta, Hamilton had seen few and far between earthen ramparts and bulwerks in and around Hawk's Gully.

"Plain to see, that if the powder works and the arsenal are Sherman's bull's-eye, swinging around from the south would make it easy to punch through Augusta's defenses. Union forces coming from Milledgeville or up from Mobile could push up through Millen Junction, with Queensborough smack in the crosshairs."

His nights became wide-awake vigils, the days more tense. Mother Greer and Ben wouldn't leave. Hamilton scrapped any notions of moving Sarah and Papa to South Georgia. Jostling Sarah in a buggy on packed roads with few places to stop and rest, plus the threat of stragglers and deserters, was not something he would risk. Least here, they were all together, out of the weather, and plenty of food.

•

Sam ambled along the bank tossin' pebbles into Peachtree Creek. Their Atlanta victory didn't surprise him. Wadn't different for other cities they'd took, 'cept bigger an' smellier. Their unit in camp, restin' an' refitted. Yesterday he'd took a stroll near the rubble of the Roundhouse sheds the boys in gray had blowed up. Stumblin' through tumbled bricks and smokin' timbers sure wadn't nuthin' like evenin's back home, times he an' Ben an' Hamilton roughhoused, evenin's on the back stoops, list'nin' to the nighttime whippoorwills and hoot owls, crickets sawin', bull frogs deep *rumphin'* down in the sloughs.

The hard-set to the eyes of Georgia's beaten defenders gave him thoughts on Hamilton and Ben. Yestermornin' he'd walked the dusty, smoke-stench Atlanta streets, tried ignorin' the sullen stares of passersby. Tried hatin' back for things they said, what they done. Bedevilments stewed him more'n more 'bout *home'*. Sam found hisself dreadful homesick.

He'd listened to here'n'there triflin' camp talk. "Seems General Billy's none too happy."

"Orders say he means to tear up railroads to Augusta. Go after the powder works."

Sam sat down on the creekbank, kicked off his shoes. Poked his toes through plumb wore out marchin' holes in his socks. It felt good danglin' his feet in the water. Sam pi'tured hands diggin' trenches around Augusta, maybe Queensborough. Wondered if Ben or Hamilton or Mister Rundell or Mister Andrew joined Hood up to Tennessee. Lazy fishin' days called to him from memory. Him an' Ben an' Hamilton, all three with cane poles an' fresh dug fat wigglers. Sam wrinkled his nose. The only smell in Atlanta was burnt. He'd had 'nough burnin'. Butternut, blue, gray no longer mattered, cities didn't matter.

He muttered to hisself, "Mama could git caught in the fightin'."

In days to come, Reb cavalry sallies kept raiding the Union supply railroads out of Chattanooga. Avenger Sherman got pissed. He burned Chattanooga bridges. Told those in Atlanta to *git*, put the torch to some of what was left. From one hill Sam watched. The burnin's wadn't near as bad as what waited for Sam soon as he got back to camp. Official orders come. Sherman was loosin' retribution to Savannah 'stead of Augusta. Sam didn't see Savannah or war or slave or Jubilation Lincoln. He was he'pin' bring smoke an' fire visions of Bible ruination, branding him deeper than any slave words with Mama smack-dab in Sherman's victory-drunk path.

"Have us a big holiday," Sam's Sergeant excited. "Rip the heart out of this traitor state—no scoundrel cavalry'll raid behind us like they're doing between here and Chattanooga."

Sam hung back after the evenin' shiny brass bugle tooted *taps*, made sure ever'body was sleepin', then slipped passed the sentries. He never looked back. He made off with clothes off a clothesline.

Sheddin' his uniform, he kept his coat for night cover. Sam knowed if he got caught he could be shot a deserter. He didn't know how far it was to home. Supposed it couldn't be much more marchin' than from Chattanooga. Spent most daylight hidin', white trash looters skeerin' him more than Reb lookouts. With all those kinds so much plumb out in the open, Sam pondered how bad home was gittin'.

.

At the Hollows, Hamilton kept his eyes peeled to the direction of Lithonia and Shady Dale. Any whiff of smoke troubled him, a farmer burning trash, a grass fire, the stench of something dead. He didn't sleep too sound learnin' Federal patrols had been spotted in parishes south of Queensborough, and county records and private property deeds had been moved out of Milledgeville.

The following afternoon, he and Ben stopped at the creek to water their horses. Ben said, "Mama says she's not leavin' her home to what she's callin' a bunch of *rowdy soldiers*."

Hamilton pulled a currycomb from his saddlebags, started brushing his mare. "I had a feelin' Mother Greer wouldn't leave. I hadn't mentioned it to Sarah."

"I've talked 'til I'm blue in the face to get her to go to South Georgia, stay with her cousin. She won't hear of it, says Papa's here. It's not safe for her. Maybe if you'd talk to her, get her to see."

"Ben, no one's going to make your mama do anything she set her mind against." Hamilton kept brushing the one horse he'd kept after selling the mules. "We've still got cavalry about. I doubt enough to matter—hopefully it won't come to that."

"I can't watch out for the house and her as well," Ben said, his gut in knots. "She'd try to stop any shootin', and with—"

"You mean she'd try to stop any shooting to keep you from being shot." Hamilton looked at Ben, kept brushing. "Besides, if you somehow managed to get her to go stay with her cousin, you figure out how she'd get there? Roads aren't safe, you'd have to go with her."

"Yeh, leavin' the place empty is like an invitation. Anyone could sneak in."

"I'd given some thought to moving Sarah, but with her time so near, she don't need to be jostled around." Hamilton asked, "None'a your hands stayed?"

"Bessie's cousin, Little Luke, and his woman with their

young'uns. He's run before, only came back when he was hungry, found out high soundin' words and fancy promises don't fill his belly. Things tighten up, he'll do it again, leave the woman and kids again."

Hamilton stopped brushing. "Might be we ought to think about all of us staying in one place. One another is 'bout all that's left."

"There's plenty room at the Bends."

"Ain't much left to hang to, is there Ben?" Hamilton lifted the hoof, brushed the withers and forelegs. "We might ought to think about putting out pickets, it'd let us keep an eye on both places. Me'n you split the night shifts with Josiah and Nat. Make sure they don't fall asleep."

"How in hell?" Ben exclaimed. "They's no way we can cover both places."

"Better than doin' nothing." Hamilton knocked the brush against a tree, pulled out the matted hair. "We picket at the fork of the Trace and along the river. That'd give us time to hide the few head of livestock and the milk cow in those caves down by the springs. I checked inside, made sure not to disturb the vines and thickets covering the opening. Unless you know where to look, a body could walk right past and never know the caves were there. Most around here don't know about the caves, that they were used to store powder and arms from the Red Coats. There's small side tunnels I've shored up, already stored a couple of chests of family crystal and the heirloom silver from Scotland and Normandy. I can help you cart yours, but we shouldn't wait if you want to do it."

"We'd have to make crates. It'd take several loads to move what Mama's got."

"Short trips, not at night," Hamilton said. "Lanterns draw attention. Hate saying it, but you cain't trust anyone now'days...too many strangers, too many hungry mouths."

Hamilton gave the brush a final knock. They mounted, rode in silence, the mellow afternoon sunlight and rustic lands of the Hollows seemed no longer quite so tranquil.

As they came in the back kitchen door, Bessie said, "Mister Ben, hadn't seen you in a spell. Set your backside down. You lookin' a tad whey-faced, like you ain't eatin' right. They's chilled buttermilk churned early this mornin', an' coolin' in the cistern. Some of your fav'rite cracklin' hardtack still warm on the back of the stove."

"Morning, little brother." Sarah was moving slow as she came in. "Thought I heard your two voices stomping on the back porch."

"How's my favorite sister and that little nephew of mine you're carryin'?" Ben pecked her cheek, patted her child-filled belly. "You're 'bout big enough to bust."

She took a short breath. "We're both doin' fine." Scooted out a chair, held her belly, as she eased spraddle-legged onto it. "Your nephew is letting his mother know he's like the rest of the men in this family, ready to take on the world."

Bessie laid a steaming plate of cream gravy and biscuits in front of Ben. "Put that in your belly." Then said to Sarah, "You got all the signs. I heard you stirrin' long before sunup. Cramps gettin' closer?"

"Deep down ones...woke me in the middle of the night."

"You having the baby?" Hamilton was immediately next to her.

"Not quite yet," Sarah shook her head. "Mother Nature just gettin' ever'thing ready."

Bessie rolled her eyes. "Lord, be patient with this new daddy." As she shoved a pan of biscuits in the oven, she added, "This daddy don't soon git his son, he drive the bothers into us all." Dish towel in one hand, she watched Ben wolf down his biscuits an' gravy, sayin', "You ain't eatin right."

"I fix my own meals," Ben said.

"No, you ain't. Don't start none'a your white lyin' t'me, you ought'a be mortified lookin' Bessie right in the eye, fibbin' to high heavens. You ain't eatin' right. You ain't fixin' breakfast, you workin' sunup to sundown, doin' what need doin'. I watch you char hardtack so hard you could pole-axed a squirrel with corn-bread pone you burnt. You not eatin' 'cause runaways stole in, empty the smokehouse, took most ever'thing?"

He didn't answer as he sopped his plate squeak-clean. "Sure is good." He wolfed down a second helping of biscuit pone an' chitlin gravy.

Bessie said, "You keep treatin' yo'self poorly, you come down with swamp fevers like a lame horse. Then who look to Mistress Corinth'a? Don't make me git to the Bends an' look after your mangy hide."

Ben and Hamilton worked out watches times with signal shots to use if they needed to alert those at the houses. Otherwise they'd keep silent vigils. As Hamilton watched Ben ride off and fade into the dusklight, he thought of dozy afternoons fishin' by the syrupy swirl of the river or danglin' their poles off one of the low bridges, overnight campin', huntin'. Things were a lot simpler than what they were shaping up to be by the time this played out. Being the eldest it was his job to look out for everyone as best he could.

Nights were unsettled. Sarah was more restless, and Bessie started sleeping in her room with her. Hamilton stayed dressed most nights, slept on the parlor sofa so's not to disturb her. Before midnight and time to relieve Josiah, Bessie had him a hot breakfast and a fresh pot of spicy succory.

"Biled your succory strong like you like. Would'a added a tetch of chocolate but I'm holdin' back what little we got in case the baby needs a touch of sweet for a sugar-tit to suck. With no bull around to keep a calf on the way, milk cow likely go dry next few weeks or so."

"We keep regular milkin's, keep her giving milk as long as possible, hope she don't dry up 'til Sarah starts making enough for the baby." He finished off his cup of chicory. "If there's a need, I'm up behind those big oaks where the Trace forks."

"There be a tin of buttermilk, chicken jerky, a few cracklins." Bessie handed him the knapsack. "Other tin be the rest of the succory."

He stopped out on the porch, let his eyes meander the moonlit frost dusting the yard and fields; in the east the sky turned deep purple-black. From her kitchen window Bessie watched him ride off ramrod straight in the saddle, remembering her last glimpse of Sam walkin' tall an' just as proud.

Hamilton stayed away from the lanes and roads, cut across a couple of miles of waist-high weeded fields before turning toward the river. Daylight was coming fast. A lone morning star winked like a solitaire diamond. Just above treetops, low inky blues, the underbellies of high wispy-nothing broom-tail clouds showed faint streaks of the coming sunburnt oranges. As though made just for him, tranquil daybreaks his favored times of day. He nudged the mare's flank with one knobbed spur, moved her up into the trees, nigh to invisible among the shrouds of Spanish moss. Nothing about this morning felt very tranquil.

Off to his left a squirrel chattered, skittered up the trunk of the nearest pine, a covey of quail whirred into the air, and a cottontail wood rabbit froze in the dry grass. As he crossed the low Big Creek bridge, a peppery wren darted in and out, fussing at horse and rider. He stopped back in the scrub brush short of the clearing and dismounted with the reins in his hand. There'd be no hobbling the mare today in case he needed to *git* in a hurry. From where he stood he could see the expanse of the river, pick up any barges or flatbottoms that didn't belong. He checked up and down the Trace, toward the fork where it left Ingram land to join the Queensborough road, and walked on down toward where Josiah sat next to a big tree up the hill a good piece from the Trace.

Josiah heard him, looked up, as Hamilton asked, "Seen anything?"

"Ole man Heberrer's wagon early this morning."

"Bessie's got you a hot meal waitin'."

Josiah climbed on his mule and disappeared into the underbrush.

Hamilton settled under the shade of the tree. Mid-morning, two lone riders came down the Trace. They didn't look army to him, but there was an air about them. Along onto an hour later, a wagon rolled passed, heading south, heaped with paltry belongings. A young boy reined the skin-and-bones horse and mule, as two doleful men walked alongside. They plodded past, never spotting Hamilton. Right about noon two Confederate Cavalry officers galloped passed, riding hard, slobber frothing the bridles and bits of their horses.

It wasn't long before a column of ragged men in missed-matched uniforms shuffled into view, two mounted officers leading. Hamilton couldn't tell whether their stripes on their uniforms were red or yellow, but what he did see struck him like nothing before. On a staff braced from one saddle, the slight morning breeze lifted the tattered standard. During three bloody years, he'd never seen the Confederacy's red, white and blue square infantry flag with its intrepid cross saultoir. He felt a gutty pride for these depleted, dogged men, wanted to say to them how proud he was, how much they were owed. As the column shuffled closer, a stiffer gust whipped full-out the shell-and-shot torn banner, flaring its defiant red.

Out into the sunshine, he walked to the side of the road, pulled himself straight, raised his hand, and saluted these soldiers of a mangled army. He knew some of them must be worried about homes and loved ones. He held his salute as they passed, wondering if they were hungry or wounded or hadn't slept. One mounted officer tipped his hat, returned Hamilton's salute, then looked straight ahead.

A cloud of dust trailed their going down the Trace and out of sight, and Hamilton's arm slowly came down. He wiped away wet streaks left by heartache tears for a wounded army in a wounded cause. He wondered where they'd marched from and the fight they were marching toward and how many would be alive when the fighting stopped.

Back at his post behind the oaks, it wasn't long before the Trace crowded up with a hodgepodge mishmash of wagons and carts, moving away from Augusta. As he silently watched, it seemed the whole of the parish was on the move. His thoughts jarred by the hurried plunge of a rider coming toward him through the canebrake. He dropped to one knee, his rifle to the ready, just as Nat an one of Ben's mules busted into the clearing.

Nat hauled up, slid off the mule. "Mister Ben said to git the word to you, Yankie patrols spotted this side of Sandersville. They burnin' ever'thing, barns, houses, killin' what they don't take. Tearin' Jericho out'a ever'thing they git their hands to."

Hamilton grabbed his mare's reins, pulled into the saddle. "Get back to the Bends. Tell Ben you found me, and Nat—keep a sharp eye out. Advance lookouts could be anywhere."

Hamilton nudged the mare faster. Wind whistled in his ears,

low hanging limbs slashed his sweaty face, horses' hooves flinging clods high behind him. Yankies moving that fast wouldn't ask questions; they'd burn, move on, Sarah and their child be refugees like the pitiful wagons he'd seen. He reined up next to the porch, his horse skidding as he swung out of the saddle.

Bessie was on the front porch. "See you comin' fast." Pistol in her hand, she threw quick glance out across the fields. "Nat find you?"

"Yeh, he's on his way to let Ben know, they might be making a wide sweep into Augusta from this side."

"Missy's cramps reg'lar, an' you be the only help. Yankie or no Yankie, Missy an' that chil' in her belly need both of us."

"If it's their main bunch they'll have bummers way ahead of their army."

"Lordy mercy, nobody gonna stop that 'ceptin' the Lord." Bessie shoved her pistol deep in her pocket. "Don't matter how many trompin' 'bout, ain't nobody gittin' twixt me'n Missy an' her chil'. When the Lord say that baby come, fightin' gonna wait, but Jehovah sure gonna have a handful."

"I'll keep watch out by the barns."

Bessie started inside and stopped. "Maybe watchin' from the barn ain't the best next thing. Mistress Corinth'a be upset we don't let her know her grandchil' comin' so she can come help. When she do, young Benjamin alone in that big house settin' there all big an' white. You knows what I means—Yankies cain't miss it. Bein' hot-headed he won't budge, an' now ain't the time for bein' spiteful 'bout which soldiers got the most bullets—git shot dead. You'n me both know how that cut down Mistress Corinth'a."

"Might be best to get Mother Greer here while we can," said Hamilton fighting his own fear.

"If Mistress Corinth'a come, she best while it daylight. Missy's cramps likely won't be reg'lar for a spell. 'Fore things git busy, time is now to hotfoot over there, an' git back here quick-like."

"Tell Papa where I'm headed."

"Don't need tellin' Mister Rundell, he been up 'fore daybreak, his gun primed and ready. We manage...you make double-sure your butt git back here in one piece." Shook her head, "Sweet Lord...what a mixed-up world you bringin' this chil' into."

Hamilton was into the saddle. Gave the mare her head, didn't bother with gates, jumped the fences, pushed her to a full-out gallop. He stayed clear of the Trace, cleared hedgerows and fences, splashed through slough bogs. Before he realized it, he burst through a squatter's camp, scattering pots, pans, campfires, ramshackle shelters, and stampeded several horses. Startled poachers reached for rifles. He spurred the mare and disappeared into the brush, leaving them with nothing to aim at. Racing faster, he finally caught glimpses of the white unperturbed columns of the Bends. As he came out onto the wide buggy road to the main house, he gave a quick glance behind. Made sure no one was on his tail.

16

Hamilton slowed the horse to a trot and swung out of the saddle as Ben stepped out of the front door, a rifle in his hands. "Heard shots. Sure glad to see it was you clearing those trees. Already had a bead on you. That sister of mine'd have my hide if I put a hole in your backside."

"Can't say I'd fancy that much myself." His smile faded. "Ran up on squatters down by the creek. Was them shooting. Surprised them as much as myself when I busted through."

"They been comin' in there over the last few weeks. I been keeping an eye on 'em, on occasion letting 'em see me with my rifle, make sure they know I'm keepin' track of them. For the most part they've let things be. Now an' then two or three've crossed back of the barns a few times."

"How's Mother Greer?"

"She's well. Come on in."

"Hamilton..." Corinthia hugged him. "It seems ages since I've seen you." The careworn lines of her face deeper, her plain cotton dress neat and pressed. She said, "How's Sarah comin' along?"

"Sarah's starting labor. Bessie says there's no problems, but you know how Bessie gets when it comes to her Missy."

"That's not what you came to say," her face pleasant, her voice, as always, reassuring.

With a hangdog look. "You're right," Hamilton admitted. "Sarah cain't be moved, I was thinking..." Not liking what he was about to say, he spit it out, "The situation being like it is, Mother Greer, it might be best if we all were together."

Her expression didn't change. "Yes, I see..."

Ben glanced back and forth between the two, then said, "Mama, you go. Sarah might need you."

"Ben..." Hamilton gulped hold of the grittiest breath he could grab, and said, "If patrols show up, start nosing around here, I know how you are. They's no way one man'll stop them, much less hold 'em off. There." The two looked at one another in the tight silence. "I didn't like sayin' that, but it's said."

Ben's eyes bored a hole through Hamilton, shuffled his feet, shifted a determined white-knuckled grip on his rifle. "I *won't* back off. Not as long as I'm drawin' a breath. It'd be like inviting Yankies to do as they please, and what they didn't steal, squatters taggin' behind them pickin' up their leavin's."

A pale Corinthia gave a fearful look at her son. "There's little we can do about what we face." Her heart sorrowed for him, knowing there'd be killing, Ben squaring off against other mothers' sons, Hamilton as well if he was in earshot.

Hamilton prayed he could get through to Ben. "Soldiers see you with a weapon, bullets'll fly all over the place with damn little to stop them, then ask questions later. They already crossed the bridges on the Milledgeville road west of here...spreading out, most with no officers."

"Raiders." Ben's words came between clenched teeth.

A frightful dread filled Hamilton. He couldn't leave Sarah, yet if the armies swung this way Ben was certain to end up dead trying to keep them from the house.

"Ben, listen to me," Hamilton begged. "Places like the Bends stick out like ever tale they've been told about us. It'll draw 'em like flies...our place as well. You give 'em the excuse to take out their hate, you end up dead, they've killed a proud name your father gave to you. Time's facing us when we have to bend 'stead of break. Yankies already took enough from our families, you gonna give them reason to do more?"

Ben swallowed at the lump in his throat. "Take Mama with you."

Corinthia spoke softly, "No." Her calm eyes an inflexible ice-blue. "I love Sarah, and I want more than anything to hold my grandbaby, but I love you just as much, and right now your need is more pressing. I won't go and leave you here by yourself, knowing what insufferable things you might be facing."

"Goddammit!" Hamilton grabbed Ben by the shoulders. "We've grieved enough for those we've lost! You start shootin' you're asking for them to torch the Bends. Don't make the rest of this family have to sorrow over your smoking carcass shot full of bullets."

"Won't be nothing left," he said heavy-hearted. "They might kill me, but no goddamn sons'a Yankie thieves are stomping through what my family worked their whole lives to have. They sure 'nough'll have to kill me first."

"One more dead Reb won't bother them." Hamilton was in Ben's face. "They get hero medals for doing that. You gonna stand there and tell me you're dumb enough to give them an excuse to do what they want to do?"

The First Lady of Wisteria Bends let her eyes sweep around the room, as though saying goodby to a loved one, garnering a lifetime of remembrances, closeting those keepsake times close to her heart.

Then, with a mother's way of softening a son's brittle, demanding honor, so to not let it cost more than it had already taken from her, she quietly said, "Sarah can't be moved here and shouldn't be. I'll go with Hamilton." With her hand this mother ever so caring lightly brushed Ben's manly cheek like those many times when he was a child, upset at some childish thing. "And I want you to come with us."

His watery eyes were pain-filled. "Mama..."

With her fingers gently against his lips, Corinthia stopped his words, then kissed his cheek. "What little surety we have is one another. Your father was so proud the way you'd handled things. He wouldn't want your life thrown away."

"He died for what he believed." A frustrated Ben felt cornered.

Tears pooled her eyes. "Yes, he did, but not like this. Your father died fighting because he felt it necessary in a cause lost long before all this pointless bloodshed began. He and I spoke of it his last time home. He knew the war was lost, but what concerned him most was how it was to affect all of us. He arranged your discharge from the Queensborough volunteers, not to leave you behind or shield you from harm, but to know while he was away someone he trusted...you...would be here."

"Why didn't he tell me?" His quiet tears matching hers.

"Because there was little else he could do and live with himself. That was the sort of man I fell in love with. Your father knew how strongly I disagreed with events. How misguided honor allowed those criminals in Washington City back us into the error of secession which I considered nothing more than an underhanded scheme of avaricious radicals South and North. Regardless, as his wife it was my place to support my husband, and I lost him to a struggle he felt honor-bound to contend. Honor is not easily held, sometimes demanding a great deal of those we love. If it were otherwise it would be of no value. But, I refuse to sit idle with your remaining here accomplishing nothing except the forfeit of your life...no...not this way, such a waste is honor misplaced."

Silence intruded among them like a ravenous ghost. "Sarah may need all of us to help to bring my gran'chil' into this disquieted world. I'd rather do most anything than leave this home so filled with your father." She ever so gently brushed a curl of Ben's thick black Irish hair. "But our staying—your staying—makes Hamilton choose between you and Sarah, possibly leaving Sarah and her baby facing a future with both of you lost to us." Her unshakable Gresham-Greer composure never wavering, she said, "Benjamin, this gran'chil', this family, we need both of you, we need each other more than ever. I don't wish to think on anything happening to Sarah or her baby when we might've helped. My wonderful stubborn son...your father was so proud of you, as am I, but we truly have no choice." She stiffened slightly, her patrician chin high, and with a pleasant face, said, "I'll gather a few things we might have need of."

Hamilton said, "We don't want to be on the road after sundown."

"Most certainly not," Corinthia agreed.

"Run off our own land by a hoard of vandals," a red-faced Ben swallowed hard. "I cain't stand the shame of turning tail an' running, when—"

"Dammit Ben, it's got nothing to do with running," Hamilton stormed. "You're one of the best chess players I've ever crossed pawns with. Moving a bishop or knight out of danger so you can use it later is no different from what General Lee does. Unstick that ramrod Greer pride from your craw. Sarah and Mother Greer are more important. Besides, there's not a helluva lot any of us can do except make the bunch of them more vengeful than they already are."

Ben fought the feeling of helplessness. "A man's got to stand up for hisself."

"That's not a bad thing to fight for, but it's damn well not the best of choices if you're outgunned and outnumbered. Didn't you understand anything Papa Andrew was trying to say in his last letter?"

"What letter?" Corinthia stood at the stairway landing, a deathly ashen look on her face.

Ben had that *caught* look like a kid caught doing mischief, as Hamilton heaved a long breath, and said, "Papa Andrew wrote a letter the night before he was killed."

Her lips pressed thin, she quietly replied, "And you both decided I was far too fragile to know of it."

"It was already open when it got here," Ben added, reached in his pocket, handed the stained envelope to his mother. "I didn't want you upset more than you already were."

"Times were bad enough," Hamilton said. "Wasn't only Ben's doing, Sarah don't know about it either. Maybe we shouldn't..."

"No, you shouldn't've." Her eyes pained. "You two figure

I'm some China butterfly unable to bear such unpleasantry?"

She held the letter, and without opening it her fingers affectionately smoothed it, lingering at the stains. Her eyes closed she smothered it to her bosom and murmured, "Oh, Andrew...my sweet dear Andrew," as though he could hear. "I think of you so very often. I miss you so."

"Mother Greer, I'm sorry."

Without opening it she folded the envelope and tucked it close to her heart. "I've only a few more things." Her soft steps fading up the grand staircase. "I shan't be long."

"I ain't going." Ben said it almost like an oath.

"Shut up and get your coat," Hamilton snapped.

"Don't tell me to shut up under my own roof," Ben flared.

"You're tearin' your mother between those she loves. Papa Andrew's death eats at my papa ever livelong day, 'specially knowing the dying's not finished, not by a long shot. God knows I been dumb enough for both of us about a lot of things, but what in hell you hope to accomplish staying here? You think you're Moses parting the sea, hold up your hand an' stop a Pharaoh's Billy Yank army? Me'n you together be no more nuisance than a feather in a hail storm. That's been beyond the doing for our ragtag army long before Papa Andrew was lost."

"I don't care." Defeat ripped at Ben.

"Yes, you do, or it wouldn't be eatin' you like it is. I'm asking 'cause I want us as safe as we can git, together is better than alone. With Papa doin' poorly, we're the only ones the others can depend on. It's hard my asking, but it's hardest for Mother Greer. This is the home your father was took from." He started out the French doors. "I'll get the teams harnessed, the carriages ready."

He quick-timed across the wide backyard to the barns, into tack rooms, passed the empty stalls to the paired grays. He buckled and snapped harnesses, noticed Ben had kept their unshod hooves filed. He tightened straps, checked doubletree and swingletrees, the buggy wheels, suspension, backed in the team, and hitched 'em up. The dusty lacquer of the carriage reminded him of Mother Greer's dress. For Hamilton, the Bends had always been everything proper, nothing less than spit-and-polish. He climbed up, took the reins, the elegant leather-top carriage rolled out of the carriage house, spider webs tangled topsy-turvy in the spokes. He swung around to the porte-cochère carriage entrance, his eyes roaming the time-honored sweep of massive white columns. The house seemed bathed in a hazy halflight, as though sad it was being left empty.

Corinthia met him at the porte-cochère entrance. "Hamilton, upstairs is a frightfully heavy steamer trunk of warm clothes I packed some time ago. Could you and Ben bring it down?"

"We'll get it loaded." He started inside.

"Hamilton…" She lightly took his arm. "It isn't right of me to burden you with what I'm about to say. You and Ben are brothers in all but blood, and with my gran'chil' you are that now as well. He looks up to you, is so pleased when you approve of something he's done, listens to you more than you know, emulates your abounding confidence."

"I'm not that confident."

"Neither are any of us. But that shall be my an' your secret." Corinthia gave him her soft winning smile that warmed the moment. "His grief for his father comes with a terrible helplessness at seeing all his father built falling apart, and being completely unable to do anything about it, seeing it as having failed his father. Our knowing that's not true doesn't help how he feels. No one could've done better, but the heart often refuses what the head tells it."

"After Sumter, if we'd lost that contention at Manassas Junction or failed in some of our earlier audaciousness, perhaps the war would've found a stopping point, and what we're facing might've never come to be."

The scrape of the trunk dragged toward the upstairs landing broke the moment. Hamilton called up, "Hold up, Ben," and he hurried up the mahogany stairs. "Let me give you a hand."

Without the usual blazing fireplace, there was a chill about Mother Greer's rooms. He and Ben grunted and wrestled the heavy trunk down the stairs, through the porte-cochère and onto the carriage.

"Weighs a ton," Ben said, dusted his hands, quickly added, "I won't be long."

Sensing Ben wanted to be alone, Hamilton watched him disappear back inside.

Minutes later Ben came out, red eyes dry, firmly shut the doors behind him with a solid thud. "Y'all go ahead. I'll fetch the gelding and the mare and catch up."

Hamilton climbed up next to a serene Mother Greer and the carriage moved off down the drive. Corinthia never looked back.

.

Ben caught up with them as they turned onto the Trace and into the trudging multitudes.

"Merciful heavens, such mournful wretches," Corinthia said, her heart going out to the hollow, gaunt faces. "And I was feeling poorly about our situation. They look as though they've been on the road for days."

Hamilton said, "Some probably longer."

She looked at clusters of twos and threes, some with children, spilling across the fields, sitting by the side of the road, in ditches, under trees, huddled with what pitiful belongings they'd managed to keep together.

"I'm glad Andrew was spared this deplorable sight," she said. "It would've been so frightfully distressing to him..." Her words trailed away.

Ben and Hamilton were on their guard, kept the phaeton and horses together. With eventide closing about them, light fading, they took the fork onto Ingram land and left most of the crowds behind.

An anxious Bessie met the carriage. "Sakes alive, sure glad seein' y'all be out of that mess on the Trace. Never hear of so many aimless wanderin' souls. Hamilton been gone so long it had me fearful worried. They's a hot meal ready an' waitin'."

As they unloaded, Hamilton told Josiah, "Go tell Nat to get on back. From the despairing looks on some of those faces, it's best we stay close in."

It was a quiet supper. No one talked much. No one had much of an appetite.

As Hamilton stoked the parlor fireplace to a steady crackle, Sarah eased out of her chair. "I think I'll turn in."

Bessie went with Sarah. By the time Bessie came back, Corinthia had the dishes washed, and the table set for breakfast.

•

During the night a heavy frost blanketed a still night, making it even stiller. Between fretful catnaps everyone was unsettled, Rundell not the only one who didn't sleep. Rifle cradled across his lap and hunched in a chair pulled next to the window, Rundell leaned on the sill for another look-see, his eyes hardly moved away from the frosted yard glowing under a bright full moon.

"Figured you'd be up." Bessie moved quietly next to him. "Brung you an extra sweater an' blanket so you don't catch a chill. Whole house astirrin'...the dead be stalkin' here'bouts." Her eyes were big, spooked.

"I feel it too," he said.

"Haints be on the move. Givin' me chilblegens all under. Dead aught'a stay put." she cast her eyes into the dark. "Cain't nobody sleep nary a whit, not this ghosty night."

"Bright moon." Rundell let the curtain drop. "How's Sarah doin'?"

"Toler'ble well. You be a Grandpa 'fore long."

"Bessie, what we gonna do if Sherman comes this way, burns the roof over our heads?" He fixed his gaze back out into the hoarfrost night. "Sarah and her baby cain't be out in this weather."

"Ain't much doin' left in our hands no more," Bessie whispered. "As for puttin' fire to this place." She gave a fierce look. "Any hand what's lifted agin this precious baby needin' a roof gonna have Bessie Mae smack in their face 'fore they can whistle a *Yankee Doodle*."

Rundell jerked back from the window sill. "Stay back!" he hissed. "Somebody yonder alongside the barn. Snuck behind them trees." The click of him cocking the hammer was loud in the breathless dark. "Caught a glint off what looked to be a rifle. Ease up front, let the boys know."

"I gittin'." Bessie moved swift in the shadows of the dogtrot hall.

In no time Hamilton appeared at Rundell's shoulder. "See anything else?" His eyes searched the frosty areas between the house and barns.

"Come this away." Rundell pointed, "Turned toward the back of the house."

"Ben's by himself back there," Hamilton said. "I'd best get back to him."

Hamilton found Ben crouched, the door cracked a bare slit, his muzzle tip right at the jamb, cocked and ready.

"See anything?"

"Just the one..." There was an edgy quiver to Ben's voice. "Can't be only one."

"Could be any uniform taken off a dead soldier, or a scout, one of those bummers I scattered down by the creek. If it's bummers they wouldn't be just one," Hamilton whispered.

"There..." Ben steadied his rifle, a kill-look set to his face. "...Yankie uniform alright. I saw the glint off the buttons."

Sights dead-on the shadowy figure creeping onto the back porch, Ben's finger steady tight on his hair-trigger, aiming his first shot to be a kill. Bessie with her pistol, was taking hard look-sees out the other window.

Hamilton braced near the door. "Mother Greer's with Sarah. I'm gonna check up front, make sure they aren't suckering us back here for a rush ambush through the front. Whoever's out there could be tryin' to find out how many guns we have in here, or tryin' to lure us to coming outside."

"Make sure nobody goes pokin' around outside," Ben cautioned. "Be a sure way for you to get shot by one of us." His sights stayed steady on the dark figure. "Whoever this sneaky bastard is, he's a dead man if he tries making it inside."

The crouched figure took a step nearer, halted at the squeak of the porch board. Ben's eyes narrowed, breath held, finger snug, pounding heart, death ready and waiting.

Ben whispered, "Bessie, your pistol ready?"

"Ain't gettin' by me." Bessie set to do what needed doin'.

The door hinges creaked. A shadowy shape backlit by moonlight, a hand at the end of a uniformed arm wedged the door a bit more open a mite.

Out of the darkness Ben growled, "You got several guns on you. Keep your hands right where I can see both of them. You quiver one more twitch, you're dead."

The figure froze as Ben demanded, "You got thieving business or you wouldn't be sneakin' around like we been watchin'."

"*Benjamin?*"

"Samuel!" Bessie cried out.

"Be goddamn." Ben lowered his rifle.

"Don't nobody shoot!" Bessie rushed passed Ben. "It be Sam!" She flung her arms around Sam, pistol still in her hand. "Lord Jesus brung my boy home!" She kissed his face, tears streaming, then pushed him back, glared at him, consternation mixed with vexation. "Why you so stump-dumb comin' quiet-like up on a house in the dark. Askin' Mister Death to put a bullet hole in your aggervatin' hide. If'n I wadn't so glad-hearted to see your sorry face, I'd whack you a good one betwixt the ears."

Lamps lit at Bessie's shout. Everyone crowded around, talking at once, all happy to see Sam—except Ben.

"Where you come from?" Ben scowled at Sam's blue coat. "How'd you get here?" He went to the window. "More night-sneaking Bluebellies out there waitin' for you to get us off our guard so they can bust in?"

"They'll git here soon enough." Sam looked toward the windows. "I wouldn't be in no big rush for them neither." He looked to his mama. "I stopped by the Bends. Nobody there, place was wide open. Only place you'd be was here."

"Yankies send their bootlickin' runaway back here?" Ben's bitterness spilled loose. "Get you to scout bridges and roads, then run tattle to your new masters?"

"Benjamin, you forget yourself." Corinthia clasped a shawl tight against the chill. "We're under Ingram roof."

"Yankies were my doin'," Sam flung at Ben. "Even if'n the doin' of it was a mistake."

"Sons-a-bitches killed Papa," Ben's pent-up sense of betrayal burst out. "Still killin' good men!"

"Gray's done its share of killin'," Sam spoke back, fierce.

"Kill ever damn foot-stompin' one of 'em!" Ben yelled. "We're not the ones doing the invadin'! Burning, stealing, driving families out into the winter with no place to go."

"Benjamin! Samuel!" Corinthia reproached. "Both of you stop this very minute before you say things you'll regret."

"Ain't saying what's not gospel fact," Ben spit.

"Sam, why did you leave? You must've known it was better stayin' home." Hamilton was anguished more than angry

"This wasn't home, not like you mean when you say *home*," Sam hung his head. "...For me'n Mama it was just a place to sleep an' eat."

"...Samuel!" Bessie grieved by the hurtful pangs bein' flung, knowed she no more upset than Mistress Corinth'a.

Sam's eyes were full of sadness. "Hamilton, how could you understand? Growin' up, ever' place I turn it be in my face. Even carin' ones, growin' up with you an' Benjamin, Mister Rundell, the Greers , y'all be the best I ever knowed, way better'n what else I saw, but so used to it you see it without seein'. You look right through it, an' don't see."

"Sam, we saw, lots'a folks saw, but most didn't see a way out."

"I reknen," Sam sighed. "What comin' sure easy to see now."

Shrapnel-raw edges slid between Sam and Ben as Sam turned to Corinthia. "I'm sorry to hear 'bout Mister Andrew."

Ben snarled, "Not sorry enough to stop you siding with his killers."

"He was a good man," said Sam, trying to ignore Ben. "I'm glad all y'all be alright."

"We're not alright!" Ben blared. "If we were we'd be in our own home instead of protectin' Sarah from the likes of bein' burned out."

"That's the reason I had to find Mama. We all got t'git."

"What's this *we* bit?" Ben was harsh. "They ain't no *we* here that includes you."

Sam cut his eyes toward Ben, then back to Corinthia. "I seen what Sherman does."

"You and others like you helping Sherman's hooligan soldiers burn towns, burn farms," Ben accused. "Don't sound much like soldiering to me, sounds like trash stealin' what they're too lazy to work for."

"Never seem to bother you livin' in your big house, wearin' new clothes, while others haul your cotton," Sam flung back. "'Sides, Rebs doin' plenty burnin', blamin' Sherman lots he don't order."

"I don't see him doing much to stop it." Ben was surly. "Leavin' nothing onct he's passed."

The words stabbing dreadful consternation into Hamilton. "It's too dangerous to move Sarah. The crowded roads are no safe place for her to be."

"Ain't nobody movin' Missy," Bessie gave a unyielding shake of her head. "Ain't no discussin' to it. That the way it be."

"Mama, you cain't stay," Sam pleaded.

"Milledgeville as bad as they say?" Hamilton asked.

Sam said, "I saw some of the torchin'."

"Good ol' Sam..." Ben said, scornful. "All he did was watch."

"Wasn't Union what torched the courthouse." Sam pulled out a chair, sat down next to the washstand. "Was lowlifes what lived 'roundabout, makin' sure land records went up in smoke. Carryin' on how with deeds gone, rich folks' land was up for grabs. That's what's comin' down on you."

"Running won't change that," Hamilton said. "Staying put here's as good a place as any to face what's coming."

"Mama..." Tears filled Sam's eyes. "You don't got to stay. I seen 'em herd runaways and freeborn in pens like we're animals."

"Samuel..." Bessie added, "You ought'a know better'n try t'git me leave'n Missy. Be like tryin' to make me turn from you, from any my chirren. Long as the Lord give this body life, any hand laid agin Missy or her baby ketch it from me. I ain't stayin' 'cause I have to. I love Missy much as I does you. Of ever'one here, you the one best see how runnin' make a problem worser."

"Ain't only Sherman's army. They's hordes trailin' them, bummers, pickin' over the army leavin's. Soldiers stand by lettin' 'em take what they want."

"Dear God..." Corinthia steeled herself.

Ben glowered. "Be plenty of 'em dead they come round here."

Sam dragged his uniform kepi off, dropped his head into his hand. "Dear God, what we all brung on ourselves?" his run-or-stay tussle turning way worse, as much a part of this, as ever'one here. With a pleading look, he said, "Mama, them soldiers don't care whether we slave or free. To them we all the same. Makin' promisin's what sound godly, then forgets us quick as they can."

"Me'n Hamilton tried telling you," Ben said. "You think we was lying, or you just too bone-headed to hear?"

"The bone-headed I learnt likely from you," Sam fired back. "But what' else did a body do, ignore bein' slave? Some of us whupped an' beaten."

Ben's ire rose fresh. "Papa never held with that."

"No," Sam admitted. "But you know it went on in woodsheds an' cabins on plenty other plantations." He turned to Bessie. "Mama, I cain't stay."

"What you sayin' you cain't stay?" Bessie frowned. "Ain't no one here call the law on you or runnin' you off. Marse Andrew seen to that."

Sam let out a sad sigh. "I left their army so to make it here ahead of 'em."

"A deserter..." Ben jabbed. "Cain't stick out nothin' you set out to do."

"I'm sick of your damn whitey's war," Sam exploded.

"Samuel!" Bessie blurted. "Ain't no call for sech foul mouthin'."

"A man's gotta admit his mistakes. Runnin' was one I made, runnin' North even worse. Learnt quick Yankies say one thing, do another."

Ben said, "'Specially after Papa gave you freedom papers."

"Bein' free didn't belong to your papa, wadn't his to give, was mine to have. You say it like he done a favor, like you throw crumbs to a bunch'a chickens. blood killin' blood, gittin' medals for the doin'. Most here'bouts call it slave to your face. I seen holy-talkin' abolitionists pocketin' war profits, then hightail for cover, when times turn rough. One'a them fools what believed all that talk was me. Home be home no matter what. Benjamin, your papa an' Mister Rundell saw lots'a things, didn't see eye to eye on what to do 'bout them. Me'n you the same. Ain't no way we ever look at this the same." Sam tapped his smudged blue coat. "Ain't what this Blue or your Gray say. Now it us facin' the manglin' an' killin' guns."

"There's plenty fools to go around," sweat beaded Hamilton's forehead. "You're free 'cause boneheads stuck their head in the dirt, refused to see how slavery hurt us way beyond what it cost. Those same pencil-necked boneheads preferred to fight instead of bullets and blood just forcing it sooner. Lives and land tore up worse than Kansas. Hunger, outlaws, and hate like I never seen."

"Samuel, Marse Andrew give me'n you papers, give us land. Benjamin done the same for the others. You a poleaxed mule not seein' what was here."

"Mama, it easy to see I run smack into a stone wall."

Hamilton asked, "Federals know you deserted?"

"Cain't see how not. Word come down how Augusta was gettin' troops from Carolina. Camp talk was Sherman didn't hanker another runnin' railroad fight like from Chickamauga, an' that's about the time we got orders to git ready to move out towards Waynesboro and the rail junction at Millen. I knowed right then y'all sit square in the middle." Sam took a deep breath, a dreadful silence settling about them. Finally he said, "Ben, I'm glad you ain't at the Bends. One man wouldn't matter to them. They wouldn't waste the time. Do what they been doin'. Roll up a cannon, blow the house to splinters, burn what was left, an' march right on."

Hamilton said, "Sam, you need some different clothes. I got some things that might fit. They find you with that uniform…"

"They shoot me."

"I'm surprised you didn't get shot between here and Atlanta. Black skin in blue worse'n copperhead poison to both sides."

"Some folks tried. I never seen hate 'fore the war like I see in some eyes. Like we some kind of biblical plague."

"To some you are. How a uniform got to be reason for killing is one more thing nobody give much thought about."

"Eats…" A tight-lipped Bessie sliced cold cuts and baked ham, didn't like this talk. "Killin' got to stop. Too many black an' white lickspittles what don't care." She shoved the platter in front of Sam.

"*Mmm*…" Sam gulped down a big slice. "Hadn't had no good home cookin'…"

"You looks it, too," Bessie gruffed. "Scrawny as last year's scarecrow...now eats."

Bessie brought more. Sam wolfed it down as howling night winds set tree limbs screaking across the roof.

Hamilton came in with an armload of clothes and stacked them in a chair. "These ought to fit."

Between bites Sam said, "Hamilton, it's bad."

Hamilton pulled up a chair next to Sam, "Paper out of New Orleans claims Washington City is passing lots of new laws, homestead and railroad acts. Promising free land to settlers, lands treatied to Indians."

"Your papa never held with bondage." Sam forked another thick slab of ham. "Still, like lots'a folk, sometimes you had a way of not seein'."

"Wasn't so much he didn't see, was more hope there'd be a change, let the Hollows show how a plantation didn't need chattels to make it work. As Kansas got worse, Papa saw time was closing in on ever'one. Big slave holders weren't in the mood to see slavery done away with. Abolitionists were right about slavers pushing hard to expand the trade, but both sides stirring politics egged turmoil and tempers," Hamilton shook his head. "Papa once sat down with Papa Andrew, showed him on paper where he could save money, how farms hiring hands 'stead of buying them were gaining ground, using money not spent buyin' slaves to buy more acreage. How even with Texas opening up, slaver farms were facing bust."

Sam said, "Time he spent hopin' meant misery for slaves."

"Not as much than what's happening now, slaves, owners, families that never owned slaves, the killed and wounded, we have anything left when this is over, it'll be a miracle. When Papa Andrew learnt you'd run, it pained him fierce. Wasn't so much your doin' that was so troubling as much as what the law'd do to you if they caught you."

"Never had money 'cept what the army paid, but it seems money causes more problems'n it settles."

"It does if you let it. A goodly number of folks see homes and farms burnin', see their whole future gone. Some never get loose from the pain."

Grief come sad over Sam's face. "Sure thankful I warn't at Fredericksburg. That it wadn't my bullet what might'a took Marse Andrew."

"Your being in blue let another Union trooper be at Fredericksburg to fire that bullet—plenty blame to shuffle 'round."

A travel-worn look came across Sam's face. "Like them stories Mistress Corinth'a used to tell us in the evenin's. Us kids would crowd around her on the floor. She'd tell tales about long ago. One I never forgot...some guy called MacBeth. Another was two lovers, a young squirt an' his sweetheart, their families dead set agin it."

Hamilton smiled. "I can see Mother Greer telling those same stories to her grandkids."

For the first time in a long while, Sam's eyes sparkled with good times they'd shared. "Seems like a whole other life."

"Gonna take a heap of understanding with folks like me'n you, who care about one another. Easy to see how the milk got spilt, but facing a body's errens is way better'n repeating 'em."

17

The mottled wintry night was breaking towards morning as Sam leaned back and patted his stomach. "They's plenty," Bessie at his elbow with a fresh fried skillet of chitlins. "You knows how happy I is you is in one piece."

Hamilton sat down next to Sam. "Bitter bones and deep poison's being sowed. Sadder is some Southrons will pit Yankie-hate against blacks." Hamilton reached for the pot on the stove, poured him and Sam tins of steaming chicory, and sat down. "Bessie means to stay with Sarah. Papa wouldn't hear of leavin'. Had I taken the women south, Ben offered to stay with Papa 'til I got back."

"Down around Selma an' Mobile, you'd likely've run into more refugees than you saw comin' out of Augusta. Word was Union forces was movin' up from Mobile."

Hamilton shook his head. "No way to tell what's coming."

Sam pushed back, went to the kitchen window, stared far off into the coming dawn. Ben came in, said nothing.

Daylight brightened. Pine tree turpentine mixed with warm Gulf of Mexico moisture to thicken the morning haze and dingy gray clouds. Hamilton and Ben leaned on the back porch handrail where they'd once contested who could tiddlywinks watermelon seeds the farthest. A pea soup lowland ground haze billowed cornstalk-high apparitions across the back yard, the foggy mist settling in low spots, drifting toward the creek—a powerful foulness riding with it.

Hamilton sniffed as Sam joined them on the porch. "Heaviness to the air...smell's terrible."

"More things dead than a body'd believe 'til you sees it. Hogs, chickens, mules, horses, anything they cain't take, nothin' left alive," Sam said. "Smell so thick it sticks to your skin, gits in your clothes. Sometimes I think I never be rid from it. Ain't only dead animals," he stared into the distance "burnin' barns, smokehouses, chimneys pokin' to the sky where roofs once been, whole world burnin' at the same time. Trees cut down, stacked, rails heated red-hot, twisted around stumps."

They didn't talk much more. As the day wore on, the smoke got thicker, reminding Hamilton of smoldering bog fires. The mingle of burning wood and animals stung his nose and eyes with smells seeming to drift from all directions.

Coming from hiding the horses and cow, Hamilton and Ben stayed to the thick underbrush, away from the roads. Hamilton snorted to clear his nose. "Those far off rumbles aren't thunder."

"Sounds like sporadic cannon fire," added Benjamin.

The two joined Rundell on the porch. "Hard to catch a breath." Rundell gave out a hacky cough.

Ben paced back and forth on the porch, with worried glances in the direction of the corduroy Milledgeville Road. At first the sound was faint, the muffled clank and rattle of harness and teams breaking the heavy stillness. Shuffling ones and twos were the first to appear, then slogging lines emerged through the murk, followed by sleek prancing mounts, bulging saddlebags, silver candlesticks poking out of more than a few. Behind them were the creaking wagons, clanking artillery and ammunition caissons pulled by well-fed hefty teams. Teamsters on ordnance wagons, confiscated farm wagons filled with pillaged spoils, war booty for a wife, a sweetheart, sold or bartered for ready poker ante or whorehouse favors. The more they stole, the more they wanted, locust scouring across fields, lanes, roads. Tents set up around cooking fires fed with fence rails, sidings from barns and outbuildings, fruit trees, hundred year old oaks and elms...part of the old order going up in smoke, part left in the ashes.

As more uniforms filled the yard beyond the front steps, Hamilton gathered everyone in the parlor, except for Sarah. "Guns hid?"

"Wrapped in oilskin, hid behind the kitchen fireplace and under the smokehouse flagstones," Ben said.

"Everybody stay inside," Hamilton ordered. "I'm going out, best to be seen. No matter what, don't make any sudden movements."

Corinthia said, "I'll go with you."

"Mama," Ben stepped in front of her, "they don't care about women or..."

Bessie said, "Mistress Corin'tha, you best not do this. Let me go."

"No," Corinthia said, a set look in her eyes. "We each must do what we can. Sarah might have more need of you than me." The tone of her words and her bearing spoke a farewell, if it came to that.

"Mama, I don't want you out there facing them."

"Ben's right," Sam said. "Them ain't Southern soldiers. They ain't been taught like we was taught."

"Benjamin..." Corinthia softly said his name as she brushed a sooty blotch from his cheek. "My brave warrior, truly your father's son. I've never spoken against either what your father or you wanted. You are strong and solid, but like a great tree in a fierce wind, such trees often break instead of bending. A woman can sometimes dull the fever in a man. Bending is the one thing we women are often good at. Right now the bearing of arms is the one thing we need least of all."

"Lord..." Bessie choked down her fear, quietly praying, "They ever be a time we needs you, now be it."

"Mama, they might shoot," Ben said, more agitated.

"Yes...they might," Corinthia said. "I do so hope not."

Ben said, "I'm gettin' my rifle."

Corinthia stopped him. "Benjamin, you do that, there will be shooting. They'll likely burn the place with us inside."

"They'll be a mess of dead Yankies to answer for it."

"...And your sister and her baby, likely us as well. Ben, be the grown man your father was so proud of. Think what's best."

Boots stomped up the steps, across the porch and a gruff shout, "In the house—open up now!" A pounding fist banging the door again and again.

A pale Corinthia said, "Benjamin, whatever happens, you and Sam must stay inside."

With a last despairing look at each of them, Corinthia accepted their lives were in hands of the Almighty and Sherman's minions.

"Whatever happens, take care of Sarah," Hamilton said.

"Takes care..." whispered Bessie, fear in her eyes. "Missy need both of you."

The door pounded harder. Hamilton and Corinthia exchanged a last reassuring look. He lifted the door latch, and they stepped out to face a Sergeant, flanked by two young sentries.

"I'm Hamilton Ingram," he said. "This is my papa's place."

"How about that," came the bellicose reply. "Here tell this spread has been raising grain, supplying horses and cattle to feed these bushwhacking Rebs. We got orders to stop that. Anyone who resists will be arrested, put in irons, taken with us, so there's none left to shoot us in the back. That what you doing? Hiding Rebs?"

"My father's not hiding, and never was in uniform."

"He one of those with Beauregard at Sumter, then run back here?" There was an exchanged snickers with the two guards. "Funny how all of a sudden there's a scarcity of Rebs down south here. Reckon we killed them all?"

"He's inside...abed." Hamilton didn't flinch at the kill slur. "Take a look if you must. My wife's also abed. She's been in labor since last evening."

"Peculiar kind of farm you got here, can't seem to find any mules or cattle," the Sergeant accused. "Our orders are to confiscate stores, chickens, grain, any cotton...any supplies helpful to

Rebels."

"Didn't plant any cotton these last two years. No way to sell it."

"We're not aiming to buy it," the Sergeant smirked.

Hamilton's lips pressed thin, held his temper, as he felt Mother Greer's grip stiffen ever so slightly on his arm. He knew Ben was listening on the other side of the door, worried what Ben might happen if push came to shove.

Corinthia lowered her head ever so slightly, then with the in-bred dignity and the upbringing of her mother an' grandmother, her eyes rose to face this uncultivated man holding sway over their lives. Dominion in this encounter wasn't unlike what she'd faced before. What she intended held only the slimmest of slim chances. She had nothing to lose, and smiled her most composed of gracious smiles. With an air of the resolute social graces, that obliged respect even from this ruffian, she waited.

The Sergeant didn't take his eyese off her. In the wordless clank of caissons and snorting horses, his lips slightly parted slightly, as though stopped in midsentence. No one spoke.

Hamilton felt his stomach quiver, remembered Mother Greer once saying, "I truly believe things happen as they should, whether we understand or not."

Corinthia was certain that by the grace of the Almighty, her upbringing had readied her for this very moment. Almost second nature, she waited for that momentary lull of fleeting vacillation in a first meeting, and saw the Sergeant's eyes give a slight flicker from her to Hamilton, then back to her.

Corinthia Gresham Greer bent every Southron fiber in her to salvage whatever she could. Deliberately leaned a bit closer to him. As though perplexed, yet curious, she studied the stripes on his uniform. Then pulled up herself ladylike and slightly aloof, gave a gracious smile, and softly asked, "You are a Sergeant?"

"Yeh..." He was baffled at her unexpected question.

"You have me at a disadvantage, Sergeant...?" She waited for him to give his name.

The sentries grew edgy, shuffled their feet, exchanged looks. The Sergeant cleared his throat, sputtered a crusty, "Max-well...Sergeant Maxwell." He pulled himself a bit regulation straighter. "Didn't find any animals in the barn, but we found where feed had been put out," his voice not quite as crusty.

"Sergeant Maxwell," she paused, held out her hand, forced him either to be rude or at the very least polite, "Corinthia Greer."

Even more flustered, he took her offered hand, quickly dropped it, as she continued, "I do wish we were meeting under more amiable circumstances. Sergeant, it's our only cow. Since we've hardly sufficient hay or feed to keep her giving milk, we let her out to graze whenever possible."

He looked away, snickered, then said, "Then you've likely already lost your cow to the men scouring these parts."

"That would be quite unfortunate. My daughter's inside birthing my second grandchild. She lost the first one last year. I'm sure you understand how all this confusion might disturb her, which certainly is no help in her having enough milk for her baby. Without the cow, the child could suffer something fierce. Sergeant, surely one milk cow cain't be that important." Without no hesitation she suggested, "It might avoid considerable confusion if you might spare a couple of men to fetch the cow back here?"

Hamilton wasn't one bit surprised at Mother Greer's audacity.

Sergeant Maxwell sure was. Her familiarity confounded the Sergeant, her request even more so. Ever since he first put foot into these secesh lands, such women as this perplexed him. There was no understanding them. He'd seen fear and hate and tears all stirred with an unbudging resolve. Underneath their flighty frills they were stronger than a good number of his battle-hard troopers. As though they never started this, they never lost their calm air of having everything completely under control.

"Mam, I can't spare any men to go looking for your milk cow," he grumbled. "I have my orders."

"Oh, I see, of course not," Corinthia replied ever so pleasant. "How thoughtless of me to make such a request."

A curtain twitched at one window, bringing the rifles of all three to the ready, as he bellowed, "Johnny Rebs inside best come out right now!"

"I assure you, Sergeant," Corinthia glanced toward the window. "There's no soldiers inside. You are the first Northerner some of us have ever seen. Havin' heard so much about you, naturally they're curious."

Lowering his rifle, he looked at her, saying, "Greer?" A gloved hand scratched his whiskers. "Related to a Colonel Greer?"

"He was my husband. Colonel Andrew Greer, he was killed."

"...At Fredericksburg. Lots of good men died there, 'specially at Marye's Heights."

"Too many good men have died, on both sides."

"Most of this company is marching from Queensborough," he said, the back of one hand wiped at the smudge across his face. "Courthouse was burning as we moved out. We tried to keeping the fire from spreading. Don't know we did much good. We was told Colonel Andrew Greer lived around these parts."

With a fleeting thought of what the Whiteheads must be going through, Corinthia said, "My husband was highly thought of."

"That may be, but he had the reputation of being quite the Rebel."

"Gracious sakes alive, of course, Sergeant Maxwell." With unassuming refinement. "My husband was a loyal Georgian, as I'm quite sure you are loyal to where you grew up. Otherwise you wouldn't be in that uniform. One's honor can demand a great deal, don't you agree?"

He muttered, "Wisteria Bends..." Melting sleet dribbled from his eyebrows as his words came through tobacco stained teeth. "Coming from such a big, fine plantation, you bring your slaves with you from your big house?" He tossed a derisive smile toward the others.

"There's no slaves here or back at my home." Corinthia was determined to ignore this ill-mannered ruffian.

Accustomed to being the vanquisher, he was feeling discomfited with this one. Through burning towns and farms he'd met considerable number of hysterical women screaming and moaning, the deeper they tore into this land, the more he saw of these threadbare wives and widows with their silk and satin manners. This one was the closest he'd come mingling with what he'd heard of so-called Southern gentry. In other towns and farms, having the upper hand had thrilled him, yet facing her left him with a touch of guilt. He pictured his mother scowling those times she'd caught him doing something.

Didn't want the men seeing him act a bully to this woman. He'd had wild carousing parties, his share of fancy women and good-time whores, pants shucked to their ankles, mauling free skin and flopping titties of willing freed women. A few good-smelling so-called high-borns bartering on their backs for food or just for the wild hell of the gutter. Years of muddy trenches, digging up skeletons in rotted uniforms, leaky tents so cold his teeth chattered. With him it was no longer about slaves, and he could see in her winter-blue eyes, she knew it as well. This one with a husband dead, likely more of her family as well. Their lives in ruin, yet still loyal to those his army was tearing to pieces every chance they got.

Long before Atlanta and the Shenandoah rampages, he'd handled hate and anger at the other end of his bayonet, yet no matter how often they were whipped, ones like her refused to look at it that way. In his heart fighting for the Union had once been what it was about, but things had changed. A kind of flim-flam was going against the whole country, and it wasn't the doing of ones like her.

Corinthia had no intention of yielding to this wolfing stealer, not if there was the slimmest chance she might sway them from burning the roof over Sarah's head. She read his confusion, knowing at the moment she was the best hope for what little ground remained theirs.

"Get with it," he hollered out. "You got your orders, times wasting," soldiers scattering in all directions. "We'll search the house, we got things to do before we move on."

As she felt Hamilton tense, Corinthia tightened her grip on his arm, whispered, "Go inside, make sure Ben knows soldiers are comin' in. That he mustn't do anything rash."

Hamilton disquieted at the thought of leaving her, gave an anxious glance toward the sergeant. "I don't want to leave you here."

"For heaven's sake go, while there's still time, and something changes his mind," she urged.

She turned back to the sergeant, her hand resting ever so

lightly on his arm, and with a look at Hamilton, said, "I'll be quite safe with Sergeant Maxwell." Knowing the house was to be spared, otherwise there was no need to search. "Sergeant, if you'd permit a simple request..."

He said gruffly, "Long as nobody gets in our way or interferes."

"My daughter's bedroom...I give you my word there's no one inside except we women."

"She won't be disturbed." He glanced toward the circling wagons and bellowed toward a teamster, "Get them wagons loaded. We got three more places on the list before we head for Millen Junction," then noticed he was short some wagons. He stormed at a driver, "Where's our other wagons?"

Lieutenant took them to that big Greer place," Corporal yelled over the clanking commotion. "Word came it's deserted."

Corinthia's knuckles clenched white against the awful dread, hoping against a frail hope. "Sergeant, the Bends is all I've left of my husband. If you've been with Gen'ral Sherman since Chattanooga, you've seen enough to know the South is beaten."

"I know that, and you seem to know it as well. And likely there's many others know it too, but some Johnny Rebs aren't as savvy as you, sniping at us any chance they get."

"Most are fighting for their homes," Corinthia said.

"You should of thought of that before you Rebs started this."

"Surely there's nothing to be gained by depriving me of my home."

"Orders is orders. I done what I can, and likely get chewed out for leaving this place standing."

A soldier at the foot of the steps said, "We got all the chickens we can pack."

"Shoot the rest."

"We already did."

"Don't leave anything to feed scrawny Reb snipers pestering us. Don't forget, empty the smokehouses, then torch them."

Corinthia held her breath, knowing Ben could hear them, praying Hamilton could keep him from storming out. She started inside, giving one last anguished look in the direction of the Bends. She saw no smoke above the distant treetops, didn't want to see it, preferred remembering Andrew and her life as it had been.

Two guards came toward them, three more met them coming from the back of the dogtrot hallway. "We got to search now," the Sergeant said. He pushed through the parlor door and found himself face to face with a sallow-faced Ben. "What we got here?" he blustered, "Another snippersnapper Reb trying to hide?"

"My son, Benjamin," Corinthia said.

"Well, well..." Maxwell said. "Andrew Greer whelped himself a male pup. Another Johnny Reb like a lot who deciding it was time to hide behind his mama's skirts."

"Where's your uniform, sonny? No guts?" a corporal sniggered. "Didn't stay long at your big fine house, once all your niggers run off."

"Ben—" Hamilton grabbed the beet-red Ben as he started toward the man. "Remember your mother and Sarah. Eat crow 'til it hurts."

All the long weeks of trekking deeper into Georgia, smashing their armies and towns, the more the Sergeant kept finding himself with a grudging respect for these proud people.

Just then Bessie burst through the parlor door. "Mistress Corinth'a..."

Seeing the soldiers, she stopped, her first thoughts was they was here for Sam.

"Well looky what we got here," Maxwell said. "Still got their slaves right outside the door. Ready to wait on you hand and foot." He yelled, "What's the matter with you, Nigger? Why you still hanging around, these people don't own you no longer. You like all the rest, too dumb to know you're free? Get out of here."

With Sarah on her mind, it took a moment for it to dawn on Bessie he'd called her a nigger, like she was a field worker. Nobody'd ever called her that, an' here was this loudmouth stranger where he hadn't ought'a be. The kind what beckoned her Sam away with lies. It got all over 'Lizabeth Mae.

"What you doin', Yankieman?" she bristled. "Stompin' in here with them filthy boots what been walkin' in Lord only know what pig sty pesthole filth. Bring the whoopin' croup against this precious baby. Messin' my clean floor I done made sure didn't track no sickliness." Hands on her hips, she fiercly glared, and demanded, "An' foul-mouthin' me a dumb slave. I ain't town trash, not that you'd know diff'rent. Marse Andrew done give me freedom with his blood. Yankies didn't spill none in the doin'. You ain't fightin' for kin. Some fool shove a gun in your hand, point you at us'ns. Now move out'a my way while we he'p a little baby come into this messed up world. An' mind you, don't pokes no guns in Missy's room. Don't disturb Missy. Bessie be all over you like a banty hen the likes a which you ain't never seen."

She turned to Corinthia, and said, "Missy comin' down hard, real reg'lar. Showin' signs we mights have to turn the baby." She started toward the door, halted, gave Maxwell a sharp look, and quietly shut the door as she left.

Maxwell, flustered by this brassy encounter, wondered if all Southern women were this single-minded when crossed. Worse than Rebs carrying a gun.

"Get a move on!" he bawled out to his men. "Don't have all day."

At the heavy smell of smoke Hamilton walked to the window, smothered his fury at the sight of the dirty gray billows. "They fired the barns."

Rolling gusts choked across the fenced lots, flames already lapping out of the haylofts, crawling across the cedar shingles. Inside the carriage barn he could see yellows and oranges licking through the spokes and bubbling the glossy varnish of the Phaeton. As soldiers chased squealin' pigs across the yard, fires licked roofs and whipped the trees.

Ben said, "Nat and Josiah's cabins'll catch for sure."

"Won't only be their cabins." Hamilton threw a troubled look toward the kitchen roof. "Won't take much more for it to spread...house'll catch. Get all the blankets and quilts into the parlor, get 'em ready in case we have to move Sarah."

"Sam!" Came Bessie's scream above the howling inferno swallowing the chicken house, barns, smokehouses. "Sam, come back!" She gave a wild shriek, framed at the back door, her face lit by the flames. "Sam took his gun, gone t'stop them burnin' Nat and Josiah's cabin! They kill my boy," she moaned.

"Stay with Sarah," Hamilton said.

Hamilton dodged through sucking flurries of flaming white-hot embers, smell of burning animals, a wall of flames sweeping haystacks, chicken coops, corn fields. Pine sap sizzling, smelly turpentine exploding in muffled yellow-orange whooshes engulfing whole trees, boiling sap speckling Hamilton's face like hot molasses. He daubed spit on the sticky blistery blobers, but didn't smear it.

The house centered in a roaring cauldron of flames and smoke. He squinted, shielded his eyes for a quick look-around, couldn't make out Sam anywhere.

A gust of hot air momentarily cleared the smoke and Hamilton spotted Sam pointing a rifle on a soldier, yelling, "Git back..." The dance of flames shimmering off his face gave him a hellfire-demon look. "Them cabins ain't secesh property," he threatened. "Shoot the first hand what puts fire to 'em."

Nat came running with buckets, water sloshing from the pails. "Roof's smokin' heavy. Cain't keep it wetted with these piddlin' buckets."

Other soldiers surrounded Sam, taken aback, none ever seen armed chattels in slave country. The inferno roared louder, heat turning winter into summer, steaming snow melt forming large puddles around the burning buildings.

"Sam..." Hamilton carefully pushed the rifle barrel away from the soldier. "You ain't saving cabins this way."

From nowhere, a soldier smashed his rifle butt across Sam's head, spritzing the air with blood and spit. Sam went down.

The soldier prodded Sam's limp form with his boot. "Yellow-belly deserter...buzzard bait." He raised his rifle butt to hit again.

"No need for that."" Hamilton stepped between the soldier and Sam. "He's not goin' anywhere."

"Lincoln's a backbiting liar for setting white folks against one another," the soldier's anger spilled out. "They traipse along, follow us, begging, getting in the way like we was supposed to take care of them. Aside from swindling sutlers, contraband is the biggest thieves we got. I volunteered for the Union, and that's all I joined for. Let him be." He looked at Hamilton. "Deserted from my company. We got orders to shoot deserters, he'll get his court-martial when we make camp in Millen. Then we'll hang the sonofabitch." He prodded Sam again with his rifle butt. "Sooner we're rid of him the better."

Hamilton said, "All he was trying to do was save the cabins."

Maxwell shoved his way through. "What's going on here?"

"Found that deserter that showed yellow outside Atlanta."

Maxwell said, "Sam Greer?"

"Greer?" Hamilton was taken aback.

"That's what his sign-up orders read," Maxwell said. "How come you was hiding him here."

Hamilton said, "He was worried about us, an' Bessie's his mother. He deserted to get here, warn us, try to get us out of danger."

"Damn if I understand you Southerners and your niggers. You act like they're family.

"They pretty much are," Hamilton said. "Some even blood kin, an' we care deeply what happens to 'em."

"Said he was from Georgia." Maxwell turned to the guard. "Chain him to that gun caisson next to the stockade wagon. Post a guard, no one talks to him without orders from me. I'll get a report to headquarters that we got us another turncoat nigger." As the barn roof caved in, Maxwell yelled over the roar, "Once Sherman learns he shucked his uniform, he'll have him shot."

"There's no need for that," Hamilton insisted.

"Deserters know what they got coming." Maxwell said.

"Sam doesn't deserve to be shot." Hamilton was more uneasy as he watched them chain Sam. "What you doing with him? Where you takin' him?"

"He'll be going with us. If it was up to me, I'd shoot him here on the spot, but General Sherman will see to it once we reach Savannah. Court-martial him there, then stretch his neck."

"Where in Savannah?"

"None of you Rebs' damn business. Wherever Sherman has his headquarters. Why you want to know for? So you set up an ambush on us?"

"I want a pass," Hamilton said.

"What?" Maxwell couldn't believe he'd heard right. "You want me to give you clearance through our lines?"

"Yes. I want to know where you're takin' Sam, where he'll be, and where I can find him. And I want to know where I can meet with Sherman."

"What?" Maxwell astounded. "I never met people as bull-headed as you Southerners." Called out, "Get me an orderly over here!"

A young soldier hurried up to them. "Yeh?"

"Give this man what he wants. And be sure and spell his name right."

Just then Corinthia came out the back door. "Hamilton..?" She pulled her shawl tight around her shoulders.

He hurried to her.

"You've got a son, a fine healthy baby boy."

"And Sarah..?"

"The baby breached. We got it turned. Both restin' fair."

"Fire's gettin' terrible, house could catch any minute," Hamilton said, worried.

"Blankets soaked and stacked in the parlor," she said

Singeing smoke and flying embers and flames roared toward the turn of the Trace and into the stand of pines beyond. Panic-eyed cavalry horses whinnied, jerked at their halters. Hostile soldiers tried to keep hold of the bridles.

Ben looked off beyond the Trace in the direction of thick smoke, flames occasionally licking above the trees. "Ever'thing Papa worked for..." His shoulders slumped.

"Not everything." Hamilton laid a hand on Ben's shoulder, juggled the bit of guilt he felt. "I'm sorry."

"Likely a godsend our havin' to be with Sarah. You'n Mama were right. You'd'a stayed with me, both of us be dead, and you'd have a son without a daddy. Bends'd still be in ashes, likely the Hollows as well."

"Papa Andrew's loss grieves my papa something fierce ever day," Hamilton said. "Neither of them wanted what happened, but once it did, both gave it their all in their own way. Whole country blind-sided itself. Don't matter who's left standing, we're faced with hard feelings likely never to be forgot."

"God, Hamilton..." Ben shut his eyes tight, then opened them. "How could it go to pieces so fast?"

The two watched the barn rafters and what was left of the roof crumble into glowing coals. "Hard times ahead. We'll survive like Ingrams an' Greers always did. Gonna name that new son of mine Cornelius after Papa Andrew...Hamilton Graeme Cornelius Ingram."

"Papa would've liked that," Ben said.

18

Late 1864

Hamilton pulled the stringer of fish out of the water. "Let's go home." He got up and brushed grass and leaves off his threadbare pants. He helped Sarah up from the creek bank, slid his arm around her, hugged her gently, and shouldered his pole. "Our son's likely got his grandpapa all wore out. Bet he's waitin' for this fine mess of fresh brim ready for the frying."

Glossary of Terms

ME = Middle English
OE = Old English
OF = Old French
SYN = synonym

aboil - (a-)prefix/in a state of boil
abyling - OE - (a-)prefix/byle, boil=abyle, aboil
afeard - OE - (a-)prefix/afeared/frightened/upper southern afraid
agin - regional/against
alumen - alum/ME from OF/Latin alumen
armoured - (ISBNpdf p153) OF - armor
arguen - ME - argue
aught - ME/OE ought
avouch - declare provable truth
Banty - Bantam
baresocked - barefooted
bespeckle - (be-)intensive prefix/be+speckle
bestraddle - (be-)intensive prefix/be+straddle
bikeren - ME - bickering
blindman's buff -blindman's bluff
blober - ME - blob
bonnyclabber - full version of clabber/curdled milk
bordelo - OF - bordello
brim - bream - related to red bellies/blue gills
bulwerks - ME/middle Dutch/middle high German - bulwarks
bummlers - bummers
buncombe - bunkum/claptrap/after NC congressman
bungtown copper - worthless copper coin
    SYN: copperhead/hard times token issue 1830-45 & 1860-65
camphor oil - camphor tree distillate
chammy - shammy/variant of chamois

chilblegens - OE blegens/chilblains
chitlin - ME -chiterling/chitterlings
chirren - children
cobeler - ME - cobbler
coco-de-mer fan - palm from Seychelle Ils
comitat - Latin comitatus/posse
corndodger - fried round cornmeal/southern
croker sack - gunnysack/tow sack/tow bag
curchief - ME - Anglo-Norman/kerchief
cut-acrosses - fords
diddery - ME - dither
didoing - mischievous prank
dozy - drowsy
draie - ME - dray
Egyptian millet - Johnson grass
erren - ME - err
Esquier - ME - Esquire
eventide - ME - evening
ferthing - ME - farthing
goose flesh - goose bumps
grubben hoe - ME - grubbing hoe
Gwyddelic - a branch of Celtic language
hankeren - Dutch - strong desire
harvest-mite - chigger
hearen - ME - hear
hostiler - ME - hostler/one who tends horses
husht - ME - hush
jack fever - yellow fever/yellow jack
Jamestown Weed - jimsonweed
johnnycakes/johnnycake pone - pone - cornbread
ketch - ME - to catch
kitty-corner - ME - cattycorner
lamp oil - coal oil/kerosene
lardy - lard
lavendre - ME - lavender
lightwood - kindling
listenen - ME - listen
mia domina - Latin - my lady

middlings - ME - midlin/ground wheat & bran
mugganess - muggy/OE dialect/Northumbrian old Norse/ME -
Muskydine - muscadine
Nordmadhr - north man - Norman
okom - ME - oakum
opine - state an opinion
padlok - ME - padlock
pencil-necked - stiff-necked
pikforkes - ME - pitchfork
pitterpatt - pitapat
poleaxed - fell with an axe
poss corn - popcorn
purty - pretty/regional
quirt - short handled riding whip
raring - dialectal raring/to rise on hind legs
rascallion - obsolete for rapscallion
redy/roede - ME/OE - ready
reknen - reckon
rendren - ME - render
rosemarine - ME - rosemary
ruche - ruffle/pleat
saultoir - OF - saltire
Scottes - Scots
shindy - alteration of shindig
skeeren - ME - scare/Old Norse skerren
sloughing - slew/variant of slough
smid'rins - smithereens/fragments/splintered pieces
smithery - smithy - blacksmith shop
smushed - combine of smash+mush
snifteren - ME - snifter
snippersnapper - whippersnapper dialectal
sorghum - grain & forage grass
southron - southerne
square-on - head-on
stead - ME - to be of service
succory - middle low German - chicory
sugar corn - sweet corn
suteler - sutler

terrine - vulgar Latin/OF - tureen
tilten - ME - tilt
torchères - torches
uisce beatha - Irish Gaelic - water of life (see usquebaugh)
uraemia - uremia (both accepted spelling)
usquebaugh - English from Irish Gaelic *whiskey* (see uisce beatha)
us'uns - us ones
vinaigre wine - vinegar wine preservative
walow'n - walowen=wallow
whyttel - ME - whittle
whisky - variant of whiskey
winder - variant of window (Upper Southern)
whey-faced - peaked synonym
whup - variant of whip
wondur - OE - wonder
wrenchen - ME - wrech/twist
yankie - Oxford English Dictionary/variant for New Englander
young'uns - young ones